EMBER

S.G. PRINCE

ISBN: 9798576070091

First Edition

Cover design by Damonza

To Mom, for everything.

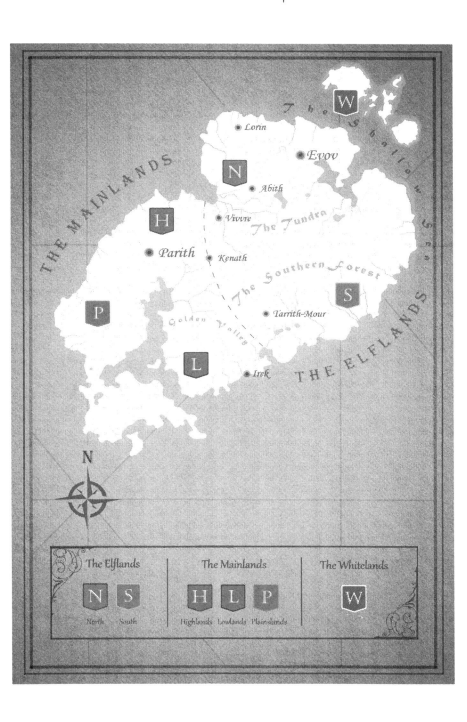

ONE

When Venick heard a rustle inside his tent and woke to a shadowy figure looming over him, he thought it was a dream.

By all logic, it should have been a dream. Venick's tent was pitched in the center of a military encampment. There were soldiers there, soldiers everywhere, six hundred elves and men with eyes and ears out for trouble. And Venick was no mere grunt among them, either. He was Commander, the god-touched, battle-born human who controlled the resistance and the highland army both. He had his own squad of soldiers to watch his back, his own personal team of fighters to guard him day and night. No one could just wander into his tent unannounced. No one would have the chance.

And so of course when Venick woke to the sight of a stranger hovering overhead, his mind resisted. It said, *dream*. It said, *not real*.

Venick had become better at separating fantasies from reality. He'd made mistakes early on, surely. He'd questioned himself, and questioned himself again, until his head was so full of doubts that he thought it would burst. But Venick saw things more clearly now. He knew he could trust his instincts, that his hunches often turned out to be true. Like: the Elder would rather give up his army than admit his daughter had out-smarted him. Like: elves and humans could set aside age-old differences to work and fight together. Like: Ellina stood beside him, had always stood beside him, had risked everything to stand beside him.

These were the truths Venick took to bed each night. They were the truths he woke with, too, as he blinked and frowned and told himself that the stranger in his tent must be a dream.

The figure produced a dagger.

Venick reacted. He rolled to his feet, reached for his knife. He'd been smart enough to keep a weapon close at hand while he slept, yet not quite smart enough to keep a *fighting* weapon. A knife. Good for whit-tling wood and chopping carrots.

So much for your instincts.

But Venick hadn't anticipated an attack like this, not here, not by a lone assassin. If anything, he was expecting battle. A full-blown, high-scale charge with all the perfunctory force to go along with it. It had been six weeks since Venick freed Ellina from Evov, another three since he'd left the highland capitol of Parith with his new—

Stolen.

—army in tow. Plenty of time for the Dark Queen to plan an attack. Plenty of opportunities to execute one. Venick's caravan was exposed out on the western plains, and they were still a day away from their rendezvous point in Igor where Harmon and the majority of their men waited for them. If Farah was wise, she would send her army to meet their contingent now, while she had the upper hand. Venick had expected *that*. Not this…sneak attack.

The figure lunged. Venick folded sideways, hit the ground. Used momentum to roll and come up again. His tent was dark and cramped, too dark and cramped to fight the way Venick wanted. Yet there were tricks he'd learned about close-quarters combat, tricks like: use the walls to your advantage. Keep your hands up, your head down. Strike hard and strike quick and be done with it already.

His attacker had not, apparently, learned the same tactics. As Venick drew his knife up in preparation for the next strike, he realized the stranger wasn't turning to face him. Was not, it seemed, following the fight at all. Rather, the figure stumbled forward into the space Venick had just vacated, dagger swiping through air and nothing.

Blind, or just stupid?

Didn't matter. Venick knew an opening when he saw one, and he wasn't about to let it go to waste. He flipped his grip on his knife, drew the green glass overhead. His eyes had adjusted enough by then to make out the shape of his attacker, the slender build, the long slope of each shoulder. Venick watched the elf—*was* it an elf?—stagger another step forward, his feet tangling in Venick's bedroll.

Venick brought his weapon down. The elf spun at the last second, lifting his arm to block the blow. No shield. No gloves or greaves. Just a pale hand jutting between them.

Stupid, then.

Venick heard more than saw his own knife whistle through the air, the *snip* as it pierced the elf's outstretched wrist. He expected his attacker to cry and jerk back, had planned to use that opening to step in closer, jab his blade into this stranger's throat. Only, the elf didn't recoil. Didn't react in any way, like Venick hadn't just sunk his weapon into flesh, like he hadn't delivered a wound that would leave anyone reeling.

Venick's mind was slow. He'd been acting, reacting, adrenaline overriding his ability to think. By the time his brain caught up with the rest of him, the thought was already there, waiting like a stage actor behind the curtain.

This wasn't right.

None of it was. The stranger in his tent, the absence of his guard, the odd, ineffectual fighting...

That's when Venick noticed the stench.

It was subtle, an acrid mix of foul breath and rot. Again, Venick's mind was slow. It strained, pulling against the end of its own chain, metal rattling. As the elf tore his wrist free and Venick fought to keep hold of his knife, the shackles of Venick's mind broke free, and he remembered.

He remembered the elven city of Evov, that high and forbidden place, overtaken last summer in a coup orchestrated by Farah, the Dark Queen.

He remembered Ellina, so brave and so strong and so *foolish*, who had used her powers of stealth and deceit to uncover the Dark Queen's secrets.

He remembered those secrets, each its own horror, but one more horrible than the rest.

The elf seemed to have forgotten his dagger. The blade hung uselessly by his side as he stretched out his injured hand to grab Venick's throat. Venick beat the hand away and moved in again, low this time. A strike to the thigh, in and out, a gash that should have left anyone incapacitated. The elf didn't even flinch.

Understanding burned through Venick. He tasted it on his tongue.

In the elflands, there were two types of conjurors: northern conjurors like Ellina, who could break through ancient magic and learn to lie in elvish, and southern conjurors like Youvan and Balid, who could move shadows and summon storms and, according to Ellina, control the dead.

Venick's knife couldn't help him. He knew that now. Yet he squeezed it in his fist like a lifeline as his attacker made a noise, a rattling hiss that turned Venick's insides to jelly. The figure took another step forward, and for the first time, Venick caught a real glimpse of its face, the hollows where cheeks should have been, the blank white eyes.

Venick's heart was wild. His breath raked up his throat.

He hefted his foot and *kicked*.

His heel connected with the creature's chest, sent it flying into the wall of the tent. The canvas collapsed over both of them, and for a moment, Venick's panic sealed over. His senses scrambled. He thrashed, cutting frantically at the fabric, ripping free into the frigid night air, desperate to put as much distance as he could between himself and that *thing*.

The commotion was finally waking nearby soldiers. Several men jogged over to see what the trouble was. Their faces were confused and sleep-heavy, their mouths a collective murmur of *Commander?* They hadn't yet seen what Venick had. Didn't yet know what Venick knew.

Behind them, the creature was struggling to free its legs from the tangles of the fallen tent, to much less effect. Illuminated by torchlight, Venick could tell that the elf had been, once and recently, alive. Its skin was supple, muscles well defined. Only its face seemed to show the thing for what it was. Venick saw better now the sightless eyes, the unhinged jaw, spidery blue veins crisscrossing over cheeks and brow.

The soldiers saw it, too.

There was a buzz of alarm, a call for an axe to behead the demon. A wasted effort. Venick knew they could cut off every one of the creature's limbs, and its head as well, and still, it would keep fighting. Ellina had been clear on this point—there was only one element that could stop the undead.

"A torch," Venick told the nearest soldier. His voice came out hoarse. He cleared his throat and tried again. "Bring me a torch."

The item was procured and set in Venick's hand. Venick touched the flame to the canvas, stepping back as fire quickly devoured the tent and the undead assassin along with it.

Now came the writhing.

The creature flailed, working its mouth as if to scream. Smoke gathered thickly, pulsing into the night sky. By the time it was done, most of the camp was awake and at the scene. Elves and men formed a loose circle around the charred remains of the now-dead-again undead, some looking stunned, others brandishing weapons.

"Commander."

Venick turned to see the elven ranger Lin Lill approaching from between the orderly rings of tents. Her eyes were pale coins in the night, her stride long and even. Unlike most of the soldiers, she was dressed in full elven armor, gauntlets and greaves and boots and shield—a warrior ready for battle.

It was this thought that made Venick say, mildly, "You missed the fight."

"We were tricked." Lin Lill looked like she would rather cut those words into her skin than admit them aloud. She peeled back her lips, a growl and a grimace both. "We received word of suspicious activity. Branton and I went to investigate. Artis was supposed to stay behind on guard, but we were gone too long. He grew worried and came to find us. I should have sent him back to you immediately. That was my mistake, a breach of duty, and I take full—"

"Lin, stop. I'm fine."

"You were attacked."

Venick glanced at the smoking heap. "I managed alright."

Lin Lill's brow creased, her skin pulling at the scar that cut across one cheek. She had taken charge of Venick's personal guard, naming herself his first and Branton and Artis his seconds. Though Venick had resisted the idea—he might be Commander now, but that didn't mean he needed special treatment—Lin Lill had insisted. When Venick tried to veto the idea by pulling rank, she'd brushed him off like he was bothering her. And she'd saddled him with a personal guard anyway.

This would have been a good moment for Lin to dig in with an *I told you so*, but instead, she merely said, "The report was valid. We confronted a southern conjuror at the east end of camp."

"A conjuror?" Venick's pulse changed. "Male or—?"

"Female. When we arrived, it looked like she was wielding magic. Her hands were moving, her eyes were closed, but we could not figure out what she was doing."

Their gazes both slid back to the undead.

Venick said, "I might have a guess."

"She was corpse-bending," Lin Lill agreed. Then, without a change in tone: "I am going to kill Artis."

"You will not."

"Then I am going to kill all of *you*," she announced, glaring at the nearby soldiers. "How could you let an undead simply wander into camp? Did no one notice a dead soldier stepping into the Commander's tent? We might as well have invited it in ourselves, offered it some tea while we were at—"

"Lin." Venick knew how it felt to be on the receiving end of Lin Lill's insults. He stopped her before she could do any real damage. "What happened to the corpse-bender?"

Lin Lill's mouth flattened into a line. "She escaped."

Disappointing, but not all that surprising, given that it was the middle of the night, with thick clouds to cover the moon. Little visibility, little light, natural or otherwise. A conjuror's dream. "I'm calling a meeting," Venick said. "Gather the others, have them meet in my…" Another glance at the smoking heap. "In Erol's tent. We'll continue this there."

Lin Lill inhaled. Opened her mouth to argue and thought better of it. She let out the breath, and with it, all visible emotion. This was an elven skill, the ability to wipe away any hint of expression. In an instant, Lin Lill had transformed back into a stone-carved soldier, ready to carry out orders. "Commander."

"One more thing," Venick added. "Where—?"

"Ellina is safe."

Venick wasn't like the elves. He couldn't hide his every thought. Still, he wasn't sure that he liked how easily Lin Lill had intercepted his question. How she had known, before the words were even out, that Venick's mind had been on Ellina, and where she was and what she was doing and whether she was safe. Venick was not supposed to be acting like he cared about Ellina…at least, not publicly.

"Find her," Venick said. "I want her there, too."

"Of course you do."

Lin Lill spoke without inflection. That could have been honest agreement, or it could have been sarcasm. Lin wasn't usually the type for sarcasm, but neither was she the type to condone anything besides an unwavering commitment to duty. And recently, Venick had been walking a fine line on the duty front. He had a role to play, one that involved his engagement to Harmon, sweetheart of the highlands and daughter of the Elder. It was this engagement—false as it may be—that allowed

Venick to command not only the resistance but the highland army as well. The arrangement was devious and political and not at all what Venick wanted, but he'd committed himself to winning this war, and that meant making sacrifices. Setting aside his own desires. Complicating his already complicated relationship with Ellina.

He might have asked Lin Lill to explain her meaning, except Venick was the one inviting Ellina to yet another Commander's meeting. He was the one worrying about her openly, with nearby soldiers listening. So maybe he was the one who should explain.

"That's all," Venick said. "You're dismissed."

Lin Lill gave a perfect salute—a gesture she'd learned from the humans—and walked away with a legionnaire's practiced detachment. She might not like Venick's choices, but she had a role to play too, that of the committed elven subordinate. Still, Venick didn't miss Lin Lill's silent message. It was in the way she snapped to attention, the way she swallowed her opinions with flawless composure, ready to carry out her duty. *You want to win this war, Venick? You want to put commitment first? Then take note; this is how it is done.*

TWO

This was going to sting.

As dawn broke cold and bright over the plains, Ellina stripped off her clothes and stepped to the edge of the winter river. Mist rose off the water's surface, shrouding the valley in a damp veil. Small grey birds flitted between shrubs along the shore, stopping here and there to dip their beaks into the shallows. On the far side of the river, an unfamiliar creature—long, thickly scaled, a wingless dragon— slid through the water, its tail swishing like the rudder of a great ship. It observed Ellina's slender form with one large, marble-yellow eye.

Ellina would have gladly traded places with that reptile. She would have traded places with any of the plainsland animals: the birds, the foxes, the tiny silver mice. Like her, these creatures were voiceless, but unlike her, they were not expected to speak. That difference, Ellina decided, was vital.

She dove into the water.

And she was right—it *did* sting. The cold shot needles of pain across her skin. It seized her breath, constricted her muscles. Ellina worked hard to make her limbs move, fighting the current and her sudden bloodlessness to hold herself below the surface.

Her lungs begged for air. Ellina ignored them.

She pushed towards the bottom.

The water—somehow, incredibly—grew colder. The chill worked its way down her arms, through her chest, where it touched her heart and paused: a finger on a bowstring. The sensation was unpleasant. Painful, even. As Ellina brought herself to sit on the river's silty floor, she thought about how she had once feared this kind of pain. Pain was, after all, something to be avoided, and what was fear if not a kind of avoidance?

She knew better now. Physical pain had a limit. It was a house with a single room, predictable and self-contained. Ellina had touched pain's highest ceiling and survived, and having done that, she now understood that it was not quite the monster it seemed.

If she was going to fear something, there were more worthy terrors.

Ellina's lungs ached. The pressure was building in her ears. She was so cold that she felt insubstantial, unfinished, like the river was running right through her. She felt like that a lot, actually.

Still, it was not exactly wise what she was doing. If Ellina wanted to press the edge of pain, there were better options than an icy swim in a frozen river. But Ellina liked this option. She liked that it demanded equal parts mental and physical concentration. She liked that it was solitary yet unconfined. She especially liked that it took her away from camp, where she could never quite seem to avoid the curious eyes of her fellow soldiers…or the suspicious ones.

The soldiers had reason to be suspicious. Ellina was a tangle of contradictions, a puzzle with so many pieces missing that, even if completed, the picture would never show clear. She was the Dark Queen's sister but also a spy for the resistance. She was a northern elf but also a conjuror. She was a defector and a liar and now, impossibly, a mute.

Ellina exhaled a flurry of bubbles. They raced to the surface, creasing the sky with their ripples.

It was not that Ellina blamed the soldiers, exactly. Given Ellina's history, it was easy to understand their misgivings. Ellina had pledged public oaths of fidelity to Farah and the Dark Army. She had championed her sister's cause among the legion. She had denounced Venick, threatened him, and called for his death.

She had done all of this in elvish.

How convenient, the soldiers must be thinking, that Ellina had suddenly learned to lie in elvish, thereby excusing her of all apparent treachery. How convenient that her voice had been stolen so that she could not even prove the credibility of her newfound power. And how utterly foolish of their Commander, for not only accepting Ellina's story, but inviting her into his inner circle, giving her further opportunity to infiltrate their ranks…if that was indeed her mission. It was one thing for Venick to rescue Ellina from Evov, but it was quite another for him to favor her so openly. Did Venick not remember Rahven, the chronicler-turned-spy who had cost them the city of Irek? Did he think that Farah, having lost one envoy, would not try to replace him? And who better to fill that role than Ellina, who was not only a famed legion spy, but the queen's blood?

Ellina touched a hand to her frozen lips. Her fingers were numb; she could not feel the motion.

If she were human, she would have already succumbed to the craving for oxygen. As it was, her body was pleading with her to resurface, wade back to shore. Part of her wanted to stay at the river's bottom, to push her limit hard enough to hear it crack, but the other part of her— the older, wiser part—warned against it.

She broke the surface with a gasp.

Cold air rushed into her face. Her eyes smarted. Ellina pressed her palms to her temples, taking measured gulps of air. When she lowered her hands, she saw she was no longer alone.

Lin Lill stood at the river's edge, staring at Ellina with an expression that was, for the ranger, as good as open bafflement. It was not Ellina's questionable decision to swim in a freezing river that had Lin Lill so affected, but rather the fact that Ellina was swimming at all. This was widely known: elves did not swim.

Lin Lill recovered, giving a small bow and an even smaller, "*Cessena.*" Though Ellina had asked the elves—or rather, asked Venick to ask the elves—not to call her by her formal title, old habits were hard to break. This was especially true for Lin Lill, who was so tightly bound by duty that Ellina could often feel its stranglehold secondhand.

"I was ordered to inform you," Lin Lill said. "There has been an attack."

• • •

Ellina pushed into Erol's tent.

It was a tight space, a modest conjunction of poles and rope and canvas, though it seemed even tighter because of the number of bodies that had been crammed inside. There were Ellina's old troopmates Branton and Artis, the legion ranger Lin Lill, the elderly human healer named Erol, and—much to Ellina's horror—the charred remains of what appeared to be an elven soldier.

Ellina blinked down at the body. Waited for her mind to right itself. Squinted and blinked again. When the corpse remained firmly in place, she had to concede that this was not a resurgence of her blood loss-induced hallucinations…though why Lin Lill had failed to mention the body during her briefing, Ellina could not guess.

She arrowed a look at the ranger, waiting for an explanation.

"Venick's attacker," Lin Lill offered. She spoke offhandedly, as if a dead body on display was nothing unusual. Then again, for a legionnaire like Lin Lill, it might not be. Ellina supposed that Lin Lill was used to these sorts of dealings, that her role as an elite killer had desensitized her…

Ellina stumbled over that thought. Brought a hand to her head, as if to check for fever. What was she thinking? It confounded her how quick she was to set Lin Lill into a separate category from herself, as if they had nothing in common. But Ellina had been an elite killer, too. She had hunted trespassers along the border, had ended the lives of more humans than she cared to count. Ellina was no stranger to dead bodies, was no stranger even to *burned* dead bodies. Had she forgotten her own history?

"Bad news," came a voice from behind. Ellina turned to see Venick stepping into the tent, taking with him what little was left of their free space. The others shuffled to accommodate the fifth—sixth body as Venick let the tent's flap fall closed behind him.

His eyes came to Ellina. His expression changed at the sight of her, then changed again, his gaze shifting to her wet hair, her blue lips. His tone was alarmed. "What happened to you?"

Ellina knew what he must be thinking: that there had been some kind of confrontation, that she had been pranked, attacked, pulled into a body of water against her will. She began to motion with her hands—

Nothing, I am fine—when Lin Lill interjected. "The princess fancied a dip in the river."

It was as if a line had been cut. The sudden release of support, the tumble into freefall. In the ensuing silence, Ellina was starkly aware of five pairs of eyes pressing into her skin.

There was nothing so unusual, really, about a travel-worn soldier seeking a cleansing dip in a river. Except that it was winter. Except that the western plains were blanketed in snow, the rivers and lakes crusted with ice. Even those rivers that had not yet frozen were treacherously cold. No one in their right mind would choose to swim in them. No elf, really, would choose to swim at all.

Venick was concerned. Ellina saw his concern, the half-formed *do you have a death wish?* on his lips. But he recognized her discomfort. Recognized, too, that this was not the time to press for answers. Reluctantly, and with a look that conveyed his unhappiness, he hauled the conversation back onto its original track.

"I talked to the night's watch about the attack," Venick reported. "It's as we thought. No one saw the corpse enter camp."

"That is impossible," Branton asserted. "Someone must have seen."

"The men are lying," Lin Lill agreed.

"Not just the men," Erol said, lifting a wrinkled finger. "There were elves on watch last night, too."

"I questioned the elven watch," Lin Lill replied stiffly. "They had nothing to report."

"You accuse our men of lying, but not your elves?"

Venick's gaze skipped sideways, caught Ellina's. This was dangerous language, the kind Venick had worked hard to smother. He did not want it to be *our men* and *your elves*. He wanted the soldiers to be a collective *us*. They had made impressive strides in that direction, but these were old prejudices, hard to smother. That was true even for men like Erol who had—years ago, before the border—spent time in the elflands.

"I questioned the elves in *elvish*," Lin Lill clarified. "Last I checked, Ellina is the only one who can—" a sidelong glance "—could lie in elvish. And anyway, all of our soldiers are traditional."

Traditional. The soldiers had white hair, she meant, indicating that they were not conjurors and therefore could not lie in elvish. Only black-haired elves like Ellina—and more specifically, black-haired elves from the north—had the power to break the bonds of their language in that way.

Venick folded his arms. "If our men say they didn't see a corpse, I believe them. They have no reason to lie."

Lin Lill was quick. "Unless there are traitors among us."

"Traitors?" The voice belonged to Artis, quiet and level. "It is a big camp."

Ellina understood Artis' skepticism. Even if a few operatives managed to sneak a living corpse past the night's watch, that did not explain how the creature had made it all the way to Venick's tent unobserved. Someone should have noticed.

"Southern conjurors can summon shadows," Branton offered. "Maybe the conjuror disguised the corpse. Covered it in darkness, made it difficult to observe."

Erol rubbed his chin. "If that was possible, why wouldn't the conjuror have snuck into camp along with it? She could have covered herself in shadows too, crept up close to Venick's tent. That would have been easier than conjuring blind from a distance."

"Maybe she was too limited in her power."

"Maybe she was a decoy, and that's what *another* conjuror was doing."

The discussion continued. As everyone took turns throwing out progressively wilder ideas, Ellina came to kneel beside the corpse. Though its uniform had lost all color in the fire, she could still make out the rough shape of it, the size of the neck hole, the reinforced stitching. She reached out to touch the blackened tunic, searching for a clue, some thread she could pull to unravel this mystery. The fabric disintegrated under her fingers.

"Well," Lin Lill huffed. "Until we have an answer, we can take no chances. Venick, I am doubling your guard."

"No." Venick's face pinched. "Absolutely not."

"It is for your own safety."

"You three are enough. I can't have someone watching me every minute."

"You are the Commander."

"And as Commander, I order you to let it go."

Lin Lill dragged her eyes over Venick's face. Ellina knew that look. It was the same way Venick had looked at Ellina earlier when he decided not to question her about her trip to the river. There was a promise there, an agreement to let things go…for now.

They called the meeting to an end. Everyone agreed to continue mulling over the problem and to reconvene if any new information was uncovered. Branton and Artis exited the tent first, their long elven braids swishing in unison. Lin Lill went next, chin high, followed closely by Erol, who gave Venick a sympathetic pat on the shoulder. Ellina was the last to come to her feet. She was halfway out of the tent when Venick's hand closed on her sleeve, tugging her gently backward. "Not so fast." He dipped his head, squinting as he searched her face. "Are you alright?"

That was like him, to ask if she was alright when he was the one who had been attacked. He caught her expression and gave a slight smile. "So it's like Lin said? You just fancied a dip in a river?"

Ellina shrugged. She did not want Venick probing into her early morning swim session. He had a way of seeing things too clearly. Of seeing *her* too clearly. And though there were times when Ellina appreciated his insight, she often wished it was easier to hide. It could be disorienting, having another person read your every thought, particularly when you yourself did not even know what you were thinking.

She turned the question back on him, motioning towards the corpse.

Venick raked a hand through his hair. The movement was momentarily distracting. Venick's hair had grown these past months. Not nearly as long as an elf's, which might reach as far as their waist, but long enough to brush his shoulders. Wavy. Thick.

"I was lucky," Venick said. "The conjuror was at a disadvantage—working from outside the camp like that, she couldn't actually see the fight, so she struggled to control the corpse. She had it facing the wrong way at one point. It bought me time. Not that time was much help." He grimaced. "It was like fighting a cloth doll. Stabbing it was useless. It just kept coming for me."

It had been the same when Ellina first witnessed the conjurors practicing their corpse-bending in the palace crypts. She had seen an elf cut off an undead's head, but it had not stopped the creature from fighting. Or rather, it had not stopped the *conjuror* from fighting. The corpse was merely a vessel for the conjuror's power, a puppet that could be manipulated on its master's behalf. A severed head was no obstacle.

"She was female," Venick said abruptly. "The corpse-bender, I mean. The one behind last night's attack. Lin Lill said she was female. I thought Balid might…" He stumbled. "I thought it might have been him."

The space around Ellina seemed to shrink. Balid, the elf who had stolen Ellina's voice. Balid, the elf who Ellina had first seen controlling a corpse in the crypts. A powerful elf, vicious in a way even Youvan had not been. If Ellina killed Balid, they believed that his conjuring would be reversed, and she would get her voice back. Yet whenever Ellina tried to imagine facing him, her mind only served her images of the prison: Balid's long, slim fingers. Farah's wicked smile. The feeling of her voice being sucked from her throat.

She looked at the wall of the tent, the way it cupped the morning light. She tried to breathe evenly.

"If Balid was with that conjuror last night," Venick began. "If there was even a chance—"

Ellina lifted a hand to stop him. She did not want Venick to finish that sentence. She did not want to hear his voice go low with resolve as he offered to turn his army around, forsaking their greater mission to hunt down Balid. And Venick would offer it. He would run his army into the ground if it meant giving Ellina her voice back, because he blamed himself, and believed it was the right thing.

He was wrong. It was not Venick's fault, what had happened to her. It was not his job to set things right. And Venick had sacrificed enough for her already. Too much. He must be aware of the problems her presence was causing among his soldiers, the way they gossiped, the mistrust it sowed. Ellina could not let Venick throw away any more of his hard-won progress on her behalf.

If anyone was going to go after Balid, it would have to be her.

A feverish shiver spread from her chest. Ellina again remembered the prison, guards gripping bruises into her forearms, Balid sliding towards her like a snake slides over sand. The blacks of his eyes had been large. His mouth was a bloodless slit. He lifted his hands, an almost delicate gesture, a conductor before his orchestra. Then those hands had squeezed to fists, and Ellina's world cracked down the middle.

THREE

The city looked familiar.

This was what Venick thought as they rode into Igor, his contingent trailing behind him like a great, muddy cloak. He squinted at the buildings, the outpost, the low stone fences, all of which looked halfway to crumbling, pried apart by time and weeds like fingers pry apart a biscuit. He tried to place the familiarity. Was Venick simply imagining things, or had he really seen this place before? In a book, maybe? Or a painting?

Unlikely. The plainslands were located on a peninsula, separated from the rest of the continent by Heartshire Bay. It wasn't the bay itself that was an obstacle—those waters were smooth enough to rock a baby to sleep—but rather, it was the divide. Plainspeople and lowlanders had been warring off and on for the better part of a century, with little trust and even less trade between them. Not much opportunity for artwork to cross the water. Not much demand for it, even if it had.

Still, as Venick urged his blind mare Eywen down packed-earth streets, he couldn't seem to shake that feeling of familiarity. It was in the block-shaped houses, the leaden glass windows, the ambient sounds of people and animals. The city itself was of middling size, remote enough to require its own farmlands and grazelands. The goats and sheep had been herded inside for winter, but Venick could see big-bodied horses out in the pasture, their necks dipping gently over frosted bales of hay.

Too many horses, Venick noted. Too many people, for that matter. Igor was large enough to support its residents, but nowhere near large enough to handle the sudden influx of soldiers who'd traveled to meet the resistance. As Venick drew towards the city's center, he saw soldiers loitering in the streets, in the alleys, even a few up on the rooftops. They smoked fat rolls of tobacco and slender pipes smelling suspiciously of jekkis, their legs dangling over gutters as they watched Venick pass.

"What say you, Commander?"

Erol rode up beside him. As usual, the healer looked well-rested, his grey hair combed neatly back, his white robes pristine, despite hard days on the road. The subject of Erol's attire had become a topic of much speculation among Venick's men. How did the healer manage to stay so clean when the rest of them looked like drowned cats? As far as Venick knew, the soldiers still hadn't uncovered his secret.

"I say I'll be happy once we're off these streets," Venick replied.

Erol cut Venick a look. "You don't like Igor?"

"I don't like *ambush*."

"We're not being ambushed, lad."

Venick drew his eyes up again. "Not yet."

Erol followed Venick's gaze to the men on the rooftops. Venick couldn't be sure if Erol saw what he saw. Then again, Erol hadn't been raised a warrior.

Venick had. And so it was easy to imagine those were enemy soldiers overhead. Easy, to see their hardened lambskin armor and double-headed spears and envision an attack. Venick had no shortage of memories to supply the vision. At sixteen, he'd enlisted as a trooper in the lowland army and had battled plainspeople bearing that very gear. They'd been a tricky adversary, emerging from the depths of their sacred rivers to strike with spears and blow darts, only to vanish again, like tigers into reeds. *Devious*, Venick's father had once called the plainspeople. *Those warriors know the land—they worship it, even—and that makes them crafty. Fighting the plainspeople is like trying to catch a fly in one hand.*

"Harmon has worked hard to lay the groundwork for our arrival," Erol said in a tone that made it obvious that he saw Venick's thoughts and disliked them. "Her missives have been clear. You've come to offer these people a treaty on behalf of the resistance, and the councilors of Igor are eager to accept. My advice? Don't go hunting monsters where there are none."

Funny, seeing as Venick had been attacked by a monster just the prior night. Yet Venick dropped his gaze. Tried, too, to drop his suspicions. Erol was right—Venick hadn't come to fight the plainspeople. He'd come to extend a hand of friendship, which the councilors of Igor did seem eager to accept. That made sense, given that the highlands, lowlands, and northern elves were already allied. If presented the choice between joining the resistance or making enemies with both the resistance *and* the Dark Army, the plainspeople would be fools to choose the latter.

Venick thumbed the leather of Eywen's reins, then kicked her into a trot, guiding their party past a line of low grey buildings and up towards the old baron's house. In the lowlands, the highest-ranking officers always rode at a formation's center, not only because it was safest, but because their commands could travel most quickly up and down the ranks.

That Venick had taken a spot at the army's head wasn't so much a show of leadership as it was a sign of faith, a peace offering in and of itself. *I'm entering your city undefended and exposed, and I'm trusting you not to kill me.*

Venick glanced back at Ellina. His wasn't the only position that seemed selected to send a message. During their journey from Parith, Ellina had often ridden by Venick's side, but now she hovered a few ranks back, her borrowed silver stallion plodding steadily between Branton and Lin Lill. Venick wondered if Ellina had chosen that spot herself. Or had Lin Lill suggested it?

He shouldn't be bothered—it was such a small thing. Yet when it came to Ellina, all Venick *had* were the small things. Every silent gesture, every glance, every inch taken or given was like a verse in a larger song. The tune wouldn't make sense if he missed a line. The tune hardly made sense anyway. And still Venick read into everything, because Ellina couldn't speak for herself. And even if she could, would she tell him the truth?

Not that he deserved the truth. Not that Ellina owed him anything.

They reached the city's center, a wide plaza paved in uneven stone that stretched between a collection of taller buildings. Harmon was there, looking less like a military leader and more like a puffed-up princess in a dress of deep green, her ankles clad in white stockings, hair piled high atop her head. Gathered in the plaza around her stood a congregation of citizens, soldiers, councilors, a full-color guard, and—to Venick's surprise and subsequent dismay—a band.

The band struck up a tune. Flags were unfurled. And dear gods, was that *confetti?*

Harmon gave a wide smile. "Hail, Venick."

Venick cleared his throat. "Hail."

"You have traveled far, brave Commander. Your return has been *much* awaited." Nearby, a group of women giggled. Venick's neck burned. "But come." Harmon closed the distance between them, sweeping her arms wide. When she spoke, her voice was pitched to carry. "Your men are weary, but you are here now, and you will find rest and welcome."

"Laying it on a little thick, don't you think?" Venick muttered.

"Play along," she warned through her teeth. Then again, in her stage voice: "Let us all convene in the tavern. We have refreshments there ready and waiting for our heroes."

Venick understood what Harmon was doing. This was a public reunion between the Elder's daughter and the lowland Commander, the perfect opportunity to showcase their union and, subsequently, bolster the alliance between their countries. Though Venick had broken off his engagement to Harmon, they'd agreed to keep up the façade while the war was ongoing. That had been the smart choice. It was still. Yet as Venick looked out over the sea of eager onlookers, he couldn't help but think that this was a punishment designed specifically for him.

"Well?" Harmon prompted.

Venick didn't reply. At that moment, he'd glanced behind him to discover that—while Ellina's horse was still standing placidly between Branton and Lin Lill—its rider had vanished from the saddle.

He turned, searching for a head of dark hair among the crowd, those golden eyes. He was met instead with a mix of faces, elven and lowlander and highlander and plainsperson, and Harmon before them all, a warning in her expression as she followed his gaze and his train of thought. Venick couldn't go running after Ellina, not when this was supposed to be a heartfelt reunion with his bride. *A show of unity*, he could almost hear Harmon thinking. *Remember?*

The pause had gone on too long. People were beginning to notice.

"I could use a drink," Venick finally admitted.

"An ale," Harmon agreed, her smile returning in full force. "I know just how you like it."

. . .

"You fool," Harmon snapped.

She crossed the room—private, underground: the tavern's cellar—in four long strides, braced her hands against a wine barrel. Spun back around in the next instant, her teeth baring like a wild wanewolf. "Whose idea was it to name you Commander, anyway? The way I see it, men usually want a leader with a brain."

"I have a brain," Venick replied mildly.

"Half a brain, maybe."

It wasn't the first time Venick had borne the brunt of Harmon's anger. Wasn't the first time he'd earned it, either. After smoothing over the almost-incident at the city's center, Harmon had ushered Venick into the tavern for a round of drinks, then into the adjoining courtyard for the official treaty signature ceremony, then back to the tavern for a celebratory performance orchestrated by the city's leaders. Venick greeted dignitaries and shook hands but faces and names quickly began to lose all meaning. It was around this time that Harmon had explained—quietly, the words fluttering over his shoulder—that the highland soldiers would be expecting a public display of affection from the soon-to-be-weds. Nothing overblown, she'd assured, nothing extreme, just a small gesture. A holding of hands would suffice, or even a fond smile.

Venick had been stiff as a wooden plank. Harmon did her best to smile for the both of them, excusing his stiffness for exhaustion, and the gatherers seemed appeased, right up until the moment when Venick asked if anyone had seen Ellina.

The room had gone still. Glances were exchanged. The vintner asked Venick to repeat himself, and Venick—tired of being paraded around like a circus animal, and suddenly resentful of his situation—had done so. Loudly.

"Honestly," Harmon continued, making fists of her skirts. "Things were going fine until you pulled that stunt. It's like you want people to figure out we're faking this engagement."

Venick didn't want that, but nor did he understand why there had to be so much showmanship. It was a political marriage, for gods' sake. Half of these men had been there when the Elder made his proposal: the highland army in exchange for Venick's fidelity. Venick didn't love Harmon. She didn't love him. Everyone knew that.

"These are highland traditions," Harmon continued. "It's what's expected, no matter how the marriage was arranged. Things might be different in the lowlands, but if you want to convince my men to fight alongside yours, to show our countries that we are truly united—which is necessary to hold this whole thing together, by the way—then this is how it has to be." A heavy sigh. "I'd do this without you if I could. But I can't."

And there it was, the twinge in Venick's belly that was regret. He gave a sigh to match hers, loosened his stance. Venick had known the challenges they faced, knew the kind of balance they'd need to strike to convince highlanders and lowlanders and elves and now plainspeople to live and breathe and work in the same space, when before that space had been filled with nothing but war and derision. Venick had thought, because he'd been able to persuade elves and lowlanders to work together, that it'd be as easy to connect the highlanders and plainspeople, too. But he'd already earned the loyalty of the lowlanders and the elves and had been able to translate that loyalty into cooperation.

He didn't have that kind of pull here. The highlanders belonged to Harmon first. As for the plainspeople…it was likely that they fell somewhere in between. They'd wait to see how things would play out before fully committing to a side. Would the newly formed resistance succeed in battling the Dark Army, or would they tear themselves apart first?

"Well?" Harmon demanded. "Do you have anything to say?"

"I'm sorry."

She rolled her eyes. "I'll say."

"I am," he insisted. "I can do better."

She blew a breath through her nose, what might have been a snort. "There's a welcome dinner tonight, hosted by the city's council in our honor. Can you at least try to follow my instructions?" She gave another sigh, but her anger was all used up now, and there was no real force behind it. "This arrangement isn't forever, you know."

Venick studied the ceiling. Music wafted from the tavern above, floorboards creaking under people's feet. Every so often, someone would stomp, and a dusting of plaster would shake loose. The cellar was coated with it, as if all the barrels had grown a second skin.

"Venick?"

"Yeah," he said. "I know."

FOUR

Ellina tipped her head back, surveying the slatted exterior of the granary. The building stood a half-story taller than any of the surrounding structures, its planking done in three different types of wood, which either meant that this granary had once burned partway down and had since been rebuilt, or the original carpenters were just poor planners. Ellina considered both possibilities, weighing the likelihood of each, though neither the three-toned wood nor the cause of its incongruity made any difference to her current problem—if she wanted up this wall, she would need a running start.

The thought made her jaw harden. Ellina had scaled hundreds of walls, but never before had she required a boost. Usually, mounting obstacles took little more than a thoughtless spring *up*, a quick release of speed and strength. Maybe—Ellina thought this timidly, like a beggar holding out a cautious hand for fear of being slapped—if she gave herself enough time and rest, that was still all it would take. But for now

Ellina's shoulder was aching, and her legs were saddle sore, and if she wanted to reach the granary's roof before dark, this was how it would have to be.

She took the necessary steps backward. Ten, maybe twelve. Ellina did not know, exactly. She did not count things like steps anymore.

She sprinted towards the building in a burst, took several vertical leaps up the wall, and launched herself within reach of the jutting roof. She caught the ledge and gripped tightly with one handhold, ignoring the hot sear of pain in her shoulder, the protest of weakened muscles. Her legs dangled wildly, her feet windmilling as she swung up her second hand, then used what was left of her strength to haul herself over the lip.

Cool, weather-warped shingles. Grimy, and therefore slick. Ellina felt that grime smear into her palms as she pushed upright, moving towards a gable and a second, smaller roof. She scaled this as well, and then she was there, clinging to a weathervane at the top of the granary and peering out over the city.

The granary was not the tallest point in Igor, but it was high enough that Ellina could see the network of muddy streets below, the little homes arranged in tight clusters, a few larger buildings interspersed between. Ellina scanned the grid of roads and public houses, spinning in a slow circle until at last, she spotted it—a flat grey river bisecting the city.

Her hand tightened on the weathervane. Ellina had smelled the musky tang of water as soon as they entered Igor, but she had not been able to ask about it, nor locate its source, until now. The river was three times as wide as any of the brooks they had encountered during their trek from Parith, and while it appeared to be slow-moving from this distance, Ellina suspected a river of that size must carry quite the current.

A flutter in her chest. An eager, reaching thrill in her limbs. Ellina wanted to test the water for herself. She wanted to see just how strong that current truly was.

She began her descent down the roof, pausing long enough to glance back towards the city's center. Though it was only midafternoon, the sky hung low, the sun hidden somewhere behind the clouds. The muted light made the day seem later than it was: an hour for calling children home and setting tables for dinner, for cozy blankets and warm fires, and four walls to shut out the night.

Ellina could have those things. She could turn around, rejoin their contingent, catch the end of the city's welcome reception. Maybe even find herself a decent meal, something hot to warm her belly. But that would mean returning to the tavern, and *that* would mean a new crowd of faces to pick her apart. It would mean restraint and confinement, judgment and side eyes and the itchy, cobwebby feel of mutters skittering up her skin.

And, Ellina admitted to herself, it would mean watching Venick and Harmon playacting the happy couple.

Ellina had known to expect that. She had envisioned it, even, in an attempt to armor herself against its sting: Venick holding Harmon's hand. Venick pulling out Harmon's chair. Venick and Harmon smiling, toasting, sharing each other's space. Ellina understood the political purpose of such displays. Harmon had explained it all quite clearly in Parith, back when the two of them had come to a sort of truce. At the time, Ellina found herself agreeing with Harmon's reasons—it *would* be better if the Elder's daughter and the lowland Commander pretended engagement. It *would* smooth a path for this alliance, show that their leaders were willing to guide by example. The mainlands had been infighting for decades. Many lowland soldiers had fathers or sons or friends who had been killed by highlanders and vice versa. *So how,* Harmon had asked, *do we get them to put all that hate aside in order to battle as brothers in arms?* The woman had drummed her fingers along her thigh, then turned the hand over, as if offering a present. *We take a shortcut.*

Ellina knew this. She should not be bothered.

Yet she was bothered. Despite its logic, the thought of watching Venick and Harmon together made Ellina cringe with embarrassment… though why *she* should be embarrassed, Ellina could not say.

She dropped off the granary roof, crouching low to absorb the impact, one hand jutting down for balance. Her shoulder gave another twinge; it would ache in the morning, but then, it always ached. Ellina did what she normally did and ignored it.

She started towards the river.

People streamed around her. There were farmers hauling hay and goatherds driving goats, nannies and marketers and vagrants and soldiers. Some of those soldiers were elves, easily identified by their hair and their height, but many more were human, easily identified by… everything else.

It struck Ellina how different humans were from each other. Some were wide and some were skinny, some had missing teeth or beards, warts or birthmarks, orange hair or black hair or yellow or brown. They spoke in different accents, dressed in different colors. Their expressions, too, were all unique. Even a simple smile might look different from person to person, depending on the face. Ellina thought about elvish, how vital inflection was to that language since elves did not allow facial expressions to color their words. Humans were not constrained in this way; expressions *were* words, each stamped with a person's identity, revealing their thoughts as if written on paper.

That was useful…usually. Now, though, as Ellina moved across a thoroughfare towards the residential district, she decided that she would not mind the humans learning a bit of elven composure. If the citizens of Igor knew how to shutter their thoughts, maybe Ellina would not have to watch as they caught sight of her, their eyes drifting first to her simple elven armor, then to her dark hair, her face. She would not have to see the moment of recognition, or how recognition soured their expressions with contempt.

Ellina ducked her head, doing her best to avoid eye contact. She told herself that their contempt was no matter. She told herself that she had survived worse. Yet her heart felt suddenly smaller.

She carried that feeling—like her heart had curled into a shell—with her the rest of the way to the river. It was only when she reached the water that some of her pain seemed to ease, her mind drawn to the object before her. The river was larger than Ellina had first thought, as wide across as ten roads and farther-reaching than she could see. More curiously than that, it was steaming, not with winter mist but with… vapor?

Ellina crouched at the river's edge, dipped a finger down to the first knuckle. The water was blood warm. A hot spring, maybe, though Ellina had never seen one of this size. Its surface was vacant. No boats. No people. No one bathing or washing or fishing. Ellina circled her finger in the water, mulling over explanations—

"Hey, you can't touch that!"

—when the answer planted itself in front of her.

The woman before her was nearly as wide as she was tall, dressed in stained overalls and hash-marked leather boots. A quick glance at her waist and thighs confirmed she was unarmed, though there were scars across her meaty knuckles that suggested violence. A brawler.

"What are you doing, touching the water?"

Ellina came to her feet. Judging by the woman's severity, Ellina had just broken a city rule, though why touching the river was not allowed, she did not know. She held up her hands anyway, giving her best impression of *apology*.

"Will you not speak?" The woman's voice rose. "Only initiated warriors are permitted to touch the river. This is sacred ground!"

Ellina made the motion again, uncomfortably aware of the attention their confrontation was drawing. *Apology. No harm intended.*

The woman's face colored. "Are you mocking me?"

She made a grab for Ellina's arm. Ellina slapped the hand aside, reflex-quick. She saw the contact register in the woman's eyes. Heard it, in the mutters of nearby onlookers. Out of sight, a dog began barking. The bystanders converged. Ellina realized that while the woman carried no weapons, most of the rest of these people did.

"Tell her how it is, Helda," someone jeered.

"The princess thinks she's above human laws."

"She thinks she's too good to speak to us!"

The press of bodies tightened. For one reckless moment, Ellina imagined drawing her weapons, flashing her green glass, driving this crowd back like Raffan had once taught her. The image fizzled in the next moment, petered and faded. These people recognized her, but they either did not know or did not believe that her voice had been stolen. Yet they were supposed to be her allies. Violence would only make things worse.

Ellina held her hands up higher. *It was a mistake*, she thought fervently, imagining the words as if they might transmute by will alone. *I did not know.* She faltered when she realized that among the crowd were several soldiers she recognized, men whom she had journeyed with from Parith. They could come to her defense, explain that her voice was lost, that she meant no disrespect. Yet they said nothing.

"Last chance, *conjuror*," the woman named Helda spat. "Either explain why you were breaking our laws, or let your silence stand for an admission of guilt."

Ellina did not think that Helda cared anymore for her answers. There was an eagerness in the woman's eyes, fueled by attention and the prospect of a fight. Helda took a heavy step closer, and it felt as though she moved for the entire city, everyone taking a collective step with her.

Without warning, Ellina's vision swayed. She forgot her weapons, forgot all tactics for driving back a crowd. She felt suddenly chilled, as if the clouds had closed over the sun, though the clouds had been covering the sun all along. And there, creeping along the edges of her awareness: a memory.

Ellina tried to stifle the memory. Failed. Helda's face loomed closer, and someone grinned, and the memory lifted inside her, transporting Ellina back over the plains and the tundra, back to a garden in Evov, and her prison, and an endless, suffocating black. She gulped a breath. Wheezed it out. Helda's face seemed to warp, her features pulling apart like taffy, and Ellina's only thought was that if she fainted beneath this woman, it would be very bad indeed.

"Give her space."

Venick burst into Ellina's vision, riding high atop his buckskin, the horse swiveling her blind eyes like one of the living dead. The crowd abruptly drew back, coiling away like a nest of snakes.

"—the size of that horse—"

"—friend of hers?"

"That's the *Commander*."

Venick wedged Eywen between Ellina and the crowd, using the horse's broad body like a shield. Helda looked like she had swallowed a toad. "Commander. Apologies. I did not realize this was your friend…"

"All of the elves are my friends."

"Of course, yes, it's just that this elf was touching—"

"I know what she was doing."

He was furious. Ellina felt the ripples of Venick's fury lap against her skin, travel out in rings through the crowd.

Helda must have felt them, too. She licked her lips, eyes darting from side to side. "Then you know why we reacted as we did. It is forbidden to touch the water."

"And how would Ellina know that," Venick asked, "if no one tells her?"

"It is not my job to explain our customs—"

"You will make it your job."

Helda had gone too far, and she knew it. She babbled something about her deepest regrets, but Venick was done listening. He swung Eywen around, raising his voice to address the city. "It's not easy to share your home with outsiders. I know that. But it looks like some of you have forgotten why we're here. Let me refresh your memory." His cheeks were ruddy with anger, his eyes like chips of ice. Ellina had never heard him speak like this: as if every word was set to ignite. "The resistance is here to fight for you. Your homes, your families, your livelihoods—it's all at stake, and right now, these soldiers are all that stand between you and oblivion. Take a good look at the men and elves around you. By the time this war is over, some of them will have died for you. We will not be in Igor forever, but while we are, I expect you to treat my soldiers—" a significant look at Ellina "—all of my soldiers with the respect such a sacrifice warrants. That's an order."

The crowd was sheepish now. There was a murmuring of *Yes, Commander*, a handful of salutes. Then, like scolded children, they all slunk away.

Venick swung his leg off Eywen, came to land beside Ellina with a soft thud. He did not immediately look at her. Instead, he peered out over the river. "I'm sorry." His voice was tired now. Worn to the quick. "I should have done that first thing."

Now that the mob was dispersed and Ellina's heart was resuming its normal rhythm, she felt wretchedly grateful...and foolish. This was not the first time memories had paralyzed her, but it was the first time they had interfered so dangerously. Ellina must learn to control them better.

But...Venick. His eyes were still hard, his shoulders tight. He was blaming himself. Again.

Ellina hesitated only briefly before reaching out to brush his hand. A light touch, three fingers along the side of his wrist. Venick blinked down at the contact. Glanced up at her. He started to say something, but stopped himself, turning back towards the water. Ellina had the sense that when he spoke next, it was to distract from the fact that he could not seem to hold her gaze. "You've found the Taro, I see."

A stab of disappointment. She let her fingers drop.

"All humans name their rivers," Venick explained, "but only the plainspeople have any true ties to the water. Every plainsland city is built along a river like this one. It's believed that the rivers belong to different gods, and that each river is the god's lifeline to the city and its people. The Taro is one of the largest. You can follow this water straight to Heartshire Bay." He peeked a look back at her. Though his voice was still tired, his expression had gentled, his mouth quirking around the words. "The citizens tend to get fussy about it, as you've seen. So, no swimming lessons here, I'm afraid."

This time, his gaze lingered. Ellina felt his gaze like sunlight on stone, warming all of her shadowed corners. She wondered if he, too, was remembering the day he had taught her to swim. The sky had glowed white. The everpool was a deep mirror. His hands had come to her elbows, then to her waist, his instructions rising and dipping like a lullaby.

Ellina had been hypnotized by them. By him. She wondered if Venick would ever choose to go back, knowing now what they both knew: that every day after was doomed.

"We should be getting back," Venick said. "There's a welcome dinner. We're expected."

FIVE

O h good," said Harmon. "You're here."

They entered a corridor outside the grand ballroom, which was within a home that had once belonged to a baron. *A relic*, Venick had called the house as they approached, peering up at the arched columns, the row of evenly spaced windows. According to Venick, the royal family had been dead for six hundred years, having either been peacefully dissolved or violently overthrown—the records were never quite clear as to which. After the monarchy was abolished, many of their manors were dismantled, the gold melted and sold, the stone reworked into shelters and roads. This home was one of the few remaining artifacts from that era.

"No one lives here anymore," Venick had told Ellina as they traveled up the curving path. "It's a public space, overseen by the city's councilors and kept up by the people. Cities sometimes use these buildings as courthouses or inns or—" his mouth had creased with distaste, "dinner venues."

Though the house was well secured with guards at every entrance, it was otherwise empty of people, despite obvious signs of occupancy: candles alight on the sidebars, half-drunk cups of tea in the sitting areas, an abandoned game of cards. As Venick and Ellina made their way through a series of long, straight hallways, Ellina began peeking through open doors, looking for guests or a staff. The home was lovely, if not a bit cluttered. The walls were obscured by portraits and tapestries, the tables stacked with books, the inset shelving stuffed with a random assortment of items that might have been period pieces and might have been junk. Ellina envisioned an overzealous collector managing the home's décor, refusing to part with a single item.

It was not until they reached the corridor where Harmon waited that Ellina finally heard it: a low buzz.

They came closer. The noise grew. There was a clatter of china, the din of conversation, the scraping of feet and chairs. By the time they reached the ballroom's threshold, Ellina had no doubt where the household had gone. They were all gathered there, behind that final door.

Harmon watched the pair approach, surveying Venick like a mother might survey a child. "Didn't you want to change out of your riding clothes?" She shushed him with a hand before he could answer. "Never mind, there isn't time. Everyone's already inside. It won't be long now before our entrance." Though Harmon looked fit for a throne—her hair woven with golden lace, her highland-style gown pleated in even folds—she sounded somewhat breathless, as if she had just dashed up a flight of stairs. "Ellina, you can go in now, find yourself a seat. Venick and I will wait for the signal. We enter last."

Ellina did not know much about Harmon's father, but this seemed like the performative type of strategy the Elder would have employed, one that set himself at center stage.

Venick appeared to share Ellina's thoughts. He spoke lightly. "Another highland custom?"

"Be grateful," Harmon replied. "If we were really in the highlands, we'd have to dance. And then there'd be the First Kiss. Oh, don't look at me like that, it's not like we haven't—"

She stopped. Glanced at Ellina.

The silence seemed to eat up the air.

"Ellina—" Venick started, but Ellina had already turned away, pushing through the doors into the ballroom. "Ellina," he tried again, but Harmon was gripping the back of his shirt, whispering something about running after her twice in one day, and that he had promised, and then Ellina heard no more, because the ballroom doors were closing between them, and she was not listening, anyway.

Her feet carried her. She was grateful for her feet, for the fact that they could move her forward while the rest of her was still stuck on that threshold.

It's a political move, Ellina could hear Harmon's voice insist. *The engagement is just for show.*

You understand that, don't you?

Well, Ellina? Don't you?

Ellina wanted a dark corner. She needed a moment to collect herself, to locate the missing parts of her armor and piece them back together. Greaves. Gauntlets. Shield and sword. However, she was given no such moment because on the other side of the door was a fully packed ballroom, the welcome dinner party and its guests. Worse, those guests all seemed to be looking at *her*, stripping Ellina of her anonymity at the moment when she most wanted to be anonymous.

Ellina fumbled. She felt a twinge of that same feeling from the river, the one that threatened to open its jaws and consume her. There were so many faces—highlanders, predominantly, dressed in their colorful garb, but also many neutrally clad plainspeople, some weathered lowlanders, a few elves, plus a guard at every door and window. Had these guests been waiting for her? But of course, it was not Ellina they were expecting, but Venick and Harmon, who would soon appear out of that same door.

An announcer began the night's introductions, his voice amplified by a speaking trumpet. Ellina forced herself to keep moving. As she searched for an empty seat at one of the two long tables, she found herself wishing suddenly, helplessly, for Dourin. Last Ellina knew, her friend was still under the care of Parith's healers, having suffered a wound to the abdomen during an assassination attempt on the Elder. Dourin might be recovered now. Or his health might have deteriorated further. Ellina had sent letters to Parith but received no reply, not from the Elder or the healers or Dourin himself.

The announcer continued his speech. Ellina listened to the words without really hearing what was said. Her anxiety was rising. This dinner was supposedly for invited guests only, but either the organizers had miscounted, or additional members had taken liberties—every chair was occupied, and people were beginning to throw her looks. *Sit down*, someone hissed. *You're blocking the view!*

Ellina abandoned her hunt and went to stand at the back of the hall. The ballroom walls were plastered with floral paper showing giant, feral-looking flowers. She pressed her shoulder blades to them, imagining that she could vanish between their vines.

The announcer's voice stopped. The doors flung open.

The ballroom erupted with applause. Several highlanders stood from their seats as the couple entered, Harmon waving like a debutante, Venick looking grim and somehow desperate. Harmon leaned her head against Venick's shoulder. The crowd oohed. She gave his arm a squeeze. The crowd sighed.

Ellina marked the distance from herself to the nearest window. She entertained fantasies about diving straight through it.

A string quartet struck up a tune. The volume in the ballroom steadily rose. Someone called for a toast, but this had not been planned, and so there was a moment of riffling while two jeweled goblets were procured, snatched straight from the hands of nearby guests. Harmon clinked their glasses and drank, but Venick scarcely touched the cup to his lips.

Somewhere beyond the clouds, the sun gave a final sigh before dropping beneath the horizon. Ellina felt that shift under her skin, a chill that reached her bones.

The celebration began in earnest. Despite this being a welcome dinner, Ellina did not actually see any food being served. Instead, wine was distributed, and there was dancing, a mix of mainland styles that Ellina could no more tell apart than she could perform herself. Harmon, with her shimmering hair and bustled gown, was easy to track as she passed from partner to partner, but Venick had vanished. Ellina did not know where he had gone.

When a servant offered Ellina a glass of wine, she accepted it and drank deeply.

"May I?" said a voice at her elbow.

Ellina startled, sloshing her drink.

Erol was there, motioning at the open space of wall beside her as if it was a seat. Ellina wiped her chin with the back of her hand, stifling a cough.

The healer set his shoulders against the wall. "I don't suppose you've seen Branton, have you? He took my water flask. You may have noticed, but the plainspeople don't serve water. You either bring your own, or you drink wine."

Ellina was not sure if this was a rebuke, and if it was, who he was rebuking? Her, for the way she had just downed nearly an entire glass, or the plainspeople, for making it possible?

She dropped her hand, sticky with spilled wine, and looked away.

"Ah, well." Erol shrugged. "I had not planned on staying long, anyway. Not that I mind a good celebration. The noise, though, I could do without. It reminds me too much of the parties your mother used to drag me to."

That brought Ellina's attention back.

"Queen Rishiana loved big occasions," Erol said, seeing her surprise. "She liked making connections, and attending galas was the quickest way to do that."

Ellina had known this. She knew, too, that Erol had spent time in the elflands. He was a friend and work partner of the elf Traegar, who had once trained alongside Ellina and Dourin in the legion. It was no secret that Erol and Ellina's mother were acquainted; Traegar's connection with the queen would have ensured that. But Erol's words seemed to hint at a deeper familiarity.

"Rishiana didn't drink much, as you must know. I think she liked to leave that part to me." Erol gave a self-deprecating laugh, the kind the old often have for their younger selves. "That was all before you were born, of course. Once Rishi became a mother, things changed."

She drew the border, he meant, which separated the mainlands from the elflands. Erol would have been banned from the east, along with all other humans. It was said that Queen Rishiana invoked these measures to protect their race, and for years, Ellina had believed that. Elves were dying out. Elven fledglings were rare to begin with, a problem made worse by the fact that elves had begun choosing human partners over elven ones. But elves and humans cannot bear children, and their population suffered as a result. In an attempt to change their fate, Queen Rishiana had stepped in, creating new laws that prohibited elves from associating with humans, among other things. Her measures were extreme and controversial. They implicated Ellina, who had been forcefully bondmated to her once-friend and fellow legionnaire, Raffan. But they had worked. In the years since, their elven numbers had greatly recovered.

Ellina ran a finger along the top of her wine glass. She could hear her own thoughts. She could hear how they echoed with empty spaces, gaps in a story that had never quite made sense.

"Venick has been asking me to check on your shoulder," Erol said.

Ellina's finger flinched against the glass.

"He's been a bit of a pest about it, actually." Erol's smile was tinged with knowing. "I told him that your shoulder is healed, and there's nothing more I can do for you. I mostly said it to get him out of my hair. But if you ever do need a healer, I want you to know that you can always come to me."

Ellina looked into Erol's face. He had fine bones, grey hair but thick white eyebrows, a delicate build. It occurred to Ellina that she had misread him earlier, when she believed he was admonishing her for the wine. Erol was not one to rebuke. There was an openness about him, a soft sort of countenance.

Kind, Ellina thought. This man was kind.

"Ah." Erol's eyes alighted across the room. "I've just spotted Branton." He pushed off the wall, switching to elvish. "*Ram aulin.*" That was an old elven phrase, one that had mostly gone out of style. It meant, *until next time*, though the literal translation was, *keep well.*

No sooner had Erol departed that the crowd split, making way for another figure.

Venick moved towards her. His shoulders were hunched, his mouth drawn in. He looked worried. Hurt, too, which made no sense. It made no sense that *he* should be the one looking hurt, after everything. This thought was so frustrating that Ellina nearly walked away again, yet she thought about how she had misread Erol. She thought about how she was allowing her feelings to dictate her actions when she had never been one to be ruled by emotion.

She stayed where she was.

Venick stopped a few paces away, abruptly, as if he'd reached the end of a lead. "Can we talk?" A poor choice of words. He sighed, pushed a hand through his hair. He had been doing that a lot lately. His hair bore permanent indents, like rows of crops. "Please."

"Why'd you need to talk to *her*?"

The voice came from somewhere within the crowd. Venick's head whipped around, but the speaker, whoever she was, had already vanished into the throng.

Ellina's cheeks burned. She hated that. She hated that she was so easily shamed, that she felt despised and powerless, and that Venick had to see it. She was preoccupied by this, and so—when someone moved up behind Venick—she nearly missed it.

She should have missed it anyway. The shift was subtle, and Ellina was distracted, and the party was loud and her head was buzzing, and there were so many people, an entire ballroom full of them. What was one more? Yet there was something about the way this particular figure moved, an unusual quality to his gait that had Ellina's hair standing up before she understood why.

Her eyes focused. She saw what she should have overlooked.

An elf lifted a blowgun to his mouth, aiming at Venick.

Ellina tackled Venick to the ground just as the dart whirred overhead. She heard the projectile land harmlessly behind her—or rather, she heard the absence of any party guests thudding to the floor. It should have been a relief. But the weapon was slight, and the room was overflowing, and for a moment, no one understood what had happened. All they saw was Ellina tackling their Commander. They saw her dark hair and remembered that they did not trust this northern conjuror. They had suspected her all along, and now their suspicions were confirmed.

The room moved to action. Many of these dinner guests were warriors, and they swarmed the scene, hands reaching for Ellina's arms, her hair, yanking her away. Ellina dug her nails into forearms, mouthing helplessly. She was not the enemy—it was the blow dart assassin, please—he was right *there*. More hands, then, more soldiers. Ellina's scalp seared painfully. A sound filled her ears. If Ellina had to name the noise, she would say it was like the ambient ringing of a piano after the final note is struck and the key is released. And on the tail of that sound: a fresh swell of memories.

No, Ellina thought furiously. She would not give in to panic. She would not be overwhelmed by past traumas. She was stronger than that.

She had to be stronger than that.

The memories ebbed, the ringing fading in time for her to hear Venick's voice, a hard command. Her arms were released. She staggered, felt a new hand at her side. This one was warmer, steadying. Callused.

The scene snapped back. Venick at her elbow, offering support. Harmon's gaping eyes. And there between them, several men subduing the correct attacker this time, pinning him to the floor. The blow-darter appeared to be one of their own soldiers, dressed in the green and gold livery favored by the lowlanders. Though…not quite one of their own.

Ellina's fingers dug into Venick's sleeve.

The attacker looked like one of their troopers, but there was something wrong with him. This was what Ellina had seen earlier, before she understood what she was seeing.

The soldier was one of the undead.

SIX

There was a cry. The *shith* of swords being drawn from their sheaths, the *shoop* of axes from their belt loops. Men began hacking at the creature, bludgeoning the body in synchronized gives and takes, like this was one of their customary human dances, like the violence had a natural place there in the ballroom. Gore began to fly. The corpse came apart. Onlookers cringed and drew back, but Ellina did not. She stared hard at the carnage, the blood. Bright red and fresh, which meant the attacker had not been dead long. Then Ellina remembered that the corpse was not the real attacker, merely a vessel.

And, apparently, a distraction.

She hauled her eyes up, swept a look around the room. A sea of faces, the tables, the doors. Of that last there were two sets, a main entrance at the back and a second pair towards the front, plus all the windows. Yet each of these was secured by a guard, with no sign of anyone slipping away, no open exit routes, nothing but a frozen audience, and the rhythmic crunching of a body being dismembered.

Venick was giving orders to someone at his side. Lin Lill's furious face swam out of the crowd. Behind them, Erol watched the mayhem, flinching at every blow. His white robes were spotless. He was too far back to catch any blood splatter. Yet he seemed somehow off-color, and Ellina had the fleeting thought that he had somehow stepped too close, that he had been compromised by proximity.

The floor was a wet mirror of red. Seemingly far off, the sounds of chopping continued. Ellina's neck prickled, and she realized that Erol had indeed been compromised. That was not a trick of the light, the discoloration, the way he seemed smudged at the edges.

That was shadow-binding.

As if sensing her discovery, Erol's shadow twitched, then promptly departed his body. Ellina watched the dark form slip across the floor towards a window, and yes, there: a face behind that window. A flicker of black against black.

She took off. She ignored the sound of Venick's surprised *Ellina?*, the protest of guests as she shoved roughly past. She gained speed, leapt, and dove straight through the window.

A crash. A shower of glass. It was Ellina's luck that the frame's cross-beams were elf-sized, that the glass was not double paned. She sailed through the air and tumbled into a courtyard on the other side, bringing a spray of debris with her. She remembered wishing earlier for this very thing and tried not to choke on the irony.

Ellina lifted her head just in time to see a dark-haired figure fleeing around a corner and out of sight.

She gave chase. Her lungs felt like they had been filled with salt. Her legs were sluggish, her skin fiery with a constellation of cuts. And some-how, even though Venick had just been attacked, even though a conjuror had managed to sneak a corpse into their midst *again*, Ellina felt buoyant, like a balloon had been inflated inside her.

She ran. It felt good to run, to pursue, to do something other than think or fret or avoid. This was as liberating as a freezing dip in a winter river, the way pain and pressure drove out all other thoughts.

Igor's streets had mostly emptied for the night, everyone wanting inside where it was warm. The people Ellina did pass were useless to her, ignorant of the conjuror, the attack, this chase. Had Ellina had a voice, she might have called out to them, roped them to her mission, but Ellina did not have a voice, and she was tired of stewing over that fact. Her blood was pumping now. Her legs were gaining momentum. She could see the conjuror—smallish, female—up ahead, swinging another corner out of sight.

She would not get far. Ellina had caught the conjuror's scent like a hound on a rabbit. More than that, Ellina could hear her, crisscrossing through an alley to the left, quick-pattering down the adjacent street. The female was trapped between buildings and growing frantic: a mouse in a maze.

And then, a new sound. Boots on pavement. Distant hollers. This was one of those times when Ellina could be glad for Venick's perceptiveness—he must have figured the reason for her dash and ordered his soldiers to join the chase.

Ellina changed direction. Runnels of snow-slush churned along the roads, kicked up with her feet. A roaring barrel fire showed closed doors and roughly nailed window frames, a line of storefronts. Ellina knew this section of streets from her earlier survey of the city, the map of them clear in her mind. She calculated which direction the conjuror had gone, how many turns it would take to head her off. She reached a fork in the road and went left, pressed through a plaza, turned a final corner between two buildings—

And was nearly decapitated.

The conjuror materialized, wielding a slice of metal. It was not a sword but a broken segment of barrel ring, the kind used to seal together casks of wine.

Ellina slammed to the wet ground, heard the metal whistle overhead. Her mind iced over as she rolled swiftly out of range, and *where* had the female found that weapon? Conjurors did not often carry blades, believing themselves above such crude methods of violence. If the elf was resorting to this—a discarded piece of junk she must have picked up in the streets—it could only mean that she was fully sapped of strength, and therefore too weak to wield magic.

Ellina shoved to her feet. The female's hood had fallen back to reveal a crop of black hair, skin like goat milk, the chin a sharp little point. Blood ran down her wrist, dripped off her bare elbow. It took Ellina a moment to understand—the sharp edges of the barrel ring had punctured the elf's palm. She was cutting herself with her own weapon.

Ellina unsheathed her dagger. Out of sight, she could hear Venick's reinforcements sweeping the city, closer now.

She knew the smart thing. Ellina had the female trapped in an alley with the river to one end and the promise of soldiers to the other. And Ellina—despite her initial drive—was in less-than-ideal condition for combat. She had yet to gain back the weight lost during her time in Evov, nor the strength, and though the wound in her shoulder had healed, it had not healed well. It hurt to move in certain positions or stretch in certain ways. It would be a hindrance in a fight, but Ellina did not have to fight. If she could stall for time, backup would arrive, and the conjuror would be forced to surrender.

Yet a dull anger warmed Ellina's belly. She remembered once aiming an arrow at the Elder's heart. She remembered facing a mob in the city. She thought of how powerful she had felt in one situation, and how helpless in the other.

Ellina switched her grip on her dagger. The green glass blade was like a dragon's scale: shimmery in the light, yet nearly colorless in the dark.

She launched forward. The conjuror's face showed quick surprise as she parried, sidestepped, and tried to retreat. Ellina delivered a series of strikes, catching her opponent's forearm, her shoulder. More blood, then. More anger, too. As Ellina drove the female backward out of the alley and towards the river, her anger seemed to swell, building upon itself like a wave.

The conjuror sensed it. She parried each of Ellina's blows but came in with no more of her own, for to do so would be to expose her own body while wielding an inferior weapon. Nor, Ellina noted, did she try to flee, for to do *that* would be to take her eyes off her adversary and open her neck to attack. As Ellina forced the conjuror up against the Taro, she saw desperation in the female's eyes, mixed with the knowledge that she was out of her element, and Ellina was in hers.

"Your sister has a message for you," the elf gasped.

A lie. An attempt to stall. Ellina had no intention of entertaining false messages, yet she could say nothing to stop the conjuror from continuing. "There are things you do not know about your mother. Things she never wanted to tell you."

Despite herself, Ellina pulled back. They were both breathing hard, their black hair sticking to their faces, their golden eyes shining in nearby lamplight.

The female's voice dropped. "Have you never wondered why Queen Rishiana was eager to crown your eldest sister Miria—an elf so ill-equipped for the throne it is a wonder she was highborn at all—yet hesitated to initiate a natural leader like Farah?"

Ellina knew better than to be drawn in by an enemy's words. Yet, she had wondered about that. Ellina never understood why their mother had forced Miria to the throne when she was not ready and might never have been ready. Miria was not like most elves. She was sweet and joyful and kind. Queenhood would have stripped her of that, so rather than accept her fate, Miria had fled, and later died. Ellina had always believed that if not for their mother's inexplicable urgency, Miria might still be alive.

Could it be true, what the conjuror was suggesting? Was there some secret reason for Rishiana's haste?

Ellina observed the conjuror. Long limbs, slim features, and again, that dark hair that was so unusual among their race. Ellina could not help but notice that she and this elf looked alike, each a close image of the other. Yet Ellina recalled, almost as if seeing it for the first time, that Miria had looked like this, too. She was shorter than most elves, her face rounder, her hair darker. It was, in part, what had allowed Miria to start a new life in the mainlands. She blended in easily with the humans, because she looked like a human…

Ellina shut down that thought. This was the conjuror's aim. She wanted Ellina confused, wanted her attention elsewhere—

So that Ellina would not notice the second elf descending from behind.

Ellina spun, hurled her dagger. Her shoulder spasmed and the blade went wide. A terrible throw, yet one that distracted this new opponent— male, white-haired, not a conjuror—long enough for Ellina to grab the knife from her boot. She might have thrown this as well, except that the female was coming in again, brandishing her metal ring with a new-made gleam in her eye.

Ellina skidded on the rocky riverbank to avoid the blow. Her side hit the earth. She tried to retreat out of range, but they were quick, too quick. The male had a sword, which he did not draw. Rather, he kicked Ellina—not in the ribs, as she expected, but up behind her shoulder. Ellina gasped. Pain broke her vision. He kicked her again, but this time Ellina reached out a blind hand, caught his leg. Her arm was on fire. It hurt to breathe. She reached up her other hand, grabbed the male's wrist, and somersaulted backward, using the strength of her legs to heave him over her body and into the river.

A splash. A gurgled cry. His head disappeared beneath the surface, one hand pawing at the air. Then the hand vanished as well, and the river fell silent.

Ellina stood on unsteady legs. The female was staring at the water as if waiting for her comrade to resurface, swim back to shore. Yet this was a fundamental truth of their race, one they had long tried to keep secret from humans but could not keep from each other—elves could not swim.

The conjuror's eyes hardened to stone. She exhaled, and Ellina had a split second to anticipate the attack before the female was raging forward in a blur of black and silver, her makeshift weapon swinging a deadly arc.

The fight changed. Ellina's arm was throbbing now. Her strength petered. Whatever anger had driven her before was gone now, replaced only with a strange sense of emptiness. As she tracked the elf's incoming attack, she thought of her mother's blood spilling across a polished stateroom floor. She thought of Miria, killed by southerners, and Venick's mother, killed by conjurors, and Ellina's own voice, which had been stolen for the sake of her sister's vengeance.

At the final moment, Ellina dropped to one knee and summoned every final ounce of her will, swinging her knife towards the elf's heart. But the female saw the blade coming. A quick recalculation, a surge of strong muscles as she twisted to dodge—

"Ellina!"

Venick's voice broke through the night. The conjuror's attention shifted. It was enough to create the opening Ellina needed. Her knife came around and slammed into the female's side.

The elf gave a cry. The force of the impact jerked Ellina's arm, but she managed to keep hold of her weapon as the conjuror stumbled, lost her footing, and crashed to the earth. Her cheek hit the damp riverbank. Her teeth snapped together. She tumbled a short distance before coming to a halt, groaning and clutching her side.

Venick sprinted towards them from between buildings. His face was pale, arms pumping. Ellina's vision steadied enough to mark the group of men arrayed behind him. They were dressed in mismatched suits and vests, but they each wore a green military cap, as if in a quick effort to unify.

Venick skidded to a stop in front of Ellina. He looked like he wanted to yank her into his chest but checked himself. "Are you hurt?"

Behind them, soldiers swarmed the conjuror. There was a fleshy *thump*, a short cough, the clink of metal chains. The elf was hauled to her feet—chalky white, bleeding from palms and ribs, but alive.

Ellina came up off her knee. Her trousers were ripped. Her entire body felt as if it had been wrung like a rag. Yet somehow, she had been spared any worse damage. She realized how lucky she had been.

And how foolish.

"Ellina?"

She blinked up. Venick's hair was in his face. His eyes were huge, hands half lifted, as if he had decided to pull her to him after all. Standing there like that, hovering and uncertain, he looked the way she felt: as if he had been squeezed dry.

Ellina took a shaky breath, then made a hand motion for *I am fine.* Venick's eyes lingered. He did not look convinced.

The conjuror was dragged before them.

"The prisons," Venick ordered, "with six men to guard her. Once she's secure, find Erol. Have him tend to that wound. I want her to live."

This command was obeyed without question. One of the men snapped a quick salute, collected the rest of the troops with a gesture. He was young, Ellina noted, which was good. His inexperience might be enough to override any questions…like why Venick wanted to keep the conjuror alive rather than simply slit her throat.

Silence settled over the riverbank. Around them, the Taro's steam suffused the air, dampening the winter chill. Ellina realized she was still clutching her knife. The hilt was sticky under her fingers. Her hand looked dipped in blood. She was glad for an excuse to avoid Venick's gaze while she cleaned the blade and sheathed it.

"Your dagger," Venick noted, seeing the empty scabbard at her hip. "Did you throw it? Here, I'll help you look."

It did not take long to find the missing blade and return it to Ellina's belt. Much less time, in fact, than Ellina would have liked, because as soon as the weapon was recovered, that same uncertain silence descended once more.

They fell into step towards the baron's house.

"I don't know how you saw it," Venick said after a time. His head was bowed a little, his hands stuffed into his pockets. "Earlier, I mean. In the ballroom. How did you notice the corpse when no one else did? Or the conjuror through the window? It was pitch black outside."

Ellina studied a nearby fountain. No water poured from its spigots, though whether that was because the fountain was broken, or because the water was frozen, she did not know.

She shrugged.

"Don't do that." He turned towards her without breaking stride. "Don't pretend like what you're doing isn't worth something. You saved my life tonight. That's—gods, four times now? Five? I'm beginning to lose count."

The baron's house came into view, nestled quietly on its hill. A red flag had been unfurled, hanging from the third-story balcony like a pronged tongue. A signal of distress, though the house itself was quiet, with no hint of the violence that had occurred there.

Now that her adrenaline was draining away, Ellina was beginning to feel the full aftereffects of the fight. Her side ached. Her eyes were heavy, her bones loose in their sockets. She had done too much too quickly. She would pay for this.

Ellina found the path and started towards the home's entrance. It took her several steps to realize that Venick was no longer beside her.

"Ellina. Wait."

Light from the house glowed over the grounds. It touched Venick where he had halted, illuminating one side of him, throwing the other into shadow. One eye, one cheekbone. Those lips. Half a man.

He said, "I think I owe you an explanation."

Ellina tucked her hands under her arms, chilled. She knew what he wanted to explain. But she did not want to talk about this.

"When I was in Parith, I thought we were enemies. You'd chosen Farah's side. You said you wanted me dead, that you'd kill me yourself. And then in Irek…you were there during the attack. That fire. The ambush. I thought…"

She saw that fire in her memory. A sky rent open with black powder.

A city up in flames.

"I blamed you," Venick admitted, wretched. "I blamed you for everything. The destruction of my home. Rahven. My mother. You *let* me blame you."

Ellina looked out across the frosty lawn. The wind was picking up. It pushed across her clothes, her face. She allowed herself to believe that was why her eyes stung, why her chest felt too tight.

"Harmon kissed me," Venick said, turning to bring his profile fully into the light. His pupils were blown wide. His throat worked as he swallowed. "I let her. I shouldn't have. But she wanted me, and you didn't, and—gods, I don't know, Ellina. Maybe it felt good to be wanted by someone."

Ellina inhaled a ragged breath. Tried to let it out softly, so that he would not hear. She did not want him to hear the evidence of her pain. He had all the power, and she had none, and this breath was one small thing, but it was something. She clung to it, because she needed something to cling to that was not him.

"It was one kiss," Venick said. "Nothing more. There are no real promises between Harmon and me. You know that, don't you?"

Ellina did know that…mostly. Yet it was impossible to ignore the gnawing doubt she felt every time she looked at Venick. The way her heart ached, and reached, and was denied. If things were as simple as he said, why was there a wall between them, thicker and higher than ever before?

Ellina stared at the path, the little imperfections highlighted by weak light. Her thoughts continued to tumble, but like water over a waterfall, they began to lose their shape. They crashed and collided, dispensing into a roaring mist.

She was exhausted. She exhausted herself.

Venick sensed it. He did not push, but said only, "You should go inside. Eat, rest. We're sleeping here at the estate while we're in the city. Someone should have already prepared a room for you."

Ellina motioned with her hands. *You, too. Eat, rest.*

He gave a rueful smile. "There's something I need to do first."

SEVEN

Venick stepped into the prison. It was a small space, an exterior addition to the baron's home that had not been built for the purpose of housing captives. Humans didn't keep captives. At least, not for long. Had Venick left it up to his men, they would have beheaded this conjuror already, maybe burned the body. They'd spit into the flames and call it justice.

They'd have a right. Centuries ago during the purge, elves had done just that to human conjurors. They'd severed their heads and—in a move that seemed wholly unnecessary and blatantly sacrilegious—burned their bodies.

Families mourned. No bodies meant no funeral rites for the dead, no prayers or tombstones. Without proper burials, many believed their loved ones were forever doomed to haunt the earth. In an attempt to give peace to the deceased, makeshift cemeteries were erected over the burning sites, piles of stone stacked atop the ashes to prevent the spirits from wandering. Those graveyards could still be seen, a reminder of the massacres that had occurred there.

Not that humans needed reminding. Mass genocide had a way of sticking to the bones of people. Humans weren't likely to forget the purge, and they sure as hell wouldn't forgive it, especially now that the Dark Army seemed intent on finishing what their ancestors had started. And yet, Venick couldn't afford to let his soldiers have their justice. He wanted the conjuror kept alive.

He couldn't question her if she was dead.

Venick let the door fall shut behind him. The prison was sparse; the floor done in grey tiles, iron bars drilled crooked over all the windows. No cells. Rather, the conjuror had been chained to the back wall, her hands pinioned out to the sides, her legs, neck, and arms all manacled to the stone. Venick's own limbs gave a sympathetic pang. The binding was designed for discomfort.

Venick spoke in elvish. "*I want to make a deal.*"

The elf kept her head down so that her black hair veiled her face. Venick could just make out her thin mouth, her close-set eyes, the three golden earrings pierced into the top of her left ear. Not only had her hands been secured, but her fingers too, each digit bound to a metal rod—a necessary precaution. Southern conjuring relied on manual dexterity, the use of both hands and all ten fingers. If this elf could twitch even the smallest joint, she might still be able to weave power.

Venick pulled up a chair and sat, which put him below her eye level. "*If you answer my questions, I will let you live.*"

She looked down at him through her hair. "*As if I would trust the word of a human.*"

Venick was instantly gratified. He'd worried the conjuror might try to armor herself with silence. If she'd refused to speak, his task would have become much harder.

He said, "*I am speaking your language.*"

"*We all know that elvish does not hold the value it once did.*"

"*Because of Ellina, you mean.*"

"*Your elven lover, yes.*"

Venick ignored that jibe. The conjuror was attempting to bait him, to crack his composure so that he might make a mistake. An old elven trick. He kept his tone conversational. "*Only northern conjurors can lie in elvish.*"

"*Of course you would say so.*"

"*It is true.*"

The conjuror forced a laugh. It was a strange sound, strained, the kind of noise someone might make if they had never actually heard a laugh before, but had been told how it was supposed to sound. Her hair fell back to reveal more of her face, and Venick was surprised to see how young she was, young enough that she might still be called a fledgling.

"*Man knows no truth,*" she said, quoting a popular elven saying. It was a phrase Venick would happily never hear again. "But it does not matter." She switched to mainlander. "I would not agree to your proposition, even if I believed that you would uphold your end."

"Oh?"

"Do not be disappointed. We both know that with or without my help, you stand no chance against the Dark Army."

Venick pretended to study the prison's ceiling. "I can understand why you might believe so."

His calm—mixed with the fact that he had both chosen a seat beneath her and taken his eyes off her—was beginning to have its desired effect. Venick was giving every indication that he did not consider this elf a threat, and it rankled.

"It is no mere belief," she hissed. "You cannot win this war."

"We won't know for sure until it's over."

"What kind of proof do you need, human?"

"I'm not asking you for proof."

She clicked her teeth, an elven sign of impatience. "Do what you want to me. It will be no less than the queen will do to you…or to the princess." Venick's gaze flicked down. The conjuror noticed. Her expression changed. She had the look of someone who'd just drawn a high hand. "Have you not heard? The Dark Queen has made special requests for her sister. Ellina is to be captured alive. She cannot be allowed to die too quickly, not after her betrayal. She will be made to pay. Would you like to hear how?"

"No."

The elf told him anyway. She spoke, and as she spoke, her words became like needles, stitching Ellina's fate into Venick's skin. He listened. He forced himself to listen so that he could remember what he was doing, and why, and for whom.

When she finished, the conjuror's chest was heaving. There was a wild gleam in her eye. She *was* young, Venick thought, but not so young as to mistake the dangers of baiting her captor.

When Venick was certain that he could speak calmly again, he said, "I can see that your mind is made. That is unfortunate. I didn't want to have to do this the hard way."

"I told you already. Torture me all you want. I have nothing—"

"I am not going to torture you."

She shut her mouth.

"You are from the southern elflands," Venick said.

"That is not hard to guess. All the Dark Queen's conjurors are from the south."

"Yet you were not *raised* in the south. Judging by your accent, you grew up in the north. You call the northern elflands your home."

The conjuror eyed him, not understanding this new line of questioning. "I speak as all elves speak. We have no accents."

"You have the accent of an aristocrat." This was true. The female spoke with a subtle lilt that Venick would never have recognized, if not for his recent stint in Evov. It was the way Ellina spoke, too—the voice of a highborn. "But the south has no aristocrats," Venick continued. "They have no class system. That hierarchy only exists in the north. Even without your accent, I can see that your ear is pierced. Another northern tradition."

The conjuror's nose flared. "What does a human know of our traditions?"

"More than you might think. For instance, I know that your earrings—the double etching in the design, the placement at the top of your ear—means *assassin.*"

She was smug again. "Well. That is what I—"

"Except that the literal translation is *gravedigger.* That's clever. A play on words. Or," he arched a brow, "a nod to the family business?"

The female had gone perfectly still. If she did not understand this direction of questioning before, she understood now. She hung frozen, employing too late the armor of silence. A more experienced soldier would have done that from the start, but she was naive. Talented, yes, and determined, *yes*, but inexperienced.

It was this fact, more than any of the others, that first made Venick wonder. Why would Farah send a young conjuror on such a high-stakes mission, risking capture and potential exposure? Was she merely a throwaway? That seemed unlikely. Farah didn't have many conjurors at her disposal—twenty, maybe thirty total. If this elf had been chosen for the assignment, she must have advantages that outweighed her inexperience.

"I think that you are from Evov," Venick said. "I think that your family still lives there. Maybe they own the burial grounds. Or maybe, given your highborn status, they run the palace crypts. Either way, I suspect they've been provided bodies for you to practice your corpse-bending. That's why you were sent to kill me—because so far, you're the only conjuror who has mastered the ability to control the dead without actually having to see the corpse you're controlling."

It would make sense. If her family had ties to the crypts, she would have extra resources to hone her abilities. And she would be motivated to hone them. It couldn't be easy, having been born in the south but raised in the north. She would have to work doubly hard to overcome her northern upbringing, to show that she belonged in Farah's army.

The conjuror looked slightly ill. "You cannot threaten me."

"I am not threatening you. I'm threatening your family."

"You do not know my family."

"No? How hard would it be to scour all the crypts in Evov? How hard would it be to narrow those down to the ones who were owned by a family with southern origins and a dark-haired daughter?"

Venick was bluffing now. He would never make it back to Evov. He'd done that once, twice, three times already, and had been lucky every damn time to make it out again. But the female didn't know that. Venick watched his words spread over her. Saw them settle and stick. When she spoke, her voice was a bare scrap. "Leave my family alone."

"Happily. In exchange for a few answers."

She seemed to struggle. She wanted to tell him no. Probably, she wanted to spit in his face, find a way to make him suffer as she was suffering. But he had her cornered, and they both knew it.

At last, she bowed her head. "*Ask your questions*," she said in elvish, an offering of faith in a world where little faith was left. "*I will answer.*"

EIGHT

I just do not understand."

Lin Lill paced the baron's attic, her boots tapping across uneven floorboards. Behind her, Artis, Harmon, and Erol sat around the room's single table, which had been dragged up from the library earlier that evening. The baron's attic was not their first choice of meeting place, but it was the only location that was both large enough to fit all seven of them while also being secluded enough to ensure privacy.

"We had the ballroom secured," Lin Lill continued. "Every entrance was under guard, with additional sentries stationed around the grounds. So tell me, where did that corpse come from?"

Lin Lill aimed this in Ellina's direction, but Ellina was only half listening. She stood at the attic's fourth-story window, squinting out across the dark lawns below. Stupid, to let Venick speak with that conjuror alone. Stupid, to send him into the prison without backup or assistance or a second set of eyes watching for nefarious movements. Ellina thought of the highlands, how Venick had pulled the same stunt in Parith, facing the Elder alone without an ounce of green glass to protect him. Venick had a way of finding trouble, of making trouble, and his conversation with the captured female would be no different. Ellina was sure of it.

"The guests were all searched before entry," Lin Lill went on. "Once the room was secured, the guards were under strict orders to admit no latecomers. A conjuror would have never made it inside."

"But the conjuror wasn't inside." Harmon spoke over the rim of an amber wine jug, which she had been nursing all evening. She looked frayed from the night's events, her shoulders drawn inward, her elaborate hairstyle now a myriad of knots. "She was standing in the courtyard behind the window."

"And the undead?"

"It was dressed to look like one of our soldiers, was it not?" Artis replied, rubbing at a scratch on the table. "It could have slipped in with everyone else."

"A dead elf just *slipped in*?" Lin Lill rounded on Artis, apparently eager for somewhere to aim her frustration. "As if a costume could conceal the fact that the elf was not breathing. I suppose you also believe the guards failed to notice they were patting down a dead body? The guests failed to notice they were sitting beside one?"

Artis was unfazed. "How are we supposed to know what is possible? It is magic."

"That is nonsense, and you know it."

Lin Lill, Harmon, and Artis continued their argument. Erol set his chin in one hand and listened placidly. The only two missing members of their group were Branton, who was standing guard outside the estate's prison, and Venick, who was busy making stupid choices.

Ellina had tried to overrule him. Had, up until the last moment, planned on forcing her way into the prison alongside him. She had followed Venick across the estate's grounds to a block-shaped building at the back, fueled by indignation…and a lingering sense of hurt that made her want to be contrary. It was not until they met Branton at the guarded prison door that Venick finally set a hand to her shoulder, his expression pained. "Do you trust me?"

Somehow, those simple words had been enough to change her mind.

"Ellina," Erol called from his spot across the room. "Why don't you come sit? Let me take a look at those cuts."

From smashing through the ballroom window, he meant. Ellina had shallow cuts all along her forearms and even a few around her face. They stung, but Ellina knew Erol was only offering because he could see her agitation and hoped to distract her from it. She gave him a small smile but did not leave her spot at the window.

"There must be traitors among us," Lin Lill was insisting. "It is the only possible explanation."

"It would take more than a few traitors to pull off tonight's attack," Artis said.

"So then there is an army of traitors."

"You really think an army of traitors is working against us?"

"Yes."

"No," Harmon argued. "That doesn't make sense. If there were insiders sympathetic to the Dark Queen's cause, they wouldn't try to kill Venick in the most crowded room in the city, with so many military members present. They would have orchestrated a nighttime assassination. Copied keys, secret passages, that kind of thing. If the corpsebender chose to attack in a packed ballroom, it's because she had no other option."

Or because she needed the cover of a crowd, Ellina mused.

Her mind snagged on that thought. Ellina blinked. Turned away from the window. She stared at Harmon, her brain reaching, gripping this new rope of an idea, pulling it towards her.

Harmon caught her expression. "Ellina? What is it?"

But Ellina did not know what she was thinking, exactly. She only knew that this revelation felt like two puzzle pieces locking together, except that the pieces were flipped so that she could not see what their faces showed, only their grey backs.

A noise from below interrupted her thoughts—the sound they had been waiting for.

Boots on a ladder. The shift of the attic's trapdoor, a hand appearing from the floor, swinging the square cutout up and out of the way. Venick's head appeared first, then his torso, then the rest of him. "There's been a change of plans," he said.

Everyone began speaking at once. Lin Lill launched into a tirade about estate security, Harmon was wondering about the status of the dinner guests, Erol prodded Venick to take a seat, and Artis was asking after Branton—who was right behind Venick, as it happened. Only Ellina was silent as she scanned Venick's clothes, the skin of his neck, his hands. Unmarked. Uninjured. And yet…Venick had not been gone long, not nearly long enough to conduct a full interrogation. Questioning a captive took time. There was convincing to be done, and mind games to be played, and threats to be made and delivered. It could take days or weeks to wear a prisoner down, like carving a hole in the wall with a rock. So what did it mean that Venick was back already?

"Alright, alright." Venick held up his hands in surrender. "Everyone, please."

"Come," Erol insisted, guiding Venick towards the nearest chair. "You look exhausted."

"He looks *victorious*," Lin Lill corrected, shouldering forward. "I take it the conjuror had intelligence to share?"

Venick sank gratefully into the offered seat. "Yes."

"Like how she has been managing to break through every one of my defenses to attack you with zombie-elves?"

Venick shot Lin Lill an apologetic smile. "Actually, she couldn't answer questions about that. She swore an oath in elvish."

An elven oath. Ellina had made one of those once. She swore an oath of silence to her sister Miria, promising to never speak of Miria's escape into the mainlands. Ellina remembered how it felt to make that vow, the strange, gritty taste of the words, the way her skin had tightened, as if with static. An elven oath of secrecy was absolute—once made, the power of their language forever prevented the oath-maker from breaking their promise.

Harmon made a swinging motion with her jug. "So what's the information, then?"

"The location of her elven encampment," Venick said. "The captured conjuror's name is Inra, and she's been working with a group of five others under Farah's orders. They're hiding out in the hills just east of here."

"Five conjurors." Artis gave a low whistle. "That's nearly a quarter of the Dark Queen's total count."

"And the perfect opportunity," Lin Lill agreed, her disappointment already morphing into new zeal. "We will stage an attack."

"It'll be dangerous," Harmon said, "but we have the numbers. We'll need to send a large force."

"Actually," Venick said. "We'll need just five of us."

Silence.

"Just five of us?" Lin Lill's face slackened. "You want to make the fight *equal?*"

"You've lost it."

"That's a suicide mission."

"Did the conjuror put you up to this?"

"Maybe," Artis said softly, "we should let Venick explain his thinking."

Erol gave a cheerful laugh. "A man of reason."

"Artis is an elf," Lin Lill snapped.

"You know what I mean."

Venick leaned forward, bracing his elbows against the table. "If we send our full army, the conjurors will see us coming. Even a medium-sized brigade would give us away. The camp will scatter, and we'll lose our chance. But if it's just the five of us, we can stage an ambush. We'll take them by surprise. They aren't expecting an attack. *They* planned to attack *us*. This way, we'll flip the plot. It's better."

"Better for the conjurors," Harmon mumbled.

"Better for us," Venick insisted. "It won't even be a real fight. We'll finish them before they have a chance to counter."

"And if they gain the upper hand?" Branton asked.

"We'll attack at the moment of sunrise. The night will conceal us until the ambush, but if something goes wrong, we'll have the advantage of the rising sun on our side." He was looking at Ellina as he spoke. She was the one who had discovered this secret: daylight weakens the conjurors' power.

"You said the five of us," Harmon interrupted. "But there are seven in our group. So, which five?"

"Oh." Venick rubbed the back of his neck. "The five of us who can fight."

Ellina glanced at Harmon. Though the woman had removed her

gilded headpiece and changed out of her wooden-heeled shoes, she still wore her ballgown, which showed the small curve of each shoulder, the undefined plain of her back. The thought of Harmon fighting was absurd. Yet there was a stubborn set to her jaw.

"Well?" Venick asked. "What do you say?"

"I have been waiting for a chance like this," Branton replied. "Count me in."

"If Branton goes, so do I," said Artis.

Venick turned to the ranger. "Lin?"

"It is risky," she said slowly. "But your logic is sound."

He cocked a brow. "It is?"

"A show of stealth and force at once. Striking in a way the enemy does not expect. Yes, Commander. You are thinking like an elf."

Venick pressed a hand to his heart. "I'm touched."

"Do not get used to it."

At last, Venick brought his eyes to Ellina. He sounded almost nervous as he asked, "Ellina?"

It was the way he was looking at her. It was the curious quiet that fell over the room, and the dim light of the moon shining through the window, and Venick's unaccountable nervousness that had Ellina remembering his words to her earlier that night. *Do you trust me?*

That phrase rattled around in her head. It became an echo of itself. Ellina felt disjointed, as if the words were overlapping, until she remembered that this was not the first time Venick had asked her that question.

Do you trust me? Yes. There had been another time, in the everpool. Then, his hands had held her waist. His touch was light at first, timid. Later: fingers digging into skin. The hot sear of his mouth. Ellina remembered that kiss, and how it, too, had been like a question. Or...so she thought. It occurred to Ellina that the kiss might have just been a kiss, and she was only imagining that it was like a question because she wanted to be its answer.

The silence went on. Everyone was looking at her. They were waiting, as Venick was, for some kind of reply, but Ellina suddenly could not remember the inquiry that had been posed, only the one still ringing in her mind.

"I want to talk to her," Venick told the others. "Give us a minute."

Ellina's face flamed. She started to lift her hands—she was just thinking, that was all, there was no need for anyone to leave. But she caught the false cheeriness in their faces and realized that the mood in the room had shifted, and that she had been the one to shift it.

Harmon was the only one who looked unaffected. She tapped the side of her wine jug with a nail, making little pinging sounds. "I don't see why we *all* must go."

Venick frowned. "That's—"

"You and I share responsibility for this army," Harmon barreled on. "We are equals. I might not be a trained fighter, but I'm a Stonehelm." She was coming to her feet, pressing her palms to the table, gaining momentum. "I've taken a risk by acting against my father, leading the highlanders west. I've taken a risk by tying myself to you. Can't you imagine how difficult that's been? And what's so important that it must be kept private, anyway? If you have something to say to Ellina, I should hear it, too."

The room, already tense, became stifling. Everyone's eyes jumped from Venick, to Harmon, to Ellina, back to Venick.

Erol was the first to break the silence. "I think we're all just a little tired…"

"I'm wide awake," Harmon snapped.

"Come, now. There's no need for fighting." Erol's voice was like a balm. His words created a lather, which he smeared over the room, soothing. "We all appreciate everything you're doing for the resistance, Harmon. No one doubts your position. But let's give Venick and Ellina a moment. We should be checking in with the staff downstairs, anyway."

Harmon's demeanor changed. The shift was instant, as if whatever demon gripped her had suddenly been exorcised. She sighed. "You're right. It's just—it's been a long day." She moved to leave, pausing when she drew level with Ellina. "Sorry," she clipped.

Harmon exited through the trapdoor. The others, sensing their moment, followed suit.

NINE

Venick waited until the others were gone. If they, like Harmon, didn't appreciate being ordered away, they showed no signs of it. Then again, Venick showed no signs of his feelings, either. Yet his stomach was swimming.

Ellina had returned to her original spot by the attic's window and was now pretending great interest in the nighttime sky. Though fat wax candles burned in clusters on the floor, the light did not quite reach the place she stood. Smudged in the dark like that, she could have been anyone. A nameless warrior. A wraith. A dream.

He went to her. She had one arm resting on the sill, her palm flat, fingers drumming lightly. He set his hand over hers to stop the movement.

"You think my plan is rash."

She looked at him. Up close, Venick could see her face better. Dark circles stamped her eyes. Her forehead was puffy with thin red scrapes. Her cheekbones were too prominent, the skin stretched taut, so pale as to appear almost blue.

Not normal, said a voice inside him. *Not normal, that she should still look so ghostly.* It had been a month since Ellina's rescue. Wartime campaigns were hard, certainly, but they had yet to enter battle. Their supplies were full, their pace easy. Plenty of food. Enough time for sleep.

If she can.

He suspected she couldn't. Ellina's lingering frailty wasn't the type to be solved with a few decent meals and a good night's rest. Venick had seen the way she watched the sun set, like watching a life raft float out of reach. It was the way some soldiers looked, too, after facing the traumas of war.

She had suffered in Evov. She was suffering still.

"It's a risk," Venick admitted, "but killing conjurors isn't the only opportunity here. Ellina." He faltered. "Balid is with them."

Ellina's hand went cold in his.

"I would rather have waited," he continued. "Planned a more complete ambush. But I don't think we'll get another opportunity like this. If you want to stay behind—"

She shook her head once, firmly. *I am not staying behind.*

Venick tried to smile. "I didn't think so."

Her hand was still cupped beneath his. Without thinking too hard on it, he slid his palm up, gently gripped her wrist. She shivered, and Venick found that his mouth had gone oddly dry.

"I wonder," he said, "what will you do if you meet Farah again?"

It wasn't a question he'd really planned on asking. Yet like his hand sliding up her wrist, he didn't think too hard on it. He allowed his mind to quiet, to open and scatter like spores. He let the breeze of the moment guide him.

A line appeared between Ellina's brows as she considered.

"More to the point," he continued, "what would you have *me* do? Farah killed your mother. She started a war. But she's the last of your living family. And I just…I know what it's like to be without a family. To have no one. I can't promise to spare your sister's life, but if you think—"

Ellina pulled back. She seemed angry that he might even suggest this. *No*, her expression said. *Farah is no longer family to me. She must not be spared.*

"And Raffan?"

Slowly, Ellina shook her head. *Not him, either.* But she looked less certain.

"There's something I never told you." Venick closed his mouth. Dragged a breath through his nose. "Something that happened in Evov. Raffan gave me the key to your cell. He created a distraction to lure the guards away from us while we escaped across the ravine. He helped set you free."

Ellina looked as if she'd been slapped.

"I'm not saying he deserves forgiveness." Venick thought of Ellina's scars and felt a throb of his old anger. "He doesn't deserve it. But I wanted you to know."

She looked back out the window. The wan light of the moon washed over her cheek and cradled her jaw, turning her neck to shadow. She had grown small again, and Venick wondered if he'd been wrong to tell her about Raffan. She had enough to worry about already. Too much. And it could be dangerous, unloading such a revelation on her when she needed a clear head for the fight ahead.

He was struck by a sudden compulsion to call off the ambush. He wanted to ask her to stay behind, let him and the others handle the conjurors. She shouldn't be risking herself for this. She'd risked enough already.

Before, he'd named her a wraith, nameless, a dream. Insubstantial things. It wasn't the first time he'd had the thought. Venick had worried about this ever since he'd pulled her from that prison. She just seemed so *impermanent*. He feared that he'd wake one morning to discover her gone. She would be taken, she would leave. She would blow away on a breeze.

Venick knew what Dourin would say if he was there. He'd say that Ellina was a capable fighter.

Better than you are.

That he shouldn't coddle her.

She can handle herself.

He'd probably laugh outright if he knew Venick wanted to leave her behind. But Dourin couldn't see what Venick saw. He couldn't see the razor edge of Ellina's clavicle, the shadows in her face. He hadn't been there on the tundra when Ellina had thrashed in her sleep, and he'd shaken her awake, and she'd sobbed into his chest. Nor, Venick thought, had Dourin heard the conjuror's threats, all the things Farah would do to Ellina if she managed to catch her alive.

"There's only a few hours until dawn," Venick said, casting around for something that would stop his mind from spiraling down that path. "We'll spend the time preparing, but I want us riding by first light. I'll explain things to the others, about Balid and…how he's the one who stole your voice. The importance of this opportunity. If you want." Venick was rambling. He took a breath. "It'll be better if they understand everything."

Ellina looked at their interlocked hands. After a moment, she gave a nod.

That should have been the end of it. Venick had said what he'd needed to say, and it was time now to find the others and resume their preparations. Yet the moments slipped by, and neither of them moved.

Venick became aware of his blood shushing in his ears. The warmth of the room. The way the floorboards creaked under his shifting feet, and how the anxious sound of them revealed his own anxiousness. Though Venick could often read Ellina's mind, this was the one subject where he felt like he was treading in the dark. He thought about the long hours they'd once spent together in the southern forests. The palace. How she had opened for him like a flower, only to close back up again, petals overlapping like armor. Venick knew she'd lied about wanting him dead, knew most of her reasons, yet she'd never really explained everything, and it felt selfish to ask about it now. Selfish to even *think* about it. Who was he, to wonder about Ellina's feelings when he was publicly promised to another woman? Even if his engagement was fake, he knew it wasn't fair.

He wasn't being fair to her.

He released his grip.

"Will you swear something to me?"

His question, or maybe the way he'd asked it, made her narrow her eyes.

"We'll find the conjuror who stole your voice. You'll have your chance to kill him and win it back. But I want you to promise, don't… do anything rash. If you're ever in a situation where you have to make the choice between risking your life or retreating, retreat, please. Can you promise me that?"

This was not, he thought, an unreasonable request. But Ellina seemed thrown.

"What is it?" It was times like these when Venick was most acutely aware of her voicelessness, when he most loathed Farah and the Dark Army and this war. "Does that bother you?"

She slanted her gaze sideways to avoid his eye. At last, she shook her head.

It wasn't until later, when Venick was alone again, that he realized he didn't know which question she'd been answering—whether his concern bothered her, or if she would promise to stay safe.

TEN

Ellina sat on a bench at the back of the baron's house, watching the sky. She was supposed to be looking for the morning's first light while the others finished their predawn preparations, but her eyes refused to focus. They darted from edge to edge, catching on stars, playing tricks. The black sky was troublesome in that it was familiar, familiar in that it was absolute.

Ellina's prison had been like that. The door, when shut, let in not even the faintest trace of light. The walls, the floor, her own two hands—all of it was lost to her. Ellina had been locked in the dark for so long that her brain began reaching for any hint of illumination, began seeing things that were not there. It was confusing and disorienting and, eventually, maddening.

The wind rattled unseen through bare trees. Ellina's fingers curled loosely around the bench's stone lip. Was the horizon slightly brighter now? Maybe. Should she alert the others just in case? Yes, except that

Ellina knew what would happen if she was wrong about the dawn. She could imagine the pitying looks the others would give her, how a mistake like that would serve as yet more proof that Ellina was slipping, that her experiences in Evov had damaged her past repair. This was not a difficult task, spotting the day's first light. She should be able to tell whether the sky was black or grey or blue. Yet it felt impossible.

Ellina swallowed a well of frustration. She glared at the sky until her eyes ached. Now, she thought. The sky was lighter *now*...wasn't it?

"Ellina?"

She turned to see Venick guiding two horses across the dark lawn: his blind buckskin, plus the dappled silver stallion that had become hers. Though Ellina had initially taken Dourin's steed named Grey after leaving Parith, she felt uneasy about keeping the beast. Dourin might need him. At the very least, Dourin would be displeased to wake and find his horse missing. After some internal debating, Ellina had slapped Grey's rump and thought the words *go home*, sending the animal back to its master.

Ellina was not *geleeshi*. She did not have the ability to both summon and send animals in a desired direction. That skill was reserved for elves like Dourin, whose bond with his homing horses was unmatched. Still, Ellina was certain Grey would find his way back, if not for her, then for Dourin.

Now, Venick handed over the silver's reins, nodding towards the horizon. "Dawn's first light. Are you ready?"

He said this lightly, yet his eyes were strained at the corners, his mouth lifted uncertainly. Venick was the one who had assigned Ellina the task of sunrise lookout. He was wondering why she had not yet come to alert them it was time to leave.

Ellina busied herself with the reins. She gave a short nod.

They walked around the outside of the house, passing the baron's solarium, which protruded from the home's façade like a crystal. The grounds were not empty at this hour. Morning workers braved the early chill to haul in bundles of firewood and bags of flour for breakfast biscuits and bread. There was a man digging a hole at one end of the yard—for what purpose, Ellina did not know—and another carrying two dead chickens by their feet, one in each hand, their heads lolling haphazardly with his peculiar hopping gait. He nodded to Venick as they passed, mumbling *Praise the Taro*, like a greeting.

They reached the entrance, where they would meet the others. The front doors opened, but it was not Lin Lill or Branton or Artis who emerged—it was Harmon, wearing a full metal kit.

Venick smothered a frown. "What are you doing?"

"I'm coming with you."

The frown, which Ellina could see lurking at the edges of his eyes and lips, threatened its hold. "You're not a fighter. This wasn't part of the plan."

"Don't patronize me." Harmon hopped on one foot, trying to adjust the heel of her heavily booted shoe. "I'm a healer. I can help."

"Harmon, no offense, but you'll only get in the way."

She continued to struggle with the shoe. "You might need me."

Venick crossed stares with Ellina. He was looking for her opinion, but the notion of Harmon joining their mission was so obviously inadvisable that Ellina frowned hard enough for the both of them. Venick turned his chin. *Just asking.* She scrunched her nose. *You already know what I think.*

"No," Harmon interrupted. "None of that silent talking between you two. I can guess what you're thinking, but listen. In the highlands, we always send a healer into the field with the soldiers."

"That's a dangerous use of resources."

"That's smart planning."

"I won't argue with you about this."

"Let me come, and there will be no arguing."

"Harmon, it's like you said earlier. You're not just a healer now. You're a leader of our resistance. If something happened to you—"

"If something happened to *you*—"

"It's not the same. I was raised to fight. I'm a warrior first."

"What do you think I was doing in the lowlands, that day you found me? Taking a holiday? How do you think I wound up your captive? I was a healer for our contingent. I might not be a warrior, but I'm no stranger to battle, and *you might need me.*"

Venick started to argue further. Glanced at the sky. "We're wasting time." A heavy sigh. "I can see that your mind is made."

Harmon was smug.

"But you'll need to find yourself some scout's armor," Venick said. "You can't wear metal."

"What?" Harmon looked down at herself. "What's wrong with metal armor?"

"We're not riding into battle. This is an ambush. They'll hear you rattling in that from a league away."

"Oh." Harmon had the decency to look embarrassed. "Right, well, don't act like that's obvious, it was an easy mistake, and we're not all commanders of great armies."

• • •

They set out on horseback. Venick took the lead, Ellina second, followed by Lin Lill, Branton, Artis, and—wearing borrowed gear and a sword she did not know how to use—Harmon. They rode single file over the grassy landscape, crouching low in their saddles, following deer trails and riverbeds and the occasional man-made path. Though the sky was still mostly dark, Ellina could map the terrain in her mind's eye. She knew where the mountains lay to the far northeast, the glades and pastures between there and here. More importantly, she knew where a cluster of boulders sprouted from the earth just east of Igor, which matched the black dot that the captured conjuror had sketched on Venick's map: their destination.

Ellina gripped her stallion's reins, silently urging Venick to pick up the pace. He was being cautious. The path was riddled with roots and cracks, places a hoof could easily catch. If they were too hasty, a horse could stumble. It would throw its rider. Arms would break, or legs, or necks.

But twilight was upon them. Soon the sky would blue and lighten. If they wanted to reach the conjurors and stage their ambush the moment the sun first peeked over the horizon, they would need to hurry.

The path opened abruptly, tall stalks giving way to a wide expanse of sand and shortgrass. Ellina imagined they had gone over a cliff; the sudden flatness felt like a void. She dug in her heels, urging her horse into a gallop, but rather than pulling up beside Venick, she passed him to take the lead. He glanced at her, his hair whipping around his cheeks, his eyes grey stars in his nighttime face.

Ellina set the pace, scanning the landscape for the smoothest route. It was only when she spotted a thick band of rocks in the distance that she finally felt it: a small knot in her belly, like a sickness.

The first twinge of nervousness.

They dismounted and continued on foot, jogging silently towards the boulders. Ellina's quiver bounced against her back. Her scabbard dug into her hip. She wished for water, but she did not want to stop for the time it would take to uncork her canteen and drink. The sky was a deep purple now. Not much longer.

The boulders were larger up close than they had seemed from a distance, sprouting from the sandy soil like the bulbous shells of giant animals. In a small clearing between them, Ellina could make out a flicker of orange light. A campfire burned to embers.

It was only then that Ellina realized she had not truly expected to find their enemy where the prisoner—Inra, Venick had called her—said they would. It did not matter that Inra had given her information in elvish; elves were masters of trickery, and Ellina knew too well how their language could be twisted in order to deceive. Yet there around the campfire were five long bedrolls, and tucked into each bedroll was a dark mass.

Venick was a solid shadow at Ellina's side. He caught her eye. There was something in his face that looked like regret, gone so fast Ellina wondered if she had imagined it. He retook the lead as they slid into camp, each approaching a bedroll where a sleeping conjuror lay. Only Harmon remained behind, vanishing into a nearby crevice where she would wait until the ambush was over.

Ellina felt as if her chest had been filled with syrup. Her heart labored. It was impossible to tell which conjuror she might be advancing upon. They were bundled deep in their bedroll, face hidden from the cold. No movement. No elf on lookout, either. That was odd, but before Ellina could question it, Lin Lill and Branton were drawing their swords, Artis his mace, Venick his dagger. Ellina drew her own dagger, angling towards her target in a way that circumvented the fire's waxy light and therefore prevented the fall of her shadow from giving her away.

All eyes came to Venick. A morning bird began to chirp, a sound that seemed both aptly timed and wildly out of place. The air radiated anticipation.

Venick gave the signal. *Now.*

Ellina threw open the covers, lifted her dagger—

And froze.

The bedroll was stuffed with cloth where a body should have been. Ellina glanced up to see Lin Lill uncovering a similar dummy, and Branton too, and Artis…

Instantly, the five of them were coming together, moving back-to-back. They reacted just in time to see the conjurors—black-clad and long-limbed and very much not asleep—sliding from the spaces between boulders, their hands lifted, hoods drawn low to conceal their faces. There were eight elves in total, not five, each well-armed with swords and knives and even an axe.

Apparently, these southerners did not share their brethren's qualms about wielding weapons.

"I applaud your efforts," said an elf to the left. Ellina flinched, expecting Balid, though she had never actually heard him speak and therefore did not know his voice. But the conjuror who lowered his hood was not Balid. He was shorter, with a wide stamp of a nose and hawkish yellow eyes. "Ambushing elves is near impossible for a human. We almost did not hear you coming. And the timing." He tilted his chin towards the lightening horizon, seemingly entertained. "Impeccable. Unfortunately, your game is up. Though…" He trailed off for effect. "I suppose I could be convinced to spare your lives, in exchange for something that I want."

"A bargain." Venick was unamused. "I've learned not to bargain with elves. It tends not to go so well for me."

"You have not yet heard my offer."

"I don't need to hear it. I know what you want, and my answer is no."

Ellina caught the look on Venick's face. The sharp clip of his mouth, the barely concealed rage. She realized what she should have known already—the conjuror was asking for *her*.

The world condensed. Yet Ellina scarcely had time to absorb her fear, because on the tail end of this realization came another, worse thought. She remembered the two elves she had battled by the Taro. She saw again how the female had hesitated to attack, how the male fought with only his fists. But he had been wearing a sword.

Why had he not drawn his sword?

And why had the female—a warrior in prime fighting condition—not used her conjuring? Was it because she was truly sapped of strength, as Ellina had believed…or because she was stalling?

Ellina understood, suddenly, what she had missed.

She had been outmatched. If those elves wanted to kill her, they could have done so easily. But they had not wanted to kill her. They wanted to take her captive.

The earth seemed to shift. It cracked, rolling, shaking her foundation. Ellina was *shaken*, because she had overlooked this, something so obvious as to be unavoidable. Doubt seeped into her vision, and that was worse, because Ellina could not afford to doubt herself, not now, when she needed her concentration and every bit of her confidence. And yet, would she have survived that fight, if not for her opponents' reluctance?

Would she survive this one?

"Give us the princess," the coven leader demanded. His shoulders were hard knobs, his boots molded to look like bird talons, a sharp claw at each toe. "Do so, and we will let you go free."

"Say it in elvish," Venick challenged.

"Would that make any difference? Our language has cracks. We all know it."

"Humor me."

Venick was grandstanding, buying them time. It was not hard to guess why. Now that their plan of ambush was in tatters, their best hope was to stall until the sun rose fully above the horizon.

The dark elves, however, had no intention of waiting. They moved closer, tightening their ring. Ellina felt Venick's shoulder press into hers. She could hear the thin sound of Lin Lill's breath at her back, the turn of Artis' feet in the sand.

"A shame," said their leader. "I hoped we could handle this civilly. Though, I am not surprised. I was told that you can be...difficult."

Venick's smile did not touch his eyes. "One of my many charms."

"Last chance, human. Is she really worth your life?"

Venick drew his sword between both hands. He gave his answer in elvish. "*Yes.*"

In a synchronized motion, the conjurors unhooked their cloaks, allowing the fabric to pool at their feet. Their faces—pale and shining, unique yet similar—were revealed, and though Ellina knew she should be marking each of them, cataloging their weapons, noting their positions, her eyes latched onto a single face and refused to pull away.

Balid met her gaze and grinned.

The conjurors drew up their hands, fingers splayed, lean muscles bunching. The shadows gathered, leaching the world of color as the sky dimmed back to twilight. Then, like ravens spreading their wings, they descended.

Ellina ripped her sword from its sheath, sliced at the nearest enemy. She felt the blade make contact, saw the elf's arm laid open from wrist to elbow. Blood sprang forth, and the elf hissed, clenching the injury to his chest. His conjured shadows dissolved around him, stripping him back to skin and bone.

"You witch," he snarled. "You traitorous, human loving—"

She cut off that thought with a blade to his throat.

Beside her, Venick sparred with a long-faced female. To her right, Artis was swinging his mace at a pair of identical elves—twins—in a graceful arc. Across the clearing, Balid was in a skirmish with Lin Lill, the two of them moving so quickly that their hands seemed little more than a blur. Ellina started in that direction but was intercepted by another conjuror, this one taller than her by a head. She swerved, kicked his knee. He grunted but did not fall, opening his fingers as if reaching towards her, his shadow seeming to reach with him. Ellina tried to skitter out of range, but was distracted when she felt her sword fly unbidden from her fist. She looked down at her empty hand. Heard the blade clatter to the ground a dozen paces away.

The elf had summoned away her weapon.

Ellina breathed around her shock. Conjured shadows could be used to steal the senses, to build storms and bring darkness, but *this*, disarming an opponent, yanking a blade right from their grasp…

This was new.

Ellina reached into her quiver, grabbed an arrow, and sank the point into the conjuror's thigh. He screamed as she blew past, unhooking her bow and nocking another arrow. Ellina's earlier doubts were not gone, exactly, but they were diminished, tamped down by the rush of the fight, and by the fact that she was now wielding her best weapon. Bow and arrows. The smooth curve of wood under her palm, the hard tension of the bowstring, the smell of hemp and wax. She drew the arrow to her cheek and set her sights on Balid, but Lin Lill was in the way. Ellina did not have a clear shot.

Venick's voice rang through the clearing. "Ellina!"

She spun. The male whose throat she had slit was upright again, a sword in hand, coming for her. Blood oozed from the open wound, coating his neck like a red tongue. Ellina jerked back a step, floundering. But, how? How could he possibly be alive when…?

No, Ellina corrected. Not alive. *Controlled.* Ellina had created a corpse, and these conjurors were corpse-benders. The elf had become one of the undead.

Ellina cast around for the wielder, but then the corpse was on her, demanding her attention. His eyes were unseeing, but his body was able, his grip firm on his sword. That explained why these elves carried weapons when conjurors rarely did. Their blades were not meant to be used in life, but in death.

Ellina ducked to avoid the incoming blow, swung her leg to catch the corpse at the ankles. He *jumped*, an agile leap to avoid her maneuver, and Ellina's thoughts scrambled. She had never seen such a fluid, natural movement from a corpse.

The conjurors were getting stronger.

The creature came in again. Ellina shot four arrows in quick succession, piercing the undead in the chest, the shoulder, the stomach, but it did nothing, did not even slow the corpse, who was past the point of feeling. Ellina knew that it was pointless to attack the dead elf—she needed to find its master. Yet, the scene was chaotic, and it was impossible to tell who was doing what. There was Balid, who was now fighting both Artis and Lin Lill. Venick, still engaged in combat with that female. Branton, sinking his sword into an elf's hip just across the low, glowing embers of the campfire…

Ellina was moving. She was unbuckling her armor, tearing her cuirass away from her body, then her tunic, leaving nothing but a tight chest wrap. She caught Venick's horrified look, saw reflected in his eyes the insanity of what she was doing, yet there was no time for second thoughts, because her opponent was still swinging, and Ellina had to duck and dodge and move and strip, all while keeping her attention on that blade, which would slice through her bare skin as easily as ripe fruit.

She threw her tunic into the campfire.

The fabric smoked. It caught. Low red embers were rekindled, springing into true flames. Ellina reached into the fire, grabbed the blazing tunic, and flung it over the corpse.

The creature wailed. It clawed at the fabric, but the shirt tangled around its neck, and its bender—whoever they were—was not dexterous enough to lift it free. The stench of searing flesh hit Ellina as the undead dropped to its knees, limp now, as if cut from puppet strings. It pitched forward like a felled tree, denting the earth where it landed.

Ellina's hand throbbed from reaching into the fire. Her whole body trembled. She swung her gaze back to Balid, still in combat with Lin Lill and Artis. He was in Ellina's range. The shot was wide open.

But—her hand.

Ellina dared to look at it. Angry purple blisters had sprouted like a fungus, reaching all the way from palm to fingertips. The pain tunneled up her arm, turning her hot all over. She fought a well of nausea.

Around the clearing, the fighting seemed to be gaining new fervor. Though they had killed two enemy elves while somehow managing to stay on their feet, things were not looking good. They were still outnumbered. The sun appeared no higher than before. The conjurors were tireless and could reanimate their dead. Ellina was hurt, and down to her last arrow.

A well of fear rooted her to the spot. Then, sadness, that she could not be stronger than her fear. She saw her friends battling for their lives. She saw Venick, the person who, when asked if she was worth it, had not hesitated to say yes. His face was stripped with exhaustion. His sword arm strained with every swing. Ellina imagined him dying there, how his grey eyes would go blank, his mouth never again quirking with amusement, or telling her secrets, or saying her name.

A memory settled over her shoulders. It was the same memory that infiltrated Ellina's mind whenever she felt helpless, latching into her skin like hooks to pull her under: a black mind in a black prison in a black night. But could that memory hurt her, really, when *this* nightmare stood before her? Could fear dig those hooks any deeper when they had already reached her bones? Ellina would not be more afraid than she was now. There was nowhere left for her terror to go.

That, somehow, seemed to change things.

She stopped trembling. She ignored the agony of gripping her bow with an injured hand, the way the blisters burst and wept. She nocked her last arrow, exhaled slowly, and aimed at Balid.

"Help!"

Ellina's attention swung to Harmon. *Harmon*, who was supposed to be safe in hiding, had somehow been discovered, and was now being dragged forward by the coven leader. He threw her to the ground. His claw-toed boots looked disturbingly lifelike as he drew up his foot, aiming the talons at Harmon's head.

Later, Ellina would think back on this moment. She would imagine how things would have gone had she made a different choice, ignored the woman's cry, finished the task she had come to finish. Ellina would touch gentle fingers to her throat and think of her own voice, the midrange tones, and how she did not miss the ability to speak so much as she missed the way speaking made her feel: like she was limitless.

Ellina switched her single arrow away from Balid and towards the coven leader. She let the arrow fly.

A clean hit, straight through his skull.

The elf jerked from the force of impact, collapsing like an under-stuffed doll. Harmon was nearly crushed beneath his weight, but she managed to shove out of range, panicked and scrambling.

The darkness lifted. Like a dissipating fog, the sky was suddenly re-vealed, bluer and brighter than before. The sounds of fighting trickled away as the conjurors spotted their fallen leader, the lifting sun. Their hands fell. Their summoned shadows faded. Whatever spell had been reversed with the leader's death, it severed their momentum, leaving them exposed.

The enemy retreated, and Balid along with them.

ELEVEN

Venick felt like his mind had been blunted. The conjurors were gone. The land was still. Yet the silence had come abruptly, like the plop of a stone into water, and the sudden quiet was jarring to his battle-heightened senses.

Ellina stood nearby, staring into the distance. Not necessarily in the direction the conjurors had fled. Not really at anything. She was wearing only a band of fabric around her chest, one bicep smeared with blood, her left hand held awkwardly at her side. As the sky pushed past dawn into a labored sort of daylight, the sun touched her face, and Venick's heart thumped painfully at what it showed.

Grief. Ellina looked the way she had in Irek when they'd stood on the beach, and she'd tried to explain things, and he'd drawn his sword on her. Or—no. She looked like she had when she'd taken a beating for him in the forest last summer. There was that same tight mouth, the same too-large eyes. A hard choice, and all its consequences.

Venick started towards her. He didn't yet know what he'd say. Didn't really think it mattered. This had been their chance to win back her voice, and they'd lost it, and now she was hurting.

He couldn't stand to see her hurting.

Before Venick had taken three steps, however, Harmon was there, drawing Ellina's attention with a word.

Venick halted. Sun reflected off the stones, a white contrast to the earlier dark. The air was crisp, a little dusty. Quiet enough to carry voices, even distant ones, even those pitched down to whispers.

But Venick shouldn't strain to hear what Harmon was saying. He shouldn't worry about the obvious emotion in Ellina's face, or the choice she'd made, or how it might change things between those two. Slowly, with effort, he pulled his attention back to the clearing where three dead conjurors lay. He focused on those bodies, the tangle of ghostly limbs, the way death stripped the elves of their menace.

A victory.

Right. A victory. Three dead enemy was better than no dead enemy. And yet, Venick couldn't quite ignore the chill that crept under his skin, prickling up his spine, over his scalp. They'd tried to spring an ambush and had been ambushed instead.

Not your fault.

Except that it was his fault. Venick didn't know if Inra had tricked him, or if the conjurors had merely figured she'd been captured and made to talk. Either way, Venick should have anticipated something like this. He should have created a contingency plan in case things went awry. Instead, he'd blazed forward with all the finesse of an angry bull. It was a mistake that belied his experience.

"We will burn the bodies," Lin Lill said, appearing at his side. There was a slice along her bicep, weeping blood. Another across the back of her hand. She seemed to notice neither. "So that the dead may not rise again."

Venick was glad for the task. For any task. He got to work searching for twigs and branches, dried grass, anything that would burn. Branton, Artis, and Lin Lill joined the effort, and soon they'd managed to gather a sizable pile of kindling. It wouldn't be enough to cremate the corpses, not like a true pyre, but it would prevent the dead from walking.

When Artis began dragging one of the bodies forward, however, Branton stopped him with a hand. "Look."

Branton crouched down and pulled something from around the elf's neck. It was a slim glass vial attached to a silver chain, filled with what appeared to be a pale green liquid. Branton uncorked the bottle. Sniffed.

"Don't *sniff* it."

Venick swung around to see Harmon marching forward, Ellina following closely behind. Harmon swiped the vial from Branton's hand, then shook it in his face. "This could be poison."

Branton raised his hands in defense. "So?"

"*So*, not all poisons must be ingested. Some are airborne. Some carry lethal fumes." Harmon looked around the group, seemingly baffled by their blank expressions. "Don't you know that?"

"Elves do not have to worry about poison," Lin Lill said. "We are immune to most toxins."

"Oh, fine excuse."

"What?" Lin Lill raised her shoulders. "We have superior—"

"Do *not* finish that sentence."

Ellina set a hand to Harmon's arm, a calming gesture. That alone was enough to raise Venick's brows, but nothing could prepare him for the way that Harmon—stubborn, fiery Harmon—actually calmed.

"Elves might be impervious to toxins," Harmon said, working for a more diplomatic tone, "but humans are not. "From now on—" she plucked the cork from Branton's other hand and stoppered the vial, "—let's tread a little more carefully around unknown substances, shall we?"

They finished creating their not-quite-a-pyre, then set it aflame, watching in silence as the bodies burned. That silence held as the last of the flames died, and they returned to their horses. Ellina walked slightly ahead of Venick, her expression inscrutable. He noticed that her left hand was now bound in a wrapping—Harmon's doing—though she was still only half-clothed, having removed her armor and burned her tunic in that insane stunt to defeat the undead.

Though the fighting was long over, it was as if Venick's mind had boxed away his fear, tucking it onto a high shelf so that it could not interfere. Now the lid of that box seemed to open, all its contents tumbling free. He thought of what Ellina had done. Its lunacy. It was one thing to play with fire, but stripping out of your armor mid-battle? She couldn't have hatched a more dangerous idea if she'd tried.

As if sensing his eyes on her, Ellina glanced back. Whatever she saw in his face closed her expression.

By the time they retraced their path to Igor and entered the welcome warmth of the baron's house, the day had matured. The others—nursing an array of minor wounds—limped towards their rooms, their minds already on baths and some well-earned sleep. Venick, however, hung back. "Ellina."

They stood in an empty hallway that split the west wing of the house from the east. They would leave each other there, him going to the master's suite on the third floor and she to another quarter in a different part of the estate.

She turned towards him, expectant.

I'm sorry, Venick might have said.

We were so close, he might have said.

I know what this fight cost you, the sacrifice you made to save Harmon, but there will be other chances. We'll win your voice back.

Yet what Venick said was, "That stunt you pulled today was idiotic."

Ellina cooled.

"I don't know what you were thinking," he continued, voice rough. "I truly cannot imagine what possessed you to remove your armor during a fight, but you have to be smarter than that. I have to know that you'll be smarter, because if I don't know that, I'll be focused on you rather than the battle. I'll be distracted."

Ellina raised her chin, defiant. *You should not worry about me.*

"Reeking gods, Ellina. I do worry about you. I worry about you *all the time*. If something happened to you, I can't, I couldn't—" He cut himself off. Took a breath. "You scared me today."

Some of Ellina's defiance faded.

"You scared me," Venick continued, "because it's not just your own life you're playing with. It's mine, too. I…care about you. I never stopped caring. If something happened to me, you'd survive, but if something happened to you—it would kill me."

Ellina, who had already been quite still, turned to stone. Venick swallowed around a sudden throb of nervousness. He'd said too much, he knew that he had, and yet…

The air seemed to shift. And maybe Venick was sleep deprived, maybe his senses were still frayed from the fight, but Ellina's eyes were growing luminous, the light from a nearby window limning her cheek. Venick saw the way she was looking at him. He saw the dirt and sweat and blood, how her hair was coming free from its braid, and how these things made her seem more real, as if every doubt he'd ever had about her was for nothing. Which was, really, all Venick wanted.

He lifted a hand. Hesitated, as he tried to recall why he shouldn't, why it would be unfair to her. Or was it unfair to *him*? He couldn't remember. He couldn't really think, because then his palm was cupping her cheek, feeling the blush rise under her skin, the curve of her jaw, her cheekbone. So soft. She was so impossibly soft, and as Ellina leaned into his hand, just the slightest bit, he wondered why he didn't do this all the time. Every day. Any chance he got.

Sudden footsteps coming around the corner made them both start. A footman appeared, wearing the uniform of a house staff. "Commander."

Venick dropped his hand. "Yes?"

"Someone is here to see you, sir. He says he's a friend of yours." Venick's heart kicked at the thought of Dourin, but the footman continued. "An elf from Evov."

Not Dourin, then. "Who?"

The servant looked uncomfortable. "I...do not know."

"What do you mean, you don't know?"

"He only asked to see you. He gave no other details, though the elves seemed to know him..."

Venick had to be careful not to raise his voice. "Did he at least give a name?"

"He didn't, but..."

"But?"

"He says you owe him. Also, he wants his book back."

TWELVE

They strode into the tearoom to find the visitor waiting in one of the elaborate-backed chairs. "Traegar." Venick was surprised to see the elf. Surprised that he was glad. Traegar had helped him and Dourin out of a sticky situation back in Evov. And Traegar's potion book—a gift that Venick was not, in fact, giving back—had assisted Venick in caring for Ellina on the tundra when she was at her sickest. The footman was right on that point, at least. Venick did owe him.

"I hear you take in refugees," Traegar said as he stood from the chair. The elf's unusually wavy hair had grown since Venick had last seen him, but his skin was still markedly tan, his eyes full of that same arched amusement.

"Only the useful ones," Venick replied with a grin, clasping Traegar's forearm in greeting.

"And you," Traegar said, turning his gaze to Ellina. "Oh, have I been hearing stories about you."

"We want to know what you know," Venick said as he chose a seat at the round table. Ellina nodded as she came to perch on the chair next to his, cradling her bandaged hand against her thighs. "I want to hear everything."

"Of course." But Traegar's attention lingered on the door. "I wonder." A pause. "Are we missing our final member?"

Venick and Ellina exchanged a look.

Traegar's expression wiped itself clean. "Do not...do not tell me..."

"Dourin's alive," Venick was quick to clarify.

You hope.

"He's in Parith."

You think.

"We separated about a month ago. It was meant to be temporary."

The truth was that neither Ellina nor Venick had been able to contact Dourin, nor anyone else from the highland capitol. Venick suspected that the Elder was intercepting their messages in order to punish Venick. That wasn't exactly surprising, seeing as Venick had conspired with the man's daughter to steal his army. Venick didn't think the Elder would go so far as to harm Dourin—not when he owed the elf his life price—but the situation was tenuous, especially since Dourin's state of health was currently unknown.

Traegar sank into his seat. He understood what Venick was not saying. "Dourin is unwell?"

"He was injured," Venick admitted. "A southerner attacked the Elder, but Dourin stepped between them. He took a knife to the stomach. We left him under the care of Parith's healers."

"I would have gone straight there..." Traegar toyed with one sleeve, then seemed to realize what he was doing and released the fabric. "That is to say, if I had known. If I thought he wanted me there."

It was painful seeing Traegar's uncertainty. More painful, because Venick knew that feeling well. Traegar and Dourin were both *geleeshi*, gifted with the ability to not only summon homing horses they'd raised from birth, but any homing horse. Dourin, especially, had a remarkable affinity for the craft; Venick had once seen him call an entire herd through the elflands' northern foothills, assembling the creatures from leagues away. It was this shared skill that first brought Dourin and Traegar together...a relationship that had since been soured by jealousy and misunderstandings.

Venick thought of the war. He thought of his own broken relationships with his mother, his father, even Miria. What had been lost between them was lost forever. But Traegar and Dourin didn't have to suffer the same fate. It wasn't too late for them.

"Go to him." Venick was suddenly fierce. "The road to Parith is clear. You could make it in a fortnight if you ride swiftly. Dourin...he would want that."

Traegar's mouth lifted slightly. "I suppose we will see."

A maid entered the room with a food trolly. The cart rattled, one wheel spinning wildly. "Luncheon," she said in a singsong voice, unaware that she was interrupting. "This is from the matron. She insisted on fresh berries, though where she expected us to find those this time of year, I haven't a clue. The rest is all here though, gravy for your potatoes, the raisins go on the pudding, and you, dear," she pinned Ellina with a look, "will be needing second servings, yes?" When Ellina said nothing, the woman kept going. "No need to answer—I know you can't speak. But you do look like you could use a bit of extra nourishment, if you don't mind my—"

"What do you mean, she cannot speak?" Traegar interrupted.

The maid's cheeriness didn't waver. "Heavens, you're sitting right beside her. Haven't you noticed? Her voice was taken. Scooped clean out, that's what they say. I thought everyone knew, it's all people can talk about."

"But that is just a rumor." Traegar looked at Ellina. His look became a stare. "Isn't it?"

"Some say she's faking." The maid bustled around the table, setting porcelain plates before them. She spoke as if Ellina wasn't there. "I can see why people might think so, given that she's the Dark Queen's sister. But in my eye, Ellina has reason to act against the queen. She is next in line for the throne, and what good would that do if—"

"That'll be all," Venick interrupted coldly. "We can take it from here."

The woman paused. Realized, belatedly, that all three occupants were frowning at her. Her cheeks took on a distinctively pink hue. "Right." She gave an overbright smile. "Enjoy."

Traegar turned back to Ellina. "It is true, then." He ran a hand over his mouth and held it there, speaking through his fingers. "I heard about your lost voice, but I did not believe it. I thought it was just another lie invented by Farah to sow fear. *Cessena*, I...I am so sorry."

Ellina held the elf's gaze. Her expression was carefully composed. Still, Venick could sense it under the surface: that deep well of grief.

"Tell us about the elflands," Venick said to change the subject. "You came from Evov, didn't you? Is the Dark Army still tormenting its citizens?"

Traegar turned his empty plate so that its avian design faced away from him. He took his time in answering. "Evov is gone."

Venick locked eyes with Ellina. "The city was destroyed?"

"Not destroyed. *Gone.* The city vanished."

Venick heard Ellina's sharp intake of breath. Her hands formed a question, moving quickly through a series of elven symbols. When Traegar failed to glean her meaning, Venick translated. "Evov was built into that mountain. It has stood there for generations. How is it possible that the city just vanished?"

"I could not quite believe it, either. It happened late one night. I woke to discover that I was no longer in my bed but on the cliffside, along with hundreds of others. Our houses, the streets, the palace, too—all gone. It is as if the buildings stood up and walked off, leaving its occupants behind."

Venick sat back in his seat, trying to imagine it. Those towering structures, the sheer walls, the scale and heft of the place just…gone. Evaporated, sucked into the void. Despite his initial disbelief, Venick found that he did believe it. The elven city of Evov had always been magical, remaining hidden to those it did not deem worthy. The city's enchantment had long protected its citizens until last summer when Farah used a loophole in the city's magic to infiltrate the royal palace and stage her coup. Venick wondered if that's why Evov had vanished. Maybe it didn't like the changing allegiances. Maybe it had spit Farah out like a bad bite.

Venick found himself speaking around a smile. "So that's why we haven't yet encountered the Dark Army. We've been waiting for an attack, but they're in no state for battle. They're scrambling."

"The Dark Army is in upheaval," Traegar confirmed.

Venick caught Ellina's eye. She made a wide gesture with her hands, bringing her fist up to her chin. It was the elven motion for *fury*.

Farah would be furious. She'd lost her base and was likely now stranded somewhere in the northern mountains. Her army might be in a state of upheaval, but they would regroup. And then they'd be coming.

Venick's glee leaked away. "We'll need to prepare our soldiers." He rubbed his eyes. They'd had two sleepless nights, and it looked like he was about to have another. "I'd hoped to stay in Igor through the end of the month, but I don't think we can afford that anymore. Farah is being forced to play her hand, which means we'll be forced to play ours."

Something about Traegar's answering smile made Venick remember that the elf had chosen life as a healer instead of a soldier. "That," he said, "is how war usually works."

THIRTEEN

Venick departed for the barracks, but Ellina stayed. She moved to the abandoned luncheon trolly, which was arrayed with an assortment of items: a tray of miniature fruitcakes, a bowl of yellow pudding, the aforementioned raisins, and—most importantly—a notepad and charcoal pencil. Ellina returned to the table with the writing supplies. She tamped down a wave of nervousness as she scribbled a single name. *Kaji?*

Traegar looked stricken. "Your fellow legionnaire. I understand that he was acting as a spy for the resistance, as were you. He was caught shortly after your escape. I am sorry, Ellina. Your friend is dead."

Ellina stared at the pencil in her unbandaged fist. The nib was blunted, the charcoal worn down to a stub. She thought of how Kaji had been an ally when she most needed an ally. A friend, when she needed a friend.

Shakily, she wrote a second name. *Livila?*

Traegar shook his head. "I do not know who that is."

It was a relief, of sorts. If Livila's name was not circulating through the elflands, maybe that meant the young servant had escaped the inquisition. Maybe she, too, had found a way free of Farah's clutches.

A knock at the open door drew their attention.

"Sorry to interrupt," said Erol, appearing on the threshold. "I heard we had a visitor."

"Erol." Traegar's face went blank with surprise. "Is that you?"

Erol marched across the room in four swift strides and pulled Traegar to his feet. Traegar went rigid, but Erol merely touched a hand to his own chest, then reached out to place that hand on Traegar's shoulder—an elven gesture of camaraderie. "It's good to see you, old friend."

The tension drained from Traegar. He huffed a small laugh and returned the gesture. They stood like that for a moment, hand to shoulder, human and elf, and despite the moment's obvious intimacy, Ellina found that she could not look away.

Erol wrinkled his nose. "You haven't aged a bit."

"I could say the same for you."

Traegar's words were light enough, yet they seemed to change something between those two. Erol's hand was still on Traegar's shoulder. His fingers squeezed, just slightly, little creases denting the elf's shirt. A friendly gesture...or a warning?

The pair broke apart, settling into seats around the table.

"Tell me," Traegar said, crossing an ankle over one knee. "What brings a lowlander like you all the way to Igor?"

"The same reason that brings us all," Erol replied. "War."

Traegar flicked a piece of lint off his trousers. "It does not bring us *all*."

"He likes to contradict me," Erol told Ellina in a mock whisper.

Then, to Traegar, "Are you going to be difficult so soon?"

"I am not here for battle."

"Of course. Wartime campaigns need healers, too."

"I have no interest in joining the campaign."

Traegar's voice had lost its lightness. But then, Ellina knew this about Traegar. Though he had trained with Ellina and Dourin as a legion initiate, he had never taken the oaths, divorcing himself from anything to do with fighting. He became a healer instead. That was how Erol and Traegar first met—they had worked together at the elven Healer's Academy called *Evenshina*, researching new herbal remedies and tonics and, Ellina remembered, poisons.

Ellina dug a hand into her pocket, pulling out the conjuror's vial of green liquid. She set the glass onto the table with a soft *click*.

"Where," Traegar said slowly, "did you get that?"

Ellina jotted a quick answer and slid the notepad across the wood. While Erol read her explanation aloud, Traegar held the vial up to the light. Though Ellina had first thought the liquid was perfectly translucent, there were actually what appeared to be little bits of sand near the bottom of the glass. On closer inspection, she could see the sand twitching, like larvae.

Traegar's mouth flattened. "This," he said, "is minceflesh."

Ellina shook her head. She did not know what that was.

"A gruesome name for a gruesome poison," Erol explained. "Minceflesh is one of the few poisons strong enough to kill an elf. Nasty business. You can't usually tell, at first, what caused the death. From the outside, an elf poisoned with minceflesh might look perfectly normal—no marks, no open wounds. But cut the body open, and you will discover that their organs have been dissolved. Chewed through, if you want to know the truth of it. That's what minceflesh do—they eat you alive from the inside."

Ellina grimaced. Erol barked a laugh. "I agree."

Traegar set the vial gingerly back onto the table. "If this poison was meant for Venick, the poisoner wanted to be thorough. It is a potent concoction. But it is dangerous for an elf to work with minceflesh. If the liquid contacts their skin, they risk death, too."

"It is a bit overkill," Erol agreed. "I would have thought the conjurors smarter than that. Why risk themselves when there are plenty of poisons that are harmless to elves but lethal to humans?"

"It could be that Dark Queen wants to send a message," Traegar supposed.

"Only the worst for her enemies?"

"Something like that."

Ellina took the vial back, careful now not to squeeze too tightly. Perhaps Traegar was right, and this was meant to be a message. Yet Ellina knew her sister. Farah *was* smart. She would not risk the lives of her conjurors unnecessarily. Then again, maybe the minceflesh was not Farah's idea. The conjurors had not always been entirely willing subjects to their new queen and her demands. Maybe they were taking liberties.

"Best keep that bottle safe," Traegar told Ellina as he came to his feet. "You would not want it ending up in the wrong hands."

"Best to throw it into the fire," Erol corrected, standing as well. "Some poisons are too dangerous, even during war. We have no use for a weapon like that."

Ellina nodded, closing the vial in her fist.

Later, after she had bid the others goodbye and returned to her prepared bedroom, Ellina stood before the room's hearth, the glass of minceflesh in hand. She tipped the small bottle over itself, one way, then the other, watching the poison swirl.

We have no use for a weapon like that.

Yet Ellina thought of Farah sitting on their mother's throne. She thought of Balid's half-moon smile, and a shadow slipping across a ballroom floor, and a slit-throated corpse blazing towards her across a clearing. His body was as lithe as it had been in life. His sightless eyes were a horror, more horrible still because that elf was a southerner, and must have once been the corpse-bender's friend.

Ellina did not throw the glass into the fire, but tucked it into her belongings.

FOURTEEN

She struggled to sleep.

As Ellina lay in bed staring up at the ceiling, she was careful not to count the number of hours she had been awake. Counting would do nothing but increase her anxiety over the rest she was missing, and that would only keep her awake longer. Rather, she thought about the nameless house servant who had prepared this room, which was one of many guest chambers in the baron's estate. She imagined a young girl folding the quilted duvet into perfect fourths, smoothing the embroidered cotton with her hand. It was this same imaginary girl who would have seen to the bedside oil lamp, refilling the oil, threading the wick, touching a match to light it. The girl would have stepped back to admire her handiwork, satisfied that the room was sufficiently comfortable for any guest.

Ellina was not comfortable. Outside, sleet tapped the window. The walls smelled of turpentine, the floor like sand and burnt wax. Even the oil lamp was a bother. The flame flickered and danced, its shadow morphing on the wall, creating shapes. One shape, actually. A tall figure, two slim hands...

Ellina pressed a pillow to her face.

She was not unfamiliar with these kinds of hallucinations. Ellina had been a prisoner the first time she saw Venick enter her cell, felt his hand on her cheek, his breath on her face. She watched him do this a dozen times before she realized he could not possibly be real. Ellina learned to stop trusting these visions, so much so that when Venick really did arrive, she was certain it was not true.

Ellina did not know what was true.

After her meeting with Erol and Traegar, she had considered seeking out Venick in the city where he was briefing their soldiers. She wanted to finish what they had started in the hallway. To see if *that* was true. Yet she remembered the look of regret he had given her before the ambush. Remembered similar looks in the ballroom, the attic, the estate grounds. Ellina's confidence had wavered at those memories, and so rather than find Venick, she retreated to her temporary quarters for a bath and a change of clothes. Though it was only late afternoon, she slid into bed, watching the daylight fade from soft grey to deep blue. Then: nightfall.

The pillow over her face was cloistering, but rather than remove it, Ellina turned her head so that she could breathe better. She wished for sleep. If she could sleep, she would not have to think about everything that had gone wrong that day. That year. Over the course of her whole life.

In the elflands, there was an elf named the Secret Keeper. Ellina had been young the first time her eldest sister Miria took her to meet the Keeper, who lived a day's ride from Evov. They had packed food for the journey and saddled their own horses rather than allow the stablehands to do it for them. To Ellina, it felt like the greatest adventure.

"When we arrive," Miria said, "you must be prepared to give the Keeper one of your secrets. In return, she will give you a secret of hers."

Ellina planned to tell the Secret Keeper that the palace's resident doe had birthed a fawn. Yet when they reached the small village nestled in the foothills, and Ellina left Miria to wait outside while she entered the Secret Keeper's small, thatched hut, she changed her mind.

"Well, youngling?" the Keeper had asked. Her eyes were lighter than was common, the palest of golds. "What secret have you come to share?"

Ellina leaned close, pitching her voice so low as to be almost inaudible. "I am worried...that Miria is not my sister."

"Oh?" the Secret Keeper asked, and though Ellina was suddenly doused in concern that this was more of a confession than a secret, and that she would be scolded, the Keeper's eyes twinkled. "What makes you say so?"

"She sings," Ellina admitted in a miserable rush. "She likes music and painting. She wants to play games. And she smiles. She *laughs*." Ellina clasped her hands together, terrified by the things she was saying, terrified of what they might mean. "People say that she acts like...like a human. But true elves do not act like humans. And if she is not an elf, she cannot be my sister."

The Secret Keeper set a gentle hand to Ellina's shoulder. Her skin was rough, wrinkled in the way of only the most ancient of their race.

"Thank you for your secret," said the Keeper.

"Do you not...?" Ellina had faltered. "Do you not have an answer?"

"I am not a seer, only a Keeper. But now, it is time for me to give you a secret in return."

Ellina had never told anyone about her visit to the Secret Keeper.

She buried any memory of the encounter, ashamed by her confession, worried that it might somehow harm Miria. And there were other worries, too. Because Ellina had felt those same urges—to sing, to smile—yet saw how it implicated Miria, how it turned others against her, some even going so far as to question her worthiness for the throne. Ellina did not want Miria's troubles to become her own, so she had hidden. Worn her elvenness like a cloak to conceal any differences. Even her decision to join the legion had been partly fueled by a desire to blend.

Miria had never tried to blend. It was Miria who embraced her differences, who wore her dark hair like a badge of honor, who was not constrained by boundaries, not in life and not in love. She was a peacemaker, a bridge-builder, a friend.

Ellina thought of Harmon, who had bandaged Ellina's hand, then extended her own in friendship.

She thought of Traegar's journey to find Dourin, the humility it would take to mend things between them.

Erol's relationship with Rishiana. Traegar's reunion with Erol. Venick's reunion with his mother.

Ellina breathed in the pillow's scent, then yanked it away.

Why them, but not her?

How much more courage would it take?

She pushed upright. Her bandaged hand throbbed, a reminder that just because she had been injured once did not mean she could not be injured again. There was no limit to tomorrow's grievances. No promise, really, of tomorrow at all.

She got out of bed.

• • •

Ellina moved softly through the lamplit house, her bare feet skimming the wood, feeling for planks that were too high or too low and would therefore creak. Up one flight of stairs, her hands touching nothing, not the walls nor the balustrade nor the small, silver-framed portraits. Up another flight, finding a soft spot on the landing, imagining it whining noisily under her weight and avoiding it. She went left, then left again. She moved as if she knew where she was going, though Ellina had never been to this part of the house before. She had never roamed these rooms.

There was a covered balcony that stretched the length of the third floor, an exterior door left ajar. Stone underfoot now, which would not creak, but could still make noise in other ways: loose stones. Plaster shaken free. Dead leaves blown in by the wind, waiting to crunch beneath her soles.

Ellina avoided it all, moving down the long line of windows. Her reflection flitted alongside her, appearing and vanishing and appearing again, mirrored in the glass like a ghost. The windows were all dark, save for one near the balcony's center that brimmed with yellow light.

She went to that window, feeling pulled. The curtains were drawn shut, though not quite all the way. If Ellina leaned forward and down a little, she could peer between them into the room beyond. She remembered having once done something like this before, looking in when he could not see out. Ellina felt the temptation. Understood its cowardice.

She tapped a knuckle to the glass, a clear, brisk sound.

A sloshing noise from the recesses of the room. A soft curse. The scrape of a chair.

Ellina felt the first stitch of nervousness. Or, that was not quite right. She had been nervous the whole way there—as she skipped up the stairs, as she counted windows, figuring which one must belong to him. Before, though, it had been easy to rename her nervousness, to call it *curiosity* or *anticipation*, which were less vulnerable words and therefore easier to carry. Yet as Ellina stood waiting, her nervousness broke clear, like clouds parting to reveal the moon. She could no longer pretend it was anything else.

Venick threw open the curtains. He saw her. His fingers tightened around the glass in his hand.

He undid the window's latch and heaved it upwards. Ellina expected the window to rattle, to make some kind of noise, but it slid on well-oiled hinges. *A relic*, Venick had called the house, but this no longer rang entirely true. The house was well kept and lived in. Loved, even.

That word, loved, made Ellina's jaw clench. She forced herself to hold Venick's gaze.

Yet for once, it did not seem like he knew what she was thinking. Venick was looking at Ellina as if he could not quite believe she was real. It took several thick beats of her heart for him to ask, "Are you…what are you doing here?" He scrubbed a hand down his face. "No, don't answer that." He stepped to the side. "Would you like to come in?"

Ellina climbed through the window, ducking to fit under the panel, her knee bumping clumsily against the frame. She had thought his room would be a suite, but there was only a single chamber, the bed high in one corner, a sitting area set before a small fireplace. Venick's pack was open, his belongings scattered: a coat, a pile of armor, a familiar-looking book that might have been a journal and might not have been.

Venick walked over to a desk, where he found a pen and parchment. He moved to the sitting area's two-person sofa and arranged the supplies over the low marble table, then picked up his drink again. The clear liquid glowed orange in the fire's light. He took a gulp.

Ellina sank into the chair opposite the sofa—cushy, velvet, a winged back—and hesitated. She was not yet ready for the pen and parchment. She pointed at his glass, questioning.

"A lowland liquor," he said. "Erol gave it to me. He distills it himself, which is apparently not an easy thing to do. Here." He slid the glass across the table. The contents sloshed, spilled a little. Ellina lifted the cup to her lips. She put her mouth where his had been.

The liquor was strong, slightly sweet. Pleasant at first, then the burn. She struggled not to cough.

"It's called winterclear. We used to drink it in Irek. When I was a boy, my parents would buy it from traveling merchants around wintertime. My friends and I would steal the bottles and run to this hidden cove near the beach. It was our favorite spot. Beautiful in the summer. Not freezing in the winters, but cold enough that you wouldn't want to swim. We'd share the bottle between us and then dare each other to jump in." His smile was wistful as he took back the glass. Ellina could still taste the alcohol on her tongue. Sweet again, with an undertone of spice. Not unpleasant. She licked her lips, saw Venick's eyes drop to her mouth.

Ellina's nervousness returned. It glowed under her skin.

"Why don't you tell me why you're here?" Venick prompted, motioning to the parchment. Ellina nodded. This was why she had come. She was haunted by the way she had left things with Venick. She remembered their last conversations before her voice was stolen, first in the stateroom, then on Traegar's balcony, and finally in Irek. Her lies. Their cruelty. It hardly seemed to matter anymore that her reasons for lying had been noble. She should have found a way to tell Venick the truth about her. She should have done it long ago.

But she could do it now. Venick might have already guessed many of Ellina's reasons, but she owed him a full explanation. She had planned to write it all down.

And yet, now that she was there, it felt wrong to write those things on paper. The awkward business of scribbling her notes and passing them to him, waiting for him to read and pass them back.

A fresh wave of jitters. Ellina's heart was straining with the knowledge of what she had come to explain and how else she might do it.

She stood from her seat.

Venick's eyes were dark as she moved towards him. She came around the table, stopped at his knees. He was still looking at her as he had been, like he was not sure she was real. Ellina remembered him looking at her like this once before, when she had stripped off her clothes to swim in an everpool. She had worn nothing but her thin shift, the fabric nearly sheer. Venick's swallow had been audible.

It was again now. Though Ellina was fully clothed—save for her shoes, which she had left behind in her determined rush—she felt utterly naked.

She reached to touch the space beneath his jaw. His pulse slammed against her fingers. He opened his mouth but said nothing. His grey eyes were clear, yet she could see that he doubted, that he was still not entirely sure of her intention. He held himself perfectly still.

She brought their lips to meet.

His mouth parted beneath hers. She tasted him, tasted the liquor on his tongue. He slid one hand to her jaw, his fingers curling into her hair, his other hand going to her hip, pulling her down to him. The kiss was not gentle. It was hungry and eager and wanting. Venick drew back briefly to look at her, his seriousness, the question working its way into the space between his brows. "Are you sure—?"

She kissed him again. She felt the rough scratch of his stubble, felt fires light where his hands skimmed her skin. She pushed him against the sofa's back, and his mouth landed on her neck, blazing a path. *This,*

Ellina thought, but could think no further, because then Venick's mouth was back on hers, and it was his tongue and his teeth and the way he smelled, his fingers sliding up her thighs, his thumbs digging into the creases of her hips, which was good, it was *good*, but also painfully far away from where she wanted his hands.

They had kissed before, but never like this. This kiss was a secret waiting to shake free. It was a hall of gemstones left for the taking.

And then, abruptly, it stopped. Venick broke away, pulling back. Ellina was startled to see that he looked unhappy.

"I'm sorry," he said. They were both breathing heavily. "It's just..." He gave a pained smile. "What were you doing before you came here?"

Ellina did not understand the question. A part of her—probably the same part of her that ached for his hands to keep going—reared its head in frustration. Why had he stopped to ask her this? What did it matter what she had been doing?

"Please," he said.

So she made herself think. Before this, Ellina had been—what? Lying awake in bed. Ruminating about her past with a pillow pressed to her face so as not to see the shadows on the walls and imagine monsters.

Venick nodded as if she had spoken. "It's just...I know that you have trouble sleeping. I know that you struggle with nightmares—visions, even—and that there are things you want to forget. And I can't help but wonder...if you didn't come here to forget them. It's not that I mind," he added quickly, sensing her dismay. "It's not that I don't want—" He stopped himself, struggling for words, before dropping his head and letting his thoughts come. "This means something to me. I need to know that it means something to you, too."

It does, Ellina wanted to insist. She wanted to say the words in elvish, the echo of an old habit rooted in a time when the bounds of that language still held her to her truths. She wanted to mouth the words now, to do it in a way that would not seem like denial or defense.

Ellina kicked herself. If only she had written that letter after all, then she could hand it to him, show him that he had it wrong. And yet…what exactly would her letter have said? There would have been an apology, certainly. Ellina would have explained the events that had occurred in Evov, her sister's threats, the reasons Ellina had convinced Venick to hate her. But had she planned to express more? Would she really have set her heart out for him, when he was engaged to another woman, and the Commander of an army primed for war, and Ellina was not even sure who she was anymore, and even if she had been, was not sure there was anything left of her to give?

Ellina dimmed. She understood why Venick had stopped their kiss.

Blushing with shame and a new sense of confusion, she removed herself from his lap. Venick's smile was sad. "I don't know what the right thing is," he sighed. "I don't know if it was a mistake asking you to come on this campaign. I want you here, but maybe that's selfish. You haven't had enough time to process what happened in Evov. You've barely had enough time to regain your strength. And I've been wondering if maybe…you should go back to Parith with Traegar. You don't have to decide just yet," Venick added when Ellina's eyes snapped to his. "I want you to think it over. Our army leaves for Heartshire Bay at dawn. If you're coming with us, meet me in the stables in the morning. If I don't see you by dawn, I'll assume you've chosen to stay behind."

Ellina understood that condition. He was trying to make it easier for her to stay, because she could do so without having to face him. No goodbyes.

"Well? Will you think about it?"

Ellina imagined what it would be like to return to Dourin. To remove herself from this war, to see her friend again. It would be a relief…at first. But the vision darkened, turned to show its second face. If Ellina left now, she might never win her voice back. She might never find her place among the resistance, or sort through her feelings, or figure out how to mend this hurt, fragile thing between her and Venick…if mending it was even possible.

Venick waited.

Will you think about it?

Ellina gave a nod. She would honor Venick's request. She would give herself the night to think over his offer. That way, when she chose to stay, Venick would know she meant it.

FIFTEEN

Ellina returned to her chamber. The lamp was still burning, the bed still perfectly made. She touched the quilted cover, thinking of dreams, but quickly abandoned the notion. If she had not been able to sleep before, she would never sleep now.

She went to her pack and dug into its inner pocket. Her fingers meet cool glass. The vial of minceflesh was where she had left it—a small relief. It was not safe to leave the poison unattended, but nor did Ellina like the idea of wearing the vial's chain around her neck. She imagined what would happen if the glass broke against her chest. The liquid would soak. The tiny creatures would burrow through her skin. They would make a meal of her flesh, munching through sinew and tendon until her insides were reduced to mush. Ellina's body would bloat with the pressure: a balloon full of blood.

She left the minceflesh where it was and went to the window. Outside, the sleet had slowed to a drizzle. In the courtyard below, a plainsperson was rolling a rainwater barrel back towards the house with apparent difficulty. There were hundreds of such barrels scattered around the city, the plainspeople's solution to their self-imposed drought. Since they refused to drink from their own river, they must collect water in other ways. And they hoarded it. Ellina had not been offered a drop of water since arriving in Igor, only wine.

She thought of the dinner party wine and how she had chugged gratefully from an offered goblet.

She thought of the corpse that had attacked Venick, the way men had hacked the creature to pieces.

Ellina rested her head against the window's casing. Though she was not asleep, the noise of the storm felt a little like dreaming. Down in the courtyard, the barrel-collector looked miserable. His shoulders hunched against the sleet. He rolled his barrel off the stone paving and down a gravel path. Likely, he was headed to the kitchens, which were located in a building separate from the rest of the house.

Ellina pushed away from the window. Though she was not cold, she rubbed at her arms in the way of someone who anticipated being cold soon. Her hands paused when she realized what she was doing.

She had not known, until that moment, what she planned.

Her feet were moving. They were taking her to her small bag of belongings, the set of gloves. She removed the bandage from her injured hand. Pulled on her boots.

The army would ride at dawn. There was still time.

She exited through the window.

• • •

The baron's kitchen was a large, practical structure set on the grounds behind the house. There was no fireplace or chimney, but rather several stout, guttering ovens, along with a ceiling high enough to ventilate the smoke. The kitchen staff, if they had slept that night, had not slept long. Workers crowded the space, busying themselves with a number of tasks, some of which involved cleaning up last night's welcome dinner. The floor was dotted with trash bins. The sink was a tower of goblets. No plates. If food had been prepared for the dinner guests, it was never served.

A woman greeted Ellina, an aged matron with thick white hair and calm, inquisitive eyes. Ellina had come ready with pen and parchment to explain her purpose, but the matron merely smiled, waving away the supplies. She did not speak, and Ellina wondered if she was mute, too, or if this was some kind of backward attempt at deference. The matron motioned around the kitchen, then surprised Ellina by making an elven hand gesture, linking three fingers but leaving the pinkies pointed out. This gesture was often used with guests, or sometimes as a sign of respect for one's superiors. It meant *as you wish* or, in this case, *make yourself at home.*

This, too, surprised Ellina. The matron had been expecting her.

Ellina peeled off her coat but left her gloves as they were. The gloves, which she had acquired in Parith, were made of supple leather as thin as skin, allowing her to retain dexterity while at the same time offering remarkable warmth. More importantly, the gloves were waterproof and armor-strong. Impenetrable.

She went to the sink and its pile of glass goblets. Her heart sank to see that half of the goblets had already been rinsed, dried, and set into a nearby cabinet. Those that had not yet been scrubbed showed the hardened, evaporated dregs of dark wine.

She thought back to the dinner party, the nasal voice of a guest calling for a toast. She thought of two matching jeweled cups, their tinny clink, the way Harmon had gulped deeply while Venick looked on, scarcely touching his own rim to his lips. He had not taken a drink of his own wine.

But that was not the point.

Ellina began searching the pile, ignoring the sting of her burned hand, riffling through glasses of varying styles and sizes. The matron, for all she had anticipated Ellina's purpose, had apparently not passed that knowledge to her staff. The kitchen workers craned their necks to watch Ellina, whispering animatedly until the matron shooed them back to their work.

Night lifted. Grey morning light filtered into the kitchen through small rectangular windows. Ellina kept at her task, moving to another cup, then another. She was aware that time was ticking by. If she did not arrive at the stables by dawn, Venick would assume she had made her choice. The army would leave without her. And then? Ellina did not have a horse of her own, only her borrowed silver stallion. If she did not claim the steed, someone else would claim him instead. Ellina would be stranded.

She redoubled her efforts, tossing each glass aside with less and less care. She thought of the way Venick's hands had come to her face when he kissed her, and of his words, the self-consciousness hidden within them.

I need to know it means something to you, too.

Through the window, the clouds abruptly dissipated to reveal a pale blue sky. Ellina blinked into the light. It was later than she had thought. Likely, the army was already assembling along the river, preparing to ride. Ellina realized with a jolt that if she did not go now, Venick would leave the city without her, his request ignored, his admission unanswered. But it was not too late. She could make it to the stables by sunrise if she moved quickly.

She began to abandon her hunt when a flash of color caught her eye.

Ellina stilled. She thought of the mosaic that had once adorned the palace in Evov. The colors were as brilliant as they were intricate, thousands of perfectly set pieces of glass. She felt like that. She felt like she was about to lay her final tile.

Slowly, she reached to the bottom of the pile and pulled out two jeweled goblets. One was smaller, with floral etchings around its base. That had been Harmon's. The other was wider, studded with rubies—Venick's.

Ellina raised Venick's cup to the morning light. There, at the bottom of the glass, swirling in the remnants of wine, was a cluster of what appeared to be grains of sand, moving back and forth like tiny, twitching larvae.

• • •

Ellina pushed outside into a blustery winter morning. She did not return to her room, did not go to collect her things. She wore what she had been wearing the night before. She was still clutching the glass goblet.

Lin Lill had been right. Someone was trying to poison Venick, and they had nearly succeeded. The goblet, though Venick had not actually drunk from it, was all the proof they needed. There was a traitor among them.

Ellina cut through the baron's home. Square corridors, a long hall, then the front doors. She drove outside in a rush, making it halfway down the entrance stairs when she was brought up short to see Harmon. The woman looked uneasy. "Ellina. I have been looking for you."

Ellina's eyes dropped to the letter in Harmon's hand.

"From my father," Harmon acknowledged. "There's been news. I'm not quite sure how to tell you this, actually." The wind pushed through Harmon's skirts. Far away, a crow cawed: a series of short, scratchy cries. "Ellina. Dourin is dead."

Ellina's hands went limp. The goblet shattered on the stairs.

"It happened recently," Harmon said. "His condition was improving, but he caught sick. An infection. He deteriorated more quickly than seemed possible. The physicians did everything they could…"

Harmon continued speaking, her voice coming from a distance. Ellina could not hear her. She had stepped over a cliff, she was falling. The depths below rushed up to meet her.

SIXTEEN

Venick arrived at the stables in the blue hours of dawn. He sat on an overturned crate, warmed his hands with his breath. Anxious. He laced his fingers, dropped his head. He shouldn't be so anxious.

As the sun struggled into the sky and burned away the morning mist, Venick watched the shadows form and change across the ground. He thought about a conjuror's ability to shift shadows, to pull them in or push them away or shadow-bind them to a quarry, enabling the conjuror to track the individual's location. He wondered what that must feel like, being tethered to another, then decided that he already knew.

After a time, men and elves began filtering into the stables. They rubbed the sleep from their eyes, chatting as they made to ready their horses. The muffled thud of hooves in hay. The creak of old hinges, the thump of saddles being dropped onto the animals' backs. Only a small fraction of their army had earned riding privileges, and of that fraction, an even smaller number had managed to secure a spot in the city's stables. Yet the space felt stifling.

Venick stepped outside. The morning sky looked like threadbare cotton. The streets were grey and damp, the city's rooftops dusted white. It had snowed again.

He waited as long as he could. Eventually, he had to concede that she wasn't coming.

Venick told himself to be glad. This was what he'd wanted, wasn't it? For Ellina to stay behind with Traegar. For her to be safe. It had been selfish of him to press her to come campaigning in the first place, not when she'd just spent a month locked away in the dark, not when she was hurting and silenced and worried over Dourin. Yes, Venick thought. He should be glad of her choice.

But Venick wasn't glad. The emotion he felt was nothing like gladness. It was small and hard, wedged beneath his heart. Rigid at the corners, and sharp, so that it hurt to move.

He scuffed the toe of his boot into the ground. Made a wet divot.

He felt the urge to go looking for her and beat it back. Ellina had made her choice. He had to respect that.

He went to ready his horse.

• • •

Soldiers gathered along the Taro, crowding up the riverbank and spilling into nearby streets. The morning was loud with military sounds, the clank and stamp of boots, the clink of armor, idle conversation.

Harmon was there. She had changed out of her flowery highland garb and back into an outfit similar to the one she'd been wearing when they first met: dune-colored, stiff fabric. Brown riding boots, a cropped overcoat, plus a winter hat lined with fur. She watched Venick as he approached on foot, Eywen trailing obediently behind him. Her expression was reserved, a little aloof. She glanced around but said nothing of their missing member. Venick decided that if she wouldn't, he would not, either.

"Ready?" Harmon asked lightly.

Venick mounted Eywen and let that be his answer.

• • •

They rode through the city, gathering soldiers as they went. Despite the early hour, citizens lined the streets. Some people waved, kissed loved ones goodbye. Others stared stony-faced, glad to see the resistance go.

Venick turned around in his saddle to watch the city disappear behind him. He finally realized why Igor looked so familiar. It wasn't because he'd seen this place before—it was because Igor, with its brown buildings and milling market and dirt-paved streets, looked very much like his home city Irek.

Sentimental now, are we?

Not sentimental, no. Poignant, maybe. There was a metaphor to be found somewhere in there. The boundaries between their countries were an illusion. The wars they'd fought, the slights they'd perceived, the hatred and fear they'd lapped onto each other, and for what? They were all just people. They looked alike. Their cities looked alike. They were even named alike: Igor and Irek. A similarity that was suddenly impossible to miss.

And the elves?

Different. Colder, harder to crack. But that didn't automatically make them an enemy.

And Ellina?

Venick shut down his thoughts.

• • •

They set a course northeast. They would follow the Taro for as long as they could before breaking north around the bay. It would be slow going; they could only travel as fast as their foot soldiers, and their supply wagons, which struggled to maneuver down unpaved winter roads.

Harmon rode by his side, unusually quiet. Venick was bothered by her silence, but he knew he'd also be bothered if Harmon felt like talking. He focused instead on the low drum of the army behind them, which filled his head like white noise. It drove out all thought. And yet, Venick still carried that emotion with him from the stables. Dense. Sharp, like an arrowhead.

Snow drifted down in flurries. The temperature seemed to drop, even as the sun rose.

Soon, Igor vanished over the horizon, leaving nothing but wide-open plains and the lazy, sprawling length of the Taro. The land, vibrant most of the year, had turned grey with the season, the poplars skinned bare, the high grass caked and brittle. The snow thickened, coming down in swirling sheets. Later, it shifted to misting rain, slowing their progress to a crawl. By the time Venick called for a halt at the end of the first day, the mood was miserable.

"Do you not have someone to do that for you?" Lin Lill asked when she found Venick on his knees in the muck, clearing a spot to set up his tent. The army would camp in the field between the road and the river that night. This was not the wisest positioning—if they were ambushed, the elven half of their forces would be trapped against the Taro, unable to swim to safety—but relocating would take time and energy, both of which were in short supply.

Venick didn't look up. "I don't mind doing it."

"You look like an underling."

"I don't care what I look like."

He could feel Lin Lill's eyes on the back of his neck. "Do you want to talk about it?"

About Ellina, she meant.

"No."

"Good. I do not really want to hear about it."

Venick glanced up.

"The Dark Queen might try to land in Kenath," Lin Lill said smoothly. "It is a central point that is already under southern control. She could move her army there to regroup, and to enforce the border. If refugees try to cross into the mainlands, she would be positioned to interfere. And it would make an excellent link in her supply chain."

"Stationing in Kenath would expose her to retaliation from both sides."

"True, but it is still the obvious move. Farah was driven out of Evov. She is being forced to change her base. Typically, that would give us an advantage, but in this case, her base is made up entirely of elves."

"And conjurors," Venick added.

"And conjurors," Lin Lill agreed.

Venick stood from where he'd been kneeling, leaving his tent in an aborted pile. He wiped the rain from his face. "I think it's about more than blunt force for Farah." Venick remembered the way Farah had staged his trial in Evov. He remembered her words to him in the cavernous prison under the mountain, how she had set them down like pieces on a playing board, rigging not just her next move, but the entire game.

A family trait.

Venick bristled at the thought. Ellina wasn't like Farah. They were both excellent strategists, yes, and skilled at deceit, but it wasn't the same.

Isn't it?

No. The sisters were different, and naming that difference felt suddenly important. It wasn't just that they looked unalike—Farah with her classic elven grandeur, Ellina darker and smaller—or that Venick happened to be in love with one of them. It was what lay within their cores. Ellina wasn't power hungry. She didn't yearn to press others down with her thumb. She viewed her abilities as a tool of war, which she used as much for others as she did for herself. Ellina was not after the throne, was not out to prove her superiority...which made Venick realize that Farah was.

"Farah likes to use trickery," Venick told Lin Lill. "She enjoys showing off her mental prowess, making you feel foolish for even trying to stand against her. She was never a warrior, not like Ellina. She doesn't care about camaraderie, and she won't go out of her way to spare her soldiers' lives. If given the choice, she'll choose the stylish strategy over the obvious one. I think that you're right—she'll move into Kenath, but not with her entire force. Half, maybe."

"And the other half?"

Venick strode to Eywen's saddlebag and pulled out a wax map, which he unrolled and spread across a nearby log. The rain was shifting to snow again, sparse flurries that melted as soon as they touched the page. "Here," he said, pressing his finger to an illustrated city. "Hurendue. Farah knows what we know. She thinks we're expecting her in Kenath, and that we'll be heading that way. But if she were to stage an ambush in Hurendue, she could trap us against the bay."

"And if we do not pass between the city and the water? She would have split her forces for nothing." Lin Lill shook her head. "It is a risky move."

"That's why she'll like it."

"If we do not send soldiers to Kenath, the Dark Army will reorganize. Southern elves will cross the border unchecked."

"We'll send a division."

"Three quarters?"

"Half, plus most of our cannons and whatever small amount of black powder we have in our supplies. They can go to Kenath, reclaim the city, cut off that point in Farah's supply chain. The rest of us will head to Hurendue."

"And if Farah does trap us against the bay?"

"She won't."

Lin Lill crossed her arms. "You sound awfully certain. But of course, you are not worried. You can swim."

Venick had been on the edge of a grin, but his smile suddenly fell away. "You're right," he said. "I'm sorry."

Lin Lill squinted an eye at him. "You should not apologize."

"I was being thoughtless."

"You have a lot on your mind."

"Your life is at risk. All the elves' lives are. I don't take that lightly."

"Venick." She sighed, clearly hating to delve into any topic that might be construed as emotional, yet unable to keep the sentiment from her voice. "No one," she said, "thinks you take this war lightly."

• • •

They fell into the rhythm of travel. This was as much a part of war as battle: the boredom, the monotony of an endless road. The younger soldiers complained, but the more seasoned fighters were glad for the tedium. They knew what would happen when it came to an end.

The Taro was a constant companion. Venick often caught his men gazing longingly at the steaming water, wondering if their plainsland allies were really so opposed to a quick dip. It was said that only warriors were sanctioned to touch the water, and so invoke divine blessings, but weren't they all warriors?

The elves did not engage in these speculations. They had no interest in the river.

One afternoon, Venick fell back to the middle lines to help dislodge a wagon wheel that had become stuck in the mud. He'd no sooner returned to Eywen's back when it happened again, another wagon wheel lodging in the divot between two rocks. By the time they'd hauled the second wheel free, Venick's trousers were caked in grime, his forearms slick with wet earth. It was somehow even in his mouth.

He remounted Eywen, only to discover that the army had stopped their forward progress. A halt must have been called.

Venick pulled out of formation, riding quickly up the line. He found Lin Lill, Harmon, Erol, Branton, and Artis all gathered together at the army's head.

"Time to part ways," Lin Lill said. "Harmon will take half of our force to Kenath. The rest of us will follow you."

Venick looked at Harmon. He waited for her to explain the customary highland parting of ways, to give their soldiers some grand speech, but she only looked as she had when they'd left Igor, uncertain and... guilty? Venick couldn't be sure. It wasn't an emotion he'd ever seen on her.

"We'll meet you in Kenath," Harmon said simply, then turned away, kicking her horse into a trot.

Their soldiers split evenly, with no distinction between country or race. Half rode north with Harmon. The others went east with Venick.

• • •

Night came. Venick sat on the dry side of an overturned crate that had been discarded by previous travelers, spinning a length of jerky between his fingers. He should eat. It was imperative that he keep up his energy. Whether or not he had an appetite was irrelevant.

He sighed and took a bite.

Erol appeared. He came to sit on the damp grass beside Venick, crossing his legs beneath him.

Venick studied the man in the light of a nearby fire. "Tell me," he started, swallowing the mouthful of jerky. "We've been traveling for days. And you do things like *that*." Venick motioned to Erol's chosen spot in the grass. "How do you keep your robes so white?"

Erol barked a surprised laugh. "I would like to hear your theories."

Venick shrugged. "Magic?" He was joking, sort of, except that as soon as he spoke the words, a window in his mind seemed to open. But…no. What Venick was thinking was impossible. Human conjurors had been eradicated by the elves long ago. There were none left.

Yet…Erol had been friends with Ellina's mother, Queen Rishiana. This meant that he'd lived in the elflands before the drawing of the border, which had occurred at least a century ago. When Venick once tried questioning the man about this timeline, Erol had waved him off, crafting some excuse that Venick had accepted because he'd been embarrassed—and rightly so. He'd all but called the man ancient. It was rude. Yet Erol *would* have to be ancient to have lived so long ago.

Erol's eyes twinkled. "I have a good stain remover, and more than one set of robes."

"Oh," Venick said.

"Oh," Erol repeated.

"Well." Venick felt somewhat foolish. "That seems obvious."

"The truth always seems obvious after it is revealed."

The scrap of jerky had gone sticky in Venick's hands. He set it on his knees. "The men will be disappointed. I've heard them tossing around some wild theories."

"Like?"

"They think you're a ghost," Venick admitted with a smile. "Or that your clothes were a gift from the gods."

Erol gave another laugh. "I think if the men wanted to know the truth, they'd have watched me more closely. But I understand. I also like to believe in magic, even when there are more likely explanations. Makes the world a little more hopeful, don't you think?"

Venick didn't answer. He wasn't sure it was wise to willfully believe in something just because you wanted it to be true. That tendency had gotten Venick into trouble in the past, on more than one occasion.

He thought of his father. General Atlas was a man Venick had respected and admired and, in the end, murdered. Atlas had betrayed Venick by revealing his relationship with Miria to the southern elves, which led to her death. At the time, Venick had believed that killing his father was the only way to ease his own pain. He'd wanted it to be. But it hadn't eased his pain, hadn't solved anything, and now that murder would always be a part of Venick, like a cut that never fully heals.

Erol spoke into the night. "What was it like, in Evov?"

Venick looked at the healer, who had turned away from the fire. His face was in shadow. Venick could not tell what it showed. "I thought you already knew."

"I haven't been back in a long time. And now it seems I may never return."

"You think Evov is gone for good?"

"It's possible. The city was built by human conjurors. Its magic is ancient, and little understood, now that the ones who built it are gone." Erol stared out across the Taro, whose far bank melted into the dark. "You know what Evov means, don't you? It's elven for *lost*. Over time, elves reinvented the word to mean *hidden*, but that's not why Evov was built. It was never meant to be a hidden city to safeguard the queen—it was meant to be a haven for those who were lost."

Erol's voice was wistful, and Venick felt a stab of sympathy. He knew what it was like to mourn a lost home.

"The city was beautiful," Venick said in answer to the man's question. "But cold."

"Like the elves themselves."

Venick nodded.

Later, though, when he was alone again in his tent, Venick found himself remembering Ellina. The flush that sometimes crept into her cheeks. The way she could look at him, and how for the length of that gaze, there was no war and no killing and nothing to be fixed. Nothing but the two of them, breathing each other's space.

No, Venick thought as he drifted, *not like the elves*.

It was the last thought in his head before sleep pulled him under.

• • •

The following morning, Venick woke feeling flat. He rolled to his knees, stared at his hands where they pressed into his bedroll. He made fists of the fabric.

Outside his tent, men and elves had begun breaking down camp, pulling on layers, gathering their tins to stand in line for rations of bread and—for the humans—roasted oxen. They cursed the cold, but the mood was lighter than it had been; the storm had cleared.

Venick went to Eywen. Her winter coat had grown in, which was good for her, but meant extra work for him. He found a coarse comb and started brushing through the most important places: behind her elbows, under her jaw, around where her saddle would rub. As Venick listened to the methodic sweep of the bristles, he remembered his dream, even though he had the sense that it would hurt him to remember. Ellina had been part of it. Most of it. He'd taken her to the cove he'd told her about from his boyhood, and even though it was just a dream, and impossible, he wanted it to be real, wanted her to see the place where he'd learned to swim, which he remembered so fondly, and loved. There was a tide of longing in his stomach.

Venick was absorbed by the frustrating memories of his dream, and so he didn't at first notice the surprised murmur sweeping through the camp. But then a lowlander said, "Dear reeking gods." Venick heard a splash.

He looked up.

There, swimming through the river, her hair a black blanket, skin grey, was Ellina.

SEVENTEEN

Venick went to her. He splashed through the shallows, water churning up to his knees, river-grime to mix with the mud. He helped haul her up the shore, their hips bumping, feet tangling in the weeds. Ellina's shoulders shook. Her hair was plastered to her face. She had been swimming for—gods, how long? Everything about her was stiff and wrong.

Once out of the water, Venick took Ellina by the upper arms, turned her to face him. She carried no belongings that he could see. No spare clothes, no map, not even a water canteen. He tried to tamp down his building panic. "Did you swim all the way from Igor?"

Her golden eyes lifted to his. Her gaze was slightly vacant.

"Ellina, I'm serious." He could hear his own voice, the raw, grating sound of it. "What's going on?"

Branton appeared with a water jug, Artis with a blanket. They wrapped Ellina in the coarse wool, then walked her the short distance to

Venick's tent, using their bodies to shield her from curious eyes. Venick dug through Eywen's saddlebag for dry clothes, a round of hard cheese. He took the water from Branton, pressed all of it into her hands. "Use my tent. Change, eat. We'll be here."

She gave a shaky nod and accepted the offered items before disappearing through the flap.

Venick paced. His boots squelched wetly with river water, his heart thrumming the way it did, sometimes, before a fight. He didn't know what he was thinking. He wasn't even sure he *was* thinking. His heart continued its insistent pounding, his angst morphing into something like dread. Beside him, Branton was staring at the tent with an odd expression on his usually blank face. "Did she really swim here?"

"I don't know. I think so."

"Where is her horse?"

She didn't have a horse, Venick realized. That silver mountain she'd been riding wasn't really hers, just one of the army's many. If Ellina had left the stallion in Igor's stables, anyone would have been free to claim him. Venick should have thought of that, but never in a million years had he considered that Ellina might decide to stay behind, only to change her mind, find herself without a steed, and choose the river instead.

"Did she know that our army planned to follow the Taro?" Artis asked softly, coming to stand on Venick's other side.

"I don't know. It wasn't discussed."

"So she took a guess about the path we would take," Branton said. "And without a horse, she figured the river's current would carry her faster than she could travel on foot." He sounded impressed.

Venick stopped pacing. He didn't understand Branton's approval. Venick felt sick.

"At least it was the Taro," Artis said, seeing Venick's agitation. "The Taro is a hot spring."

As if that was supposed to make him feel better. Sure, fine, Ellina hadn't frozen within the first few minutes of her journey, but they'd been on the road for days. She couldn't have swam that far from Igor nonstop. She would have exited the water at various points to rest. Venick imagined her pulling herself up the Taro's rocky bank, trembling from cold and fatigue, alone on the winter plains without so much as a bit of flint to start a fire…if she'd even bothered to light one.

She's not stupid.

Venick gave a hoarse laugh. Branton and Artis glanced at him worryingly.

She's survived this far.

They could thank the gods for that, or some impossible stroke of fortune. Not Ellina's own planning. Not her will or her smarts. Hell and damn, she used to be smart, but this stunt went beyond stupid, beyond anything Venick could comprehend.

He listened for her inside the tent and heard nothing. "Ellina?"

No answer.

Venick called once more. Still nothing.

His worry was eating its way down his arms. His veins looked huge on the backs of his hands.

She's fine.

She was so clearly not fine.

She'll come out when she's ready.

But Venick recalled the look on Ellina's face when they'd walked her through the camp, some anguish in her eyes that he didn't understand.

He couldn't take it. He pushed inside the tent.

She was there, standing quietly beside his bedroll, looking no less rigid but now partway dry and dressed in his things. His shirt was too big on her. The trousers were secured with an extra coil of rope. She held the water jug in one hand and the cheese in the other, but it didn't look as if she'd touched either item. Her fingernails were distinctly blue.

Venick took the objects from her weak grasp and set them aside. He touched her shoulder, and when this failed to elicit a response, he cupped her jaw, rubbed his thumb across her cheek. She raised her eyes. They were no longer vacant, but swimming with tears.

Her pain. The sight of it, like a wound to the gut.

"I don't want to push," Venick started, trying to find a way to speak without allowing his own growing anxiety to hijack the situation, "but I just don't understand. I thought you'd chosen to stay behind. You were going back to Parith with Traegar, but now you're here, and you swam the whole way and—" He brought both hands to cup her face, his gaze darting between her eyes. "Something happened. Please, tell me what happened."

She was shaking again, and not just from the cold. Her eyes were shining pools. *Dourin*, she mouthed.

A fresh wave of dread. "He isn't…?"

She nodded, and that seemed to be the last of her strength. She dropped her head, her hands coming to her face, tears escaping between her fingers. Venick pulled her into his chest, holding her upright even as his own knees slackened and his breath escaped him and the world went wobbly at the edges. Dourin. Dourin was dead.

Venick rocked Ellina as she cried. He told her he understood how much it hurt. He told her that he wished he could take her pain away. He said he knew it wasn't the same, but that Dourin would always love her, and he would, too.

• • •

Afterwards, Ellina was exhausted and looked ready to drop straight to sleep. Venick settled her into a folding chair within the tent. He poked his head outside to ask for Erol, but the healer was already there.

"Please," Venick said.

Erol was efficient, but gentle. He asked Ellina a few questions, checked her pulse, peered into each eye. He coaxed her to drink a brew of tea mixed with an herb called *grivinita*, which he said would help with the muscle spasms that had begun wracking her thighs and back. Venick hovered over Erol's shoulder, oscillating between a feeling of furious protectiveness and one of deep loss. Erol gave Venick a look, and when Venick chose to ignore this, the healer cleared his throat. "Venick. You are blocking my light. Perhaps it would be best if you waited outside?"

Venick wasn't blocking the light. It was midday, and they stood inside a closed tent—there wasn't a singular light source to block. But Erol's expression was turning severe, and Venick had to choose, very deliberately, not to be difficult. He slunk outside.

The day had shifted, the sun shining weakly through tumbling clouds. Somewhere in the brush, a dove chirped a single, throaty note. Men and elves lingered nearby, but like eavesdroppers caught in the act, they quickly turned away, pretending great interest in a number of menial things: the gloves in their hands, the dirt under their fingernails.

Branton and Artis were gone. Lin Lill was nowhere in sight, either. Venick felt glad for that without really understanding why he was glad.

He resumed his pacing. His boots worked to tamp down patchy grass. Then he realized Erol could probably hear him, and that he was being distracting again, so he forced himself to sit. He stared into his open palms. They were filthy, a raw strip in the centers from where he'd been clutching Eywen's reins—a reminder to relax, to stop holding on so tightly, learn to loosen his grip on things.

Think you can, Venick?

No.

The sun moved in the sky. Though Venick had given no exact orders, the soldiers knew enough to realize they would not be traveling again that day. Tents were re-erected. Fires sprang back to life. The mood lifted further at the prospect of a day of rest.

When Erol finally emerged, he took one glance at Venick and crossed his arms, ready to reprimand.

Venick said, "I feel like I'm losing my mind."

Erol softened. He dropped his arms, gave a sigh. "She'll be fine, Venick."

"She swam all the way here."

"I know that."

"She could have been hurt."

"She wasn't."

"She had no food. No shelter."

"She's stronger than you think."

Venick grabbed the back of his neck, stared down between his knees. He knew he was supposed to believe that, because Ellina had been strong before, and because she was a legionnaire, and an elf. Not helpless. Not someone who needed saving. But it was so hard to reconcile these facts with the image of Ellina as she had been in his tent: brittle and empty-eyed and breaking down in his arms.

Erol picked his way delicately across the earth, came to sit in the yellow grass at Venick's side. "She's sleeping now. The sleep will be good for her. Much of what you're seeing is merely exhaustion, easily remedied with a bit of rest."

"I'm not sure exhaustion is the whole of it." How much more could Ellina take, really? It had started with her sister Miria, whom Venick had known as Lorana, someone they'd both loved. But then Ellina had lost her mother, and her country, and her voice, and now her best friend, who was perhaps the last person on this planet whom she truly trusted.

"I'm worried about her," Venick said. "I'm worried about everything she's been through and the way it's making her act." Venick had an image of a different water-soaked Ellina, followed by Lin Lill's dry, *The princess fancied a dip in the river.* He remembered looking up in Igor to see an empty saddle, later finding Ellina caught in the center of a growing mob with hands on her weapons. He saw her diving through a window in the ballroom. Pushing her horse full speed across a dark landscape. Ripping off her armor mid-fight when Venick had asked her, he'd *asked* her not to put her life at risk unless absolutely necessary, and really not even then.

"She shouldn't have followed us," Venick said. "That was so foolish. And for what? She's making decisions for the wrong reasons."

"Not for the reasons you think she should, you mean."

"Not for any reasons that make sense. I've never known Ellina to be so reckless."

Erol gave Venick a candid, almost melancholy smile. "She's not who she used to be."

Which was exactly Venick's point. It sometimes seemed like Ellina was determined to throw her own life away merely so that she could feel more like the elf she'd once been. But Venick didn't care if Ellina was different than she'd been. He only cared that she was safe.

Venick voiced his deepest fear. "She's going to get herself killed."

A shadow touched Venick's boots. He looked up to see Ellina stepping out of his tent, her chin lifted, eyes pooling dark with defiance. She wasn't asleep after all—she'd heard their conversation.

Venick came to his feet. "Ellina—"

"There she is," a voice interrupted. Lin Lill sauntered into sight, her hair pulled back tightly, her golden eyes reflecting the afternoon light. Venick tensed. He felt an absurd impulse to throw himself in front of Ellina, protect her from whatever venom Lin planned on spitting. Lin Lill had never been one to hold back her scorn, and this time, Ellina might even deserve it.

Except, the ranger didn't look ready to start hurling insults. She was studying Ellina as you might study an unusual piece of artwork, trying to decide if it'd fit in your home. "The rumor is that you swam all the way from Igor."

Ellina didn't break the ranger's gaze. She nodded once, which elicited a mumbled reaction from the onlookers, who were no longer pretending not to listen.

She swam here?

Is that even possible?

Did you know that the princess could swim?

Lin Lill was still looking at Ellina in that way. There was a pause, an audible breath, and then: "Will you teach me?"

Ellina's brows went up.

Venick's did, too. And yet, he felt it again: the urge to step in. To explain that Ellina needed time, that she was drained from her journey, and grieving, and not up for swimming lessons. But Erol caught Venick's eye and gave a slight shake of his head. *Let her handle this.*

Ellina looked the ranger over. Lin Lill—larger than most elves, and not used to being sized up by anyone—allowed herself to be scrutinized. She held herself elven-still, awaiting Ellina's verdict. The entire camp, it seemed, waited along with her.

Some of the clouds cleared from Ellina's eyes. She did not smile, but there was something gentler about her mouth, an easing of her posture as she gave a single nod. *Yes.*

EIGHTEEN

Venick found Ellina a horse, taken from an unwilling soldier who wondered—peevishly, loud enough for those standing nearby to hear—why the princess couldn't just use her own two feet. There was a time when Venick would have dealt with the man's insolence with diplomatic composure, but Venick found that he was fresh out of diplomacy. He asked the soldier—

What did you say to me?

—if there was a problem, and when the man tried to backtrack, Venick reminded him—

No, really, say it again.

—that insubordination would not be tolerated. There was a tense moment when the soldier seemed to weigh his next words, rolling them around like candy on his tongue. In the end, though, he simply handed over the reins.

The army set out again the following morning, and by midday, they were within sight of Heartshire Bay. Twice, Ellina tried riding up beside Venick. It didn't go well. Every time he looked at her, he couldn't help but think of the way she'd been when he pulled her from the river, her skin tinted grey, her eyes like glass marbles. His mind would take the vision further: Ellina on the battlefield, lying dead in the dirt. Ellina in the bay, floating lifelessly on its surface. He'd chosen the strongest warhorse for her that he could find, thinking that it might give her an edge in battle, but even this seemed to have been a mistake. She looked vulnerable atop the animal's high back. Exposed. Venick realized that while he'd been disappointed to learn that Ellina had chosen to stay behind with Traegar, a greater part of him had been relieved. At least with Traegar, she would be safe.

She wasn't safe anymore, and there was nothing Venick could do to fix it. Each time she tried riding towards him, Venick would see the gentle sway of her body in the saddle, the little snow flurries hitting her cheeks, and fear would grip his throat. The lull of travel was at an end. Battle was upon them. Soldiers would die in the coming days, and Ellina would surely be one of them.

His fear was only made worse in that no one seemed to share his concerns. The elves reacted to Ellina's reappearance as Branton had, with a kind of bewildered approval. The humans, too, seemed a bit taken by the whole ordeal. Her voicelessness, which had once been a source of suspicion, now seemed to lend her an otherworldliness. It was as if people believed Ellina had undergone a transformation, like she'd entered the Taro an elf but had emerged a different creature entirely. This was particularly true for the plainspeople, who'd begun to whisper that the gods must have used their sacred river to deliver her back into their arms. It was a sign, the plainspeople said, a divine message. The princess had been marked and should be treated accordingly.

Venick wanted to shake them. He wanted to make them see what he saw. He remembered Miria's death, his father's murder, banishment. He remembered standing at the edge of a windy cliff, contemplating the value of his own life. Ellina looked exactly like he'd felt then: as if he didn't care whether he lived or died.

Yet what were his options? Venick couldn't ask Ellina to turn back, and he couldn't shield her from what was coming, so he avoided her. Whenever he saw her moving towards him through the ranks, he would spin away, find an excuse to look busy. He felt like a coward, but he wasn't handling this well and couldn't think of what else to do.

• • •

She continued to shine in his periphery as they moved east, making their way through a meandering line of trees and out onto Heartshire Bay's wide, sandy beach. The water was a vast stretch of blue under the afternoon sky. Beyond the horizon, not visible, was the Golden Valley and the rest of the lowlands. Venick might have marveled at the bay's size, large enough to be mistaken for an ocean. He might have contemplated his homeland on the opposite shore, a journey that would take weeks on horseback, but by ship, mere days.

But he was distracted.

Ellina's lean frame slid across his vision as she and Lin Lill headed to the water. While the rest of the army made camp, the pair stripped down to their underthings, leaving their weapons in a neat row along the shore before moving into the tide. Lin Lill showed no hesitation as she followed Ellina's lead, tackling her swimming lessons with the same ferocity as she tackled everything. Soon, Lin Lill had progressed to floating on her back, and soon after that, she was treading water. It was the first time Venick had ever seen the ranger's genuine smile.

But this was not what held his attention.

His eyes kept skating back to Ellina. The gentle arch of her neck, the shadows at her hips. Muscled arms, long legs, acres of creamy skin. Those scars. From his vantage point on a slight hill, she looked like the elf he'd first met, the one who knew herself. It was this thought that made Venick realize that in the water, Ellina did know herself.

His blood stirred. His breath felt oddly shallow.

He tore his eyes away.

• • •

The swimming lessons continued. During the day, the army pivoted away from the beach to travel on surer ground, but each evening they returned to the shore to make camp, and Ellina and Lin Lill would head to the water. Heartshire Bay wasn't a hot spring like the Taro, but neither had it frozen over like most of the smaller streams and rivers; the bay was large enough that it still held some of summer's warmth.

Elves began gathering along the shoreline to watch Lin Lill's progress. After a few days, Artis asked if he, too, might join their training, which prompted Branton to join, which soon inspired more elves to take part. Ellina—unable to teach so many at once—enlisted the help of the humans. She organized groups by ability, pairing stronger swimmers with weaker ones. Though she could not call out instructions, she was becoming more efficient at making her meaning clear, and others were becoming more skilled at reading her intentions. It was like watching a great machine whir slowly to life, gaining speed as it went.

When she wasn't conducting swimming lessons, Ellina kept close company with Erol and Lin Lill. Venick watched from afar as the healer teased her, Lin Lill tossing out casual insults. Ellina grinned, making a complicated series of elven hand movements that had surely never been used together before, but that were nonetheless a clear rebuttal. After sunset, the three of them would build a fire in the sand and sit around drinking one of Erol's brews. Not medicine. Venick knew that it wasn't by the way Ellina's cheeks pinkened with every sip, her smile going hazy and free.

• • •

One evening when they were about thirty leagues from Hurendue, Venick found Erol up near the beach's tree line, stirring a pot of stew over his fire. Beside the fire was a gourd of the same liquor Erol had once bequeathed Venick and three tin cups. Three bowls.

"The elves say it's good luck to gather in groups of three under new snowfall," Erol commented.

"Elves don't believe in luck," Venick said. "And it isn't snowing."

"They did, once. And it will."

Venick peered doubtfully at the sparse clouds. "So you're throwing a dinner party?"

"I wouldn't call it a *party*."

"You've set a table."

"I wouldn't call it a table, either, so much as an overturned crate. But yes, I have invited a few friends."

"Ellina?"

Erol paused his stirring. "Ellina will be here, yes. And Lin Lill." The man looked up from the stew. He seemed older in the dark, his wrinkles deep under the fire's light. "Would you like to join us?"

"I'll ruin your group of three."

"I'm sure Ellina wouldn't mind."

Venick gave no reply.

Erol poured some of the liquor into a cup and handed it to Venick. "Lin Lill has raised the issue of what happens if Farah's forces haven't split, and we end up meeting her entire army in Hurendue. That would be disastrous for us, seeing as we've split *our* forces. But it doesn't have to come to that. We could send scouts ahead to observe Farah's numbers."

"We don't have the supplies to extend this campaign. We'll send the scouts, but by the time they return with their report, it'll be too late to turn back. We need to keep moving."

"That's what Ellina thinks. She doesn't want to delay. She's confident that her sister will split her forces."

"If Ellina thinks so, I'd trust her judgment."

"I agree."

Venick took a sip of the liquor.

"Have you seen the progress she's made with the elves?" Erol asked. "I've never seen anything like it. She'll have this entire army swimming by the end of the month."

Venick didn't doubt that. If anyone was going to break down a barrier as ancient as this, it would be Ellina. Yet any pride Venick might have felt was overshadowed by that same, looming mist of anxiety.

"She told me about Dourin," Erol said, seeing the look on Venick's face and misreading it. Yet at the mention of Dourin, whatever Erol thought Venick's expression showed became true. Venick's heart fisted. His thoughts took a dark turn.

Dourin had been in bad shape when they'd left him in Parith, yet somehow, Venick had believed the elf would survive. This was largely thanks to Ellina's discovery of a late crop of *isphanel*, a weedy plant with a miracle-like ability to speed healing. Venick had personal experience with the plant. It had saved his foot from amputation, and he figured that if the *isphanel* worked on him, it would work on Dourin, too. But he'd been wrong.

"Dourin and I had our troubles," Erol said gently, "but he was a good elf. I was sorry to hear his fate."

"Traegar was supposed to return to Parith." Venick spoke into his cup. "He wanted to be there with Dourin. To help with his recovery."

"This war has prevented many reunions," Erol agreed, "and much mending. Ellina said that when Harmon told her the news—"

"Wait." Venick's gaze darted up. "*Harmon* is the one who told Ellina about Dourin?"

"Yes."

"But Harmon didn't tell me."

Erol frowned.

"Why wouldn't she tell me?"

"Maybe," Erol said, "she was afraid."

"Harmon isn't afraid of me. She's not afraid of anything."

"She's afraid of her father."

"That's not—" *True*, Venick almost said, but stopped himself. He scowled at his boots.

He didn't know what to think.

"Before you jump to conclusions," Erol cautioned, "you should speak with Harmon."

Which Venick wouldn't have the chance to do until they reunited in Kenath. Even then, could Venick trust what Harmon had to say, knowing she'd kept something like this from him?

Venick set down his cup. He moved to leave.

Erol said, "I'll tell Ellina you were looking for her."

Venick paused. "But I wasn't."

The man merely smiled.

$$\cdot \ \cdot \ \cdot$$

Yet when Venick returned to his tent, Ellina was already there, waiting.

Venick slowed. The night had chilled past the point of comfort, sneaking through his outer layers. The camp was a dark landscape across the beach. He couldn't see Ellina clearly, just her shadowy outline against the moonlit sand.

She held out a letter.

Venick took the offered paper, which was just a single piece of parchment folded into thirds. No envelope. He ran a finger over one sharp corner. "For me?"

She nodded.

"We'll need some light."

Venick disappeared into his tent, rummaging for a blanket and his flint. He returned to the dark fire pit, which had been dug earlier by an over-helpful trooper, and laid the blanket alongside it. He struck the flint to kindling. The kindling caught. Then the logs.

The scene sprang to life. Ellina wore a jacket Venick had never seen before: faded leather, two sizes too big, rolled up at the sleeves. A man's jacket. Her hair hung loose, her collar pulled tight. She looked...better. Her golden eyes were bright in the flame's light, her cheeks pinched with color. There was a smudge over one eyebrow, like she'd rubbed the spot with a dirty hand, and her hair was salt-tangled, having dried in kinks from her most recent swim.

Beautiful, Venick thought.

And then, *uncertain.* He wondered if her uncertainty had to do with what was written in her letter, or whether it was him that made her uncertain. She hadn't been to his tent since her first day back. In fact, they'd barely spoken.

And whose fault is that?

He opened the letter.

Venick turned the page towards the light and read her account of what she'd discovered in Igor. Someone had tried to poison him at the banquet. They'd done it using the same poison they'd found on the dead conjuror, a concoction called minceflesh. Ellina explained how the poison worked, its deadly efficiency, and how its discovery confirmed Lin Lill's theory about traitors among them. Until the traitors were uncovered, Venick must always be careful to keep his canteen at his side, to never accept water from an unknown supply.

It wasn't the first time someone had tried to strike the resistance by poisoning its Commander. The chronicler Rahven had been found carrying poison, too, though that had been of a weaker sort. According to Ellina's letter, minceflesh was one of the few substances strong enough to kill an elf. The poison was rare, but the Dark Army didn't need much of it. If even the smallest drop found its way into his cup, he wouldn't stand a chance.

Ellina's letter finished with, *I should have come to you with this sooner. I'm sorry.*

"No," he said, and saw her flinch. He waved the letter. "I mean, no, Ellina, you shouldn't be the one apologizing. I didn't give you the chance to tell me." He folded the letter back into careful thirds. Quietly, he added, "I've been unbearable."

Worried, she motioned.

"It's no excuse." He met her gaze. "I'm sorry."

Together, they sank onto the blanket. Campfires glowed along the beach in both directions, as far as the eye could see. Somewhere nearby, a group of men broke into song. Separately, their voices might have been unpleasant, but together they managed a nice chorus.

Softly, Venick asked, "How are you?"

She smiled a little, made the elven hand motion for *better*. It was what Venick had thought earlier—she did look better. Yet he saw the way her eyes strayed from his. He heard the sound of her clasped fingers, the sound of everything she couldn't say. Venick sensed her sorrow. It splashed around them like a tipped bucket.

He said, "I miss him, too."

Her clasped hands tightened.

"Dourin would be proud if he could see you." A long pause, in which Venick considered not saying what he was thinking, and then decided that if he didn't, he'd be going back on the promise he'd made to always tell Ellina the truth. "I think your mother would have been proud, too. And Miria."

Once, the mention of Ellina's eldest sister might have brought them both heartache. Now, though, there was comfort to be found there.

Ellina tucked a strand of hair behind her ear. She offered another smile, and Venick became suddenly aware of how close they were sitting, close enough that he could smell the soap she had used to bathe. If he leaned in, he could put his nose to her neck, inhale that buttery, floral scent. He imagined how she might drop her head sideways. Arch into his hands.

But then Venick remembered the things he'd said to her in his room the last time they'd kissed. The things she hadn't—or couldn't?—say back.

It was selfish of him to worry about this in the face of her larger grief. His own selfishness reminded him of the other thoughts he'd been having recently, and how this was like him, putting his heart before the greater issue of war.

He was ashamed. The letter hung loosely in his hand.

He wouldn't push her. He wouldn't ask.

But maybe…?

No.

"I wonder," he said, shoving a different question into the space. "Do you ever think about what it'll be like once all this is over?"

She tipped her chin. He knew she couldn't fully answer a question like that without pen and parchment, but they'd grown accustomed to speaking this way. How Venick would pose a thought and Ellina would shrug or nod, responding as she could.

She gave a little shake of her head.

"Me either," he admitted. "When I think about the war, I only think about the actual fighting. I can't imagine what it'll be like after. I can't even try. And for you." He dogeared the letter's top right corner, then the bottom left. "If we defeat Farah, that would make you…well, you'd be…"

Ellina set her hand to his knee. It was meant to be a comforting gesture, an indication that it was safe for him to say the word *queen*, but Venick's entire body responded to her touch, like he was sixteen again. His free hand made a fist of the blanket.

"Right," Venick said hoarsely. "You'd be the elven queen."

She took the letter from his hand, undid the creases he'd made, then pulled a quill and ink from her jacket's breast pocket. It took a moment for her to uncork the miniature ink bottle, dip the nib. The metal tip scratched and splatted as she scribbled. *I will not accept the throne.*

Venick frowned. "You wouldn't?"

More scribbling. *I see now why Miria chose to escape to the mainlands. Power destroyed my family. I do not want to end up like my mother, or Farah.*

"What do you want, then?"

Ellina stared at the page. Her eyes became distant. Venick had the sense that she was gazing into the past as she wrote, *I want to be free.*

Venick looked at her looped cursive. Thin ink, long *p*'s and *y*'s, all the empty space around the writing. "That's what I want, too."

She set down the supplies, dropped her chin into her palm. Overhead, the stars wheeled on their axes.

Venick's eyes fell to her lapel. He kept his voice light. "Whose jacket is that?"

Her smile turned coy.

He shrugged. "Just a question."

Sure, her face seemed to say.

"It's new. I wonder where it came from."

Maybe it was a gift.

"*Was* it a gift?"

And if it was?

Venick gave another shrug. Quietly, with that same sense of saying too much, yet holding himself to honesty: "You could wear my jacket. You can have anything of mine."

Ellina's smile softened. She reached again for the quill. *The jacket is Erol's.*

"But it's not white," Venick blurted. Ellina blinked, and then they were both laughing—he, in a loud burst, and she, with silent shudders. And even after they'd quieted again, and Venick asked Ellina another question, something lighthearted that had nothing to do with the war, that laughter seemed to hover in the air around them for a long time after.

NINETEEN

W hat is going on here?" Lin Lill demanded.

Venick woke with a start, squinting into the morning light. His clothes were damp, his boots tightly laced. To the left of his vision, his tent swayed in the wind, unoccupied. To the right, Lin Lill's head loomed like a black eclipse, a moon to block the sun.

Venick pushed to his elbows, glancing over to see Ellina looking similarly disoriented. He remembered, as if waking up again, how he and Ellina had talked late into the night, lying back on the blanket and staring up at the starry sky. They'd fallen asleep like that, side by side.

"Did you two sleep together?" Lin Lill asked.

Venick choked. "Lin."

"You know what I mean." The ranger crossed her arms, fingers drumming along her biceps. Her hair was plaited in three long braids that day, each end knotted with a strip of leather. Venick had the fleeting thought of a head of snakes. "The soldiers are all talking," she continued, throwing Ellina an apologetic glance, "and I hate to be the one to bring this back up—"

"So don't."

Lin Lill gave him a narrow look. "You would have me shirk my duty?"

"Babysitting me isn't your duty." Venick spoke around the rising heat in his cheeks. "And even if it was, you'd have already failed."

She blinked, open-mouthed. "What?"

"Ellina and I have been here all night. As the head of my guard, you should know that. Yet you seem surprised."

Lin Lill's face flashed with something stormy, then schooled. "Branton and Artis were on watch. You were not undefended."

"So you did leave your post." Venick pushed to his feet, squaring off. "Would you like me to ask where you went? Do you want me probing into every detail of your life? Maybe it's *me* who should be questioning *you.*"

He didn't mean it. Venick trusted Lin Lill implicitly. But he was tired of feeling like an ant under a magnifying glass, tired of all the sidestepping and tiptoeing and motherless pretending. He wanted to deflect. Get under her skin a little.

Which he had. Lin Lill's eyes were cool granite. Her back was straight, her legs shoulder-width apart, hands clasped in parade rest. To an outsider, she would seem the image of composure, but Venick knew elves well enough to know that her poise was merely a mask meant to cover stronger emotions.

She said, "My only aim is to win this war."

He knew that. But he was still too angry to relent. "That's all any of us want."

"I would never allow my actions to put you in jeopardy."

"Good. Anything else?"

Her voice was a bare hiss. "No."

"Then we're done here."

He gave her his shoulder. Heard her tight exhale, which he ignored, and the deliberate slap of her feet as she stomped away, which he also ignored.

Ellina lifted a brow.

"I know." Venick rubbed his eyes, pressing hard enough to see spots. "But she's getting on my last nerve." A sigh. "She wants me to quit playing favorites with you."

Ellina blinked. *Oh.*

"I won't," Venick added.

Ellina bent over to relace her shoes, which she must have kicked off at some point in the night. Her expression was measured. But Venick could see her fighting a smile.

• • •

Later that morning, the supply tenders were ordered to search the water vats for signs of minceflesh. Though no poison was found, a soldier was assigned the task of boiling the Commander's water before every meal, and Venick was instructed to carry his canteen with the same care as he carried his weapons.

"I feel I owe you an apology," Erol told Ellina. Behind him, a landscape of men and elves could be seen readying for the day's journey. "This is something I should have thought of right away, as soon as you brought us that vial. If the Dark Queen is trying to attack Venick in this manner, the minceflesh could have found its way into the water supply. We're lucky that no one has yet been harmed. We're also lucky that minceflesh is a delicate poison—if you can really even call it a poison. I suppose it's more like a parasite. Boiling Venick's water will be a hassle, but it is better that we take all precautions."

Ellina was returning from her swimming lessons that evening when she recalled Erol's words. Her boots sank into the sand, leaving dark stamps. Her hands paused in their movements, halfway through braiding her hair. The memory shuffled around in her head like birds making room on a branch.

We're lucky that no one has yet been harmed.

Ellina paused, turning over those words as if there was something within them she was meant to find.

But what?

. . .

The bout of clear weather held as they continued north. Dry skies meant dry roads, and they were able to pick up their pace, covering ground by day, swimming and sparring by night. Elves and humans intermingled, but this had become commonplace, and hardly registered Venick's attention. It wasn't until he saw an elven soldier and a human wagon-tender sneak up towards the tree line one night, hand in hand, that he began to understand exactly the degree to which things were changing.

He smiled to himself and went to find Ellina.

. . .

It was on the eve of their arrival to Hurendue when the news came: Farah's forces had been spotted east of the city.

"It is exactly as we predicted," Lin Lill told their group where they had gathered near the shoreline. "The Dark Army has split its forces and is heading towards the bay, but they are late. If they meant to trap us against the water, we will beat them into position. We can choose our moment. That is good. And, better—there are reports that the Dark Queen is with them."

Venick glanced at Ellina. She and Erol had both removed their shoes to stand in the tide. Their eyes were closed, the sand slowly swallowing their feet, pulling them deeper with each passing wave. A balance exercise of some sort.

If Lin Lill's news affected Ellina, she revealed no sign of it.

"The Dark Army does not appear aware of our current position," Lin Lill continued, unrolling a map. "And—can you two pay attention?"

"We are paying the *most* attention," Erol replied without opening his eyes.

"You cannot see the map."

"Ellina has the region memorized, and I do not need to see it."

Lin Lill scrutinized Ellina. "You have been studying?"

Ellina—eyes still closed, arms out for balance—nodded.

"How many cities sit between here and Kenath?"

Ellina flashed her fingers. *Six.*

"How many roads lead into Hurendue?"

Two.

"How much black powder does Farah possess?"

Ellina peeked open an eye, shooting the ranger a scowl. She had no way of knowing that from studying the map.

"It was worth a try," Lin Lill said, shoving the parchment into Erol's hands. He swayed but did not fall, clutching the map outwards for the others to view. Lin Lill tapped the page with a finger. "There are two roads leading southwest from Hurendue towards the water, as Ellina correctly guessed."

Ellina's scowl deepened.

"One of the roads is paved," Lin Lill went on, "but unrestricted, therefore exposed. The other is unpaved, which would make for more difficult maneuvering. However, the unpaved road winds through a small woodland. We need the Dark Army to choose the woodland route. Otherwise, we will have to face them in open battle."

"An option best avoided," Artis said.

"At all costs," Branton added. "So how do we ensure that the Dark Army ends up where we want them?"

"We must give them a reason to avoid the open road," Lin Lill replied. "Or a reason they *should* take the wooded path."

"An incentive often works better than a deterrent," Erol said from behind the map. "We could find something to act as bait."

Lin Lill's eyes came up. "Or someone."

"No." Venick spoke through his teeth. "That's a hard *no*."

"Lin has not even explained her plan yet," Branton complained.

"I know her plan," Venick said, then speared Lin Lill with a glare. "We are not going to use Ellina as *bait*."

Silence.

Erol lowered the map. His eyes were open again. "Lin?"

The ranger spread her hands. "The Dark Queen wants Ellina. The conjurors made that clear in Igor. If Ellina allowed herself to be seen, she could lure the elves after her, turn it into a chase. We would be waiting under the cover of the trees, ready to strike. After we dispose of the first round of elves, the rest of the army will realize that their comrades are missing. They will send another brigade to investigate, and then another. They will be unorganized. The Dark Army will not know that we are hiding in the woods. We can pick them off little by little. It will be easy; we just require a catalyst. Ellina would hardly even be in danger," Lin Lill added when she saw Venick's expression. "The conjurors need only spot her from a distance. Just far enough for them to recognize her and use their shadow-binding to catch her trail. After, she'll shake the binding—"

"You can't shake a shadow-binding," Venick snapped. "Not unless the elf who conjured the binding decides to drop the conjuring, or is killed. Ellina would be permanently marked."

"Then we will make sure to kill—"

"And that's to say nothing of the fact that if a conjuror is close enough to shadow-bind Ellina, he'd be close enough to do more."

Lin Lill wavered. "More?"

"He could blind her. It happened to me once. They push their shadows over you and the world just…goes dark."

More looks exchanged.

"How did you get your vision back?" Branton asked.

"I killed the elf who blinded me."

"See?" Lin Lill said, as if this proved her point. "You got out."

"I got *lucky*."

"This is an opportunity."

"It's too dangerous."

"Ellina was trained for this."

"It's a suicide mission!"

Ellina set a hand to Venick's shoulder.

He couldn't look at her. He knew what he would see if he did. She wanted this. She had always wanted it, maybe now more than ever: to risk herself for a greater purpose. Maybe even to risk herself for herself alone.

Venick remembered, suddenly, a different forest. Summertime. A band of conjurors, a raging storm, shadows crawling down the trees. He remembered the elf Ellina had killed in that fight, how she'd broken her own laws to do it, how she'd done it for *him*. Later, her lies. The way she'd risked capture and torture to work as a spy. The way she had been captured and tortured. How she was always doing exactly what she wanted, no matter the danger, no matter the consequences.

Ellina gave his shoulder a squeeze. She was trying to catch his eye, to express without words what this meant to her, that she was strong enough, that he had to trust her. But how could Venick possibly do that when trusting her meant this?

He saw it again: Ellina lying dead in the dirt, stripped of everything that made her.

He saw what would happen if he let her go.

And he saw, suddenly, what would happen if he didn't.

Like a rock tumbling into a pond, his vision broke, rippled, and changed. Ellina had always been a prisoner, and not just in Evov. She'd been enslaved first to the legion, then to her bondmate Raffan, her mother, Farah, her own sense of duty. Her life had been nothing but a series of commands, her hands forever tied by limited choices.

He thought of her words written on the back of a letter. *I want to be free*. A promise, a story, and also simply itself. A life of freedom. Ellina now had a chance at that life, the opportunity to choose her own path. If Venick tried to stop her, wouldn't that only make him another kind of cage?

She's stronger than you think.

Venick knew that. But he could know that, couldn't he, and still fear for her? She might be strong, but she wasn't endless.

He turned to face her. She looked exactly as he'd known she would:

like the first slice of sun on the horizon, brilliant and brimming with fire.

"It's your choice," he said.

A smile split her face. The sight cut into his heart. Venick couldn't bear it.

He yanked his gaze away.

Lin Lill's lips peeled back in a warrior's grin. "We move at dawn."

• • •

Night fell. The plan was polished and sent through the ranks. Lin Lill—agreeable again now that she'd gotten her way—asked for permission to begin assembling their soldiers. Venick granted the request.

He found Ellina sitting on a lichen-covered rock near the tree line, lacing up her boots. Her torso was bound with cloth. Venick could see the exposed plain of her stomach, the jut of her clavicles, the soft skin at the base of her neck.

She knew he was there, but didn't look up. She jerked the laces, pulling them tight, then switched to the other foot. When she reached for the plainsland-style tunic draped over a nearby rock, Venick caught sight of the jagged scars along her back, a lash carving up over one shoulder, the dagger wound in the other.

Her hands stilled, and Venick wondered, could she hear the painful thump of his heart? Or sense his thoughts, which had begun to keen? He became caught in the memory of her scars and how they'd come to be, some of which he'd witnessed himself, others he'd only imagined, or dreamed about, in nightmares.

She drew the tunic over her head, pinching the scene from sight.

He wanted to speak. He wanted to ask again if she was sure, to beg her to reconsider. There were other soldiers who could do this, others who could be dressed to look like Ellina, who would be eager to risk themselves for this mission. He wanted to grab hold of her, beg her to stay, *stay*. Stay alive, stay safe. Stay there, with him.

His fear felt wretchedly close to misery.

She reached for her chest armor. Venick found himself stepping forward to help lace up the armor's sides before he'd consciously chosen to do so. She met his eye over her shoulder. Hers were still bright, still burning with purpose. But they had settled a little, too, brimming with everything he knew about her...and the things he still couldn't guess.

He let his hands fall. It felt as if they'd had an entire conversation, though neither of them had said a word.

She hesitated, then lifted her palm to cradle his face.

He thought about the last time she'd done this, and how poorly it had ended. He wanted it to go better this time. He didn't want to repeat his mistakes. Yet he was drowning in uncertainty, suddenly sure that he'd ruin this, because he'd ruined everything he'd ever loved. Marred it by greed and his own inability to see things clearly.

She's not the elf she used to be.

Venick tried to do something he'd never been good at doing: to quiet his mind and simply see Ellina as she was. There was a spark of surety in her eyes. A determined set to her jaw. Perhaps it was her voicelessness, which required her to use expressions more than she ever had before. Or maybe it was something else. She *wasn't* the elf she used to be, but only then did Venick consider what that might mean. Ellina had adapted. Softened in some places, toughened in others, like a tree split by lighting that continues to grow. No longer was she the rigid legionnaire staunchly set in her beliefs. She had changed. Her ability to change had saved her life.

Venick would always worry about her, because he loved her. He would always wish to keep her safe. But if she could adapt, then he would, too.

Ellina watched him. Her expression grew radiant, and Venick wondered if she saw it: the moment he gave her back his trust.

He slid a hand around her neck, drew her close. He made a soft sound into her mouth, which was pliant as it opened beneath his.

I can't lose you, he was saying as he kissed her.

She made fists of his shirt. *You won't.*

TWENTY

Ellina dug her knees hard into Eywen's sides. She sped across the flat earth. The sun hung like an ornament on the horizon, shivering orange and seemingly huge, yet Ellina knew how the sun would appear to shrink as it climbed higher into the sky, tightening from a wide orb into a small, hard disc. Its enormity was merely an illusion.

Ellina was under no illusions. She knew the danger of what she was doing. Knew its foolhardiness, its likelihood for disaster. Worse: she had done this before. She had faced her enemy and failed.

She stood in the saddle, crouching low, allowing her body to move with the horse's long gait. Venick had insisted that Ellina take Eywen, saying that he did not trust any other steed to keep her safe. Though Ellina was not sure what he meant by that—how could any horse keep her safe, let alone a blind one?—she could appreciate the mare's ability. Rather than act as a hindrance, Eywen's blindness made her more tuned to handling; the slightest pressure in Ellina's knees or smallest pull on the bridle elicited an instant response.

The mare had been Dourin's. As a *geleeshi*, Dourin had raised and trained horses for the legion, using his summoning abilities to give their troop an edge during border skirmishes. Eywen had been a favorite of his. In fact, Dourin seemed to prefer the horse because of her blindness.

Ellina did not know how Eywen had lost her vision. She had never asked.

She looked at her hands gripping the reins. The bounce of the horse's mane.

Why had she never thought to ask?

Ellina's lungs tightened. Her chest was fossilized bone. This was a familiar feeling, one that seemed to float over her skin like a settling of dust. Sister, mother, friend. Yes, Ellina knew well the bleakness of grief.

But it was easier, with these new challenges ahead. Easier, to keep her mind on the mission, which required her full attention. Speed was of the essence, and so in addition to her new riding gear, Ellina had donned the lightest armor she could find, opting against a full warrior's kit. She carried a borrowed bow—ashwood, longer than she was used to wielding, already strung and strapped to her back—plus two daggers at her waist. No sword. It was her least favorite weapon and would only weigh her down.

The sun continued to lift. On the horizon, Ellina could see the sprawling outline of Hurendue, and beyond that, a blot of blue mountains, their snaggletooth peaks capped in snow.

A rabbit darted across her path. The wind shifted and sighed.

Ellina thought of Venick's mouth moving over hers. How his kiss had filled her like a jewel fills with light. The way he'd looked at her.

This thought was more distracting than the others. It promised a seductive sort of comfort…and pain. As Ellina wavered, deciding whether to dip deeper into this memory or shut it out, she came around a knoll and saw several things at once.

First, a natural rock formation, which expanded across the hilly landscape to the northeast, marked by sandstone arches that looked as if they might have been man-made but were more likely the result of an evaporated salt bed.

Second, the city of Hurendue, closer now, with two distinct peaks built on identical hills divided by a river.

And finally, between the city and the rock formation, a massive black shadow that was not a shadow at all, but an army.

Ellina had never seen her sister's army. She heard tales of it passed around campfires, stories of its immensity, but it was not until Ellina actually saw those ranks that she finally understood. *Dark Army* was not merely a title. It was a description. The elves wore black armor, rode on black horses. Their cannons were black, their wagons black, their black flags snapping in the wind. The effect was striking, as if Ellina faced not a horde of soldiers, but a single, great titan.

Her hands stiffened on the reins. Sweat trickled between her shoulder blades. She urged Eywen around the knoll and out of sight, riding as close to the army as possible without being seen. Ellina could hear the enemy better as she came nearer, boots and hooves and wagon wheels, the creak of wood, metal against metal.

She eased along the rounded slope of the knoll. Glanced at her own shadow, which looked crisp under the sun's harsh light. And then, against all her legion training, against every ounce of self-preservation, she walked Eywen into plain sight.

• • •

Venick waited with a host of archers behind a thin layer of trees spanning either side of the road. The wind was low. The trees glistened with ice. The archers, mostly elven, scanned the lane with steady eyes. Behind them, deeper in the trees, more men crouched alongside cannons, which had been covered in brown cloth to blend into the brush.

The wind shifted directions. It smarted Venick's eyes.

Maybe the Dark Army would recognize Ellina's appearance for what it was.

Maybe they wouldn't take the bait.

A twig crunched under someone's shifting weight. Everyone tensed, only to slacken again when they realized it was nothing.

The soldiers had pulled scarves over their noses and mouths to hide their streaming breaths. Venick had a cloth over his own face, which had grown damp with moisture. He yearned to remove it. He felt like he couldn't breathe.

He left the cloth where it was and watched the road.

• • •

Ellina knew the moment she was recognized. She sensed it in the air like an electric charge.

Three horses split away from the Dark Army's ranks, kicking up dirt as their riders charged towards her. Ellina's elven vision sharpened. Each elf was a conjuror, marked by their black hair, the bruised rings around their eyes. They were several hundred yards away. Closing in.

Ellina tugged Eywen's head around, preparing to take off back towards the trees. It was a straight shot—all that mattered now was speed.

Or, that's all that *would* have mattered…had her path not been suddenly blocked.

Ellina yanked Eywen to a halt. Dread shallowed her breath. She did not know how the Dark Army had predicted her arrival—she herself could not have predicted it, until a few mere hours ago. Yet, they must have known she was coming, because at that moment, a long line of southerners—ten, maybe twelve elves in total—appeared along the path, blocking her way back to the trees, and Venick, and safety.

Ellina's heart surged even as she calculated, scanning the windy field, marking the distance between herself and the riders, herself and the city. If Farah was giving orders, she did so from a safe distance. Ellina could not spot her among the ranks.

With a silent *ya*, Ellina urged Eywen into motion. The elves gave chase from both directions, pinching Ellina between them like teeth around a morsel. As Ellina's gaze swung from side to side, her mind was quickly enveloped by a singular word, one that seemed to vibrate out from her core: *escape.*

She had been Farah's prisoner once. She could not do it again.

She made for the rock formation.

• • •

Venick was restless. His eyes continued to rake the empty road even as worry burrowed into his heart.

He didn't know how much time had passed. It might have been minutes. It felt like ages. But maybe that was better. If time was passing, it could mean that Ellina was being careful. She was figuring the best way to lure the conjurors back into the trees, choosing to work slowly, being smart *about her options.*

Tell yourself that.

Venick drew his sword. He had no reason to do this yet. There was no enemy in sight, nothing but the fidgety sounds of his own soldiers and the low hum of the breeze through chattering trees. Behind him, Venick heard ranks of men and elves drawing their swords as well, responding to his action as if it had been a command.

Venick sometimes forgot what it meant to be Commander. That his orders—even his perceived orders—would be followed by everyone without question.

Not everyone.

No, not everyone. Not Ellina. She was always doing exactly the opposite of what he wanted, and now, as he waited in the trees, worry gnawing at his chest like a flesh-eating mite, he wondered if he'd been mistaken to trust her, if his trust was wrongheaded and softhearted, and it would have been better to lock her up for her own good.

Don't be a fool.

But he was a fool. Who was he, if not the person who felt too much, who worried about the wrong things, or the right things at the wrong time?

Venick flung this question into the void, but the voice that always seemed to inhabit his head—the one, he was beginning to realize, that sounded suspiciously unlike his own, yet still familiar—went silent. He strained to listen, and when still he heard nothing, Venick took this as permission to turn his eyes skyward and speak for himself. *Please*, Venick prayed, *keep her safe.*

The gods laughed and laughed.

• • •

Ellina sped between sandstone arches. She could hear the band of horses racing in pursuit, the clatter of tack, the explosive sounds of the steeds' breaths. She could hear her own gasps tearing up her throat.

Thin, towering boulders blew past on either side. Though Ellina had not dipped below ground level, it felt as if she had entered a deep canyon. Some of the rocks were huge, their sheer faces a dazzling mix of purple and red. Others were craggy, twisted, like the hands of crones.

Ellina raced between them, keeping her knees in tight, her head low. She tossed a glance backward, but she could no longer see the conjurors. Could no longer tell, either, which direction they were heading, if she had lost them or if they were in close pursuit; Eywen's thundering hooves echoed between the rocks, making it impossible to discern their own noises from those beyond them. It sounded as if Ellina was surrounded on all sides.

She tugged Eywen to a halt. This was not going to work. If before speed had been of the essence, now stealth was. And yet, as long as Ellina was on horseback, stealth would be impossible.

She was grateful, then, that Venick was absent. He would hate what she was about to do.

She swung her leg over the horse's side and dropped to the ground.

Go home, Ellina thought, giving Eywen a slap on the rump. She did not know if the command would work. Venick was not *geleeshi*, and Dourin was…gone. That meant Eywen was a homing horse without an anchor. Like a dingy far out at sea, the mare would have no sense of the horizon. And yet: *go home*.

Though her milky eyes were unseeing, Eywen turned her head as if to look at Ellina. There was a tense moment when Ellina thought maybe the mare would refuse, that Ellina's mind link had failed to reach the animal, but then, mercifully, Eywen flicked her ears and galloped away.

Ellina tried to ignore the sense of vulnerability that fell over her in the mare's absence. She tried not to think about how she had just inadvertently created a diversion, or what the enemy would do to Eywen if they discovered her without her rider. Rather, Ellina moved to the balls of her feet, sliding quietly between boulders in the opposite direction.

She paused to listen.

Nothing.

Inch along, pause, listen, inch.

Though she was not lost, exactly, the overlapping layers of rock felt like a maze, some of the crevices so thin that Ellina had to turn sideways in order to squeeze between them. She considered climbing up one of the nearby peaks to catch her bearings, but thought better of it. Ellina did not know if she had shaken her pursuers, or if they, too, had stopped to listen. Likely, they were still nearby. Hunting her.

She continued forward. The day was bright enough to hurt her eyes. She closed them. Listened again.

And heard something.

A shift of feet. The whisper of an inhale.

Ellina froze. Her eyes came open.

She turned her head slightly and saw him through the slit between two rocks: a lone figure standing under one of the sandstone arches. Ellina's vision tightened to a point.

His back was to her. His face was concealed. Yet she would know that form anywhere.

Balid.

• • •

Venick felt it before he saw it: a shuddering through the trees.

Trunks began to shake. Clumps of snow fell from branches overhead, mulch clattering around Venick's feet. The soldiers tensed, yet held their positions.

A messenger came panting through the woods. Venick knew what the boy was about to say, even though it couldn't be possible, because Ellina wasn't back yet. She wasn't back, and so how did the Dark Army know where to find them? Yet the messenger's words were clear.

"They're coming."

• • •

Ellina's heart ratcheted. She held herself perfectly still.

Balid turned slightly, revealing his profile. Long nose, sharp chin. Those small, sunken eyes. He still had not spotted her, hidden as she was in a thin crevice between two boulders, though he appeared to be listening. His face was rapt with attention.

Ellina knew how to be silent. She knew how to step, to move with the earth rather than against it, to make herself weightless. She could turn around, go back the way she had come. *Escape.*

Yet she still wore her bow. Her arrows seemed to strain against her back.

Ellina slid the weapon—slowly, so slowly—from her shoulder. She did not have much room to draw. Her elbow butted against the stone. It would affect her aim. And this bow did not belong to her—she had left all of her possessions in Igor. Ellina had borrowed the bow from a fellow archer, meaning she did not know the weapon's temperament, was not accustomed to its handling. That, too, might affect her accuracy.

Escape.

She did want to escape, but not from this clearing. Ellina was a prisoner. She had been, ever since Balid had stolen her voice, which was more than merely a voice. It was part of her identity. Precious to her.

She wanted it back.

Ellina allowed herself to imagine it: how she would sink an arrow into Balid's skull. How his death would come quickly, without time even to gasp. After: the return of vibrations in her throat. A waterfall of words. If Ellina killed Balid, she would regain the ability to speak lies, yes, but also truths.

The wanting poured over her like rain over a desert. She yearned to speak the truth. To Venick. To her new friends, her comrades, even her sister. Ellina had spent her entire life hiding behind a wall of lies. She did not want to do that anymore.

She nocked an arrow. Pulled the bowstring tight.

The bow creaked. Balid whipped around, seeking the source of the noise as Ellina ducked back out of sight.

A silent curse. Did the bow's owner really not oil her weapon? That oversight had just cost Ellina her chance. But she had been lucky, too. Though Balid surely heard the bow's creak, surely recognized it as *hers*, given the hollow reverberance of this place, he could not tell which direction it had come from.

Realizing that he was exposed, and under fire, he darted out of sight. Ellina followed.

• • •

The Dark Army came from all sides, sweeping through the trees like a howling wind. It was an instant, vicious attack.

The sounds of battle became deafening. The boom of a cannon. The clash of steel against green glass. Venick lost sight of the road in the initial crush, and though their original plan was clearly out of play, terror spiked through him at the thought of Ellina reappearing without forewarning. She'd be riding straight into a massacre.

You fool.

It was a sign of his stunned mind, that he fixated on this rather than on the onslaught before him. Ellina wouldn't ride blindly into this massacre. Reeking gods, she'd be able to hear the fighting from leagues away. Yet he couldn't stop looking for her.

It wasn't until an arrow whizzed through the air by his head, piercing the eye socket of the soldier to his right, that Venick snapped back to reality.

Their line was devolving into an unsteady wave. Enemy elves began breaking through. Venick watched a southern elf slide past the resistance's front ranks, slit the tendon behind a man's knee, and take his horse for herself. More enemy elves followed suit, swarming through their defenses like termites into wood, exploiting the weak points, the openings.

"Hold the line!"

Venick blocked the swing of an incoming sword, then gripped the green glass of his own blade with his gauntlet, punched it sideways into the enemy's neck. A burble. A jet of red. He ripped the cloth from his face and shouted again. "The *line.*"

This time, his command seemed to catch, rippling down the ranks. Men shored up their shields, closed gaps. The resistance, adjusting to the situation, began to reform into a layered circle facing outwards.

To an untrained eye, this formation seemed logical. The Dark Army had them surrounded, so in order to hold their position, they needed to create a ring. Yet Venick knew that a circle was the worst kind of formation in this situation, one that would only make it easier for the Dark Army to press them in, blocking their ability to regroup or escape.

They'd have to fight their way free or be trapped.

"*Line,*" Venick shouted furiously, hauling his sword up again, sinking the point into another enemy. His arm pumped. His lungs dragged in a gulp of air. "*I said line, not cir—*"

An arrow struck him in the chest, cutting off his breath.

• • •

She followed the sound of Balid's footfalls.

Ellina did not know where the other southerners had gone. She did not know where the Dark Army was. These thoughts should have registered in her awareness, should have alerted her to what she was not seeing, but Ellina was full of something tense and frightening. Her focus had narrowed to a pinprick.

A tumble of scree up ahead. Fabric shuffling against dry rock.

Ellina crept forward, her ears tuned to every noise, the shift of the breeze under stony arches, the smell of cool sand. She exhaled slowly, rounded a corner, and froze.

Balid was there, standing in the center of an opening with his eyes on her, but he was no longer alone.

Ellina was not surprised by this, exactly. She anticipated a fight—she was practically quivering with it. What did surprise her was the identity of these two additional elves. One was a slim, chiseled beauty, his moon-white hair stark against the backdrop of rusty red sandstone. *Raffan.*

And beside him: Farah.

• • •

Venick stumbled backward from the force of the arrow. Looked down at himself.

A wooden shaft protruded from his chest armor. He could feel the arrowhead on the other side, nudging his ribcage without breaking the skin.

He gripped the arrow just beneath the fletching. Snapped the shaft. Observed the red currigon feathers for the count of one heartbeat before tossing the broken shaft aside.

Venick wasn't afraid anymore. He usually wasn't in battle. Yet there was an uncomfortable awareness lingering around the edges of his mind. It told him to look up.

He did.

His soldiers had, somehow, reformed the line he'd wanted and were holding. The Dark Army was no longer squeezing them in, his men weren't falling in droves. Except, Venick had the sense that they *had* somehow fallen, that while he was concentrating on the arrow in his chest, he'd missed something vital.

The elf next to him turned her head. She was around Venick's height, dressed in golden chainmail. A resistance member. Venick recognized her to be the soldier who'd been felled by an arrow at the start of the battle. That arrow was still firmly lodged in one eye socket, deep enough to spear her brain.

The other eye was open, and looking at him.

• • •

"I admit," Farah said to Ellina. "I am disappointed."

Ellina's hand tightened on her bow as her sister stepped forward. Farah looked as she always had: those proud golden eyes, the smirking mouth, her ears glinting with the fifty rings that signified her rank as queen. To one side, Balid stood hunched, crow-like. To the other, Raffan was expressionless, holding the reins of two massive black stallions.

Farah continued. "I had thought your evasion skills better than—"

Ellina let her arrow fly.

It should have been a clean hit. The arrow was balanced. The shot was wide open. Yet at the final second, a gust of wind interrupted the arrow's arc, knocking it away from Farah and off course. Ellina's eyes snapped to Balid's raised hands.

Conjuring.

Farah appeared momentarily stunned. Her lip curled. When she spoke next, her voice held none of its former amusement. "I do not know why I ever thought I could win you over. You were poisoned from the start. If your mindless sense of morality was not enough, your sympathy for *them* should have been my clue." Farah prowled a half circle, her boots releasing dust with every step. "You had the chance to rule by my side. We could have conquered the world together. But you threw it all away, and for what? *Humans*, the most pathetic of species." She spit out the word like a curse. "You and our mother had that in common, it seems. And she is dead now, isn't she?"

Ellina's face flamed. *Only because you killed her.*

Farah's anger vanished. The change was immediate, startling. There was an unfamiliar twist to her smile, which widened at the sight of Ellina's pain. "Have I upset you? Well, I do understand. Rishiana doted on you, even after you trotted off to join the legion. She doted on Miria, too, despite how odd she always was." Farah flipped again, darkening. Her words were like claws on stone. "But never me. Never the daughter meant to rule, the one who actually knew what to do with such power."

Ellina did not like the hazy sheen to her sister's eye. She did not like the quick switches in mood or the strange tilt to her smile. There was something…off about Farah.

And she misremembered. It was true that Queen Rishiana had pushed Miria to the throne. It was true that after Miria disappeared, she denied Farah that same right. But Rishiana had never favored Miria, who resisted anything to do with elven customs, and she had certainly never favored Ellina, who defied her wishes by joining the legion. Their mother had been a levelheaded, albeit cold, arbitrator. Her decisions were always reasonable.

Forcing Miria to the throne early was not reasonable. Banishing the entire human race to the mainlands was not reasonable.

Ellina kept her expression neutral, even as her thoughts began to stir. Only recently had Ellina learned that the border was not her mother's idea, but that of Rishiana's sister, an elf named Ara. Most elven queens began producing heirs immediately after their initiation, but Rishiana wanted to wait. Yet this had been around the time of the hundred childless years, and Ara—concerned by the example their queen was setting, and about the future of their race—began pressuring Rishiana to make changes.

By all accounts, Rishiana had listened. She became pregnant with her first daughter. She invoked laws to bolster their population. She drew the border between the elflands and the mainlands, thereby separating humans from elves and encouraging intraspecies couplings, which resulted in more elven offspring.

Yet the sisters had argued anyway. Their final fight—one concerning Ellina's father, an elf who had died when Ellina was young—was so terrible that it had become nearly legendary. The matters that stood between them could not be resolved, and eventually, Ara moved away.

This, like many aspects of the story, had never made sense to Ellina. Why would Ara leave when she had Rishiana's compliance? Why abandon her highborn position after having won everything she wanted?

Unless there was some other reason for the fight. A reason that could help explain why, years later, Rishiana had seemed unduly hurried to push Miria to the throne…

Ellina felt it again—that strange sense of coming unraveled, as if she was picking at a knot. She remembered the conjuror's words in Igor. She remembered their mother's hard, lovely face, so much like Farah's. So unlike Ellina's.

There are things you do not know about your mother. Things she never wanted to tell you.

"I like you better this way," Farah mused. "Unable to speak. I can see your mind spinning, but I must say, I am glad to deny you any final words." She snapped her eyes to Raffan and Balid. "Kill her."

• • •

Venick froze for one dumbfounded moment as he stared at the undead elf, and the undead elf seemed to stare back at him.

His first coherent thought was, *fire*.

His second thought was, *no*.

He couldn't set fire to these woods, not without risking the death of his own soldiers. Venick envisioned it: the way flames would catch on the barren trees, jumping from branch to branch, creating a canopy of red. The fire would spread. Smoke would strangle the air. Elves and men would break formation, trampling each other in their rush to escape the blaze.

The dead elf lifted a slow hand to the arrow in her eye. She yanked the arrow free with a wet *pop*. Gore from the hollow socket splattered Venick's face.

She raised the arrow like a dagger, and came for him.

• • •

Balid moved. Everything about him promised violence: the set of his jaw, the rapacious twist of his hands. Raffan released the stallions' reins. Farah's smile grew teeth.

Ellina began to retreat. As she watched Balid close the distance between them, old memories brushed against her consciousness. She could feel them expand, like a ravine yawning beneath her. One wrong step and she would tumble into their depths.

She took a deep breath. Forced the memories back. Ellina reminded herself that it was full daylight. Balid would be clumsy with his power, slower, more likely to misstep. She reminded herself that she had asked for this, had asked Venick to trust her, and he had, even when trusting her had proved disastrous in the past. She wanted to be worthy of his trust. She wanted to be worthy of her own desires.

She nocked an arrow, holding the bow down by her thigh as she matched Balid step for step, circling. Balid's fingers curled. His eyelids drooped. Yet there was a pause, and in that pause, Ellina realized she was right—it *did* take him longer to summon his power in the full light of day, and the extra effort left him momentarily occupied.

An opening.

Ellina rushed forward. She released her arrow without breaking stride, pulled a dagger from her waistband. Her speed and the unexpected connection of these maneuvers caught Balid off guard. He blinked his eyes open, dropping the conjuring to dodge the assault. One step, skip and spin. Eyes narrowed now, elbows bent, long robes catching the breeze. Ellina had never understood why conjurors preferred soft cloth over armor, their own hands over weapons, particularly when they had no direct way of killing an opponent with magic. It was overconfidence, maybe, a haughty superiority. They were tricksters, using light and shadow to confuse their foes, blinding them or distracting them until someone else came in with a blade—

As Raffan was doing now. His green glass sword made a peeling *hiss* as he rushed forward, four quick steps that brought him within striking distance. Ellina raised her bow overhead on instinct, caught his downswing. Saved herself from being speared, barely, but nearly cleaved her bow in two. Ellina cringed and released her hold on the weapon, which was now firmly lodged into Raffan's sword.

Everyone's eyes were on her mistake. They had forgotten, maybe, that Ellina still had a dagger in her other hand. They did not anticipate her next move, how she did not dwell on the loss of one weapon, but swiftly changed strategies, hurling her dagger at Farah.

At the final second, Balid was there yet again, lifting a hand to block the blow. This was not conjuring—it was simple, bodily shielding. The dagger caught him in the wrist, carving a red slash. He gave a strange, muffled croak.

"*No*," Farah cried.

Ellina floated back out of range. Raffan succeeded in dislodging her bow from his sword as Balid doubled over, hugging his wound. He lifted his face and made that noise again, his lips parting in a gurgled moan. That was when Ellina saw.

He had no tongue.

The truth vibrated from the crown of her head all the way to her toes. Balid, who had muted her, was a mute himself.

"*Kill her*," Farah screeched.

Rage curled through Ellina. She did not know Balid's history. She did not know if he had lost his tongue recently or long ago, if he had been born this way or deformed as an adult, or if he had bitten it off himself, as spies sometimes did to avoid being forced to speak their truths in elvish. None of it mattered. What mattered was that Balid knew the precise degree of pain he was inflicting when he stole her voice, the exact state of purgatory to which he had condemned her. The knowledge was like a brand to the skin. She seared with fury.

Ellina pulled her second dagger from her waist and launched towards Balid, but Raffan was already there, intercepting her attack. He turned her weapon away easily, their blades meeting in a clash of green glass. Ellina's fury swelled. She doubled back, raged forward again. Dust began to swirl as their weapons met, hers a flurry of sharp little movements, his slower, more calculated. Not the style of fighting Raffan usually favored. Not aggressive, or forward, or sly. Ellina was just beginning to wonder if Raffan even wanted to win this fight when he caught her dagger's cross guard with the tip of his blade and flicked it from her hands, then brought his sword to her neck.

Their gazes locked.

"Do it," Farah snarled.

Raffan's chest was rising and falling, his cheeks full of color. His face was not void of emotion, as he so often made it to be, but pooling with something stricken and angry and—hurt? Ellina could not tell. In all the years she had known Raffan, had trained beside him in the legion, had been his friend and later his enemy, she had never seen him like this.

"Raffan," Farah snapped. Beside her, Balid continued to writhe. "What are you waiting—?"

The earth began to tremble. Little chips of rock jumped around their feet as the ground shook, swelling with the sound of a distant rumble. Ellina looked down, then up again. *The Dark Army*, she thought, except when she met Raffan's bewildered gaze, she knew that could not be right. *An earthquake*, she thought instead, until Farah's gasp made them both turn their heads.

A stampede of horses—hundreds of horses—was rushing through the narrow byway, heading their way.

Rocks began to topple. Nearby, a little tree shook so violently it shed all its needles. Farah pulled Balid onto one of her own black stallions, digging her heels into the animal's sides as they swiftly galloped away. Raffan lowered his sword from Ellina's neck. Their eyes both jumped to the only remaining steed.

Ellina moved. There was no time to ask questions, no time to understand where the stampede had come from. She had to make it to the stallion first, she *had to*, because the boulders were sheer on all sides, impossible to climb, and the crevice through which she had come was now clogged with tumbling rocks. She would never be able to outrun the stampede on foot. If she did not ride out of there, she would be trampled to death.

Raffan caught her arm and shoved her in a different direction. Ellina gave a silent cry, thinking that he meant to push her to the ground, but he only moved her into a small crack in the rocks that Ellina had not seen, wedging her out of the stampede's incoming path.

"It has to be you," he said. Ellina blinked up at him, dazed. "If you want your voice back, you have to be the one to kill Balid. Otherwise, the magic won't be reversed."

He gave her a last, haunted look before racing away.

Ellina wanted to follow him. She wanted to demand to know why, *why* had he saved her? Yet then the animals were upon them, and there was nothing for Ellina to do but close her eyes and hold her breath as the horses flew by, storming past with such ferocity that Ellina's teeth chattered in her head.

· · ·

Venick was lost in the gore. He couldn't tell how many undead had appeared around him—three? Four?—only that as soon as he spun to engage one, the corpse would go limp, dropping lifelessly to the earth just as another corpse rose up from behind to take its place. Venick had the vivid image of a demon jumping from body to body. The conjurors were switching their puppets at frightening speed, leaving the resistance befuddled and exposed, unable to focus on a single target.

Venick ground his teeth. Just as he was about to behead his nearest foe—an elf whose guts were spilling from the stomach—*that* body crumpled, and a new one sprang to life beside it, sword swinging. Venick didn't have time to reorient. The blade caught his shoulder, the green glass glancing harmlessly off his armor. Close to his neck. Too close.

Venick struggled to contain himself. This was an unexpected development, one they hadn't planned for. They needed to regroup, to devise a strategy that involved *not dying* so that their soldiers couldn't be reanimated and used against them.

Good plan, Venick.

A surge of frustration, bitter in his mouth. He knew what he had to do, even if he hated to do it.

He gave the signal.

It took several moments for his command to register. But then: the sound of a distant horn, calling for the resistance to retreat.

· · ·

The rumbling slowed to a stop.

Ellina's forehead was pressed to the cool wall of her rocky crevice. It was exactly her size, just large enough for one. She had the wild thought that it had been made for her, like a coffin for a body. Yet she was alive.

She peeled her eyes open.

Dust covered everything. The air smelled like chalk, the ground churned to such a degree that it resembled a sandy beach. The little tree was reduced to splinters.

It took three tries before Ellina could make her legs move. She maneuvered off the crevice wall, steadied herself, then let go. Outside, more dust hung in the air. The stampede was gone, the horses having run deeper into the rock formation…save for one.

A pure white stallion, unmarred by the dust. Braided mane. Bright black eyes. Atop that horse: a rider. Ellina saw him there as the air cleared. His face, as familiar as her own. Long hair, the arch of his eyebrows, that pouting mouth.

She ceased to breathe.

Impossible.

The elf dismounted his steed. For a long moment, Ellina simply stared. Then she ran, heart flying, and crashed into him, her arms going tight around his neck.

Dourin *oomphed* as the breath punched out of him. He wheezed a chuckle. "Miss me, did you?"

Ellina choked out a silent laugh, which might have also been a sob. She had the fleeting yet terrifying thought that Dourin was a hallucination, that he had died in Parith after all, or she had died in that stampede, and this was some sort of horrible and wonderful afterlife.

Yet she felt Dourin's arms come around her. The solid surety of his grip. "Ah, Ellina. I missed you, too."

TWENTY-ONE

The others will try to claim that we were lucky. This will insult me. You must not let them use that word."

Dourin's expression was stern as they emerged from the rock formation into the open field between the city and the woods. The scene was still, the land empty. The Dark Army had vanished, as had any trace of the horse pursuers. Ellina might have been relieved by that, had she not been otherwise preoccupied. She was looking at Dourin. She had scarcely taken her eyes off him.

A pair of speckled wrens chased each other through the grass. Clouds hung over the northern mountains but did not reach as far as the plains; the sky overhead was clear. Dourin tipped his head as if to feel the sun's warmth on his face, even as the winter air nipped their skin. He looked well. Happy, even. An outsider might have never guessed that he had ever been gravely wounded and fighting for his life.

It was not until Ellina heard the familiar whuff of a different horse that she finally pulled her gaze from her friend. Eywen was there, looking calm yet alert, her tan coat rippling in the afternoon light.

"She found me," Dourin explained. "Or, let me start from the beginning. Traegar found me. He was on his way to Parith when our paths crossed. He is the one who told me of Venick's plan to lead the resistance east along the Taro. We changed course, thinking to rendezvous in Kenath, and were passing through Hurendue when Eywen appeared. You can imagine my surprise." Dourin's mouth lifted, as if recounting a fanciful tale. "I have never felt such panicked energy from that mare. I thought something must have happened to Venick—he does have a propensity for trouble—but Eywen led me straight to you. And then, of course, once I realized what was happening, I led them." He nodded towards the rest of his enormous herd, which had reappeared shortly after their reunion. The animals were placid now, bumping shoulders, trailing after Dourin as ducklings trail their mother. "Thoroughbreds," Dourin explained. "Every one of them. They were a gift from the Elder. He likes me now. I am very likeable."

Ellina's eyes were back on Dourin. She was trying to follow his story. She wanted to marvel at their good fortune, the timing of Dourin's arrival in Hurendue, her decision to dismount Eywen and send her *home*, which had led the mare to Dourin. Ellina wanted to wonder at her friend's mastery over these horses, and the skill it would have taken to create a stampede, which went beyond the ability of any *geleeshi* Ellina had ever known. But it was difficult to concentrate on anything beyond the mere fact of Dourin's existence.

She decided that she did not need her voice back. She did not need anything, so long as she could have this.

He threw her a tall look. "Stop *smiling* at me."

She beamed brighter.

As they picked their way through the field towards the woods, Dourin was quick to summarize his understanding of Ellina's silence. "Traegar said that Farah took your voice. Or one of her minions did. I have seen the conjurors' abilities. They can steal one's vision, and now voices, too?" He frowned. "I want the full story, and you cannot even tell it. That irritates me."

Ellina lifted a brow as if to say, *That irritates* you?

"Indeed." Dourin turned his head, giving her his profile. "I have questions. It will take forever to write down your answers. You are being very inconvenient."

They were just pushing through a row of dense, shrubby bushes when their attention was drawn by Traegar, who approached at full speed on a rose-grey stallion. Dourin made a noise of disapproval. "He rides that animal far too hard without reason." Yet when Traegar pulled up beside them, his face was tight with concern.

"Your plan worked," Traegar announced. "The Dark Queen and two others have fled for the woods."

"No," Dourin pouted. "My plan did not work. If you saw them flee, that means they escaped. But what good is a stampede if no one is stampled?"

Traegar's expression did not change. "You are lucky Ellina was not *stampled.*"

Dourin shot Ellina a look. "See what I told you? There is that word, lucky. Bah. Luck had nothing to do with it. The herd was under strict instructions. They would not have harmed you. In fact—"

"There is more," Traegar interrupted. "The resistance passed through here as well. They have gathered in Hurendue."

Some of Ellina's giddiness bled away. Hurendue was the location they'd chosen in case a retreat was called.

Dourin, too, appeared to sober. "A change of plans?" He clicked his teeth. "And here I was hoping for good news."

They found the road—stone-paved and flanked by a footpath on either side, but poorly maintained—and started towards the city. Hurendue appeared to have outgrown its original design; a thick stone battlement circled each of its twin hills, but the city's buildings spilled far beyond these walls, tumbling along the riverbank and trickling into the adjacent fields. Ellina could see the modest homes of pasture workers on the outskirts of the city, as well as the workers themselves, busy pulling out last year's crop. Something about the way they hacked at old corn stalks with long machetes, seemingly unfazed by the arrival of Dourin's massive herd, had Ellina remembering that these people were born for war.

They had just reached the outermost row of homes when Ellina heard her name. She caught sight of Venick tearing out of the city down the street, his figure small but quickly gaining ground.

Ellina frowned. She wished he would slow down. The road was like a mouth full of bad teeth, some stones jutting upwards, others missing from their sockets. Venick would trip if he was not careful. He might twist an ankle. A wrist. Yet he continued at his breakneck pace.

He reached her, apparently oblivious to the sudden addition of several hundred horses, or the two elves positioned just behind her. "You look okay," Venick said, breathless and hopeful. He gripped Eywen's bridle to slow the animal, tipping his head back to peer at Ellina in the saddle. "Are you okay?"

"I am fine," Dourin said dryly. "Thank you for asking."

Venick's eyes skipped to the elf. He did a double take. "Dourin?"

"Hello to you."

"But..." Venick teetered back a step. At last, he seemed to take in the scene: Dourin astride his pure white horse named Grey, Traegar to his left, the plod and stamp of the herd behind them. Venick made a choked sound. "How?"

"How did I get *better* looking after a sword to the gut? Well, it is a funny story—"

"How are you alive?" Venick appeared too stunned to temper his tone. His words sounded like an accusation. "We thought you were dead."

"Is that why you refused to answer my letters? You did not want to entertain the missives of a ghost?"

Venick and Ellina exchanged a look. "We didn't get your letters."

"A likely excuse."

"It's true." Venick slid his teeth sideways, and though he didn't say it aloud, Ellina knew what they were both thinking: Harmon.

Harmon had lied about Dourin's death...or someone had lied to her. Either way, she had proven her propensity for meddling when she told Ellina of Dourin's supposed demise, but not Venick. And now this.

Had Harmon intercepted their messages? And if so, why?

Venick caught Ellina's gaze again. His brows drew a hard line. *It's my fault*, his face seemed to say. *I should have suspected something was not right with her.*

You could not have known, Ellina tried to convey back. *You cannot always blame yourself.*

"While I am sure you two are enjoying your private little conversation," Dourin cut in, "the rest of us have had a busy day of saving lives, and would like to get out of these saddles."

"Dourin." Traegar closed his eyes, as if seeking patience on the back of his lids. "We have discussed this. It is not always about you."

"No, Dourin's right," Venick said. When Ellina and Traeger frowned at him, he elaborated. "I mean, he's right that we shouldn't stay here. We should move inside."

"So that the others may congratulate me," Dourin asserted.

"In case the Dark Army returns," Venick corrected.

"Semantics," Dourin replied, kicking his horse into a trot towards the city.

• • •

"It is not broken," Lin Lill insisted, frowning at Erol as he secured her foot with a wooden box-splint.

Ellina, Dourin, Traegar and Venick were all gathered in the city's infirmary around the ranger's cot, which was one in a long line of identical white medical beds. Upon their arrival, Venick had attempted to warn the others about what lay behind the infirmary doors, explaining in clipped tones how they had battled the Dark Army in the woods, the bloodshed that had ensued. Ellina understood Venick's attempt to brace them, even if she believed it was unnecessary. None in their group were strangers to gore. They would not be shaken by what they saw.

She was wrong.

The smell hit her first. Blood and excrement. The tang of urine and sweat. Healers swept back and forth between rows of narrow beds, each occupied by a wounded soldier. Ellina saw a man with a hand missing, the severed tendons hanging freely. An elf whose leg had broken at a disturbing angle. A woman with a deep slice down the center of her face, her mouth split in two, nose spilling loosely to either side. It was not merely the horror of the injuries, but the scale of those who had been maimed. The number of wounded far outstripped the number of available cots, and so many patients were forced to sit along the walls, clutching bloodied rags or cradling broken limbs while they waited their turn.

Lin Lill lay propped against her pillows in a relatively secluded corner of the infirmary. Though the ranger's injury was not life threatening—her foot had been crushed under a horse's hoof—Lin was inconsolable, not only because she deemed the method of damage utterly embarrassing, but because Erol maintained that the bone was broken.

"We will need to wait for the swelling to go down to assess the severity of the break," Erol said patiently as he finished splinting her foot.

"It is not broken," Lin Lill repeated. "How could it be? I was wearing a metal boot."

"You must keep it immobilized," he continued, unfazed. "Six weeks, minimum. Maybe longer."

"Even if it is broken, I cannot stay in this bed. I will go mad."

"Lin," Venick tried. "Think about this reasonably."

"If Dourin can come back from the dead, I can fight with a broken foot."

"For the record," Dourin said, "I never actually died."

Lin Lill's glare was razor-sharp. "Whose side are you on?"

"Venick's, usually."

"Venick is a lovesick fool with a hero complex."

"Hey." Venick frowned. "I'm right here."

"Prove me wrong," Lin Lill challenged. "Call in our troops. Announce our departure from Hurendue."

Ellina guessed by Lin Lill's tone—and by the sudden jump to a topic that had not even been mentioned—that this was not the first time they had argued about this.

Venick set his teeth. "We're not done here."

"Not done here? Venick. The Dark Army destroyed us. We need

time to replenish our supplies and our forces, and we will not have a chance to do either if we stay in this city. You called a retreat, so let us retreat…to Kenath, where the rest of our army awaits."

"You would leave the people of Hurendue undefended?"

"They can handle themselves."

"No, they can't. They don't have the numbers. You say we need to retreat, but that's what the Dark Army expects. It's what they want. When they strike next, they'll do to Hurendue what they did to Kenath and Evov. They'll overtake it, kill or enslave all the citizens, and claim it for themselves."

"If we stay, they will overtake *us*. It's a pointless endeavor."

"It's the *right thing*."

They glared at each other.

"I hate to interrupt," Erol said, "but I am needed elsewhere. Lin, can I trust you to stay off that foot?"

Lin Lill grumbled a reply.

"A little louder, if you please."

She sighed, then spoke in elvish. "*I will stay off the foot.*"

"Good." Erol turned his eyes to Traegar. "I know you said you have no interest in wartime campaigns…"

"That is right," Traegar cut in firmly. "I do not."

"Our soldiers are suffering," Erol continued, "and we are woefully understaffed. We need every healer we can get. I ask you to reconsider."

Traegar's face was set. Yet he hesitated.

"I will help, if you do," Dourin said.

Traegar's gaze swung sideways. The air thickened, though Ellina could not tell if the sudden tension came from Traegar, who had chosen the Healer's Academy over Dourin, or Dourin, who had effectively ruined Traegar's healing career by reporting his illegal experiments, or

Erol, who had been tangled up in that entire mess. Maybe all three.

Traegar's next words were a clear insult. "You were not trained in healing."

"Every elven legionnaire knows the basics. I will be your assistant." Dourin shrugged, as if this offer was not entirely out of character. "You can tell me what to do."

Traegar continued to hesitate. Yet his mouth twitched. "A chance to boss you around for a change. Tempting."

The tension eased, like a sigh. Erol was hopeful. "So you agree to help?"

Traegar looked skyward, not so much a roll of the eyes as another attempt to find patience in unsuspecting places. "I will help."

TWENTY-TWO

In the end, they all stayed to help, even Venick, until he was pulled into a meeting with the city's councilors to discuss the practicalities of the resistance's arrival, and to plan their next move. He paused on his way out of the infirmary, his gaze slipping towards Ellina in a way that made her think he might ask her to join the meeting. Or was there some other reason he was looking at her that way? Before she could ask, however, he was gone.

Ellina threw herself into her work. No matter how many wounds they tended, there seemed always to be another mouth crying for relief, another face pleading for deliverance. Though all elves knew of death— they had a long practice of hunting and killing humans who entered their lands—the elven legion did not historically engage in battle, and therefore was not accustomed to destruction at such scale. The immensity of the operation was dizzying. How did humans do it? How could they stand to see their own comrades maimed as often as their enemy?

And they must see it, given the size of Hurendue's infirmary. Such a place would not exist, unless necessary.

Without commenting on it, Dourin and Ellina tended patients near each other. Dourin seemed to sense that Ellina needed his closeness as much as she needed not to speak of it. It was a bright spot in one of the longest days of Ellina's life; Dourin was there, alive, at her side.

As Ellina worked, she found her mind drifting back to Farah. Seeing her second eldest sister had been like seeing her own past. Even as fledglings, Farah had always been a schemer. She liked to play tricks on the palace maids, stealing their most treasured keepsakes, releasing mice into their cupboards to eat their limited food supplies, even once going so far as to kidnap one of their infants. When Miria confronted her, Farah called these stunts harmless pranks, but Miria had a different idea.

"There is an energy inside our sister," Miria once told Ellina. "It fills her like water through a pipe. Usually, Farah can keep her energy contained, but sometimes the pressure becomes too great, and the pipe bursts. Her schemes are harmless enough for now, but I fear they will not always be."

It was nearing midnight when Erol found Ellina standing in the center of the melee, staring blankly at her bloodied fingers. He ordered her to retire, and when she tried to protest, he set a kind hand to her shoulder. "It has been a long day. You've done what you can for now. Best to accept when you've reached your limit." His smile was tired. "We will not be far behind. Go. You've earned your rest."

Reluctantly, Ellina washed up and exited through the infirmary's small reception hall. Outside, leaves eddied along the street. Cool air touched her face.

She would do as Erol asked. She would rest. But not yet.

Ellina found Venick standing alone on the city's western rampart, leaning into a rectangular cutout on the parapet. Hurendue stretched beneath them, rippling over its two low hills like a brick-and-stone quilt. The inner rings of the city were denser, shops and homes stacked like stepping-stones up each hillside, thinning as the rings expanded into the working sectors and farmlands. A clear, straight line ran between the hills, like a tear in the city's seam: the river.

Ellina came closer. Venick's profile was outlined by the glow of the nearby lanterns, which did not burn orange, but blue. A quick glance at one of the lantern's bowls confirmed that it did not contain oil, but rather a thick black substance that gave off a faintly woody scent.

Venick spoke without looking at her. "I think one of us must be shadow-bound."

Ellina halted.

"The Dark Army didn't need a lure today," he continued, gazing out towards the woods. "They uncovered our location without you to bait them. Maybe that means there are spies among us, but we've been careful about potential traitors since Rahven. We track every hawk—currigon or otherwise—that comes within sight, and no messenger birds have been seen flying in range. We've passed no everpools. So what other explanation could there be?"

Ellina was alarmed. But of course, the Dark Army had good reason to shadow-bind members of the resistance, if given the chance. Such a binding would allow them to track the resistance's movement and location. They could anticipate possible ambushes, and counteract them, striking at the most opportune times, just as they had that day.

Ellina's eyes dropped to Venick's shadow, stark in the blue light of the lanterns.

"I've already looked," Venick said, pushing away from the wall. "As far as I can tell, my shadow looks unbound. But it's hard to know for sure."

That was because shadow-bindings were difficult to detect, even without the strange bluish light of the battlements to contend with. Ellina should know. She herself had once been shadow-bound by the conjuror Youvan, and even then, even knowing she was bound, and studying her shadow in the full light of day, she could not quite see a difference.

And yet…Ellina worried. Her worry was a small, hard gem refracting the light. It changed the color of things.

"Even if one of us is shadow-bound," Venick said, "it wouldn't have changed the outcome of today's battle. It was a mistake to fight under the canopy of the trees. They offered us cover, yes, but the branches also provided shade from direct sunlight. The conjurors were able to summon their full power." He braced his hands against the parapet. "I didn't think of that. It didn't occur to me that of the two battlefields—the open field or the woods—Farah might also have reason to want the woods." A sigh. "The Dark Army doesn't lack for bodies. They'll strike hard when they strike next. Worse, there have been reports that they've been stealing black powder from human cities, whole stores of it—another dangerous advantage in their favor."

He relayed his conversation with the city councilors, which included ideas on how to secure Hurendue against the coming invasion. As he spoke, Ellina's eyes drifted back to the lanterns. She realized that she recognized the black liquid in their bowls. It was *rezahe* sap, which came from trees used to make alcohol by that same name. That explained the fire's odd color, as well as the aroma. Though Ellina had never seen *rezahe* sap used in place of lantern oil, she could quickly surmise the benefits. The sap was viscous, slow-burning. These lamps would likely not need to be refilled for weeks. And the bluish light was pleasant, calming to the guards who patrolled here. Easy to look at. To spot.

The edge of an idea.

"I want you with the archers," Venick was saying. "They'll be stationed here along these battlements."

That drew Ellina's attention back. She frowned. If Ellina was on the battlements, she would be away from the main battle. Venick was putting her in the safest location.

"I know," he said, anticipating her objection. "But it's not about keeping you safe. I need someone to lead the archers, and I've seen your skill with bow and arrow. You're the best."

Her frown only deepened.

"Lin Lill is injured," Venick reasoned. "Dourin will be with me on the front lines. Traegar and Erol are healers—they don't fight. So who does that leave? Branton, Artis, and you. I want it to be you."

Ellina did not care what he wanted. She was not going to leave him to lead the assault while she hid atop the rampart. She lifted her hands to express her refusal…when something made her pause.

Ellina's eyes were again on the lanterns. They were simple, cased in glass. Clear bowls filled with sap. The flames, dancing gently.

She thought of a group of conjurors in Igor, their campfire, its low burning embers.

She thought about the coven leader's demands, and Farah's desire to take Ellina prisoner.

Her idea began to grow. It swelled like larvae in its cocoon. If Ellina commanded the archers, Venick believed she would be in the safest location. But he did not see what Ellina saw. How she would be in a position to do more.

She gave Venick a nod to accept his request.

He peered at her. "That was…easy."

She shrugged. *You want me to lead the archers, so that is what I will do.*

His eyes narrowed. "I want you to lead the archers, *and* I want you to promise not to do anything reckless."

It was absurd for him to make that request when he himself was taking the front lines. She motioned, encompassing the whole of him, then pointing to the place they stood. *Only if you stay here with me.*

His expression fell. "I can't. I need to be down there with my men." She could tell by the look on his face that he already knew he had lost. "But—"

She pushed past him, having made her point. She would make no promises to him that he could not make in return.

• • •

On her way down the keep's spiral staircase, Ellina nearly collided into Artis.

"Sorry," he said, catching her by the arms. She waved off his apology, but before she could continue down the stairs, he cleared his throat. "Actually, I was looking for you."

Ellina paused. Though they had been troopmates in the legion for years, Artis never actively sought her out. This was fueled partly by his deference to her—she, being a highborn princess, and he, a commoner from a tiny village in the north—but also because Artis was shy. He and Branton were close friends, and between them, Branton did most of the talking.

Now that he had her attention, Artis looked suddenly unsure. He gave a timid smile. "I just…wanted to check on you. Ask how you are doing."

Ellina could not hide her surprise.

"I have been wanting to ask for a while," he admitted in that soft, almost musical voice of his. "I worried you would think me intrusive. But I know…I know today was long for you. Your fight. Dourin. The infirmary. And you, being unable to speak about any of it…"

Ellina was not prepared, not for Artis' tender concern, nor for the rush of emotion it drew forth. She swallowed, wondering if she should don a cool elven mask to cover the emotion, wondering if she even could. It had been a long time since Ellina had summoned her icy exterior. A long time, since she had wanted to.

"Do you know," Artis started slowly, "that the elves talk about how you do that? How your face does so…much. Not just smiles and frowns. Skepticism, annoyance, delight. We can read what you are thinking just by looking at you." Ellina was suddenly wary, recalling how her facial expressions had once been used against her, but Artis continued. "The elves are trying to learn how you do it. It is useful, to know how to speak without words. Still…" He moved down a step, so that they were at eye level. "I do know what it is like to struggle with communication. I have a voice but—ah—do not often use it." He pulled at an earring, toying with the golden loop. "The others are understanding, but they do not really *understand*. How isolating it can be. How lonely. But I do."

Ellina pulled her lips between her teeth. Artis was right. She did sometimes still feel lonely, even when surrounded by friends. She made a series of hand motions, which took several tries for Artis to interpret.

"Ah," he said, bobbing his head. "How to cope. It gets easier, once you learn to accept what is. To let go of how you thought things were supposed to go, or who you were supposed to be. That is the key, I think—you have to let go. And," he continued valiantly, "you must lean on friends. That is really what I came to say. If ever you need someone to, well, to *not* talk to, you have a friend in me."

Ellina held Artis' gaze. Dark pupils, golden irises, the most common of shades. Yet kind, and open, and therefore not common at all. She did something she had never done before, something that felt very human, yet perfectly appropriate. She took his hands in hers, and kissed his cheek.

TWENTY-THREE

Come to raid the good people's pantry?" Dourin asked.

Venick looked up from where he'd been rummaging through a drawer in the storeroom beneath the keep. Dourin leaned against the bare doorframe, wearing a tunic Venick had never seen before, billowy and human-made. Wearing a smile Venick had never seen before, either, a little cocky, a little ironic. His hair was damp from a recent bath, skin clean, each of his nails filed to a perfect crescent.

Something about the way Dourin stood there, all good humor and ease, put a knot in Venick's chest.

Venick went back to his rummaging. "I'm searching for a bootlace, actually." His old one had snapped. It was a strangely ordinary problem given the greater issues of war, but Venick couldn't exactly walk around with one shoe undone, so he'd come hunting for a spare.

"This storeroom is for food," Dourin replied. "You will not find bootlaces here."

Venick pulled a lace from the drawer.

Dourin huffed. "A lucky find."

Venick sat on the storeroom's bench and got to work unthreading the broken bootlace, centering the new one. Dourin regarded him. That feeling in Venick's chest—tangled, briar-like—began to grow.

Venick said, "You really didn't get any of my letters?"

"No."

"I was starting to worry." Venick kept his eyes on his task. "I mean, I thought the Elder might be intercepting them."

"The Elder would not withhold something of mine."

Venick heard Dourin's tone. He glanced up, seemed to again see Dourin's clothing. Though the elf's outfit was not flashy, the stitching was tight and even, the embroidery done in the highland's colorful style. Its quality was unmistakable.

Dourin said, "The Elder and I have come to an understanding."

"He gifted you those clothes."

"Yes."

"And the horses."

"The Elder has many resources," Dourin replied. "I saved his life. In doing so, I won his life price. These are mere trinkets—so he says—compared to what he has gained."

"That doesn't sound like the Elder."

Dourin shrugged. "The man may be stubborn, but he is not a heretic. A life price is binding. He would not risk offending the gods."

"You don't even believe in our gods."

"What difference does that make?"

"None, I guess."

"Yet you are upset."

Venick finished tugging the leather laces through the boot's eyelets.

He pulled back the tongue, shoved in his foot. Though he couldn't see them through his sock, he knew if he pushed down the fabric, there'd be a series of scars running crossways from ankle to heel—his souvenir for getting caught in a beartrap last summer. The wound hadn't bothered Venick in ages, but he felt a pang at the thought of it, the phantom pain of an old injury. He remembered how blood loss from those gashes had rendered him delirious and how fever had set in, which quickly became more serious than the wound itself. Venick had skated near death that night; the black veil had been close enough to touch.

He said, in a voice that was more gravel than actual tones, "I thought you were gone."

"You knew where I was."

"I mean, gone forever."

"You *mean* dead."

"We shouldn't have left you," Venick blurted, eyes flying up. "You were injured. Dying. We couldn't transport you—it would have been too dangerous. I thought I'd taken enough precautions. Left soldiers to guard you. The healers. You were in good hands—"

"Venick."

"But I shouldn't have left." The briar had outgrown Venick's chest cavity. It ballooned against his ribs, drawing blood. "The Elder. He was furious. He could have done something to you. Even if not, you were hurt. Alone. We left you *alone*—"

"*Venick.*" Dourin pushed off the doorframe. "You only chose for yourself what I would have chosen for you. And for me. You owe me no apologies."

Venick stood from the bench. "But I am sorry."

"A sorry sight, surely."

"I'm being serious."

"You are always serious. But fine. Be sorry. Wallow in your regret. Heavens knows it is what you do best. Just know that if you are going to anguish, you suffer for nothing."

"You should blame me."

"I forgive you," Dourin said simply. "You are my friend, and this is war. Hard decisions must be made. You are merely the unlucky human who must make them." He went back to leaning on the doorframe. Sighed. "This is not what I came to talk about."

Venick eyed him. "Was there something else?"

"I dare not bring it up now."

"Just tell me."

"Harmon."

Venick grimaced, and Dourin gave him a look that seemed to say, *I did warn you.*

Slowly, Venick said, "We've broken off our engagement."

"The Elder does not know that."

"No one does, yet. Harmon and have I kept up the ruse—a fake engagement—to help unite our people. It's been working, but it's not forever." He sank back down to the workbench. "I'm not marrying her."

"I should say not," Dourin agreed. "But things are not quite as simple as that. The Elder has been touchy about the subject of his daughter. He has not yet tried to call back his men because of Harmon. Though her duplicity wounded him, I think a secret part of him is proud. Who else would have the cunning to undercut the most powerful man in the highlands, let alone steal his army? He has not wanted to move against her. But his restraint will not last forever."

"He doesn't have the power to stop us now."

"Not so. As I have said, the Elder has many resources."

"He'd infiltrate our forces?"

"Perhaps. The Elder never wanted his men out fighting this war. He hears of your escapades, how you've been parading his soldiers around the mainlands. The longer he waits, the more it rankles."

"If given the choice, the highlanders would choose Harmon's side," Venick said. "They'd choose to fight."

"Ah," Dourin said. "But what side would Harmon choose?"

Mine, Venick started to say, then caught the word between his teeth. The truth was that he didn't know if he could trust Harmon anymore, not after she'd lied about Dourin's death, and may or may not have been intercepting their letters. He didn't understand her motives, and that was worse, because he *didn't* know what she was thinking. What she'd choose.

Dourin read Venick's thoughts. He hitched a sharp little smile. "From what I have heard, things between you and the highland's sweetheart have been…sticky. Harmon is like her father. She will make whatever choice suits her in the moment. That is not to say we do not still need her," he added, "or that I do not have my own debts to repay. She was there the night of the Elder's attack, you remember. She helped save my life when I was actually quite determined to die. And yet…" Dourin made a show of looking around, "she is not even here."

"She led a force to Kenath."

"Where she has undoubtedly had time to rethink her stance on your relationship."

"Regardless of what she thinks of me, she wants to put an end to the fighting. She once told me that she doesn't want any more daughters to lose their mothers in battle, like she lost hers. I have to believe she means that."

"And leading the resistance is her answer?"

"Yes."

"Saving mothers by killing brothers." Dourin drew his eyes upwards. "What fools war makes of us."

TWENTY-FOUR

Day came, then night, then day again. The city tied itself into a collective rope of tension as everyone began readying for a siege. Catapults were rolled out of long, wide storage shelters and set in a row along the river. Weapons were sharpened, armor distributed. Dourin devised a series of signals that would be used to communicate with their soldiers once the fighting began, and Erol organized the distribution of rainwater barrels to douse potential fires.

Scouts were sent to observe the Dark Army's location. They never returned.

Preparations began in earnest. During the day, the streets came alive with the sounds of stone grinders, hammers on metal, the tap and clack of activity. As soon as dusk fell, however, the chatter and buzz seemed to solidify, hardening like an insect in amber. Though the Dark Army would surely return to finish what they'd started in the woods, it was impossible to say when, and so each night must be treated as *the* night.

Foot soldiers took their positions along the road. Women and children vanished into underground shelters. Archers on the ramparts, cavalry at the wall. And then: the silence. The waiting.

On the third night, they came.

There was no obvious warning. No blow of war horns or cry of battle. Yet a change seemed to creep into the breeze, what might have been bats on a hunt, and wasn't. A tuft of clouds shifted to cover the moon. Dusk fell early that evening, as if a sheer curtain had been drawn over the sky.

There was no need to tell the soldiers what everyone already knew, yet runners were sent to deliver the message anyway: the enemy was coming.

Hidden along the main road near the outskirts of the city, Venick looked at his soldiers. Elves and men, mostly, but also a few women, those from the lowlands or the plainslands who had learned—either by desire or necessity—how to wield a sword. Some of the elves had cropped their hair close to the scalp in the human way. If asked, they would say it was a practical choice. Short hair was convenient, less likely to be caught or pulled. While this was true, Venick couldn't help but see a deeper meaning in the elves' shorn hair, which was yet another tradition they'd adopted from the humans.

It pleased him. This was what Venick had wanted all along: for elves and humans to meld, for the barriers between their races to fade. Venick liked the way the elves had begun to show facial expressions, to smile or laugh, tell jokes. He liked how they played cards and swore. He even liked how they had learned to swim.

Venick picked up a pebble from the ground, squeezed it between thumb and forefinger, then peered across the city towards the western rampart where Ellina was stationed with the archers. Hurendue wasn't perfectly fortified. Aside from the fact that there were two separate walls rather than just one, much of the city sat outside of those walls. Furthermore, the river, called the Angor, split the city in two from north to south, then curved sharply west. It wasn't as large as the Taro, but it was still too wide and too deep to traverse easily. It was, in many ways, like a third wall.

Venick went utterly still.

An idea.

It began to grow. Venick's idea was like the pebble in his fingers. There was a sensation of being squeezed between two things.

He saw, suddenly, how they might win.

• • •

Ellina was given command of the archers, who gathered around her on the rampart like wide-eyed schoolchildren. Dourin appeared, dressed in fitted armor that looked custom made, and which Ellina suspected was another gift from the Elder. Dourin was not an archer, and he would soon leave to meet Venick at the city's entrance, but he had come for a purpose.

"Hear me now," Dourin told the archers. "Ellina has a plan. She has explained it to me, and I will explain it to you. You would do best to listen closely."

He told them what she had in mind. Ellina watched the archers' round eyes grow even rounder, then narrow. By the time Dourin finished, they looked like Ellina felt: as if forged in fire.

Before departing, Dourin regarded Ellina under the soft blue light of the lanterns. "I hope that will be the only time I must ever speak for you." His tone, so often flippant, was steel. "Let's get your voice back, shall we?"

. . .

Venick heard the Dark Army advancing towards the city from his hiding spot along the road. Boots and hooves. The wheels of carts, cannons.

Venick glanced at his soldiers. He held up his hand. *Hold.*

He edged around a building to peer down the road.

The Dark Army's cavalry. Slim, quick-footed horses. No conjurors, not in the front lines where they would be open to attack, but many officers, elves armed with swords and crossbows. Milk-pale skin to contrast black armor. Those faces, all beautiful. Terrible.

Marching closer.

Dourin appeared.

"Where were you?" Venick asked.

"Helping."

"With what?"

Dourin wagged his finger. "Always so nosy."

"Tell me this, at least. Is her plan a good one?"

Dourin flashed a smile. "It is brilliant."

"What about *this* plan?" Venick asked, then explained what he had in mind.

Dourin listened, and then he laughed.

. . .

From her position atop the western rampart, Ellina watched the Dark Army approach the city. She could see where resistance soldiers were hidden behind buildings along the road. She could see how, as the enemy marched up the street, those soldiers did not move to attack.

Why did they not attack?

Ellina's fingers dug into the parapet's stone. This was not part of the plan. The battle was supposed to happen *there*, on the road outside the city. The cannons and catapults were already in place, trenches dug in strategic locations, archers at the ready. Allowing the Dark Army to move into Hurendue's streets would be as good as inviting defeat. Yet the resistance remained hidden.

The torches flickered in an undetectable breeze. Behind her, the archers shifted, their arrows tapping against wooden bowgrips as they readied but did not draw. Ellina ground her teeth, wishing for a voice, if for no other reason than to vent her frustration.

She watched, appalled, as the Dark Army crossed unopposed into the city.

• • •

Venick tracked the southerners as they drew even with his position, then passed beyond the city's border. The wide road funneled into a plaza, which butted up against the Angor River. Meanwhile, the twin hills, though not steep, provided enough of an obstacle to dissuade access. The Dark Army poured between them like water into a divot.

Venick kept his hand lifted in a signal to hold. More enemy elves, then. Green glass weapons. Helmets stamped with the Dark Queen's insignia, a black and red raven cupped between twin flames. Infantry, to mix with the cavalry. Some of the horses were fitted with armor. Others had currigon feathers tied to their manes and tails. The red plumes flipped in the wind.

Within the Dark Army's center ranks, Venick could see a tight ring of soldiers encircling a small band of elves. There weren't many—eight, maybe nine in total. The last of Farah's conjurors. And there among them, sitting astride a tall warhorse, dressed from head to boots in gleaming armor: Farah herself.

A pulse of hot anger. A murderous longing.

Venick hadn't expected to see Farah riding with her army. Previously, she'd seemed content to wield her power from a distance. Venick didn't know what it meant that she'd chosen to join her ranks now, only that the sight put a hard, cold feeling in the pit of his stomach.

Cut the legs off the beast, Venick had once said to Dourin, which was something his father had once said to him, *and you stop it in its tracks.*

Yet why go for the legs, when you could sever the head?

Venick waited until the Dark Army was fully inside the city before giving the signal.

The resistance emerged from hiding to close them in from behind.

• • •

Ellina watched the clash from above.

Horses reared. The rearguard—or was that now the front line?—disintegrated. The scene devolved into chaos. Yet deeper in the Dark Army's ranks, Farah's forces held.

The wind picked up, tossing Ellina's hair. Overhead, clouds thickened. The streets below were going dark, the torches all pitching black as if someone was rubbing them out. A boom of thunder.

And Venick?

Buildings blocked her view. Ellina could not quite see. Even with her elven vision, the streets were too dark and the battle too chaotic to discern anything more than the general shape of things. And Ellina did not like the general shape.

Presumably, there was a reason Venick had allowed the Dark Army to enter the city they were supposed to be defending. Though she often called him a fool, Venick was smart. Cunning. Blind, sometimes, though never in battle. He would not change the plan for nothing.

Unless something had gone wrong. Unless he was unable to deliver his commands.

Ellina realized that she had begun to imagine Venick immune to harm. Some part of her must believe what people said, that he was god-touched, because what else could explain how he had become so invulnerable? Or maybe it was that she had become too vulnerable. Her weaknesses made him seem untouchable by comparison.

But Venick was not untouchable. He was human. He could bleed and he could die. She might even watch it happen there, tonight.

Fear worked its way through her heart.

• • •

In the first wave, Venick nearly lost his sword. When an enemy's horse came crashing forward, Venick threw out his arm, sliced the animal across its chest. Tossed the rider, yes, but nearly wrenched his weapon from his grip.

Idiot.

Venick heaved back, shoulder twisting. Lucky, that he didn't dislocate the joint. Lucky, that he did keep his sword, because then the rider—female, seax in hand, her face like a fox—was on him, blade swinging. Venick let her strike slide down the length of his weapon, then buried his sword in her armpit, into the gap between cuirass and shoulder plate.

Blood ran down the blade. Venick's hand was sticky and warm.

Thunder rumbled. As Venick yanked his weapon free and turned to engage the next opponent, he felt like he couldn't see straight. Every time he tried to focus on an enemy elf, his eyes would dart to the next, and the next. He knew his men were taking hits. Knew that the opponent, rather than releasing their conjurors or their queen, was keeping their ranks tight. Their human-height shields formed a barrier. Their metal-plated greaves closed the gaps. The rearguard was a wall of horses, thick and high.

Venick shouted above the fray—not words, just a general cry that got the attention of his men, had them dropping what they were doing to crowd in behind him.

They needed to push the Dark Army deeper into the city towards the river. And Venick needed to break through that center ring.

He gripped his sword with both hands, slid under the legs of a warhorse, and sliced open its belly.

• • •

Lightning flashed. It illuminated the scene below, the tangle of two forces, the steady slope of each hill, which descended to the river. A split second to take it all in before the world snapped back to black. In the ensuing darkness, Ellina heard what she could not see: the shink of metal, the *shh* of green glass. Cries of exertion and pain. Flesh against flesh.

Ellina leaned so far forward she was practically lying on the parapet. She could tell that the conjurors were in the center of the fray, and that the southerners surrounding them were not breaking ranks. She could see a commotion near the rearguard, which had indeed become the front lines. A horse fell, and another. But their own soldiers were falling as well.

This was taking too long.

Ellina pulled a blank torch into her hand. The archers looked on as she unscrewed the glass bowl from one of the battlement's blue-glowing lanterns.

"Steady," said an archer.

She nodded. Slowly, careful not to let the black *rezahe* sap contact her skin, she poured the liquid over the torch's rag, soaking it through. A second archer struck a match and set it to the rag. The torch whooshed and came alight, blazing blue.

She met the eyes of the archers, whose faces hardened.

She was going down.

• • •

It began to rain. The sky split and emptied, taking much of what was left of their light.

Venick pressed forward. Dourin—who'd disappeared in the initial wave of battle to relay the new plan to their generals—was back at Venick's side. His sword cut a perfect arc, his movements graceful and practiced. He'd shown Venick the scar on his stomach where the Elder's would-be-assassin had gutted him, the long, clean line carved into smooth skin. It was the *isphanel*—that scraggly miracle plant—that allowed Dourin not only to survive, but to recover as if the wound had never been.

Venick was grateful for that. Doubly grateful, when a southerner came forward wielding a massive hammer—not a typical elven weapon, not something Venick wanted to face alone—that Dourin could spring into the space between one swing and the next, his blade catching the female's forearm. She stumbled. Tried to reel back. Before she had the chance, Venick closed in on her other side, slapping the flat surface of his sword against the crown of her head. She went down.

It was like that all around. Guttural screams. The flail of a fallen horse. The rain: a hazy blanket. Venick's attention returned to the conjurors, and to Farah still sitting among them. There was an unhealthy sheen to the Dark Queen's face, a wild look in her eyes that had Venick remembering his own first experience with war. *Battle-shocked*, Venick thought, except then he saw Farah witness a southerner decapitate a resistance member. The head went flying. Farah's mouth curled a smile.

A cannon boomed. The Dark Army's ranks wobbled. The world was a roar of noise.

One of the conjurors—male, slim golden eyes, a freakishly long neck—went suddenly rigid. His gaze darted towards the western rampart. Venick watched as he caught his queen's attention, speaking quickly. Farah's expression changed. She gave a command, and the male vanished.

Venick felt something pull at his belly. He wanted to follow that conjuror, and he would have had Dourin not chosen that moment to make a low, strangled noise. Venick turned.

Their fallen comrades began to rise.

• • •

Ellina slid on slick pavement as she came down the hillside, dagger in one hand, blue torch bobbing in the other. Though she could see the swell of battle better now, her position on the western rampart had set her on the wrong side of the river. There was no way across, not with a live flame in hand.

Or—there was one. As Ellina reached the water and stared down into its choppy current, she recalled a bridge located on the far northern side of the city. It was old but sturdy, wide. She could sprint there, cross the bridge, and double back down the river's other side.

Ellina glanced at her torch, which guttered and smoked in the rain but did not extinguish. She had suspected that *rezahe* sap would be viscous enough to withstand the downpour. She did not have similar confidences in the sap's resistance to river water. If she crossed the Angor using the bridge, she could ensure the torch remained alight, which was imperative to her plan. But that would also take time, and more time meant more soldiers dead. It meant more of the city taken or destroyed.

Ellina sheathed her dagger, hoisted the torch, and jumped into the river.

A splash. The swift jerk of her body into the current. As the Angor wrapped itself around her waist and tried to tug her under, Ellina fought back, swimming with one arm while holding the torch above the tide with the other. Though not as large as the Taro, the Angor was still wide enough that a human would have to squint to see across its banks—a long swim, even with both hands free.

The rain intensified, grasshoppering off the water's surface. Mist swirled in thick sheets. Ellina pumped her legs, swallowed a mouthful of water, coughed it out. By the time she reached the opposite shore, her muscles felt as if they were caked in wax. Yet her shoulder did not ache as it once had, and the torch—held aloft by that very arm—still burned brightly. The sight of its steady blue light steadied Ellina. The river might be strong, but so was she.

Ellina hauled herself up onto solid ground. The torch cast a soft halo, illuminating a plaza separated from the main surge of battle…and a figure there on the riverbank. Ellina squinted. Blinked the rain from her eyes.

A conjuror stepped into the light and raised his hands.

• • •

A strange bluish light danced at the edge of Venick's vision. He had the odd thought that it belonged to Miria. If he looked, he'd see her ghost.

But Venick couldn't look. Not when an undead soldier was charging towards him, green glass rapier slicing quick x's through the air. Venick sidestepped the attack, twisted. Pushed in again, hacking the undead's arms off its body in two clean slices. There was a moment's pause in which Venick imagined that he could sense the corpse's shock—

Not likely.

Or read the doom in its expression—

He's already dead, Venick.

Before the creature went limp. Not defeated, and hell, certainly not aware of it. Only abandoned by its bender. Whichever conjuror was targeting Venick didn't have to stick with this corpse, now that it had been relieved of its arms. The rapier-wielder dropped to the wet pavement, and just as quickly, a different undead rose up in its place.

The world was a rush of color and sound. Blood. Rain in his eyes, his mouth. A bellow, from him or from someone else, Venick didn't know. He'd lost sight of Farah. Dourin. Things were happening too quickly for him to really understand anything beyond what his sword had done, and would do again.

His muscles were on fire. Calluses split his hands. The river, nearly within reach, surged with rainwater.

• • •

Ellina scrambled sideways up the riverbank. The conjuror—a male with an unusually long neck—made fists of his hands, summoning a corpse from the nearby forest of bodies. At first glance, the dead elf looked whole, untouched, and Ellina's mind went straight to minceflesh. But then the undead bent to pick up a dagger. Ellina saw the crown of her head had been smashed in. Her back was a cape of blood.

The conjuror pushed his hands forward and the corpse obeyed, moving towards Ellina in long, purposeful strides. Ellina backtracked, avoiding the attack without engaging the corpse. Her eyes were on its bender.

Ellina had known all along that their only hope of winning this battle would be to target the conjurors. She had known, too, that targeting them would be difficult. Farah—having lost more than half of her conjurors already—would be careful not to risk any more. Most likely, she would keep them protected in the Dark Army's center ranks where they could wield their magic with the least amount of interference. Breaking through would be costly, and time-consuming…if it was possible at all.

But then, Ellina did not have to break through.

Ellina had always liked the idea of using herself as bait. This was not so different from a swim in a winter river, the way it required equal parts mental and physical concentration. And it was fitting, that Farah might try to set a trap and be trapped in turn.

Yet *how* had always been the question. It was one thing for Ellina to reveal herself to the Dark Army in an open field. It was quite another to lure conjurors out during the havoc of battle. Ellina had chewed on this problem, seemingly without a clear solution…until her meeting with Venick on the ramparts, when she realized that she already had her answer.

She seemed to see with new eyes her sprint across the field four mornings ago. The Dark Army, like a black plight. The knoll. Eywen's lathered sides. She thought of how she had stepped into plain view, only to discover that the southern elves were already in position, appearing out of seemingly nowhere to block her path.

Ellina recalled the way Venick sometimes looked at her, as if with regret.

His regret made more sense now.

She wondered how long he had known she was shadow-bound.

It explained much. *That* was how the coven of elves had anticipated their ambush outside of Igor, with enough time, even, to hatch an ambush of their own. *That* was how the Dark Army had known where to find the resistance in the woods and Ellina in the fields. It might even be how the female named Inra had managed to catch Ellina by surprise in Igor's streets, cornering Ellina when it should have been the other way around.

The shadow-binding itself was not a great surprise. There had been plenty of opportunity for a conjuror to capture Ellina's shadow within their own. The true problem was that if anyone had discovered Ellina was shadow-bound, they would have cast her from the resistance. Venick surely knew this and had stayed silent in order to protect her. The fool. Had Ellina realized the truth, she would have cast herself. Being shadow-bound, and therefore trackable, created a sea of complications.

But that was a blade that could cut both ways. If the conjurors sensed Ellina nearby, she could tempt them away from the safety of their center ranks. Farah had already proven that she would go to great lengths to capture or kill her youngest sister. Ellina had humiliated Farah. Undermined her power. Farah wanted to make Ellina pay—she only needed the opportunity.

On the riverbank, the long-necked conjuror's hair was plastered to his face. His golden eyes looked strangely green in the torch's light. He stood a safe distance away, his corpse positioned before him like a bodyguard. Ellina could see the sleek confidence in the bender's eyes, the way he believed himself invulnerable. After all, they stood apart from the main battle. If Ellina tried to break through to him, he had an endless number of bodies at his disposal. If the fight became difficult, he could call forth more conjurors. He did not believe Ellina could possibly beat them all, and he was right—she could not. At least, not alone.

Ellina swiped her bright blue flame through the air in a high, deliberate arc, as if drawing a line from the rampart to her opponent.

An arrow whizzed by, striking the conjuror through the neck.

· · ·

A spray of arrows hailed from the sky. Venick didn't see them, but he could hear them as they whistled overhead.

The Dark Army vanguard was switching strategies. They began to pull back, attempting to gain the space they needed to reform their lines. In doing so, they passed the resistance's semicircle of catapults, which remained abandoned, unlit. Their wooden beams looked like skeletons in the low light.

As the Dark Army was driven beyond the catapults and up against the storm-surged river, Venick thought of Ellina's stunts. He wondered if this was how she felt when she did something any rational warrior would consider insane: like her heart was cased in fire.

· · ·

Ellina continued to draw the conjurors out. She remained relatively isolated from the central grip of battle, which raged farther down the river. The elves came one by one, and each time Ellina lifted her torch, an arrow—or really, dozens of arrows—found their way into the enemy's flesh.

Ellina did not know how many conjurors were left alive. Farah's coven had started with thirty last summer, whittled down to twenty, ten. What Ellina did know was that as the night wore on, the rain began to ebb, slowing to a fine spray that irritated the eyes, then ceased. The clouds broke apart, the moon peeking shyly through. The corpses within Ellina's line of sight were just that. None stirred to rise.

Her plan was working. Yet there was one conjuror Ellina had not yet seen, and was desperate to see. Her desire for it burned a hole in her heart.

• • •

The enemy was in position. It was a miracle, a god's given gift, that the resistance had managed to corral them so quickly, admitting the Dark Army into the city and pressing them towards the river, all while allowing them to believe that's where they wanted to be. The Dark Army, though massive, and vicious, had a flaw—it was comprised entirely of elves.

Elves were trained in solo fighting. They concerned themselves with the elegance of their own blades and not their neighbors'. Oh, they'd learned a few tricks along the way. With Farah as their leader, they'd managed to organize themselves into the semblance of a real army, capable of doing serious damage. But there were oversights in their training, chinks that only experienced human warriors would know how to spot and patch.

The Dark elves didn't consider the catapults a danger. Not as they were then, unlit and unmanned.

Venick's soldiers knew the plan. As they pressed their enemy beyond the catapults and towards the water, their eyes began to stray to their Commander, awaiting his signal. Dourin, too, reappeared long enough to give Venick a final, "Try not to die, will you?" then vanished again. He would not stay for this part of the scheme.

And yet...Farah.

Venick could see her there, still tightly enclosed within a halo of elven soldiers, still looking as if she'd swallowed a mouthful of blood and wanted more. She had not yet crossed the threshold of catapults, which encircled a sector of the city in an expansive arc, dropping off on each end at the river. If Venick gave the signal now, Farah would escape.

And if he waited?

His army would continue to struggle. More soldiers would die. The southerners might even recognize the threat and switch their position.

A true Commander never hesitates.

Venick turned to the nearest soldier and gripped the boy by the arm. "Gather six others. Run to the gunners. Tell them to light the catapults."

"But," said the soldier, "the enemy has already moved beyond the catapults. They aren't in range."

"Not the missiles." It was just Venick's luck that he'd chosen a soldier who'd missed the message. "I want you to light the catapults themselves. The wood."

The boy's eyes bugged. "All of them?"

"All of them."

"Sir...that will create a massive fire. The smoke alone will be suffocating. And the catapults block our way back down the road. We will be trapped here in the city to be burned alive."

Venick spoke in his Commander's voice. "Not if you know how to swim."

• • •

She walked among a garden of dead.

Ellina's arms, though they had done little more than lift a torch, shook from fatigue. She felt strained, strung out, and though she sensed how the battle tipped, how *she* had tipped it, she still wrestled with those twinned feelings of emptiness and desire. They beckoned her like the song of a siren. If she listened closely, she could hear them sing her name.

Ellina moved along the river towards the main surge of battle. Whatever lines had existed between their sides were dissolved now, the two armies weaving together like a tapestry. The colors, too, like a tapestry: green and gold, brilliant red. As the inky shadows continued to lift, Ellina scanned faces, riffling through them as if through a drawer. She cared not for the general content, only for what she sought.

She saw him from a distance.

Balid stood on the river-most edge of the fight, battling a human resistance member. The man—a hulking giant of a person—windmilled his sword through the air, then brought the blade down with an audible *swoosh*. The weapon cut close enough to sever the end of Balid's outstretched sleeve. A slice of fabric fluttered to the wet road.

Ellina's stomach took a hard twist. She tossed her torch into the river. Pulled a dagger into each hand.

The giant surged towards Balid. His sword was steel, double-edged, etched with ancient human symbols. It came up and then down, cutting perilously close to Balid's neck. As Ellina moved towards them, she wanted to say, *stop*. She wanted to say, *mine*.

Balid's cloak spiraled around his ankles. His fingers came together. The giant dropped his sword with a raucous clatter and covered his face with his hands. Ellina did not have to see his eyes to know that he had been conjured blind.

Balid pulled a little knife from his sleeve, stepped forward, and drove it through the man's jaw.

• • •

When Venick was a boy, his father had taken him to see the traveling circus. He still remembered the red and white striped tent, the garish costumes, the oily slip of buttered corn on his fingers and around his mouth. As part of the final stunt, the ringmaster had set fire to his ring. He stood in its center, waving his baton as the flames rose, dancers twirling long ribbons around him in intricate circles. But one of the ribbons came too close to the blaze. It caught fire. The other dancers tried using their own ribbons to bat it out, which only helped the flames spread.

It was like that.

The catapults were set aflame. They created a ring of fire. The heat was instantly suffocating, trapping both the resistance and the Dark Army against the river. In the chaos, the flames began to spread, leaping onto the bodies of the dead, eating their way through the ranks. It was as the young soldier had said—they were trapped, with only one way out.

Humans dove into the river. The sounds of splashing mixed with the rumble of the fire, the screams. The southern elves watched, masks falling away to reveal blatant shock as their northern brethren did what elves simply did not do, and followed the humans into the water.

Though only about a third of the Dark Army was captured on the wrong side of the catapults, it was more than enough to shift the battle. As the fire blazed, everyone tripping and rushing to escape the heat, Venick stayed back, ushering his soldiers to safety. Soon, however, the smoke became too thick. Venick's eyes burned. He'd waited too long; it was time to join his troops in the river.

A slice of pain, hot through his skull.

Venick fell to his knees. His vision spotted. It took him a moment to understand—he'd been hit with something from behind.

He glanced back to see a southerner holding a shield, which she was using like a club, swinging in blind, haphazard circles. She had the wild look of someone who knew they were doomed and was intent on taking as many victims as she could down with her.

Venick swayed. Something warm trickled down the nape of his neck.

Get up.

He closed his eyes.

Get up, Venick.

He frowned at the voice in his head. Gruff tones, brusque, edged in disapproval. That voice had always been a part of him, always lurking around his mind, but it no longer felt quite like his.

Don't give up now, you hear me?

Venick pressed a palm to the road. Blinked. When he looked up again, he found himself hunting for that blue light. He wanted to see it one more time. He thought, if he saw it, he might have the strength to understand why the voice in his head sounded like his, yet wasn't.

The world closed over, and everything went black.

* * *

Flames sprang to life in the distance. There was a clamor of running feet, the hollers reaching a previously unmatched pitch. Then, bodies to match those feet and those hollers, a host of southerners speeding by.

Ellina was aware of this without really understanding that she was aware. The greater scope of the war had ceased to matter, fading like mountaintops into the fog. Her focus was much more singular.

Balid had climbed onto a low stone wall near a rocky section of the river. He craned his neck towards the fire, his expression indiscernible. He seemed to understand something about the fire that Ellina did not, his eyes pressing back to it again and again. Ellina wondered if maybe the heat and the light were close enough to hinder Balid's conjuring. Maybe that was why he was so preoccupied.

It wasn't. He spotted Ellina, marking her weapons, her expression, the lithe slide and step of her feet. His face changed again, turning hungry, almost luminous as he drew his fingers together and lifted them above his head. Ellina could see his bandaged wrist from where he had intercepted her dagger. The wound had missed the hand.

There would be no monologues between them. No insults or exchanging of threats. Then again, the silence was its own exchange, loaded with all the words they could not speak.

Ellina saw the corpse rise to life in her periphery. Though conjurors were masters of shadows and storms, they had no magic that could kill an opponent directly. Balid's best weapon, besides that little knife up his sleeve, was his corpse-bending.

And yet, Ellina felt a tingle of something, that same sense of being aware without understanding that she was aware. Instinct told her to keep her eyes on Balid, not to allow him out of her sight, but another, stronger instinct told her to look at the corpse, so she did.

Her hands went loose. She nearly dropped her daggers.

Balid's chosen body—his articulated undead—was Artis.

• • •

Venick's eyelids felt glued together. His ears rang. He pushed to his knees, vomited. Wiped his mouth, told himself to move, move, or else he'd burn alive.

He looked up at the sky and wondered if he hadn't died already. It was raining fire. The belly of smoke glowed like the eye of a god.

As Venick struggled to make his legs work, he spotted the elf who had hit him. She had dropped her shield and was lying motionless on the ground. Flames caught the hem of her trousers. They worked up her legs, swallowing her midriff, her chest.

The sight was enough to spur Venick into motion. He rose to his feet. Limped to the water's edge. Gasping, flames nipping at his heels, he sank into the safety of the river.

• • •

Ellina was frozen.

Artis looked in death much the way he had looked in life. A gentle face. Moon-white hair, round chin, a dimple in one cheek. The only differences now were his eyes, open but unseeing, and his side, which was stained dark with blood. Yet Ellina could look past all of that, and see her friend.

She wanted to sob for him. For herself. Easy, soft-spoken Artis. He, more than any of the others, would hate how his body was being used against her.

Artis—controlled by Balid—raised his sword and sprang forward. Ellina twisted sideways, aimed a kick at his knee. She caught him in the thigh instead, tipped his balance. It created the opening she needed to peel around his body and rush towards Balid, who slithered away like flames over oil.

Up close, Balid looked gaunt, his skin stretched tight across cheeks and chin, his eyes dark in their sockets. He bared his teeth, open-jawed, his severed tongue on display. Then he scrabbled farther up the bank, four quick steps while he worked his dark magic, hauling Artis upright and back between them.

Artis' stance was different than it would have been had he been alive and in control of himself. Balid's puppeteering was a poor replica for the real Artis, who was elegant, precise. He had always been the last to enter a fight and the first to leave it, never minding violence, but nor wishing for it needlessly. Nothing at all like corpse-Artis, who surged forward again, his sword hacking a careless shape.

Ellina's eyes blurred as she parried and evaded. She did not want to fight Artis. She did not want to desecrate his body, to go for his limbs or his head. This was not like fighting any nameless corpse. This was her friend.

It occurred to Ellina that Balid had chosen Artis for this purpose, that he wanted to hurt and distract her enough that she might make mistakes, maybe even refuse to engage. And he was right—Ellina did not want to engage. It was wrong, the way Artis' dead body jerked with silent commands, his head snapping a beat too late as his torso changed direction. The wound in his side leaked blood. Yet even knowing Balid's intentions, even understanding how he must relish in Ellina's misery, it was not enough to change her mind, which bristled at the idea of doing anything more than deflecting Artis' attacks.

Artis sliced his sword towards her neck, backhanded now. Ellina brought her daggers together. Caught his blade and thrust it away.

It gets easier, said the memory of Artis' voice, *once you learn to accept what is.*

His sword came in again.

To let go.

Spun and struck.

You have to let go.

The feeling, when it came, was familiar: that building swell of memories. Yet this time, the memories that pulled at Ellina's attention were not of hardship, or suffering, but of Miria.

Ellina had been a fledgling the first time she heard her sister sing. Miria's voice was light, agile, capable of switching quickly between notes without correction or delay. Miria never saw a reason to hide her singing, but Ellina saw a reason to hide how often she listened. She would follow her sister through the palace, crouching behind pillars or under tables, closing her eyes to absorb the vibration of Miria's voice, which carried through the halls like bells. *She sounds like a drowning cat,* Farah had once scoffed, but they both knew it was untrue. Miria's voice was beautiful.

The first time Ellina tested her own voice, she was alone in her room. Nervous, even only with herself. Afraid, too, of what would happen if she was discovered. Yet Miria's singing had lit something within Ellina, and the urge to attempt this, to make something, something lovely and true for its own sake, had become impossible to ignore. That day in her bedroom, Ellina hummed her first low note, then another, her voice rising to meet the ceiling, then higher, up to the clouds and beyond.

She was too good. Her talent was almost cruel. Ellina's voice was pure and easy: a gift she must never use.

She had hidden her ability, singing only on rare occasions when she could not manage to fight the impulse, and only when she was certain she would not be overheard. Still, Ellina used to spend long hours thinking about singing, and about what it would sound like for her and Miria to harmonize, how they would come together and break apart again, whose voice would take which refrain.

Ellina still imagined how their voices would sound, though imagining was all she would ever have—Miria and Ellina had never sung together, because Ellina never told Miria that she could sing.

One more regret, to sit with all the others. As Balid spread his fingers and Artis continued to batter Ellina with his blade, she saw her own life laid out before her, all the years she had spent hiding from what she was and what she wanted. Ellina did not want to hide anymore. She did not want to be the kind of elf who was afraid to face the truth, who became paralyzed by the difference between what should be and what was, who refused to step into the light and make herself known. Refusal had once felt like a choice, and thereby a kind of freedom, but a caged bird who chooses its perch is no less caged.

Artis was dead now. There was nothing more Ellina could do for him. But Ellina was still alive, with so much left to fight for.

She gave a silent cry as she burst forward, chopping at the back of Artis' leg to sever the hamstring. He went down crookedly, unable to catch himself.

Balid seemed thrown by Ellina's sudden attack. As she swept forward, he clapped his hands together, the start of another conjuring, but Ellina was faster and would reach Balid before he managed to call forth another corpse.

He knew it. As Ellina drew back her dagger, Balid's gaze sharpened. He pulled his knife out of his sleeve: short, plain, no longer than his longest finger. Ellina curled to dodge the blade, ramming her green glass through his belly. Her weapon went in cleanly.

His did, too.

His knife caught her thigh. Ellina did not feel the wound, at first. She leaned into her dagger, needing to watch Balid die, to see it. She felt a heady surge of energy as his eyes bulged, his lungs wheezing a final breath. Balid collapsed sideways, and as he did, his knife in her thigh pulled free. There was a rush of wet pain. Her hand went automatically to the wound.

She sucked in a breath, and screamed.

TWENTY-FIVE

Venick heard a scream in the distance. He knew that voice. Heard in, sometimes, in his dreams.

And yet, it couldn't be.

Could it?

He began treading against the river's current, turning in one direction, then the other. Smoke. The air like a black lung. Fire: a bright orange mouth to swallow the Dark Army whole. Along the shore, enemy elves attempted to escape the flames. Some jumped into the water. This, too, like a mouth. Their heads were quickly swallowed by the tide.

Venick saw this as if someone else was seeing it. Cool water blanketed him on all sides. The river's surface reflected the colors of war, red and yellow, dazzling orange. Any Dark Army soldiers who were not trapped by the fire thundered back up the road. A retreat. Venick hadn't heard the call for one, but then, his mind was still echoing with that earlier scream...

He reached a wet hand to touch his brow. His vision was blocked by two bright spots. He lowered the hand, realizing that if he had a head injury, he'd likely imagined the voice. It hadn't been real.

A snuffed feeling, like a candle. The drop into disappointment.

He turned away from the brightness of the fire, which had begun to irritate his eyes. He didn't want to leave the water. It was peaceful there, the current gentling now that the rain had stopped, a basket of silence among the rage. Yet he'd begun to feel dizzy, and if he was going to black out again, this was the last place he should do it.

He put all of his energy into reaching the opposite shore.

Muddy bank. The smell of sweat and grime. Human hands reached down to haul Venick out of the water, then tightened to steady him on his feet. He swayed, blinking into the concerned faces of strangers who weren't entirely strangers, because *they* knew *him*. Their clothing was wet. Their skin was streaked with blood and dirt. They were looking at him in a way that was familiar to Venick, but only because he remembered once looking at others in this way: generals in the lowland army, mainly, or heroes from his regiment. Their eyes, as his had been, were lit with awe.

And then, again. That voice.

"Venick."

He saw Ellina stumbling out of the river and up the bank. Her armor shed water. Her face was a cloak of soot, her eyes rimmed in white, as if she wore a mask. She drew a wet hand down her brow, and the image smeared, leaving a dirty imprint across her nose and mouth.

Her mouth. Those lips, which had spoken his name.

But…she'd spoken his name?

Ellina moved towards him, picking up speed. She spoke again, like a sob. "*Venick*."

He caught her to his chest, and though the impact sent a spike of pain

through his skull, he held on tight. That scream. Her words. Could...
could Ellina speak?

"Your voice." His pulse pounded in his temples. He drew back a
little, hands trembling, hardly daring to believe it. "You won it back?"

She nodded.

"Say it."

"I killed Balid." She wasn't smiling. He sensed this inside her: a sav-
age kind of energy. "I won back my voice." Her expression shifted. She
pulled out of his arms, as if seeing him more fully. "You are hurt."

A gift. It was a gift, to hear the concern in her voice, to watch her lips
move and make sound. Even as Ellina began shoving up his sleeves, feeling along his ribs, seeking the injury, Venick couldn't help his smile, or
the buoyant feeling that started in his stomach and worked its way down
to his toes. "I do not see a wound," she said, fingers flying. "Where—?"
She stilled. Her eyes jumped to his. "Your head."

He wanted to tell her it was nothing. He wanted to reach up and rub
away the line between her brows, to make her recount the story of how
she'd killed Balid and won back her voice. Yet Venick suddenly wasn't
sure that he *could* reach up. His arms felt weighted with rocks. His eyes
did, too. They began to droop.

Her expression went tight. "We need to find Erol."

She tugged on his arm, and when he stumbled, she supported him
with her shoulder. His head was filled with nails. Every step was agony.
Venick tried to separate himself from the pain, tried instead to focus on
Ellina, the feel of her slight form beneath him, which surely couldn't
support his weight, yet did.

The distance between the river and the infirmary seemed to stretch
wider the farther they went, like a door at the end of a hall in a dream.
Twice, Venick tried to stop, but Ellina wouldn't allow it. "Almost there,"

she said, then appeared to notice how the sound of her voice gave him strength, and kept talking. "We are nearly there, Venick, you will be able to rest soon, don't stop just yet, not yet, only a little farther."

Eventually, Venick couldn't follow what she was saying anymore. Her words became like the shush of ocean waves, one folding over the next. They lulled him. His body slackened. Every step beat a wedge into his skull.

• • •

The voice was gentle, but stern. "You walked him here?"

"There was no time to fetch a litter," Venick heard Ellina reply.

"You should have come for me."

"I did not want to leave him."

Venick peeled open an eye. The infirmary. Tall windows to hold the night, a sea of white beds. Erol was stepping forward to squeeze himself under Venick's other arm, his bushy eyebrows dancing as he spoke. "This was unwise," he told Ellina as they pulled Venick towards the nearest cot. "Are you aware that head injuries can be made worse with movement?"

Ellina gave no answer, and Venick couldn't tell if this was because she hadn't known that and was ashamed, or because she had known, and chose to move him anyway.

Erol said, "You can speak."

Venick drew an angry breath, but Erol spoke over him. "Easy. I didn't mean it as an accusation, merely an observation."

"Yes," Ellina replied. "I can speak."

They pushed Venick into bed. He didn't resist, exactly, but strained to stay upright rather than fall back onto the pillows. He wanted to see

Ellina's face. He hadn't recognized her tone when she said, *I can speak*, and he wondered—was that because her tone was new? Or was it because he'd become so used to reading her expressions that hearing her voice was like listening to a language whose dialect was unfamiliar, and required extra concentration?

But Venick couldn't concentrate. His head was so heavy.

"He must stay awake," Erol said. "Sleep is dangerous for him right now."

"Venick." The bed dipped with Ellina's weight. "Talk to me. Tell me something."

He gave a sleepy sigh.

"The cove," she blurted. "In Irek. Your homeland. You said you and your friends used to swim in a hidden cove."

He remembered recounting that story, but he wondered what it meant to her. Did she know how he had dreamed of sharing that place with her? Why did she think of it now? "Yes."

"Was it deep?"

He might have smiled at her obvious attempt to keep him awake, if smiling didn't hurt so much. "It wasn't too deep." Another sigh. "But it was beautiful. The grove. The flowers."

"Fish?"

"Fish," Venick agreed. The words came from deep in his chest. "Tiny, colorful minnows. Urchins. Giant *shroopa*. You would like it." He did smile then, a little, despite the pain. "I always did."

She kept him talking, asking questions, calling forth memories from boyhood he thought he'd forgotten. As he spoke, Erol drifted away to tend other patients, leaving the two of them together. Soon, though, speaking became too difficult. Venick's eyes fluttered closed.

"Venick."

"Just resting."

"You shouldn't."

"Mmm." He caught her hand. "Stay with me?"

He heard her hesitate. Felt the warmth of her body fit alongside his. She gave her answer in elvish. "*Always.*"

• • •

"This is a nice change," Dourin said.

Venick peeled open his eyes to see Dourin stepping through a thin privacy curtain, which must have been installed around his cot while he slept—a Commander's privilege. Ellina was there, too, no longer tucked in bed beside him but perched on a wooden chair near his head. A section of her trousers had been cut away, a wide bandage wrapped around her thigh.

"Dourin." Ellina's tone was stern. "Don't."

"I like to see him bedridden for once."

"Not funny."

"Everyone is talking as if he is a god of some sort. They do not know Venick like we know him. They were not there for the beartrap or the poisoned dagger. And then there is all that time he spent *moping* just because you told him you wanted him dead—"

"Can we talk about something else?" Venick interrupted, angling himself up against his pillows. It was still nighttime. He didn't know how long he'd been asleep—a few hours? A day?—but his head felt clearer, despite the throbbing. He closed his eyes, pressed fingers into the sockets. "The battle."

"What is there to say?" Dourin spoke like a jester for a crowd. "Ellina managed to kill nearly all of Farah's conjurors with her brilliant little trap while you decimated their remaining ranks with fire and water. The Dark Army retreated. You suffered a blow to the head, which has made Ellina snappy, despite Erol's conclusion that the injury is not severe. And, of course, there is the matter of Ellina's voice."

Venick's eyes came open. Ellina's face was drawn closed. She said, "Dourin is leaving now. You should rest."

Venick shook his head, then winced. "But, your voice."

"Shh."

"Ellina. I don't even—"

"I know," she relented.

"It's like—"

"Yes."

"And you didn't even—"

"I *know*."

Dourin made a disgusted sound. "What is the point of being able to speak if you two can just read each other's thoughts?"

• • •

"Your voice," Venick said again, later. Outside the infirmary windows, sunlight streamed hazily through smoke from extinguished fires. Citizens could be seen clearing the streets of ash and debris, singing old tavern songs as they worked. Earlier that morning, wine barrels had been rolled out of storage, the pale liquid passed around for all to share. The mood, despite the gloom, was celebratory.

"How did you win it back?" Venick asked. Ellina had moved from the chair back into bed with him. Her shoulder pressed against his. A slow, heavy warmth.

"It is a long story."

"We have time."

She readjusted her shoulders against the metal headboard. She must have bathed at some point—her clothes were dry, her skin clean. Yet she looked unhappy.

"What is it?"

"Your head. The wound."

"I feel fine."

"You have been awake too long. Before, Erol said you should stay alert, but now he wants you to sleep."

"I'll have no hope of sleep as long as you're here."

Surprise. A swift look of hurt. She moved to stand.

"Wait." He reached for her sleeve. "I didn't mean it like that. I only meant…it feels good. You, here. This feels good." He swallowed. "It's hard for me to sleep because I don't want to miss this. Please, don't go. Tell me what happened. How you won your voice. I want to hear the story."

She looked unsure.

"I'll sleep after," he said. "I promise."

Softly, careful not to jostle him, she returned to his side. She set her head on the pillow next to his. As she began speaking, he closed his eyes. He hadn't noticed, at first, the way her voice scratched slightly from disuse, or how she struggled with certain words, the ones far back in her throat like *sword* and *mourn*. A new kind of vulnerability. But courage, too, in her willingness to trust him with it.

He slipped his hand into hers as she told him everything.

• • •

He didn't sleep. Even after Ellina finished speaking, and her head came to rest on his shoulder, and day sunk back to night and her body warmed against his and everything went impossibly soft, Venick's mind wouldn't stop working. He thought about what Ellina had risked and won. The battle. Artis, and the remorse that gripped Ellina as she recounted his death. Farah. Her escape, and what it might mean for the war.

Venick's relief mixed with his worry, conspiring to keep him awake until eventually, he couldn't stand it anymore. He spoke into the dark. "Your sister is alive."

Ellina lifted her head from his chest. Though they'd been quiet for some time, he'd known by the rhythm of her breathing that she wasn't asleep.

"The Dark Army will strike again," Venick went on, drawing his eyes to the ceiling. Though the initial post-battle rush had calmed—inpatients settled into beds, pain tonic distributed, minor wounds tended and discharged—the infirmary's late-night noises and the slim hang of the curtain provided a measure of privacy. "As long as Farah is leading them, they'll have a reason to fight. This battle was a victory for us, but it won't be the end."

"Farah will be careful from now on," Ellina said, pushing fully upright. Her hair was undone. A lock snaked over one shoulder, falling forward. "Exposing herself was a mistake. She wanted to establish her position as a leader on the front lines, but she is no warrior, and the fight surely went worse than she anticipated. She will not risk herself again. It will be difficult to target her directly."

"But not impossible," Venick said. "As you said, she has made mistakes."

"And learned from them."

"Maybe." Venick scratched his chin. "Have you noticed? The way she looks a bit…"

"Different?"

"I was going to say deranged."

"If that is true, it will only make her more dangerous. She is determined."

"Well." Venick shrugged. "So are we."

They sank into silence. Ellina, rather than moving back down next to him, stayed upright. She inhaled a breath, flexed her jaw. Then: "I have been angry with you."

Venick's surprise almost made him laugh. "Oh?"

"You knew that I was—" she faltered, swallowing the syllables. "That I was shadow-bound."

He'd thought she might bring this up. In his imaginings of this conversation, they were both stone-faced, serious. He would apologize and try to explain. Ellina would motion, nonverbally, that he was or was not forgiven.

But Venick didn't feel serious. He still couldn't quite believe that Ellina no longer had to struggle with hand symbols and scribbled notes. She could accuse him directly, tell him what an idiot he'd been, how angry she was. He wanted her to.

He said, "I told you of my suspicions."

"Your suspicions, yes, but nothing direct. You have known about my binding for weeks."

"I knew nothing for certain."

"Fool."

His smile pulled free. "Gods, I missed hearing you say that."

"That is not an apology."

"Ellina." He sat up, took both of her hands in his. "I am very, very sorry."

She frowned. "Could you say it in elvish?"

"Probably not."

"You *are* a fool."

"But it's true that I didn't know anything for certain. It's like I told you the other night—I suspected one of us was shadow-bound. At first, I thought it was me. And then…" He shrugged. "I wasn't going to turn our soldiers against you for the sake of a hunch."

"They would not turn against me now."

"No," Venick agreed, "I don't think they would. Not that it matters anymore. You killed, what? Half a dozen conjurors? Whoever had you bound is surely dead."

"We cannot know that."

"We can assume based on the odds."

"I do not like to assume."

Another shrug. "If I'm wrong, we'll know soon enough."

"You seem unconcerned."

"You're safer here among us than out on your own."

"I meant you seem unconcerned about *you*. About what happens if a conjuror uses me—my location—to find you."

Venick paused. "You're talking about the corpse-benders."

"They have smuggled dead elves into our midst before. Until we figure out how they are doing it, and how to stop them, the risk remains."

"Even so, they don't need shadow-binding to guide them. My whereabouts are hardly a secret." A half-smile. "Unless you've had enough fighting? Maybe you'd prefer to be absent the next time a corpse tries to slit my neck?"

"You are insulting me."

"I'm teasing you."

Ellina's mouth popped open as if her argument had been snatched clean from her throat. She looked at her hands, still clasped in his. "I wanted to apologize, too."

"For what?"

She shifted a little.

"Ellina?"

"You grew out your hair," she blurted.

"What?"

"I…noticed." Her cheeks were two bright apples. "Your hair. It is longer."

Venick peered at her. "You're apologizing for my hair?"

"No, not—" She screwed her eyes shut. "That is not what I meant to say."

Venick, now thoroughly confused, tried for a smile. "I can cut it, if you don't like it."

"I like it."

"Do you?"

"Yes."

Yet he saw how uncomfortable it made her to admit this, the way she struggled to hold his gaze. Understanding poured into him. It had always been difficult for them to speak plainly, and especially about this. But: "Look at me," he said. She did. "You're beautiful. You always have been, to me."

Somehow, this seemed to make things worse. It baffled him, the way her eyes filled with sudden tears, or how she sucked in a ragged breath, then held it.

"I'm sorry," he said automatically. "I didn't know—I didn't mean to upset you. I take it back. You're not beautiful. You're wretched."

She sniffed an almost-laugh.

"Tell me what's wrong," he said softly. When she struggled for words, he added, "Or don't. You don't have to say anything."

"I know." She made frustrated fists.

"You know?"

"I have my voice back. I can say anything. I *could*." She pulled her lips in. "I thought it would be simpler than this. To speak about…things. What I am thinking."

"It's not easy." This, at least, he knew for certain. "Not for me, either. And you've been voiceless for…well, for too long, Ellina. It's not going to be easy. But you have time."

"Time," she repeated. Her breathing evened again. The tears were gone. She lifted her gaze to his. "Yes."

TWENTY-SIX

When she woke again the following morning, the bed was empty.

Ellina's pulse tripped as she scrambled upright, stumbling over the sheets in her haste. She flung back the curtain, which was not truly a curtain, but a bedsheet knotted to a rod. Her gaze landed on Erol changing pillowcases a few beds over. He looked up.

"Venick—?"

"Is fine," Erol said smoothly. "He's just been discharged."

"But, his head…"

"The damage isn't as serious as originally thought. He'll have a headache, but there is no further reason to limit his activity. I examined him myself just this morning." The ghost of a smile. "You, on the other hand, need to be careful with that thigh."

The awful feeling in Ellina's stomach began to settle. "My thigh is fine. It did not even need stitches."

"Only because you refused them. You're as bad as Lin Lill."

"It is a minor wound." Ellina was eager to finish this conversation. "A scrape. I would gladly suffer a thousand like it."

Erol seemed to understand the unspoken, *Given what I have gained.* He opened his mouth to respond. Stopped himself. Wrung out another smile. "Venick is in the reception corridor, I think." As Ellina turned gratefully away and began striding in that direction, Erol called out to her once more. "*We are all glad for you, Ellina,*" he said in elvish. "*And I am so proud.*"

Ellina's boots squeaked to a halt.

There was a pause, which lasted just long enough for Ellina to find the courage she needed to turn back around and meet Erol's gaze. She could count the number of times anyone had told her they were proud of her, so she was not expecting the sudden lurch of shyness…or pleasure.

Erol was smiling. He appeared comfortable, despite the sudden heaviness of the moment. Comfortable, despite having made the moment heavy.

Ellina did not like to think about her father. She saw no point in contemplating the would haves or could have beens, particularly when her own mother hardly cared to speak of him. Ellina's father was dead. He had drowned in a river when Ellina was little. Even if he had not died, there was a good chance that Ellina would never have known him; after she was born, he chose to move back to his home city, Vivvre, rather than remain among the court. His story was long over.

Yet Ellina wondered, suddenly, if this was how it would have felt to have a father. She wondered if he would have been proud of her, and open enough to say so.

Ellina thought back to her last conversation with Venick. She was not like Erol. She had never been good at expressing difficult feelings. And yet, things were different now. Ellina understood better the preciousness of certain moments, how they must be grasped immediately, or else lost forever. And she saw, too, how she might be brave enough to grasp them.

"Thank you, Erol," she said. "I am glad, too."

• • •

When Ellina pulled open the door to the infirmary's small, brightly lit antechamber, she found Venick and Dourin engaged in a whispered argument. Dourin was speaking animatedly while Venick was closed tight, his expression adamant, bordering on angry.

"This isn't a circus," Venick told Dourin through gritted teeth. "You can't parade us around."

"Would you deny the citizens of Hurendue a chance to thank their savior?"

"I'm not their savior."

"Don't be modest."

"I didn't fight the army singlehandedly."

"No, but it was *your* stubborn and ill-advised decision to remain here with a weakened force. Had we not, these people would be reduced to rubble."

"I don't expect to be praised for it."

"I know," Dourin said in the same way he might have said, *exactly*.

When Ellina reached the place they stood, they both turned to her, imploring.

"Ellina." Dourin flashed his white teeth. "Talk some sense into your boy here."

Ellina ignored the punch of pleasure at hearing Venick called *hers*. She looked between them. "Sense?"

"The time has come for us to move on to Kenath. Venick wants to gather our ranks and leave later, after sundown, like thieves in the night. I am in favor of a more public departure."

Venick shot Ellina a desperate look.

She asked, "Is there something wrong with a public exit?"

"See?" Dourin flourished a hand. "Ellina agrees with me."

It was announced that the resistance would depart that afternoon. This—predictably, and to Venick's obvious discomfort—brought the citizens of Hurendue out in droves, everyone lining the streets in order to thank the soldiers for their bravery and sacrifice. Flowers were thrown. Babies were kissed. Venick—after more strong-arming by Dourin—led the procession atop his blind mare, but soon the press of bodies became too dense, and he was forced to dismount and continue on foot.

He threw Ellina a look over his shoulder: a silent plea.

She dismounted as well, doing her best to keep him in sight. It was not difficult. Even on foot, Venick stood a head taller than most others. He wore his usual sand-colored tunic, a winter jacket, leather boots with different colored laces. His sword was broader than most green glass weapons, heavier, the sheath as wide as Ellina's two hands cupped together.

She kept looking. Strong shoulders. The narrow taper of his hips. That hair. Venick looked like a warrior, like exactly the kind of man these people would choose as their hero. And they had chosen him. Ellina saw the way Venick's appearance set the crowd abuzz, roping the city with a band of elastic energy. People began reaching for him, wanting to touch him, shake his hand, ask for his well wishes. They did not seem to notice the lines around his eyes, the uneasy set to his mouth. Likely, the people of Hurendue would never guess that their praise made him uncomfortable, or worse—that he did not believe he deserved it.

Ellina understood why Dourin had insisted on this. Yes, it was good politics, but it was also a chance for Venick to greet the people he had helped save, to see the fruits of his efforts. *I'm a warrior first*, Venick had once said, but it could not only be battles all the time, always one after the next. There must be room for celebration, too.

They continued forward, funneling past the battle zone with its ruined catapults and blackened streets. A swath of buildings had been demolished, both by cannon and by fire, and the eastern rampart was partway crumbled. Yet Ellina could see stonemasons already at work on the walls, and lumberjacks—some of them cheerfully drunk on shared wine—hacking at the catapults with double-headed axes. The city would rebuild, and survive.

Soon, people began to notice Ellina as well, and it was not long before she was inundated with as many greetings as Venick. As the crowd closed in on her, she felt the smallest spark under her lungs, like her heart was being held to a stone grinder: the whisper of an old fear.

She caught Venick looking back at her. His face was sketched with apprehension.

He reached for her hand. His warm fingers squeezed hers. Venick was still looking at her, asking without words if she was alright, seeking the answer in her expression as if she had never regained the ability to speak.

But Ellina could speak. She could explain that she was better now, that she did not need his protection anymore, yet wanted it anyway, because his protection felt a lot like love. She imagined saying that word aloud. How his face would shift in subtle ways, darkening, turning serious. All the ways it would change things between them.

At that moment, someone pushed something soft and loose into Venick's hands. His arms came up automatically to cradle the thing to his chest. Ellina leaned forward to see what it was.

"A banehound puppy," said the owner, a thick-haired woman with a straight blade of a nose.

Venick blinked. His face went soft. "Incredible." He looked down at the sleeping banehound, which resembled a wolf pup. Jet black fur. Two pointed ears. Each pink paw pad like a little stamp. "I've only heard tales of banehounds. I never thought I'd meet one."

"She is yours."

Venick's eyes snapped up. "What?"

"A gift."

Venick stared at the woman as if she was mad. "I can't accept this."

"You saved our city."

"I didn't—"

"Our life prices are yours."

Venick pressed his mouth shut. He looked at Ellina, who asked, "Are banehounds dangerous?"

"Not dangerous," Venick said hoarsely. "Just, valuable. Rare." He spoke to the woman. "The gift is too much."

"In repayment for our lives? It is not enough." The owner was stern. "The gods require that you accept."

Venick shifted the puppy more securely against his chest, careful not to wake her. The woman—probably to prevent Venick from handing the animal back—vanished into the crowd.

Later, after they'd exited the city and remounted their steeds, Ellina asked what she did not understand.

"Banehounds are unique," Venick explained. The puppy was tucked into his jacket, her head lolling softly in sleep. "She's tiny now, but they grow to be huge and fiercely protective. They're also intelligent, but more than that…" He trailed off.

"What is it?"

"They have uncanny abilities," he admitted. "Some call them mind readers. And like I said, they're rare. Really rare." A pause. "They're an interbreed. A mix between dog and wanewolf."

"Dogs and wanewolves cannot make puppies," Ellina said. "They are two different species."

"That's what everyone thought for a long time. We were wrong. It's not common," he added. "That's the point, I think. Mostly, it does seem like dogs and wanewolves can't interbreed. But if the conditions are exactly right…" He shrugged. "You get a banehound."

Ellina looked at the puppy. Silky fur, wide black nose, little tufts between her eyes. "If what you are saying is true, she would be an outcast among her pack. Not a dog, not a wolf."

Venick surprised Ellina with a laugh. "If she's an outcast, she'll fit in here just fine."

• • •

The hound grew quickly as they traveled west, settling into her big paws. Though Ellina did not know much about puppies—elves did not keep pets—the animal was different than expected. She was not playful, nor did she show any interest in bones or sticks. Rather, she preferred to sit in silence, often switching between Venick and Ellina, leaning against their legs, staring—glaring—at any who came too close. *Fiercely protective*, Venick had said, yet the puppy was not aggressive, either, and the horses did not seem to mind her. That was curious. Had the horses encountered a true wanewolf, instinct would have sent them fleeing. But of course, the puppy was not a true wanewolf.

A mix. An interbreed of two unlikely species.

One afternoon, as Ellina was carrying her small wash bag to a nearby stream to bathe, puppy trailing at her ankles, she thought of her visit to the Secret Keeper. She recalled how Miria had led them to a little hut in the northern foothills, the wizened elf waiting within, followed by Ellina's tearful confession, her fears that Miria might not be her true sister.

People say that she acts like…like a human. But true elves do not act like humans. And if she is not an elf, she cannot be my sister.

The Secret Keeper had leaned forward. Her brow was painted with golden stars. They seemed to make her eyes shimmer.

Ellina remembered, vividly, the secret she had shared in return.

The world is not merely divided into humans and elves, the Secret Keeper had said, *just as it is not divided into day and night. There is dawn and dusk, too.*

Ellina looked at the pure black puppy that was half dog and half wanewolf.

She thought of Miria's black hair.

She thought of conjurors, and how they, too, were marked by black hair. It had long been said that only southern elves could conjure, yet had Ellina not proven this assumption false? Had she not broken the bounds of their language by learning to lie in elvish? What other rules could be broken? What rules *couldn't* be?

Humans were the original conjurors. Centuries ago, before the purge, it was humans, not elves, who bore the ability to wield magic. Elves—worried about what humans might do with such power—chose to destroy what they could not possess. They conducted the largest massacre of their era, eradicating human conjurors from the earth for good.

It was only a few years later when the first elven conjurors began to emerge. Some supposed that the magic, without human conduits, jumped to elves. Others called it coincidence. No matter which theory one believed, there was no mistaking the truth. Elves—in an ironic twist of fate—had somehow discovered the very ability they once sought to destroy.

That word, *discovered*, hung in Ellina's head like a star during the day. It drew her eye, lovely in its simplicity, but not quite right.

TWENTY-SEVEN

Y ou'll need to name her," Erol said one afternoon as they stopped to water their horses. A stream spun down through the meadow, its shallow edges bordered by young grass. Somewhere in the brush, a liralin bird chirped a high, trilling song. Their group was all gathered, the seven of them crowding around to watch the puppy sniff the water.

Venick crouched down, flicking the water's surface to entice the hound's interest. "Any ideas?"

Lin Lill—who had stubbornly chosen to ride with a broken foot rather than stay behind with the other injured soldiers—came to sit heavily on Venick's other side. "How about Big Paws? You know," she went on when the others merely stared at her, "because her paws are so big."

"Thanks, Lin," Venick said. "We'll consider that."

"You need a strong name," Traegar said. "Something she can grow into."

"But a meaningful one," Dourin added.

"There is a word in elvish," Ellina offered. "It is pronounced *bournmay*."

Venick didn't know the word. "What does it mean?"

"That depends. If a mother calls her child *bournmay*, it means my loved one. A teacher to a student means my star. If a master calls his hound *bournmay*, it simply means *mine*."

"So many options," Venick teased. "What does it mean if I call you *bournmay*?" But Ellina turned bright red, and when Venick looked around to figure out what he'd said wrong, the others all looked away.

• • •

The army moved from the road into a pasture situated on a ridge. It slowed their pace, and caused trouble for the horses carting the supply wagons, but Venick wanted the high ground. Bournmay—May, they called her—had already grown too big to ride in Venick's jacket, so she was left to trail Eywen's heels as they traversed the ridge, disappearing occasionally to find Ellina, then back again, as if drawing an invisible tether between them.

Though Venick had grown up hearing tales of banehounds' uncanny abilities, he didn't truly understand until he saw it happen.

They'd paused to rest on a hillock overlooking a village. The day was breezy, the clouds puffy and sparse. Venick sat on a low rock with a bone needle and some thread and began stitching a hole he'd discovered in the seam of his vest. He wasn't an expert sewer—really, not very good at all—but his mother had taught him the basics. *If you can't manage neat seams, at least double back on your work. It'll be strong, even if it isn't pretty.* He'd been a young man when Lira had said this, already a fighter. Impatient, and hell, ornery. He hadn't wanted to learn to sew, especially not when he could see the other boys sparring outside through his kitchen window. But Lira had insisted.

You'll be sorry when you're in the field and you can't repair your own clothes, Lira said. When Venick rolled his eyes, she'd added, *Your father knows this skill.*

Your father. Those had always been the magic words, and Lira knew it—Venick wanted to know anything General Atlas knew. After that, he'd been nothing but attentive to Lira's lesson.

Now, Venick squinted past the shadows his own hands were making and threaded the needle, stabbed the cloth. The task—and the day, the balmy breeze, so much like Irek's weather—brought his memories to life. That kitchen, with its decorative plates hanging on the walls. The clock, which chimed off schedule. The worn table, where his mother had spread her sewing supplies, explaining the purpose of each item. Even given everything that had happened since then, even after his mother's death and his banishment, after killing his own father in that very kitchen…it was a nice memory. Venick smiled a little, wishing Ellina was nearby so that he could tell her the story. It was something he wanted to share.

Venick finished his patching, then held the vest up to the light. Gods, it *wasn't* pretty. But it would hold.

As Venick was packing away his supplies, Bournmay appeared over the ridge, pulling a bewildered Ellina by the sleeve. Venick was instantly alarmed. "What—?"

"I don't know," Ellina replied breathlessly. "She just started whining, but May never whines. Then she began tugging at my clothes. I thought—" Ellina pushed back her hair, which had blown into her face. "I thought something must have happened to you."

"I'm fine," Venick said quickly, eyeing the banehound.

"What is it?"

"I think…well." He cleared his throat. "I was wishing you were here with me. May must have known," he continued, trying for lighthearted-ness and mostly failing. "She could feel it. Sense it, somehow."

They quieted. Bournmay looked between them with bright yellow eyes, placated now that she'd brought them together.

Venick breathed a laugh. "You're as persistent as Ellina," he told the hound, who gave a single thump of her tail. Venick peeked back at El-lina. "Is this what it feels like to be *geleeshi*?"

Ellina's answering smile was small, but quickly growing into some-thing larger, big enough to hold Venick's question and all its implica-tions. "Let's not ask Dourin." Her voice was halting, and not just from disuse. Timid. But pleased, too. "He will tease us mercilessly, and we will never hear the end of it."

· · ·

The terrain grew rocky as the army continued east, winding over Heartshire Bay's northernmost finger before angling up towards the border. As they retook the road, several elves pulled Dourin into con-versation. They wanted to hear the story of how he had wooed the highland's most powerful man into handing over as luxurious a gift as three hundred thoroughbred horses. Dourin motioned at himself, grin-ning devilishly. "Is it not obvious?"

Traegar was there. He and Venick rode in silence beneath an egg-blue sky. Traegar watched Dourin from the corner of his eye, his gaze drawn back and then back again, as if against his will.

Venick said, "You could summon away his horses. Might shut that mouth of his."

Traegar shook out a smile. "Dourin would never forgive me if I made him look the fool."

"Have you forgiven *him*?"

The elf pushed a hand through his wavy hair, let the locks fall forward again. "I will never regain my status within *Evenshina*, the elven Healer's Academy. I have been blackmarked by all practicing members. It is Dourin's fault." Traegar sighed. "But it is mine, too. Dourin has always been forthcoming. He knows what he wants and asks for it. I am not like that. I have known him nearly all my life, yet I was never brave enough to express my feelings."

"Dourin isn't blind," Venick argued. "And it's like you said—you grew up together. He should have known how you felt."

"Should have, but did not. Dourin is explicit. He needed me to be explicit. When I was not, he made his own assumptions, and grew hurt, and wielded his hurt like a weapon. He informed the *Evenshina* about the illegal experiments Erol and I were conducting. Erol suffered no consequences—he is human, and was therefore never a member of the *Evenshina*. My career, on the other hand, was ruined. And yet," Traegar lifted one shoulder, "I ended up forging a different path. And Dourin and I understand each other better now."

"You undid your past wrongs?"

Traegar's brow quirked, not so much in amusement as in awareness of Venick's true reasons for asking. "We did not undo them. We learned to accept them, to understand that they are a part of us." Traegar tracked a bird gliding overhead. "That was half of it."

"And the other half?"

"I said things that long needed to be said. I forgave Dourin. And most of all, I forgave myself."

• • •

The next time they stopped to rest, Venick found Ellina sitting with Bournmay at the base of a lone tree. The broad leaves dappled her face, creating a collage of sun and shadow. He came to sit beside her and uncorked his canteen.

Ellina frowned. "Did you boil that water?"

"It came from the stream."

"So you didn't."

"No one's going to poison the entire stream."

"Venick."

"Fine," he sighed, recorking the flask. "Let me have yours."

She pulled out her canteen and handed it over. Venick was aware of the way she watched him flick open the cap, set his mouth to the rim. He paused. Raised his brows.

Ellina said, "Dourin has told me his concerns about the Elder."

Venick lowered the canteen. "You think the Elder will try to intervene?"

"Truthfully, I am surprised he has not tried already. He does not have the power to stop us directly, but he could attempt to persuade his daughter to rejoin him. And yet…"

"You don't think Harmon would."

"No."

"Even after she lied to us. To you."

Ellina gripped Bournmay's tail, gently swung it back and forth in the mime of a wag. The banehound eyed Ellina but did not pull away. "Harmon has much to answer for. I do not know why she lied to us, though I think whatever the reason, Harmon…believes in herself. She believes that whatever she chooses is the right thing. Or, let me rephrase that. She believes that winning this war is the right thing, and that any decisions she makes to that end must be good, because they are guided by those morals. She told me about her relationship with the Elder."

"That day we fought the coven. When you saved her life."

Ellina nodded. "She loves him, even if they do not see eye to eye. He is her only living family, and she took a big risk by moving against him. It would not make sense for her to quit now."

"People do things that don't make sense all the time."

Ellina's mouth lifted. "So I have seen."

Venick scowled. "And elves. Elves do, too."

"Untrue. Elves are perfectly rational."

"Overly analytical."

"They make no mistakes."

"They're obsessed with rules."

Ellina plucked back her canteen. "Humans could learn a thing or two."

• • •

Three days later, the city of Kenath emerged in the distance: a dense, grey pebble.

"I feel like we've done this before," Venick mused.

"Hmm," was all Ellina said.

Like a plainsland city, Kenath was built on a river, a wide valley to the south, hills to the north, buildings stacked on either side. But Kenath wasn't a plainsland city—it was a border city, set across the invisible boundary between the elflands and the mainlands and one of the few places where, during Queen Rishiana's reign, elves and men had been allowed to meet freely.

They rode closer. Venick, Ellina, Erol, Traegar, and Dourin took up the army's head, Bournmay sliding like a shadow between them. As they approached the city, more details emerged: the watchtowers, the streets, the rust-and-slate buildings. Kenath looked like Venick remembered, save for one, glaring difference.

A ring of soldiers encircled the city's perimeter. These weren't mere troopers on patrol—this was a veritable *barricade* of bodies, all human, and highlander, if the color of their uniforms was any indication. The soldiers stood shoulder-to-shoulder, six people deep, everyone armed with crossbows…

Which came up at the sight of Venick's party.

Venick tugged Eywen to a stop. Held up his hand to order a halt, then glanced sideways at Ellina, who had shut her expression down to near-blankness. Still, when they crossed stares, Venick knew she was thinking what he was thinking.

Harmon had retaken control of this city. Those were her warriors. So what did it mean that they were barring Venick's entrance with their crossbows trained on his heart, hundreds of arrows watching him like eyes?

"We should dismount," Erol suggested, "to show that we are not a threat."

"We should turn back," Dourin corrected, "and forget this entire plan."

"We cannot turn back," Traegar said, exasperated. "Those are our own men."

Venick was already swinging out of his saddle. "I'll go."

"Not alone," Ellina replied. "We are coming with you."

As they walked down the uneven hillside and approached the line of bodies, the crossbows didn't lower. Venick relaxed his shoulders, un-clenched jaw, doing his best to don the countenance of a man whose heart wasn't sitting in his throat. He counted one breath, two, before a headless voice said, "Stand down. It's the Commander."

A gap appeared in the bodies. Venick recognized the man who emerged through it: a middle-aged highlander named Oppan, short in height but wide in girth, with a handlebar mustache that tended to flap when he spoke. Oppan was one of Harmon's captains.

"Commander," said Captain Oppan. "Apologies for the—ah—wel-come. The men are under orders."

"To shoot their fellows?" Dourin asked dryly.

"We had to be sure you were who you appeared to be. Can't be too careful these days. Kenath's wall was destroyed during our fight for the city. We haven't yet had time to build a new one."

"Oh, I don't know," Dourin went on in that same, parched tone. "It looks like you've built a new one to me."

Oppan looked confused. "Sir?"

"Let us in," Venick said.

"The soldiers will need to be searched. And the wagons."

"For what?" Dourin seemed unable to contain himself. "Weapons? You may not have noticed, but we are an *army*."

"Not weapons," Oppan replied. "Messages. Or symbols. The Dark Queen's spies have been known to carry black and red jewelry…"

"Oh, for love of the gods."

"It's fine," Venick said, shaking his head at Dourin in a silent *lay off*. "Do your search."

"And—apologies, sir. But your friends must be searched as well. You, of course, are exempt…"

"I speak for them," Venick said, with a prick of his own annoyance.

"You don't need to search these four."

Oppan shifted his weight. "It is protocol."

"And I am overruling it."

"You cannot…"

"This is the Commander," Dourin snapped. This time, Venick didn't intervene. "He outranks you, so he can, in fact—"

"Come now." Erol stepped between the three of them, hands upraised. Venick blinked back into his body, his irritation swirling away. Dourin looked similarly disoriented, as if he'd been shaken. "Let them do their search," Erol continued in that same, soothing voice. "It won't take long."

Venick moved aside as Captain Oppan called several more men out of formation to help pat the others down. When Oppan tried to step forward to search Ellina, however, Bournmay shoved her body between them, lips pulled back in a silent growl. The hound, though young, had grown at a frightening pace, her wide, boxy head already reaching Ellina's hip.

Oppan eyed Bournmay uneasily. "Is that…?"

"A banehound."

"I see," he said, and nothing else.

"Captain?"

"Yes, right." He dipped a nod at Ellina. "You are…also exempt." He snapped his fingers, and once again, a gap appeared in the bodies. Then, to Venick: "Your soldiers should find beds where they can. Space is limited, but we're making do. As for you, I've been instructed to escort you straight to the Mistress Commander. Your bride is anxious to see you, sir. She has been awaiting your arrival."

• • •

"Venick." Harmon motioned him into the brothel's workroom from her spot at the desk on its opposite side. "You made it."

Venick stepped into the room, which was one part office and two parts lingerie closet. He'd nearly laughed when Oppan first revealed the location their Mistress Commander had chosen as her headquarters. Turned that laugh into a cough at the last second, nearly choking on his own saliva for the effort.

Keep it together.

No easy task, given Venick's memories of this place. But of course, Harmon couldn't have known that this was the same brothel where Venick and Ellina had taken refuge from a band of conjurors last summer. And Venick couldn't have known that Harmon was old friends with the brothel's mistress, a fair-haired woman named Fryva who, unfortunately, remembered Venick.

"So you're the Commander," Fryva had said when he'd arrived in the brothel's antechamber. Her lips hooked a frozen smile, her eyes two icy pools. "Isn't that something."

Now, Venick listened to the *snick* of the door shutting closed behind him as Oppan exited the workroom, leaving Venick alone with his fake bride, surrounded by lace panties and garter belts.

Venick stayed by the door. "We need to talk."

"Of course," Harmon agreed easily, rifling through a stack of parchment spread out before her. She looked at ease in a tunic and trousers, her smooth hands nimble as they shuffled paper. "Much has happened since our—"

"You lied to me."

Harmon's hands stilled. She lifted her eyes. "Did I?"

"You forged a letter from your father back in Igor. You said Dourin was dead."

"I never said that to *you*."

Venick locked his jaw. "Are we really going to play that game?"

"I'm not playing."

"You let me believe Ellina wanted to stay behind when we went east," he snapped, at last leaving his spot by the door to stride forward. "And you lied to *her*. You pretended a letter had come from Parith, that her best friend was dead. From the looks of it, you even went so far as to intercept our messages, cutting off all communication between Dourin and us." Venick's voice, which had been steadily rising, reached its full volume. "How? How could you do that?"

"I did it for your own good."

The air whooshed out of his lungs. "My *what*?"

"Your own good," Harmon repeated, pressing her hands to the top of the desk. "And for Ellina's own good, too."

"You're going to have to break that down for me."

"I mean, *really*. The two of you were a catastrophe. You, because you were so preoccupied by her, and her, because she wasn't ready to join us. She should never have come to Igor in the first place, and being around you was only making things worse. So I...helped a little."

Venick gave a disbelieving laugh. "You meddled."

"I thought that if Ellina believed Dourin was dead, she would go to Parith. Once she was there, she'd realize he was still alive, that there'd been a mistake. But the time apart would have been good for you. For us. This war."

Venick didn't think he could be any more furious. "Reeking gods, Harmon. Ellina didn't go to Parith. She tried to catch up to us instead. Only, she was stranded in Igor, so to make up for lost time, she swam the Taro." The words, like dust in his throat. "It nearly killed her."

It wasn't often that he could render Harmon speechless. Wide eyes, round mouth, utter astonishment. "I didn't know she would do that."

"And somehow, you're still not sorry."

"No, Venick, I'm not. When we set out for war, I promised to do whatever I could to win. To protect my people. My father, too, even if he'll never see it that way. So yes, if that meant deceiving you for the good of our cause, then that's what I had to do."

"You couldn't have talked to me about this?"

"And said what?"

"I don't know." Venick threw up his hands. "Anything would have been better than the lie."

"Really? You lie all the time for the greater cause. You're lying to half a world right now about our engagement."

"Yeah, well, the engagement is off."

"The engagement was already off."

"The fake engagement."

Harmon rolled her eyes. "Now you're just being petulant."

"I'm not doing it anymore, Harmon. All this deception—you're right. It's too much. The engagement has served its purpose, but I'm putting it to an end."

"Because of Ellina."

"Because I'm *done*."

"We need this—"

"We don't need it!" Venick burst. "Maybe we did at first, but I've seen our warriors battle together. I've seen them learn from each other, adopt each other's ways, form relationships. They don't need us to hold them together anymore. They've already figured out that their differences are less significant than what they have in common. Let's not pretend that's not *worth something*."

For the second time in as many minutes, Harmon looked perfectly stunned. There was a long moment when she merely stared at him, chin pulled back, fingers gripping the desk's edge. Then: "I can see you feel strongly about this."

"I do."

"Is there nothing I can say to change your mind?"

"No."

Harmon gathered her papers, tapping them against the desk to line up their edges. Venick expected her to storm by, maybe spit names at him on her way out, so he was surprised—hell, baffled—when instead she came to sit on the front of the desk, her expression one of casual diplomacy. "We've retaken the city, as you've seen. It took two days, and cost us a fair number of lives, but—why are you looking at me like that?"

"Because." Venick continued to eye her. "That's it?"

"That's what?"

"We're just going to move straight to strategy? No argument? No big speech?"

"I think you've given enough speeches today for the both of us. But no, Venick. I'm not going to argue with you, and I'm certainly not going to bind you against your will. If you want to quit faking our engagement, we will." That was guilt in her eyes, easier to pinpoint now, having seen her guilt before. She blew out a breath. "I really am sorry for what happened to Ellina. I couldn't have known about the river. I'll have to apologize to her. Again. And just when I was beginning to think she didn't absolutely hate me."

It wasn't Venick's place to speak for Ellina, especially not anymore. And selfishly, a part of Venick wanted Harmon to believe she was despised, to suffer some consequence for her lies. Gods knew *they* had suffered.

This is bigger than you.

Venick found himself sighing, too. He was still angry with Harmon. He couldn't trust her not to make more foolish choices for the greater good. But continuing to argue about it wouldn't solve anything. It was like Dourin said: they needed each other.

"Ellina doesn't hate you."

"No." Harmon gave a self-deprecating shake of her head. "She only thinks I'm completely evil."

Venick set his hands loosely to his hips, squinted up at the ceiling. He studied a wobbly crack in the plaster and thought of things like redemption sacrifices and murdered parents and second chances. "You've made some stupid choices, Harmon." Another sigh. "That doesn't make you evil. Only flawed. Just like the rest of us."

TWENTY-EIGHT

Ellina did a quick sweep of the city, starting at the outer edge
and working her way in. Bournmay trotted at her side, nose to
the road, black coat rippling in the spring breeze.

Ellina was glad for Bournmay's presence, especially there, especially
then. It was strange to be back in this city. To remember the last time she
had come here, when she was still legion-bound, and Venick was no one
to her but a ragged outlaw. She felt the memories weave into her vision
of this place, catching on the similarities…and the differences.

Battle had clearly taken place here. There was little left of the old
market, the scene a mess of splinters and fragmented armor. Ellina saw
a steel sword, snapped in half. Arrows, protruding from wood. Grey
buildings and grey people, who were busy sorting through the debris,
shoveling crumbled stone, trying to coax the space back into some semblance of normal. As Ellina turned towards the city's central inn, her
eyes skated from the workers down to their shadows, though this was

more out of habit than any true concern. Ellina did not care how wily the conjurors had become—the idea that anyone might sneak a corpse through Kenath's warrior wall was ludicrous.

As they turned towards the central district, Bournmay worked her head up under Ellina's hand. The banehound was a predator by nature, often quiet, never nipping or wiggling. This—her head seeking to comfort, or perhaps to be comforted—was rare. Ellina pushed her fingers through Bournmay's thick fur, encouraging the sentiment.

The inn had begun as a simple block of human masonry, meant to house passing travelers. Further work had wrought the building taller, wider, with additional details done in the elven style. Vendors and merchants lined its width, their stalls encircling the structure like rays around the sun. This section of Kenath was livelier than the rest of the city, everyone more at ease out of sight of the battle's destruction.

When Ellina entered the inn's wide, low-ceilinged great room, Dourin was the first to spot her. He tossed her a smile, tipping his head towards where he, Traegar, Branton, and Erol had pulled their chairs into a circle. The inn was busy but not crowded, groups of people milling about. There was a fireplace burning merrily on one wall. An enormous rug woven in iziri goat fur that was coarse, but better than cold stone. Mugs in everyone's hands.

Ellina moved to claim the seat beside Dourin, pulling Bournmay into the space between her knees.

"It's interesting," Erol said, breaking off his conversation with Traegar to turn his eyes on Ellina. "That hound answers to both you and Venick."

"Is that not normal?"

"Banehounds are meant to serve only one master. And…" Erol's pause was brief, but unmistakable, "only humans."

"What Harmon has done here is ingenious," Lin Lill interrupted, appearing with a cane under one arm, her splinted foot thunking with every step. She plopped into the chair opposite Erol, ignoring the way he scowled at her injury. "The city is quite secure."

"Who resplinted your foot?" Erol asked.

"I would have never thought to use bodies to create a wall," Lin Lill continued, ignoring the healer. "The elven legion does not have those kinds of numbers. You humans, on the other hand—"

"Was it an *eondghi*?" Erol pressed.

Lin Lill sighed. "Does it matter?"

"The wrapping is all crooked. You should let me…"

"The wrapping is fine, old man. Now, as I was saying—the wall. I am impressed."

"Lin is impressed?"

The voice was Venick's. Ellina looked up to see him entering the great room with Harmon at his side. As the pair moved forward, Venick caught Ellina's eye and gave a small, encouraging nod, which Ellina could not interpret. Harmon's expression, on the other hand, was clear. She looked like someone had dropped a spider down her shirt.

There were not enough chairs for everyone, so Traegar stood, shuffling into the way of a nearby group of soldiers to offer Harmon his seat, ignoring Dourin's good-natured, *Such a gentleman.* Harmon, however, did not sit.

"Ellina." The woman squirmed. "I was wondering if we could…"

Bournmay let out a snarl.

"May," Ellina reprimanded, feeling the banehound's hackles puff under her fingers. Ellina was not exactly happy with Harmon, either, but for Bournmay to—

Traegar choked out a gasp.

Dourin said, "*No.*"

Then: a beat of silence that lasted an eternity.

It took Ellina the entire length of that beat to understand what had happened. She saw Dourin's stricken face, the way he mouthed, *Traegar, Traegar.* She saw the dagger protruding from Traegar's back. And she saw the elven corpse—empty eyes, jaw hanging—that had put it there.

The room broke into a frenzy. Bournmay lunged forward, gripping the corpse's arm between her powerful jaws. There was an awful *snap.* The distinct sound of muscle tearing. As the banehound worked to relieve the corpse of its arm, Venick rushed in, gripping the undead by the head, his fingers digging under its jaw. The creature fought back, windmilling its free arm, but it had already sunk its only weapon into Traegar, who lay motionless on the floor.

"Impossible," Harmon was saying, her voice swallowed by the havoc. "That's *impossible.*"

The corpse—besides the blank eyes, and the network of blue veins peeling over cheekbones and forehead—looked disturbingly lively. There were no visible signs of damage, no hint as to how the elf had died. The male himself had been young, barely out of his fledgling years, unremarkably dressed, hair done in a simple braid. Ellina could have passed him on her way in and never looked twice.

The corpse snarled wordlessly, alien sounds sliding past Ellina's ears as Venick continued to haul its body backward. Others moved to help, some twenty soldiers all crushing together as they dragged the corpse outside. One man yanked a torch off the wall on his way out. The smell of burning flesh permeated the air.

But…Traegar.

Dourin was bent over Traegar's body, making fists of his shirt. "Come back," he cried, pressing his forehead to Traegar's chest. "Traegar, come back.'"

Ellina felt her breath trickle to a mere wheeze, then cease. She was not rendered numb by the scene. Shock did not save her from the moment. She was crushed, instantly, by the horror of what had happened.

She spun on Harmon. "Save him," she demanded.

"Ellina…"

"Save him," she repeated, swinging her gaze to Erol. But the healer was grim.

"There's nothing we can do," Harmon said.

"There is always something you can do."

"It doesn't work like that."

"You saved Dourin. In Parith. After the attack. His wound—he told me. He should not have survived that first night. He would not have, except for you. So do it again."

"I'm so sorry, Ellina." Harmon was shaking her head. "It's too late. Traegar is already gone."

Ellina wanted to lift her hand to block Harmon's words. She wanted to go to Dourin, to comfort him as Venick had once comforted her. But a terrible feeling rooted her to the spot, reaching up like vines to trap her legs. "He can't." Ellina's throat clicked. Her tongue was too dry. She could not get enough air. "He can't just be gone."

The smell of burning flesh dissipated. Outside, the clear, bright day mocked them. Dourin's agony was a melody, begging Traegar back.

• • •

Ellina sat on the inn's rooftop overlooking the crumbled section of Kenath's wall, and beyond that, the tight barricade of soldiers.

She hated those soldiers. She hated how they were like a mirage, creating a false vision of safety. She especially hated how—even after allowing a living corpse into the city—they continued to stand sentry, as if they had not already proven their worthlessness.

Venick appeared. He pulled himself up the rickety trellis and onto the roof, cursing softly as his clothing caught the dry twigs. Night had descended. Venick's face was a dark landscape. Behind him, the city's lights slowly blinked out, its residents settling in for sleep.

Venick said nothing at first, simply pulled her into his arms.

It had been painful, wrapping Traegar's body in cloth, carrying him to the gravesite. Elves did not perform burial rites, but it felt wrong to simply leave Traegar in the ground without ceremony, so Venick had helped improvise. He showed Dourin how to wave incense over the body, which gods might be appeased by which scents. How to mix rose petals with water, where to sprinkle the liquid. Dourin had remained silent throughout the ceremony, allowing Venick to speak in his place. After the others had retreated, Ellina watched Dourin sink to his knees in the freshly dug earth, bow his head, and grip the stone that had been placed over Traegar's grave. She had intended to wait for him, but he stayed like that for so long that Ellina began to suspect he was waiting for her to leave, so she had.

Traegar's death was worse than his death alone, because Ellina felt it through Dourin, like a refracted mirror. Grief for a loss, and grief for the one who grieved.

Venick's voice was hoarse when he said, "That dagger was meant for me."

Venick's habit of self-blame was familiar, but this time, Ellina could not deny it. That dagger *had* been meant for Venick. The corpse-bender, whoever they were, had misaimed, likely because they were wielding their magic from outside the city.

"I believed we were secure," Venick went on. "Those soldiers. That wall."

"That is what we all thought."

"I just don't understand. How are the corpse-benders doing it?"

It was the worst kind of mystery, one with an answer that sounded too much like magic. But conjuring was not mere magic. It was not unexplainable. There was always a process, a series of events that could be traced and understood.

"If the conjurors can attack us here," Venick said, "they can attack us anywhere. None of us are safe. Not our soldiers, not the citizens."

Ellina hugged her knees and gazed up into the dark sky. Three times now, the conjurors had managed to infiltrate their defenses, first sneaking past the night's watch outside Igor, then by the guards in the banquet hall, and now here, through a fortified wall of highlanders. Each time, the corpses had been fairly unremarkable. No significant features. No wounds, either, to explain how the elves had died.

Ellina went still.

Venick noticed. He leaned back a bit, as if trying to better see her face, which must have been as shadowed to him as his was to her. "Ellina?"

"The corpses were all in perfect condition," she said softly.

"I suppose…"

"And all recently dead," she went on. "No decay. Fresh blood, when we cut them open. The undead were not dug up from gravesites, not like the ones I first saw in the palace crypts. The conjurors wanted new bodies. But how did they die?"

"How does anyone die?" He brushed his hands on his trousers. "A knife to the throat usually does it."

"There were no wounds."

Minceflesh works quickly, Erol had explained. *From the outside, you cannot tell what has gone wrong.*

Ellina was pushing to her feet, her body pitching to match the angle of the roof. She remembered hunting for Venick's goblet in the baron's kitchen, holding it up to the light, discovering minceflesh in the wine dregs. The squeeze of vindication, that her hunch had been confirmed. A waterfall of relief, that Venick had not drunk from the cup.

Yet Ellina remembered that goblet had not really belonged to Venick. The banquet toast had been unplanned. That jeweled cup was plucked from a guest's fingers—a guest who had already taken a sip.

Ellina had gone hunting for proof that someone was trying to poison Venick, and she had found it. She believed the conjurors were sneaking living corpses into their midst from the outside, and that these two dangers were unrelated. But what if she was looking for the wrong thing?

Ellina remembered Harmon's argument that corpse-benders would not choose to attack in a packed ballroom unless they had no other option…or needed the cover of a crowd.

She remembered Erol's words. *We are lucky no one has yet been harmed.*

Ellina's mouth dropped open. "I know how the conjurors are doing it."

TWENTY-NINE

So you are saying that the conjurors are not sneaking the corpses through our defenses," Lin Lill started. "They are poisoning our own soldiers, waiting for them to die, and using those bodies to attack?"

Ellina had roused the others from their beds and gathered them in the inn's great room. Without commenting on it, they each claimed their prior seats, leaving Traegar's chair empty, and Dourin's, too. Harmon remained standing.

"It makes sense," Lin Lill continued. "All along, we thought the conjurors were slipping corpses past our guards when in truth they were merely sneaking poison past—a much easier feat."

"It also explains the purpose of the minceflesh," Erol agreed. "It's the only poison strong enough to kill an elf. We assumed that these two threats—the undead attackers and the minceflesh—were unrelated. We thought an assassin was in our midst, maybe even living among us, trying to poison Venick. But the minceflesh was not for Venick at all, at least not directly. It was being used to create corpses."

"That still does not explain how no one recognized the corpses," Branton argued. "If I was a soldier, I would notice if one of my fellows became an undead."

"In the elven legion where troops remain small, yes," Ellina replied. "But we are an enormous resistance. Many of our elven fighters are wildings, or from small villages in the far north and east. It would be easy for a lone soldier to go missing."

"And," Harmon added, "even if the victims did have friends who might recognize them, the corpses have always been destroyed quick-ly—dismembered or burned—before anyone could have a chance to identify them."

"A weapon that must be destroyed in order to be defeated." Erol did not seem put off by this revelation, but rather impressed, as if this was another one of his experiments. "We have been erasing the enemy's evidence for them."

Ellina imagined it: the way the conjurors would have planned ahead, slipping into the kitchens to poison a cup at random or confiscating a canteen when a soldier was not watching, then waiting for the unknow-ing victim to get close to the Commander, and to drink. The poison would need to be fast-working, yet subtle enough that the soldier did not appear to be dying. Then the conjuror would take control of the body and attack.

"We must alert the city," Lin Lill said. "All water sources need to be searched, the ale and wine poured out."

Harmon made a skeptical noise. "The citizens will be up in arms about that."

"The citizens should be thankful. We are saving them from a grue-some end. And they are lucky, too, that we discovered the truth now, before the conjurors grew tired of waiting and decided to start poisoning the entire water supply."

"I believe that is unlikely," Erol said. "Minceflesh is difficult to procure. The conjurors likely do not have much of it. Even if they did have enough to poison the entire water supply, it would dilute the toxin. It might not have the desired effect."

"On elves," Lin Lill emphasized. "But humans, being weaker—"

"Here we go again," Harmon groaned.

"What?" Lin Lill gave an innocent shrug. "Most poisons *will* kill humans but not elves. For those few rare poisons that can harm an elf, it only makes sense that a larger dose would be needed to achieve the same effect."

"I should invent a poison that works the other way around," Harmon said, "just to shut you up."

"Actually," Erol admitted, "I already did."

Everyone looked at him.

"That was the project Traegar and I spent years working on together," he explained. "We created a poison that could kill elves, but not humans. We named it lace powder due to the toxin's dust-like properties. That was the key. Lace powder is not ingested like most poisons, but rather blown into the air. It is inhaled."

Ellina was stunned. "Why have I never heard of this?"

"Well." Erol scratched his neck. "It was the experiment that got Traegar expelled from the Healer's Academy. All records of it were destroyed."

The room fell quiet.

Erol said, "One of us should check on Dourin."

"Allow me," Lin Lill said.

"No offense, Lin," Venick said, "but Dourin might need someone a little less…abrasive."

"I'll go," Harmon offered.

"Ah." Venick gave an uncomfortable smile. "Thanks, Harmon, but when I said we needed someone less abrasive—"

"I can do it," Branton interrupted. He spoke quietly, in a way that reminded Ellina that Branton, too, had recently lost someone he cared for. Artis was his best friend. "I know what to say."

Branton left. The others stayed a while longer, discussing their plan to protect the citizens from further poisonings, but eventually exhaustion won out, and they called it a night. Venick was slow to leave, touching Ellina's shoulder as he passed. The look on his face nearly had Ellina hurrying after him, but she made herself stay. Unlike the others, she was not quite finished.

Soon, she and Erol were the only two remaining.

"There is something that I do not understand," Ellina said.

Erol waited.

"You knew Traegar before he was expelled from the Healer's Academy."

"I did," Erol acknowledged.

"That was over a hundred years ago."

Erol studied his fingers. Through the window behind him, the moon was bright. It glowed against the back of his chair. "Yes, it was."

"Humans cannot live that long."

"Most humans cannot."

Ellina saw Erol's perfectly white robes. His slim, clean hands. She remembered the times he had tended her wounds and the wounds of others, how his presence brought a sense of peace, the way fights tended to fizzle when he was around. She thought about his relationship with her mother, and what kind of man could have caught the attention of the elven queen.

Ellina thought about how she no longer believed in impossibilities.

She said, "You are a conjuror."

Erol's smile matched the moon: soft, yet still bright. "A human one."

"But, the purge…"

"Did you think elves eradicated all human conjurors? They decimated our ranks, certainly, but many of us escaped into hiding. We have been there ever since."

Despite having guessed this, Ellina was astounded. "If there have been human conjurors among us all along, where are they? They could be helping us fight."

"Our numbers are few. And we do not fight. Didn't you know? Human conjurors were masters of the earth, able to shape rock and stone. We could pull minerals from the ground, lift wells, unearth plants with medicinal properties. Historically, we were builders, or healers." Erol leaned to the side, resting an elbow against the chair's armrest. "My people live nomadic lives in the mountains now. They survive off the land. Herd goats."

Ellina remembered something Venick had once said to her. "Iziri goats?"

"Yes, actually."

Ellina shifted in her seat. The cushion was old, the leather torn in places. It creaked a little as she said, "You spent a lot of time in the elflands with Traegar."

"Yes."

"And my mother."

"Her, too."

"But if you knew Traegar for all those years, and my mother, then you must have also known my father."

Erol blinked down at his knees. "I knew Rishiana's bondmate, yes."

Ellina studied Erol's face. Deep lines, straight nose, those almond-shaped eyes. "You switched my words," she said. "That is not what I asked."

He appeared distracted. "What's that?"

"I asked if you knew my father."

Erol's smile was different now, caught between two places. "Indeed, you did."

Ellina thought of the cove Venick had described from his boyhood, and how he and his friends used to climb the nearby rocks, daring each other to jump from greater and greater heights. She felt like that. She felt like she was about to dive off a new peak, that the hunch that had been growing within her since last summer would soon be confirmed, or denied. This was the moment when Ellina would toss her question from the cliff, and listen to the sound it made as it hit the water below.

"My life has been nothing but a series of lies," she said. "Some of those lies were the kind I used to tell myself, because I was afraid. Others were truths that have been withheld from me. My mother kept secrets—about why she really created the border, why she fought with her sister Ara, why she wanted to initiate Miria early into queenhood. I think you know those secrets, and now, I would like you to share them with me."

As Erol considered her, Ellina's suspicion continued to grow. Fragile. Hard to look at. Harder, to know that this man had the answer to so many of her life's mysteries, and that if he trusted her enough, he might be willing to share them.

At last, Erol gave his reply. "As you wish."

• • •

When the night reached its peak, Ellina set Bournmay out into the city to hunt for rats and rabbits, then went to find Venick. She had so much to tell him. Yet when she ventured to the inn's second floor and knocked on his door at the hall's end, there was no answer.

She tried the door. It was open.

Ellina entered the small space, which was strewn with his things, everything dropped in a rush, most of his bags yet to be unpacked. She moved to the balls of her feet, then realized that her desire to move quietly felt too much like snooping and dropped back onto her heels. She walked deliberately across the room. The floorboards groaned.

Hesitating, yet remembering the way Venick had touched her shoulder earlier, and finding confidence in that, she perched on his bed to wait.

Time slid by. He did not appear.

Ellina told herself not to worry. Most likely, Venick was with Dourin, or back on the inn's roof. Maybe he was waiting for her somewhere as she waited for him. Yet when the moon began its descent and Venick still had not appeared, Ellina could no longer ignore her concern. She stood. There was a cloud of anxiety in her stomach.

She would set up a search party. They would scour this inn, the city, the entire continent if they must. Ellina grabbed her coat, marched out the door—

And straight into Venick.

She reeled. "Where have you been?"

He looked down at his hands, which held a basket of food.

"You went *shopping?*"

"Well." A shrug. "I was hungry."

"It's the middle of the night."

"There's a market," Venick said. Then, seeing her agitation. "I paid for this. We won't be one of those armies who demands free room and board."

"I was about to gather a search party."

He started to smile, then realized she was serious. He bit his lip, hoisting the basket in offering. "Can I make it up to you?"

Ellina stepped backward into his room, and Venick followed, shutting the door behind them. As he moved to set the food on a low table, Ellina became aware of how small his quarters were, and how much space Venick seemed to occupy in comparison.

She slid away to open the window. A breeze rushed in, dissipating his scent.

He moved up behind her. "Are you angry?"

"I wish you had told me where you went. I thought—" She kept her back to him, fiddling unnecessarily with the window's clasp. "I thought you might have—" She could not say it.

"Hey," he said, catching her elbow. "I'm fine."

She turned to face him. "You need to be careful."

"Bournmay was with me."

"She cannot protect you from everything."

Venick's gaze darted between Ellina's eyes, the room's low-lit fire gilding his face. "I understand that you were worried."

"Of course I was worried."

"It's been a long few days. Everything that's happened. It would make anyone anxious."

"I was worried because I love you."

He froze. His expression folded in on itself. "You didn't mean to say that."

"Yes," she said. "I did."

His gaze came back to hers. The moment was like an empty glass, open to whatever Ellina might pour into it. She thought of all her missed chances. Her voice, lost and then returned. Her heart broken open, but sweetly, sweetly.

Ellina set a hand to Venick's chest. His pulse was wild. Hers was, too. She could not quite keep her voice from shaking as she said, "I never explained what happened that day, after the everpool."

"No," he said. "You didn't."

"Did you know," she started, spreading her fingers wide, "that the first time I lied in elvish was the day of your trial? I had been practicing. I knew about the rumors. Elves were talking about us. I worried what that might mean for you. That day in the stateroom, I was terrified..."

"Of what would happen if you were discovered," Venick finished.

"No." Ellina shook her head. "No, Venick. I was terrified of what would happen if *you* were discovered. The everpool. That kiss. All the things you had just admitted to me about...about how you felt. What if they made you say it in elvish? My mother forbade humans from pursuing elves. That was law, punishable by death. I thought I was going to watch you die." A hard swallow. "You once told me that if you died, I would be fine. That's not true." She closed her fingers, fisting his shirt, and said it again. "That's not true."

She continued speaking. She told him everything. How difficult those first lies had been, how painful. The way she had lied again on Traegar's balcony to prevent the conjuror Youvan from discovering Venick's secrets. Later, on Irek's beach, how she had tried to tell Venick the truth about her. How everything had gone so wrong.

Venick listened to her story without interruption. She might have kept talking, continuing her seemingly endless list of recountings and regrets, except at some point, she caught the look on Venick's face. His expression had changed. Ellina thought of how a stained-glass window changes, seemingly unremarkable at night, but glorious with the dawn.

Her voice trailed away.

Venick reached a slow hand to touch her face. When Ellina did not pull away, he closed the remaining distance between them, slanting his lips over hers.

A noise, deep in his chest. His hands, everywhere: at her hips, her ribs, the back of her thighs. Then he was speaking, too, whispering against her neck all the things he wanted, the things he needed. Her. Now.

Her answer came on a breathless exhale. Venick pulled back a little, toying with the hem of her shirt before lifting the material up and away. Then his shirt was gone as well, and they were stumbling towards the thin mattress, peeling off more layers, lips coming to skin. Ellina's head was hazy. She thought, blurrily, that she should try to focus, try to re-member these details, but her mind could only offer meaningless words, like *ah* and *here* and *this, this*.

She stopped trying to think. She found an old scar on the back of his hand, traced the pink ridge with her open mouth. Venick watched her do this, color rising to his neck. He seemed torn between the desire to study her and the desire to drag her mouth back to his. His torment was a pleasure. Hers was, too.

As his weight finally settled over her and Ellina's cheeks pinkened and he moved inside her, Ellina was glad that words were not needed. So often, she struggled to make herself seen and known and understood. But not then.

Outside the room, the city was drifting like a boat on a wave, rocking softly to sleep. Beyond the city, the enemy was on its way, bringing shad-ows and darkness. But there in that room, illuminated by the embers of the dying fire, it was only the two of them, finding each other at last.

THIRTY

Ellina woke with a sigh.

There was a heavy arm across her body. Morning rays streaming in through the open window. The tickle of breath in her hair.

She turned over.

Venick squinted open an eye. Smiled. His voice was soaked in sleep. "Morning."

"Good morning."

He came more awake. Ellina was awake, too, to the quality of his gaze, the way it caught on her form, which was naked beneath the covers.

He touched her cheek. "Sleep well?"

"No."

"Ah." He winced. "My fault."

She studied his face in the light of morning. Strong jawline, strong nose, eyebrows that were slightly darker than his hair. His chin looked different up close, more square. His eyes, though. They were as she had always known them: deep and clear as winter.

"We should be getting up," he said, though it sounded like a question.

It took two tries for Ellina to reply. "Or we could sleep in."

"Hmm." He drew his thumb across her bottom lip. Ellina's pulse rose to meet the point of contact. Venick's eyes gleamed.

They stayed in his room a while longer, but did not sleep.

· · ·

Later that morning, Ellina found herself in a daze. She moved through the city like a spore on a breeze, stopping here and there to pin leaflets onto doors and boards before continuing on her way. The leaflets were Erol's idea—they explained the threat of minceflesh, as well as the new protocols that must be followed in order to prevent further poisonings. It was an important task. Vital to the city's survival. Yet even as Ellina pulled a fresh page from the pile and secured it onto soft wood with a little tack, her thoughts were not on minceflesh. She was not thinking of corpses or conjurors or the war. Her mind was on Venick, and a low-lit bedroom, and the flush of her body and the noises they made and the sweet tide that had filled her from the crown of her head to the tips of her toes.

She pulled another leaflet from the pile. The flyers themselves were simple, done in bright red ink and stamped with an image of a walking corpse. Ellina's hands seemed to float in front of her as she pinned the paper to a wall. She realized she was smiling, and that smiling at an image of a corpse surely looked odd. Yet she could not make herself stop.

There was a commotion among the citizens. Ellina might have

moved past the disturbance altogether, drifting along with her tacks and her leaflets, if not for the fact that she heard someone speak her name.

"Asking to meet with the princess," a red-haired woman was saying. "Insists he has a message that could help the resistance."

"As if anyone would believe him," another woman tutted.

Ellina came more alert. She moved towards the crowd, which had gathered along the curb to watch a small band of guards march some-one down the street. The sky was clear that morning, the spring sun shining harshly. It was in Ellina's eyes. She could not quite see.

"Who?" Ellina asked no one in particular, squinting into the light. "Who is it?"

Yet at that moment, the guards passed through a shadow, and the prisoner came into focus. Silvery white hair, a plain silk vest, that nose and those cheekbones. Ellina inhaled, one hand jutting sideways as if to catch her balance. Sensing her shock, or maybe hearing her sharp intake of breath, the captive lifted his head and met her gaze.

Raffan.

· · ·

He was taken to the prisons.

Venick was already there when Ellina arrived, his boots tapping an anxious beat as he paced the prison courtyard. There were four guards stationed on either side of the building's thick doors, with more men patrolling the structure's perimeter, but aside from those guards, the courtyard was empty; the rest of the area had been cleared.

"He wants to speak with you," Venick told Ellina, shaking his head as if to dispel water. Bournmay hugged his side, looking as if she had grown another few inches overnight. "Alone."

"Why is he here?"

Venick frowned. He didn't know.

Ellina tried a different question. "How was he captured?"

"He…wasn't, exactly. The barricade soldiers say he just walked up to their line, held out his hands, and asked to be taken captive. He didn't even put up a fight."

"That does not sound like Raffan."

"No, it doesn't." Venick's eyes narrowed on the grey doors as if he could see right through to the prisoner inside. "I don't like this."

"I know."

"It feels like a trap."

"It could be." Yet Ellina remembered the way Raffan had pushed her into a crevice to shield her from an incoming stampede. His words, spoken in a rush. *It has to be you. If you want your voice back, you have to be the one to kill Balid.* She thought of how he had given Venick the key to her cell.

Venick was watching her. She could tell by the way his features darkened that he knew what she was thinking, and hated it.

"He hurt you," Venick said. "Again and again, he chose to hurt you when he could have done otherwise."

"Like I hurt you," Ellina replied. "By choice, again and again, when I could have done otherwise."

Venick's voice went hard. "That was different."

"I am not so sure."

"He's a traitor. He wanted this war. He chose Farah's side."

"He regrets it, I think."

"Are you saying that you want to hear him out because he feels *guilty*?"

"I am saying that he was given a choice, and he made the wrong one, and now he is asking to speak to me."

"He doesn't deserve forgiveness."

Ellina was angry then, too. "I never said he did. But if not for him, I might still be trapped in that prison."

"If not for him, you wouldn't have even *been* in that prison."

"I know. I can know that and still want to speak with him."

Bournmay pressed harder into Venick's leg, echoing his agitation. He gripped the scruff of her neck, not so much to control her, but more like a child gripping a favored blanket.

"You shouldn't go alone," Venick said. "He shouldn't be setting the terms. He should never again order you to do anything."

Ellina saw how Venick struggled to restrain himself, and how the mere act of his restraint revealed the depth of his anger. Her own outrage drained. She was reminded that their histories with Raffan were different, and that if she was in Venick's place, she would hate this, too.

Ellina reached for the hand that clutched Bournmay's scruff, opened his palm to the sky. "I have upset you."

"Yes, I'm upset. It's upsetting to hear you defend someone who has hurt you."

"But that is not the only reason."

Venick watched her trace the lines of his palm with her finger. He looked miserable. "You and Raffan share a past. You were close, once. And he was your bondmate. He has a certain…claim to you."

Ellina brought Venick's hand up and kissed it. "He did once. But not anymore."

· · ·

The prison was a cool, rough-walled building with cells spanning its entire length. The floors looked recently swept, but the lamps were dusty, cobwebs clogging the ceiling's high arches. If there had once been other prisoners kept there, they had since been moved. Every cell was empty, save the last.

Raffan sat on a three-legged stool at the back of the farthest prison block, watching Ellina approach. Though Venick claimed that Raffan had come quietly, this could not be entirely true. There was a cut across his left cheek, the skin around his eye the color of an eggplant, and though Ellina saw no evidence of blood, his once perfect nose now jutted right.

"That will need to be set," she said.

He wheezed a little, what might have been a laugh. "I do not suppose you are offering?"

No, Ellina wanted to say, she was not. Let his nose heal crooked. Let him bear the reminder of his fights, as she bore hers.

Yet this vengeful thought quickly dissolved into another. She thought of Raffan coming to *her* prison cell. How he had risked exposure and possible punishment to tend to her wound in Evov…a wound that he himself had inflicted.

I wonder why you have risked coming at all, said the memory of Kaji's voice.

It was never supposed to be this way.

Ellina's pulse was in her head. It was in her hands. She saw Raffan as he was then, face marred but golden eyes untouched. He was looking at her like he still knew her, like she was the same elf she used to be, which made her feel like the same elf she used to be. It was something Ellina had once longed for, but no longer did.

She halted a few paces away from Raffan's cell so that even if he came to the bars and reached all the way through, he would not be able to touch her. "Why are you here?"

"Farah sent me."

"Whatever message she asked you to deliver—"

"Not with a message. She sent me here to scout."

"That is a lie."

When Raffan merely looked at her, Ellina groped for the right words to explain. "I saw the way you two were in Evov. My sister favors you. She likes to keep you close."

"Does she." He spoke as if they were sharing a private joke.

"Besides," Ellina went on, "Farah has enough spies. She would not have sent you on a scouting mission. You are too valuable to be doing her grunt work."

Raffan touched the side of his broken nose, an absentminded gesture. "Your sister has been...displeased with me. She has begun to doubt my loyalties."

Ellina eyed him. "Why?"

"Hesitating to kill you outside of Hurendue might have something to do with it." He dropped his hand. "Farah has been attempting to punish me by assigning me tasks that are below my rank. But I wanted to come."

Ellina ignored the question pushing at her ribs. It was a wide funnel, dark, sucking in all the light. She was not yet ready to face it.

Instead, she repeated her earlier question. "Why are you here, Raffan?"

"I wanted to speak with you."

"And here we are," Ellina said. "Speaking."

Raffan twitched his mouth, then winced, as if the movement caused him pain. "You despise me."

"Is that what you came to ask? If I despise you?"

"No." He stood from the stool, a great unfolding of his limbs, then stepped carefully closer, his hands curling around the bars of his cell.

His broken face reminded Ellina of a living corpse, all deep gashes and purple bruises. It was difficult to look at him directly.

He said, "I came to ask that you surrender to your sister."

Ellina laughed. She turned to leave.

"Ellina, please. Hear me out."

"You have gone mad."

"I am begging you."

She glanced back, then spun all the way around. He had dropped to his knees.

"This war has been more costly than Farah expected," Raffan said, hands still clutching the iron bars, knees pressing into the stone floor. "Our losses in Hurendue were heavy. Most of our conjurors have been killed. *You* killed them. Your sister is…worried. She is beginning to think that she cannot win this war."

"And yet you ask us to surrender."

"Because Farah never will." Raffan's voice went sheer. "She will turn this war into a massacre, for both sides. She has been gathering black powder from every human city we conquer. I have tried to warn her that it is not safe to keep so much black powder in one location, but Farah does not want to be safe. If victory becomes too hard to grasp, she will detonate her entire supply at once. The explosion alone will level everything for leagues, and the ensuing fire will do the rest. She would rather destroy us all—elves and humans, her enemies and her allies—than live with the humiliation of defeat. You have not seen the way Farah has been acting lately. How this war has…consumed her."

Yet Ellina had seen this. She remembered facing Farah outside of Hurendue, her sister's strange smile, the harsh, shrieking quality of her voice. *Deranged*, Venick had said, though Ellina was not entirely sure that was true. Farah was awake to her own desires and their consequences.

She merely no longer had any reason to hold herself back.

"You can change our fate," Raffan insisted. "If you proposed a peace treaty, you could surrender on certain conditions. The mainlands would have their freedom. Farah would own the territory, and humans would recognize Farah as their queen, but they could govern independently."

"You would have them answer to a queen who aimed to steal their homes and kill their families?"

"It would be better than sure destruction." Raffan worked the bars between his fists, his shoulders bunching under his shirt. "Farah is currently hiding out at Revalti Manor. It is an elfland estate surrounded by a moat, just inside the border."

Ellina knew of it. She had spent time at Revalti during her legionnaire days. It was a popular meeting point for legion members, not only because of its centralized location, but because of its impenetrability. Revalti had originally been built as a getaway for the elven queen, and as such, the place was designed with security in mind—there were no windows, and only a single door.

"Why are you telling me this?" Ellina made a frustrated noise. "You have just revealed the location of your queen."

"I am hoping that you will go to her."

"What is to stop me from going to her and killing her?"

Raffan spoke carefully. "You could try. But you know Revalti. It is a fortress. Even if you did somehow manage to kill your sister, you would be trapped within its walls, and then Farah's guards would kill *you*."

"You speak as if that would bother you."

The words sliced through the space between them, and for a moment, Ellina imagined that her words truly did have the power to cut, that they could carve through the skin of unspoken things and bleed out the truth.

"Actually," Raffan said, "it would."

Ellina's earlier question was still in her chest. It battered against her ribs like a bird trapped in the rafters. She swallowed, finally, and gave it a voice. "My death would bother you."

"Yes."

"Even though you have hurt me."

"Yes."

"Even though you are the one who relished in my whippings, and you conspired with my sister to kill my mother, and you put a dagger in my back and landed me in that prison where—" Her throat closed. "Where I was so lost, and I—" She held her breath against the pain in her chest. "And I nearly *died*."

His voice was like sandpaper. "Yes."

"*Why?*"

"Because *I was wrong*," he choked, then looked sharply away. When he spoke next, the words came short and quick, as if a noose was tightening around his throat, and he had only moments to gasp the words. "The way we met. You, a highborn, and me, a merchant's son. I rose through the ranks. So young. So stupid. Hoping to catch your attention. When we were bondmated, I thought you would finally want me like I wanted you. I was shamed by your rejection. So righteous. The ways I punished you. How you let me. It was wrong, and I just—" He dropped his forehead to the bars, exhaled a hard breath. "*I do not expect your forgiveness*," he said in elvish. "*I do not deserve it. But I hope that you can hear the truth.*" He lifted his eyes. "*I am sorry.*"

Ellina felt as if the floor was tilting beneath her feet. She was dizzy with his confession, dizzy with all the things she had never understood. She had been prepared for Raffan's arrogance, for his disdain, but not for his remorse.

"I hope you will consider what I have told you about your sister," Raffan said. "You can change things, for all of us."

Ellina did not even attempt to reply. She needed to leave, to escape his presence before he could upend her any further. She turned towards the door.

"That human would walk to the ends of the earth for you," Raffan called after her. "He loves you. I think he was destined to love you from the moment we found him in the forest."

Ellina halted.

"I sometimes think about everything that came to be," he went on. "How it was my fault, for letting you two make that foolish bargain. I wonder how different things would be if I had just killed him then."

Ellina turned back to face Raffan. She could no longer keep the emotion from her voice when she said, "Well, I am glad you did not."

THIRTY-ONE

Venick was waiting where Ellina had left him in the courtyard, looking ready to crawl out of his skin.

"I am fine," she said, though he could surely see the dried tears on her cheeks.

"Come here," he told her, and tucked her into his arms. She allowed herself to be held, inhaling his scent in deep lungfuls until she was calm again. When she finally pulled away, she did not like the way he looked: mouth drawn stiff, hands tense, as if he expected her to shatter and must be ready to catch the pieces.

"Truly, Venick. I am alright," she insisted, smiling, hoping that he would smile back. He cupped her face instead, his expression full of something profound. It was the way one might look at a natural marvel, like the cresting of a great whale in the ocean, or a shooting star.

Shyness rose within her, occupying the space between her stomach and her heart. Foolish, that she should still feel shy after all they had already shared. And yet, Ellina was not used to being looked at this way: as if she was a miracle.

"We should find the others," she said. "They need to hear this."

• • •

"You must be joking," Lin Lill said after they had all gathered back in the inn and Ellina explained everything. "Raffan wants us to surrender?"

"He believes Farah is a greater danger than we imagined," Ellina replied. "He thinks I could convince her to speak with me. We could come to an agreement."

"That is absurd." Lin Lill puffed out a burst of air, as if spitting. "What an offensive thing to suggest."

"If what Raffan says is true, we might not have a choice."

"But *is* it true?" Dourin asked from his place in the chair that had once been Traegar's. There were heavy bags under his eyes. A bloodless pallor to his skin. Yet when Ellina had suggested that Dourin sit this meeting out, Dourin shook his head. "Traegar would hate to see me isolating myself. Besides," he had added with a shimmer of his old smile, "you need me."

"Do you believe Raffan?" Dourin asked now.

"Yes."

"We can't just surrender." Venick had pulled out his dagger and was switching it from hand to hand, squeezing the hilt with each pass. "Not after everything. There has to be another way."

Ellina watched Venick's dagger shift between his fists. They all knew their victory was dependent on keeping Farah contained, but if Raffan was to be believed, Farah would soon be uncontainable. She would not go down without exhausting every last ounce of her power. The resistance might still be able to claw their way to victory, but at what cost?

Ellina thought of the infirmary in Hurendue. Its packed beds, the endless rows of patients. Many soldiers had been wounded in the battle for Hurendue, and those had been the lucky ones. Ellina hated to think of how many had died in the woods, or the streets. Their bodies spitted on swords and spears. Their corpses left to decay in the sun. This image made Ellina think of other corpses, those that had been poisoned with minceflesh, and *that* reminded her of Traegar and Erol's poison, the one that could kill an elf, but not a human.

Ellina felt strange. Her skin tightened, as if drawn with a cord.

"Farah has always felt as though she belonged on the throne," Ellina said, speaking more to herself than to the others. "Even though she was not a firstborn daughter, she envisioned herself a queen. As if her elvenness…entitled her to it."

Farah had always believed that elves were the superior species, and that among their own race, *she* was superior, because she was even colder and less forgiving than most. Farah would be horrified to learn that there existed a poison to which humans were immune.

"Erol," Ellina said. "I am wondering about the poison that had Traegar expelled from the Healer's Academy. The lace powder."

"What about it?"

"Is there no way to recover the recipe?"

Erol shook his head. "Traegar had a copy, I believe. The recipe was written in a journal, which he kept secret. But I do not know what became of it."

"I do," Venick said.

Everyone's eyes darted to him.

"Traegar gave me the book in Evov," Venick explained. "*Jouvl-aian Rauam*, right? That's what's written on the cover."

"That's an old phrase humans and elves once used to express friendship," Erol said. "It's a promise, really. *I will keep your secrets.*" He smiled. "I'd forgotten about that."

"Traegar seemed to know that the book might come in handy." Venick shrugged. "I've had it ever since."

Ellina stared at Venick. The cord within her cinched tighter.

Venick noticed. His expression changed. She wondered if she had gone pale, if that was why he was looking at her like that. He cleared his throat. "Ellina, can I speak to you for a moment?"

In the hallway outside the inn's great room, he set his teeth. "Something's wrong."

"It has been a long day."

"No. I've seen you like this before. It's how you look when you're about to spin a lie in elvish. Like you're...plotting something."

Ellina blinked. Her skin was still tight with that unnamed thing, which she realized was an idea.

Venick's eyes went dark. "Whatever it is, whatever you're thinking, I want to know. Don't lie to me."

"I haven't. I won't." She set a palm to his chest, felt his furiously pounding heart. Her idea scared him as much as it scared her, and she had not even told him what it was yet.

"This could be a trap," she began. "Farah could have sent Raffan; we have no proof of his loyalties. They could be trying to get me to go to Revalti, where they could capture me, and then use me to capture you. But we know from prior reports that Farah has been gathering black powder. I also believe that Raffan's reasons for coming were honest. He...admitted some things to me. Things that he regrets. And he risked his life to deliver his warning—he knew we would take him prisoner, yet he came anyway."

Venick's expression morphed into something resolute. "If what Raffan says is true, and Farah is hiding out at Revalti Manor, I'll lead a team there. We'll infiltrate the building and assassinate her."

"Revalti is a fortress. Farah will be buried deep inside, surrounded by guards. You will never find her without her consent, and even if you did, you would not make it out alive. But we do not have to force our way in. I will do as Raffan suggested—I will request to speak with my sister."

Venick drew back. "You'll agree to surrender?"

"No," Ellina replied. "I have a better idea."

THIRTY-TWO

The following morning, Venick sat on a stool in Ellina's room, methodically tearing one of Erol's minceflesh flyers into tiny pieces. He wasn't usually one to waste supplies, and he had nothing against the flyer, but if he didn't do something with his hands, he would rip out his own hair.

Ellina, who sat at a nearby writing table, glanced up. Lifted a brow.

Venick set the mangled flyer aside. One, two, three seconds before he picked it up again. Kept at his tearing.

Ellina's hands were busy, too, but unlike his, hers were steady. She dipped the nib of her quill into a little jar of ink, continuing her letter where she had left off.

"Ellina."

"Hmm?"

"I'm worried Farah won't accept your request."

"She will."

"Even if she does, she could do so with other intentions in mind. She could still contrive a trap."

"That is possible, yes."

"If you're wrong about this—"

"I'm not."

"But you could be."

"I don't think so."

"You're going to get yourself hurt. Your sister is going to hurt you."

Ellina blew on the parchment, then rolled it into a small tube, which she secured to the leg of a waiting messenger hawk. The hawk was not a currigon. It was smaller, a western species commonly used by mountain nomads. She pushed open the window and set the bird aflight.

"No," Ellina said, "she won't."

• • •

Venick smelled the woody scent of the *rezahe* in Dourin's glass before he saw the elf enter his room. The window at Venick's back showed a golden sun setting over the ridgeline of roofs, the pink and gold clouds like a swath of tiger stripes.

"We have a problem," Dourin said. The glass in his hand was down to its ice, as if Dourin had come straight from whatever he was doing and hadn't thought to set it down. "The Dark Army is on its way."

"What, here?"

"They have been spotted beyond Heartshire Bay, heading east."

"That's not possible. We wiped out half their ranks in Hurendue, and most of their supplies. How are they already attacking again?"

"I don't know." Dourin waved his drink through the air, an airy motion that was at odds with his expression. "It might have something to do with that insane female they call their queen."

"Farah has to know her soldiers aren't ready for another battle. She'll never win."

"Unless she is moving forward with her black powder plan, in which case *winning* is subjective." Dourin studied Venick. "Do you want the other bit of good news, or shall I keep it a surprise?"

"Just tell me."

"The Elder is coming," Dourin said. "He sent a letter this morning to announce his arrival."

"He sent a letter to Harmon?"

"To me."

"But why?"

"He did not say. The letter only mentioned wishing to—how did he put it?—*reunite with his brave heroes.* I think we both know what that means."

"The war isn't over yet." Venick could hear his own voice, pitching high with desperation. "The Elder can't take back his men."

"He can try."

"Harmon…Harmon wouldn't let him."

"Right." Dourin's reply was pointed. "And how *are* things between you and Harmon?"

"We've come to an understanding."

"Does that mean we are back to trusting her now?" When Venick gave no answer, Dourin said, "You see the problem this poses. If the Elder comes for his men, and you aren't around to stop him, he could reestablish control. And if Harmon sides with him, that will only make reclaiming power all the easier. The Elder arrives tonight." Dourin tipped his head. "You see where this is going."

"No, Dourin—"

"You must stay in the city."

"I can't."

"It's the only way to ensure that the Elder doesn't seize back his army, exposing us to the incoming attack."

"Ellina leaves to meet Farah this afternoon. I'm going with her."

"For moral support."

"Yes."

"Sorry, little human. The resistance needs you here for actual support."

Venick was shaking his head, despite already knowing its futility. If the Elder was on his way to Kenath, Venick *did* need to be there. And yet: "The Elder owes you his life price. You could bargain on the resistance's behalf. Ask him to call off this visit, return to Parith."

"His life price has already been repaid."

"Those damn horses."

"Do not blasphemy. The horses are perfect."

"They were a bribe."

"I am not above bribery."

Venick steepled his fingers, set their tips between his brows. Eyes closed, he gave it one last try. "You could still help. Talk to him. He likes you."

"Everyone likes me."

"Is there really no other way?"

"No." Dourin rattled the ice in his glass, a grim parody of a toast. "I am afraid not."

• • •

Venick found Ellina in the stables with a currycomb in hand, brushing dirt out from under the bottom of Eywen's saddle pad. Gently nudging into her way, he took over the task, working the brush through the wool as he told her what he'd learned in agitated tones.

Ellina looked thoughtful. "Dourin is right."

Venick shook out the comb. "I don't want to leave you."

"You are not *leaving* me."

"It's just…" He paused. "What you're about to do…it'll change you. More than I think you realize."

Ellina watched him knuckle the comb. "You are talking about your father."

"I ended his life," Venick said. "I killed my own father, and even though he betrayed me, betrayed Miria, and I hated him for it, I've had to live with that ever since. I've—" Venick dropped his gaze.

"Venick. Talk to me."

"I hear him," Venick admitted, at last giving name to the suspicion that had been chipping away at his own conviction ever since facing the Dark Army in the woods outside of Hurendue. "I hear his voice. In my head. He speaks to me."

Ellina looked uncertain. "Your father speaks to you?"

He knew it sounded crazy.

She spoke gently. "Are you sure the voice is not your own, and that you are not imagining that it is?"

"I'm not imagining it."

Ellina took the currycomb from Venick's grip and set it aside, then squeezed his hands. "I know you fear this will haunt me. And maybe you are right, maybe it will. But I have to do it anyway."

"You're not worried?" Venick asked. "You're not scared?"

"I am both of those things. "I am both of those things. But I know better who I am now. And," she added with a smile, "I have you."

THIRTY-THREE

Low clouds blew in from the west. The air, despite having warmed these past days, held a chill. Venick's skin shivered as they finished readying Eywen to ride.

Ellina squinted at the sky. "It smells like snow."

Venick lifted his own nose, but smelled only the scents of the stables, hay and leather and horse. "Not to me." A pause. "Erol said something like that once. The sky was clear, but he was certain it would snow."

"And did it?"

"No."

Venick could only hope that the sky continued to hold. Ellina had enough obstacles ahead without the addition of a spring snowstorm. He imagined what would happen if a storm did blow in, how wind would sweep through Ellina's hair, how she would carry it with her into the dark fortress of Revalti Manor. All the ways it might affect things.

He handed over Eywen's reins and tried to be alright.

Ellina touched his arm. "The clouds do not worry me."

"Come here."

He kissed her, doing his best to be gentle, though the urge to deepen the kiss was there. He wanted to crush his mouth to hers, pull her in tight, yet he worried if he did, it would be the same as revealing the depth of his fear.

She murmured into his mouth. "You do not always have to do that."

"Do what?"

"Hold back."

So he didn't. He let go, angling her head where he wanted it, pulling her body flush against his. He didn't let himself think about why he needed this, didn't consider the possibility that this kiss might also be a goodbye. He kissed her, and kissed her, and then he let her go.

• • •

Branton and Lin Lill rode with Ellina. They had discussed sending a larger contingent along, but Ellina did not want to waste the resources. "They will be useless at Revalti," she had told Venick, watching him worry his lip between his teeth. "You need a strong force to defend the city against the coming invasion. The soldiers should stay with you."

As they rode through the countryside, storm winds ripping through the grass, Ellina tried to quell the angst in her belly. She had no reason to doubt herself. After all, what could Farah do that she could not? Was Ellina not the one who had joined the legion, who honed her skills as a spy, who knew the art of fighting with blade and mind? Farah was hungry, but she was blinded by her own convictions. This was the difference between them, as simple as it was vital: Farah did not see things clearly, and Ellina did.

• • •

The ground was dry and hard. Dust kicked up around Venick's boots as he helped load a supply wagon. It brought to mind thoughts of the black powder the Dark Army was currently carting towards Kenath, which brought to mind thoughts of the powder in a pouch currently strapped to Ellina's waist. Venick had worried that pouch might tear, that its contents would leak. It was an unreasonable fear, the kind his mind impulsively offered up as a way to cope with his anxiety. Yet he had checked the bag twice, just to be sure.

Is a leak really such a bad thing?

Venick paused halfway through lifting a coil of rope into the wagon.

He considered his enemy. According to their scouts, the southerners were moving towards Kenath with a half dozen horse-drawn carts packed with explosives. Though this was only a fraction of Farah's reported supply—there'd been speculation that the rest of her explosives could be sent to an array of other mainland cities—it was still a worrying quantity. That much black powder in one location would be enough to reshape the region. But what could Venick do? If he met the enemy on the road, they would detonate their black powder and kill them all. If he did not meet them, they would reach Kenath and detonate their supply anyway.

His father's voice spoke again. *Well, Venick? Is it?*

• • •

They crouched in the twiggy, overgrown gardens surrounding the manor. Tiny green leaves clung to everything. The scene was dazzling, interwoven, yet unfinished: a world on the cusp of blooming.

Though Ellina had seen Revalti Manor many times before, only now did she appreciate the uniqueness of its design. The windowless exterior, though devised for safety, looked like a prison; the stone façade was smooth and unbroken, save for a short series of black grates running down the manor's center. The grates, each no larger than a hand, were part of the ventilation system that had been installed within the walls to help counteract the lack of natural airflow.

"A moat." Lin Lill clicked her teeth. "How quaint."

Ellina dropped her eyes from the grates to the manor's base. Revalti was indeed surrounded by a moat, which was scarcely half as wide as the Taro. Lin Lill's tone—part humor, part distain—summed up Ellina's own feelings well. For all the elves' abilities, it was ridiculous that they had ever been stopped by something as harmless as this.

Branton nodded towards a small dock where a rowboat had been secured. "That must be for you."

"I should swim," Ellina mused, "to set the tone."

"Better not," Lin Lill replied lightly.

"You have until sunset," Branton went on, peering up at the midday clouds. "If you are not back by then, we are coming for you."

Ellina fingered the small pouch at her waist. She began to move out of the brush.

A soft hand on her arm. Ellina turned to see Lin Lill's lightheartedness had bled into something darker, more earnest.

"I know you have faced your sister before," Lin Lill said, "and that things did not go as you had planned. But you must trust yourself, Ellina. You are your own best weapon."

Ellina looked into Lin Lill's face. Their golden eyes met briefly before Ellina's gaze shifted to the scar on the ranger's cheek. *My mother dropped a plate on my head when I was a fledgling*, Lin Lill had once offered in explanation, though Ellina suspected this was a lie. She sensed it as one senses a breeze, a gentle breath on the skin. It was a feeling Ellina knew well.

An inborn trait. A learned one.

An instinct for deceit. Liars and lies. Her mind, studded with metal teeth like the jaws of a bear trap.

Once, Ellina had looked at Lin Lill and felt only the breadth of their differences. Now she looked at the ranger—sleek in her power, purposeful—and saw someone who was like her.

Ellina abandoned her hiding spot and walked towards the rowboat.

• • •

They halted their preparations. The supply wagons were left as they were, the soldiers given leave to return to the city. Venick found Harmon in the brothel's workroom to explain their change in plans.

She wasn't happy. "If we don't send our men to meet the Dark Army now, they will be free to approach the city. They'll travel as far as they want without opposition."

"I know."

"But you're changing the plan anyway."

"Yes."

"And what are the rest of us supposed to do while you're off playing the champion?"

"You can prepare the soldiers to defend the city, though truthfully, if my plan fails…you'll need to evacuate."

Harmon exhaled an angry breath.

"There's something else," Venick said. He handed her Dourin's letter. Harmon's face paled at the sight of the Elder's insignia stamped into the envelope's wax seal. "Your father sent this. He's on his way here to Kenath. He'll likely arrive while I'm away."

She stared at the envelope. "My father."

"Dourin—that is to say, we—worry he's returning to summon back his men."

"Or to summon back *me*." The letter crinkled in her grip.

Harmon's relationship with her father had always been complicated. As a girl, she'd wanted to become a soldier in the highland army, but the Elder refused; after Harmon's mother was killed in battle, the Elder forbid women from fighting. Harmon had become a war healer instead, and the Elder allowed it, but he'd never gone so far as to acknowledge Harmon's rightful position as a Stonehelm military leader. In his eyes, Harmon was most useful as someone he could marry off to gain more wealth and influence, as he'd tried to do with Venick.

Venick didn't know what Harmon would do if the Elder tried to bargain for her cooperation. Though the man could be cold, he was also shrewd, and he'd always doted on his daughter, even if doting wasn't what she wanted. The Elder still had power over Harmon, and much to offer. Autonomy. Knighthood. A place at his side.

Venick withdrew the letter from Harmon's stiff fingers and smoothed it on his thigh. "I need to know," he started, pushing the parchment back into its envelope, "that I can trust you."

Harmon's eyes came to his. There was anguish there, and shame, but determination, too. "I know we haven't always seen eye to eye," she said. "My mother would say we're too alike, though I'm not sure that's even true. Regardless, I'm on your side, Venick. I have been ever since you risked redemption to pull me from that fire pit in Irek. You saved my life that day."

"Your father—"

"I love my father," she interrupted, "but he wants the wrong things, for this war and for me. I will not abandon the resistance. You can trust me." She was steady as she said this, just as she'd been when they first met. This almost had Venick thinking about the elven trick of hiding true emotions behind a stony mask, and about his own inability to spot deception, and about all the ways she had deceived him…until Harmon said: "Tell me how to say it in elvish."

Venick's thoughts scattered. He swallowed his first reply, and his second, until he finally managed, "It's pronounced, *uro en emasthi*."

"*Uro en emasthi*," Harmon repeated, the words coming easily, with no hitch or hesitation—proof that she spoke the truth. And again, softer this time, in their own language: "Flawed, but not evil, right?"

He exhaled an almost-laugh. "Right."

She held his gaze. "I swear to you, Venick, I am seeing this through to the end. You can trust me."

. . .

Ellina rowed. The oars dipped steadily into the water, droplets flinging across its wind-rippled surface. There was a second dock on the moat's opposite side situated at the base of a narrow staircase leading to the doorway. Ellina eddied the dingy alongside that dock, roped off. She peered around, first along the waterline where Revalti's base sank straight into the moat, then up the manor's sheer four-story height, the stone block like a fist punching up through the water.

Ellina exited the boat and started up the stairs. She wore only a simple cloth tunic and trousers. No armor, no weapons. This had been a necessary part of her strategy, though Ellina was beginning to doubt its wisdom; she felt like a newborn, naked and defenseless.

At the top of the stairs, Revalti's iron-studded door creaked open, and a figure emerged.

Ellina was shocked by the sight of her sister. Farah appeared to be wearing what she had worn during the battle at Hurendue: blood-streaked armor, a torn cape, her hair singed on one side. No weapons, as far as Ellina could see. No shoes, either. Farah stepped away from the shadows of the doorway, and when she smiled, Ellina saw that she had sharpened her teeth to points.

"Hello, sister."

Ellina paused halfway up the stairs. Her blood hummed in anticipation. "*You received my letter?*" she asked in elvish.

"*Clearly.*"

"*And my conditions?*"

"*Have all been met. I ordered my guards away from Revalti, along with all of our weapons. We will be meeting in private and may take as much time as needed. There is no one here, but us.*"

Farah paused, as if waiting to see if Ellina had any more objections. When she did not, Farah's smile returned. "Come, then."

Ellina saw Farah watching her and knew they were both thinking the same thing. It was not too late for Ellina to turn back. She could abandon this plan, give up her hopes of reasoning with her sister, return to finish this war with blood and fire as it had begun. It did not matter what conditions Ellina set for this meeting—as soon as she entered the windowless fortress of Revalti, she would once again be at Farah's mercy.

Ellina's throat was dry. Her boots seemed too heavy for her feet. She licked her lips and heard herself say, "Lead the way."

It was only later, when southerners swarmed into the manor and the trick in Farah's words was revealed, that Ellina would remember that Farah had always been a liar, too, and the question was not whether the sisters would lie to each other, but who would do it better.

• • •

Venick rode swiftly with Dourin and a group of four others. The soldiers had been specially chosen for this mission, having proven themselves most adept in the skills of stealth and deceit. "Quick and quiet," Dourin had said before starting off in the direction the Dark Army was last seen, as if discussing an amusing game rather than their own possible demise.

It was midday by the time they reached the thin crescent of trees that lined the road west of Kenath. Beyond, Venick could see a caravan of elves moving up the path, though at first he did not recognize them as the enemy. The southerners trudged along in a loose line, some in armor but most in civilian clothing, looking more like a haggard band of travelers than a fearsome army.

"The reports were right," Dourin murmured, shifting to gaze through the trees. Overhead, the clouds continued to gather, shading the world grey. "This is not the Dark Army's entire force."

"But that's a good thing, isn't it?" said one of their members, a plainsland boy with a shock of red hair named Alfrick.

"That depends," Dourin replied. "How many elves does it take to light a match?"

Venick pulled out a spyglass to peer at the approaching elves. None rode on horseback. Rather, their steeds had been grouped into pairs and harnessed to a series of covered wagons. The wagons were unmarked, their canvas tops stretched tightly over hidden contents, like skin over ribs.

Quick and quiet indeed. They'd need more than a little stealth to reach those wagons unseen, especially in the full light of day. Though Dourin had first suggested waiting for nightfall, Venick dismissed the idea; in order for their plan to succeed, they needed to act while there was still as much distance between those wagons and Kenath as possible.

Dourin met Venick's gaze through the trees and lifted one perfect eyebrow—a movement that seemed to encompass both his estimation of their Commander as well as his own willingness to follow his lead—before turning back to Alfrick. "Do you believe in the gods?" Dourin asked. The young man nodded. Dourin returned his gaze to the approaching southerners. "Best you start praying."

• • •

Revalti Manor was even darker inside than Ellina remembered. The chandeliers remained unlit, many of the candelabras missing from their corners. Those that remained provided only enough light to illuminate the nearest objects: an empty cabinet, a doorway, a suit of armor.

As Farah led the way through square corridors and up a flight of stairs, Ellina called forth her other senses, smell and touch and sound. There was a marble balustrade, cool under her palm. A hint of candle wax, light in the air. The patter of their own footfalls, soft as a breeze on the stone.

Despite its apparent disuse, Revalti was surprisingly free of dust; Ellina's hands, when she ran them along sideboards or railings, came away clean. This was surely due to the ventilation system, which kept air moving through the rooms. Ellina did not know if Revalti's original creators were human or elven, but they must have known that they could not make Revalti perfectly airtight, lest the smoke from fireplaces suffocate its occupants. And indeed, when Ellina and Farah stepped into a fourth-story corridor with a balcony overlooking the dining hall far below, Ellina could see the network of air vents set into the walls, some covered with decorative grates, others open, like the burrows of animals.

They reached a door at the end of the hall. Farah produced a key. While she worked the lock, Ellina reached out to touch one of the air vents. She slipped her hand inside, felt the gentle wash of air flow over her fingers.

"What are you doing?" Farah asked.

Ellina pulled back. "I am wondering why you chose Revalti as your hideout."

"It was built for the elven queen." Farah replied, pushing open the door. "Why should I not choose it?"

They entered a study, which appeared to double as a bedroom. Ellina could see the evidence of Farah's occupancy, clothing draped over furniture, parchment scattered across the desk, a jar of oil, a file. Still no windows, but the candles were all lit, including a small one on the desk with little notches in its side to measure time. The candle was nothing but a nub, burning down to its final notch.

Farah shut the door.

"Lock it," Ellina said.

Farah did, the bolt driving home with a definitive *thunk*.

"Well," Farah said, sweeping out her hands. Her armor creaked with the movement, flakes of dried blood shaking free. "You have requested a meeting with your queen, and she had graciously accepted."

Ellina attempted to calm her racing heart. She turned a slow circle, pretending to study the room's contents while she worked up the breath it would take to say, clearly: "I want you to call back your forces."

Farah's razor smile went stiff. "That," she said, "is not what you suggested in your letter. You said you wanted to discuss surrender."

"Yes," Ellina replied. "Yours."

Farah flung a finger towards the door. "If you only came here to waste my time—"

"You are losing the war," Ellina interrupted. "Running an army is like running a city. Your elves need food and clothing and shelter, yet you have lost your base, and your supplies are dangerously low. Your conjurors are all but dead, your warriors weary. Many of them are beginning to wonder if they made the right decision by coming west with you. The elflands are massive enough as they are. Why must you conquer the mainlands, too?" This last bit was a guess, yet Ellina saw her sister's eyes narrow with her words, and knew them to be true.

"You cannot win," Ellina continued, "and I think you know it. But you still have a choice. You can surrender. Call off your army. Give up your title as queen."

"Why?" Farah snapped. "So that you may step into my place?"

Ellina shook her head. "I do not want the crown."

Farah spat, the glob skating across the floor. It was tinged red, and when Ellina looked up, she saw blood on her sister's lips. Her pointed teeth were cutting her own mouth.

Farah said, "You are a liar."

"Not this time."

"If you do not want the throne, then what is your purpose?"

Ellina spoke deliberately. "To end this war."

"To save the human race," Farah corrected, wiping her mouth with the side of her palm. "You shame me, sister. The way you care for humans as if they were your kin, choosing them over your own country. How has it come to this? I thought you would have learned better, if not from me, then at least from our mother. She hated humans."

"That is not true."

"Of course it is. Why else do you think she created the border?"

"Because," Ellina replied, her pulse beginning to rise once more, "she was afraid of what would happen if anyone discovered that she loved a human."

Farah's expression closed. "This discussion is over."

"Rishiana never wanted the border," Ellina pressed. "It was not even her idea. Her sister, our Aunt Ara, was the one who pushed Rishiana to divide our races. She knew the truth of Rishiana's affair with a human. It was dangerous. The scandal alone could have cost her queenship. When rumors began to spread that the elven queen had abandoned her bond-mate to court a human male in secret, Ara stepped in. She insisted that Rishiana create the border, and therefore distance herself from humans in the most public way. From then on, our mother acted as though she believed humans were beneath us. But it was a lie."

"Our mother was the queen. She would not have allowed herself to be pushed around by her younger sister."

"Maybe not," Ellina agreed, "except that Rishiana had another secret, which Ara knew and threatened to reveal. You have heard the story, I am sure. Shortly after Queen Rishiana became pregnant with Miria, a huge fight broke out between the two sisters. It caused Ara to leave the court for good. Yet have you never wondered what they fought about?"

Farah had begun to look slightly pale. Her upper lip glistened with sweat. "That is all ancient history," she said. "I cannot see why it matters."

Ellina did not feel well, either. A cold hand seemed to come down on her shoulder, fingers digging into the muscle. "It matters," she said, "because we were wrong about our mother. We were wrong about humans."

"Enough of this." Farah lifted an angry fist. "How dare you come to me with more lies. I thought I was being merciful when I silenced you, but now that your voicelessness has been undone, I see my mercy was wasted. I should have silenced you for good."

"Silence," Ellina said darkly, "was no mercy."

"It was for me." Farah raised her chin. "I will hear no more."

"But you—"

"I said, *I will hear no more.*"

The study door—which Ellina had watched Farah lock—swung open, and through it, eight elven guards rushed in with swords drawn. Ellina reacted, hurling herself over the desk and out of range, but there was nowhere else to go, no widow by which to escape, no weapon to use in defense.

The truth poured icy over her skin, like the breath of death herself. Ellina was trapped, defenseless, and surrounded.

Farah's face seemed lit from beneath, all shadows and bones. "This is the end, sister."

• • •

When the Dark Army passed their location in the trees, Venick and his party emerged.

The storm rolled overhead, the wind tossing dirt into their faces. The cloud cover wasn't the same as nightfall, but it gave Venick an excuse to keep his head down, his hood drawn as he slipped from the trees into the southerner's ranks. Behind him, each on a short delay, Dourin and his four other soldiers did the same, choosing gaps in the caravan, picking their moments carefully. Within a bare minute, they were in.

Venick had done this before. He remembered a windy mountainside, the push and call of an elven market. He'd once smuggled his way back into Evov to hunt for Ellina, doing his best to blend in with the elves, to hide his obvious humanness.

And how'd that work for you?

Poorly. Not that Venick expected it to go much better this time. He knew the risks, knew that even with the storm, his upraised hood did more to announce his presence than to conceal it. Their plan was a desperate one, the kind that had been forced upon them at the last minute when no better options were available. Venick's jaw ached from clenching it, his shoulders creeping to his ears, certain that any moment he would be noticed…

Except?

Except…these elves were exhausted. As Venick and his team slipped into their midst, blending among their unorganized ranks, he could see their downcast eyes, the heavy drag of their feet. Then Venick remembered that this contingent had been sent on a suicide mission, tasked with carting and later detonating their supply of black powder, and things began to make more sense. Venick had expected a bunch of zealots, but what he saw was a band of southerners who hadn't recovered from the battle at Hurendue, who were running on the last of their strength, and walking to their deaths besides.

Venick risked a glance behind him. He caught the eye of his five waiting infiltrators and twitched his hand: *now.*

In unison, each resistance member slid in a different direction and approached one of the supply wagons, which were manned by an elf in the front but unguarded at the back. Venick did the same, peeling sideways, stationing himself behind a wagon. Once in position, it was a simple matter of waiting for a moment when no one was looking to grab the handrail and hoist himself up through the curtain and into the wagon's cabin.

Which Venick did, swiftly, with as much elven-like grace as he could muster. Once inside, he flung back his hood. Before him was a heaping pile of black powder contained within cloth sacks. Working quickly, Venick cut small holes into the corners of the sacks, directing the flow of black powder down through cracks in the wagon's planking. The sacks would slowly drain through the floor as the wagon moved, the powder blending with the dirt road below. Once the sacks had all been bled, Venick turned his attention upwards, slicing several notches into the wagon's canvas ceiling. Before, he had hoped the storm would hold, but now he wished for rain. It would handle what the leaks did not—black powder, when exposed to water, was rendered useless.

Venick was sheathing his knife and redrawing his hood when a voice said, "Hello?"

He looked up.

A southerner had appeared at the back of the wagon. His golden eyes slid from Venick's knife up his arm, to his face. He said, "You."

Venick moved, ramming the pommel of his dagger against the elf's temple to knock him unconscious.

• • •

"You lied." Ellina's voice threaded high as she watched the guards secure their position, blocking her sole escape path. "You said we *were* alone. The door—"

"We were alone," Farah replied. "These eight were waiting on a launch hidden in the moat behind the manor. It was only after we were inside that they returned. As for the lock," Farah tipped her chin, "did you really think this door had only a single key?"

Ellina's heart was trying to batter its way out of her chest. Her plan was sand through her fingers, scattered around her feet. She thought of Branton and Lin Lill waiting outside, the odds that they had seen the guards enter the manor, whether or not they might try to follow. She glanced at the candle, burned halfway down its final notch.

She needed more time.

"What will you do once I'm dead?" Ellina asked. "Killing me will not end this war."

"Killing you holds its own appeal."

Farah, despite having every upper hand, still looked unwell. Her eyes had gone bloodshot, her completion shifting from white to sickly grey. When she took a step forward, her thigh trembled, as if straining to bear her weight.

"You have always had everything you could possibly want," Farah said. "Every advantage, every opportunity. You were bondmated to Raffan—"

"Against my will."

"—and you turned up your nose at him. You were a highborn princess—"

"Not by choice."

"—yet you renounced your status to join the legion. And still, somehow, you were our mother's favorite, and Miria's. All those years, I had to watch the two of you together, the best of friends. You never cared to invite me into your games—"

"You hated games."

"I hated *you*. So ungrateful. So spoiled. Last autumn, I made the mistake of believing that we could be sisters at last. You agreed to pledge me your support—"

"You *blackmailed me*."

"—and what did you do? You betrayed me. Do you think your dark hair makes you special? That your conjuring entitles you in some way?"

"Sister, you have it all wrong."

"No." Farah's lip curled. "This is my vengeance, sister. You are a disgrace. Miria was, too. Why our mother ever wanted to crown her but not me, I cannot fathom. The three of you." A laugh. "So weak. I was glad of Miria's death. My only regret was that I was not the one to wield the weapon that killed her. I did not make that mistake with our mother. I will not make it with you."

A guard passed Farah a dagger. Ellina watched the blade exchange hands with a sense of unreality. She had been reckless, her plan had been reckless. As Farah moved forward, Ellina tried to think, to scramble for some new idea, even though it was hopeless, and she was out of time.

Her eyes dropped back to the candle on the desk between them, which was nothing now but a thin sliver. Farah's blade caught its feeble light, orange melting over the green.

Ellina thought about how Venick could hear his father's voice in his head. The tragedy of General Atlas' murder, and how—though Venick would never admit it aloud, and might not even know it himself—the truth was as obvious to Ellina as the sun in a clear summer sky: Venick regretted killing his father. He would take it back if he could. It was a mistake he would carry with him for the rest of his life.

Just as Ellina carried hers. She remembered her own voice as it had been before, without hitch or pause, singing her heart into words in the company of no one because there were elves like Farah who saw such things as too passionate, too odd, too human. She wished she could hear Miria's voice like Venick heard his father's. She wished they could sing together, just once. Just one time.

But Ellina's mind was a deep ocean. Nothing in it but shushing waves. Her mother's demands. Her country's expectations. How Miria had touched Ellina's cheek on her way to freedom and said, *Be happy.*

Ellina had not known how to be happy. She thought happiness meant following the rules, blending seamlessly into her role as a princess and a legionnaire. She was like Venick in this way. She had hidden herself so deeply for so long that she was not even aware she was hiding.

Yet she had been found anyway, and known, and loved.

As Farah rounded the desk to touch the tip of her blade to Ellina's neck, Ellina did not flinch away. She looked into the gleaming eyes of her sister and said, "You are wrong about me."

Farah smirked. "Are those your final—?"

Farah convulsed. Ellina took several quick steps out of range as Farah dropped to her knees, blood spouting from her nose, the dagger clattering to the floor. Behind her, Farah's guards were doing the same, seizing, stumbling.

Ellina took another step backward, finding the edge of the desk and gripping hard. Her own legs threatened to give, the muscles too loose. When she sniffled, she tasted blood in the back of her throat.

"What..." Farah wiped her nose, looked down at the red smear. "What is happening?"

"Lace powder. It is an airborne poison. I put it in the walls. The manor's ventilation system has been filling this room with it. Once the poison is inhaled, it works quickly."

"But you—" Farah's pupils were tiny, her golden irises like two floating suns. "You are inhaling it, too."

"Lace powder is different than most poisons. It will kill an elf, but not a human."

Farah's expression said that she did not understand.

"It won't kill me," Ellina continued, taking a deep breath, feeling the poison grate her lungs, "because I'm half-human."

Watching Farah was like watching sunlight dawn over a mountainside. Her face was drawn in shadows but quickly gaining color, the shapes and ridges all coming clear. Behind her, the guards were attempting to flee the room, their limbs scrabbling uselessly over stone tiles.

"I asked if you ever wondered what Rishiana and Ara fought about," Ellina said, still clinging tightly to the desk. "It was this: Rishiana was in love with a human conjuror named Erol. He was Miria's true father… and mine, too."

"That is not possible." Farah's words came out garbled. "Elves and humans cannot…"

"Make babies? You are right. However, elves and human *conjurors* can, and when they do, they produce black-haired offspring. Elven conjurors. That is where elven magic comes from. It is also the reason why our mother wanted to crown Miria early. Miria was half-human, too. Rishiana wanted to establish Miria as queen before the truth came out—before elves like you, elves like Ara, had a chance to act against her."

Farah was breathing heavily. Her jaw worked. Her fingernails dug across the floor.

"You were wrong," Ellina said, "when you said I was weak. My humanity does not make me weak. It's going to save my life."

Farah's eyes began to fade. Her mouth foamed.

This is for our mother, Ellina might have said.

This is for Miria. For Venick. For everyone who has suffered for your prejudice and greed.

But in the end, none of that was true, or if it was, it was not the whole truth. Ellina ground her teeth. She spoke deliberately, made sure the last thing Farah heard would be these words. "This is for me."

THIRTY-FOUR

I t began to rain. As Venick slipped out of the Dark Army's ranks and returned to the trees where they'd left their horses, he turned his face to the sky and closed his eyes, allowing the downpour to wash the gritty black powder residue from his skin. The storm was just a storm. There were no hidden meanings to be found within it, no black magic at play. If there had been conjurors among the Dark Army's caravan, they'd abandoned their post; Venick hadn't seen a single black-haired southerner since leaving Hurendue.

The others reappeared. Alfrick was smiling, clearly pleased with their handiwork, but when he began spouting about their success, Dourin cut him off. "Do not be so self-congratulatory. It was not merely our stealth that won us this day. Those elves knew we were among them."

"But then…" Alfrick's boyish face turned a pout. "Why didn't they stop us?"

"Revolution sounds nice in theory, but the reality of self-sacrifice is much less glamorous. My guess? The southerners turned a blind eye because by destroying their black powder, we were saving their lives, too."

By the time they returned to Kenath, the storm had blown itself out, the late afternoon sun washing yellow over the city. The Elder had not yet arrived. But neither had Ellina.

Venick's worry simmered. He stalked around the inn, glaring at anyone who tried to approach. He hated to see Harmon, who'd grown quietly anxious over her father's impending arrival, because he couldn't understand how that possibly mattered when Ellina was still missing. Yet he also hated seeing Erol, who *was* worried for Ellina, which made Venick feel absurdly possessive. Erol was Ellina's father, but he hadn't really been a father to her, hadn't been in her life, and seeing his worry was like seeing a reflection in a lake, distorted and colorless. It did not compare.

It was in this frame of mind that Venick went to the prison.

Raffan was awake. He sat on a little stool at the back of his cell, his face a motley purple, hands hanging loosely between his knees. He tipped up his head as Venick approached but did not stand, and Venick wondered, was that meant to be a slight? Or was this Raffan's way of showing submission? Raffan would have never willingly submitted before, but then, he'd also never been a prisoner. By choice. To a human he hated.

Venick shouldn't have come.

But he couldn't leave, either, now that he was there, so he approached the cell, bringing Raffan's face into clearer view. The elf's expression was unusually open, and concerned. "Is she—?"

"I don't know."

Raffan fell silent.

Venick said, "Your crimes haven't been forgiven just because you've had a change of heart."

"I know."

"What you did to Ellina, what you've done for years—it would earn you a death sentence in the mainlands."

"Yes."

"Ellina will be the one to decide your punishment."

"That is fair."

"I wish you weren't so calm about all this."

"I am not calm, inside."

Venick shoved his hands into his pockets to stop himself from unlocking Raffan's cell and adding a few more bruises to his face. He'd come to vent his frustration, but this didn't feel like venting. It brought him no relief.

Venick gave Raffan his shoulder and said, "You're lucky my men only broke your nose, and not your neck."

"These bruises are not from your men."

That drew Venick's eyes back.

Raffan motioned at his jutting nose. "Farah did this to me. It was part of my punishment for allowing Ellina to escape our last fight."

Venick would have been surprised by that, maybe, except talking about Ellina with this elf was starting to drive him a little crazy. Venick's scalp prickled. His shoulders felt too wide for his jacket. If Ellina wasn't back by the time he walked out of here, he'd ride to Revalti.

He turned to leave.

"Ellina has always drawn attention to herself," Raffan called after him. "Not on purpose. She does not even know that she is doing it. But some elves just burn brighter. It can be hard to look away." His face had closed over again, that classic elven stillness. "I tried to look away, and we both suffered for it. I hope you will not make that same mistake."

Raffan's words burrowed like an arrow into Venick's back. The truth was that Venick *had* looked away from Ellina once, except it wasn't the same, their situations were so clearly different, and Venick didn't know how to explain that difference without finishing with Raffan's face what Farah had started.

He kept walking.

• • •

Erol found Venick in the barn readying a horse. The stallion was a plainsland breed, built for swift travel. Through the open door, the evening sun blazed over wet streets, drawing humidity up thickly from the pavement.

Erol frowned. "The Elder will be arriving any time now. Where are you going?"

Venick didn't reply. If he replied, he would snap.

"Ellina will be fine," Erol said.

"She should be back by now."

"The lace powder will work."

"What if you're wrong?"

"You have to trust her."

"I hate when you say that."

"We won," Erol said. "Our men confronted the southern caravan outside the city. The enemy surrendered almost immediately; they had little choice, given that their last and final weapon had been leaked across the countryside, and further destroyed by the rain. The conjurors have fled. Whatever Dark Army ranks remain will soon be dissolved, now that their queen is gone—"

"We don't know that she's gone."

"Yes," said a voice, "we do."

Venick spun.

Ellina sat astride Eywen in the barn's wide doorway, looking pale and rain-soaked, but unharmed.

Venick rushed forward. He helped pull her out of the saddle and into his arms, gripping the back of her head, inhaling the scent of her hair. It took several breaths before the frazzled energy that had claimed Venick ever since returning to Kenath finally abated, allowing him to release Ellina and study her more fully. Her eyes were rimmed in red, her jaw locked as if to prevent it from chattering. But her eyes. Those were fiercely alive.

"The poison worked?"

She nodded.

"And you—?"

"I am okay," she said, though her voice was even hoarser than usual. Venick continued to stare. She saw how he didn't quite believe her, so she said it again. "I am okay, Venick."

Lin Lill appeared in the doorway. "A messenger just delivered the news. The Elder has arrived. You will need your horses," she continued when Venick, Ellina and Erol tried to move past her out of the barn.

"Really?" Kenath was large, but not large enough to justify the use of horses. "Why?"

"Because the Elder has not returned to *this* city. Not to Kenath." She took a moment to find her words, as if they'd been strewn around her feet and must be picked up and rearranged in the correct order. "Apparently, he has taken residence in a different city, one that is not on any map. The messenger confirmed its location on the border, a short ride to the south."

"An unmarked city?" Ellina asked. "But how?"

"It seems," Lin Lill said, "that Evov has reappeared."

THIRTY-FIVE

Evov looked different when not set in the mountains, but Ellina, who had lost herself in that city, and found herself again, understood the nature of lost things that are found. She understood how the act of finding changes them. She recognized Evov immediately.

They were not the first curious travelers to follow the long gravel path into the city's streets. People and elves wandered the flat roads, squinting up at the buildings, which were made of shapeless stone. The avenues were winding, following old paths that no longer made any sense given the new terrain. Most of the homes were empty, but some were already being reclaimed by their prior occupants, old keys fitting into locks, elves stepping excitedly over thresholds. Ellina could see it in their faces: the relief of coming home.

"The abandoned houses will need to be handled, eventually," Venick told Ellina as they moved up the wide path. "We don't want people fighting over property, especially not so soon after our victory."

Ellina nodded, though she was only half-listening. Her attention was on Erol where he walked with Harmon and Dourin farther up the street, his white robes a beacon in the blue light of dusk. Though the five of them had ridden to Evov together, and Ellina could have spoken to Erol at any time, she felt strangely separated, as if there was a sheet of glass between them.

"You could go to him," Venick suggested gently.

Ellina's lungs no longer grated with poison. The pain of the inhaled lace powder had abated as soon as she exited Revalti Manor and drew in her first breath of fresh air. And yet, her chest seemed to pinch and tighten as she said, "I would not know what to say to him."

"Say whatever you would have said before."

"Things are different now."

"They don't have to be."

"They *feel* different." Ellina looked around for Bournmay, wishing to push her fingers through the banehound's thick fur, to find comfort there. Bournmay, however, was off hunting again. Ellina gripped the hem of her shirt instead, twisting the fabric. "Before, it was easy to be around Erol. He was just another member of the resistance. Then, after, it was still easy, because we had a mission. The lace powder. A purpose to draw us together. Now there is no purpose, only this…expectation."

"*He* doesn't expect anything."

"How could he not? He is my father. He has been all along, and I never knew."

Venick fell silent as they continued towards Evov's center. It was only after they passed under a stone arch and into a courtyard that he finally said, "I'm not saying our situations are the same. You didn't grow up with your father. For most of your life, you thought he was dead. But in a way…it's like he's come back to life. And I just know that if my father came back to life, if I had another chance with him, I would take it." He looked at his boots where they crunched into the gravel. "Is that wrong of me to say?"

A quiet feeling slipped into Ellina. She imagined Venick as he had been as a child, that gentle, hopeful boy, and though she had not known him then, the image was vivid enough that it felt as if she had. She tugged Venick's sleeve to pull him to a stop. "No," she said. "It isn't."

• • •

Midway through the city, they were approached by one of the Elder's footmen, a young fellow dressed brightly in purples and blues. "The Elder requests the honor of your presence," he intoned, though Ellina could hear how he must be rephrasing the Elder's original words, softening what had likely been a threatening order into something more like an invitation. That alone should have been grounds for refusal. Yet this was why they had come.

The footman gathered Harmon and Dourin as well, and together, the five of them made their way into one of the unclaimed elven homes in the lower quarter. A part of Ellina was unsurprised—this seemed like the Elder, staking claim to someone else's property just because it suited him—yet a different part of her was surprised, because the Elder's chosen house was only a single floor, quaintly wrought, unassuming. No throne room or stateroom, not even a proper entryway, just a little antechamber that led into a library, where the Elder waited.

He sat behind a desk in the library's center, his hands steepled, a highlander guard stationed against the wall to his left. The room's shelves had been relieved of its books, but there were a few of the man's belongings, a bell, a coat, a tapestry. At the sight of their approaching party, the Elder stood.

He was shorter than Ellina remembered, though it was possible her memory deceived her; she had never met the man up close. He wore a stiff hat that covered his thinning hair and a set of heavy robes, which seemed more suited for winter than the mild spring. His eyes caught on Harmon as she, Dourin, Venick, and Ellina came to stand before the desk.

Tension drew the room closed, like a lid sliding over a box. It trapped all the air so that when Harmon inhaled to speak, Ellina could hear her breath struggle in her throat.

"Hello, Father."

Despite the room's many occupants, the Elder had yet to look away from his daughter. "Harmon…"

"Your army has done well," Harmon said, keeping her tone formal. "The Dark Queen is dead, the southern conjurors defeated. The war has been won. Our men fought bravely, and new heroes have emerged among them. I have promised many of them land or wealth in honor of their courage. You will help me see to the distribution of these re-sources."

"I don't—"

"Furthermore," she continued, speaking over him, "my engagement to Venick is no more. You will not fight me on this. The lowlanders and highlanders have found other ways to ally without the need for such a union. The battles between us are over, Father. I hope you can learn to accept—"

"*You're alive.*" The Elder made a gruff, resentful noise. "Do you know how worried I've been?"

Harmon, who had been doing her best to appear unaffected, seemed to teeter. "What?"

"Dourin could not get in touch with you. With any of you. He sent letters. I did, too. All unanswered."

Because Harmon herself had intercepted them, Ellina thought. In her attempt to trick Venick and Ellina into believing Dourin was dead, she had blocked all communication to and from Parith—including her own.

It was clear from the sudden defensiveness in Harmon's tone that this was not a consequence she had intended. "You have spies at your disposal. Scouts. Any one of them could have reported on my well-being."

"They will not speak to me." The Elder sounded angry, but his posture had gone loose, as if he might sink right back into his seat. "I could not get a clear answer from anyone."

"I find that difficult to believe."

"You aimed to steal my army. Is it so unreasonable to think that you succeeded?"

"I aimed to borrow our men, yes, but not the loyalty of your scouts."

"They are one and the same."

"How can you say so? They have served you for years."

"Men are like streams," the Elder replied. "They tend to flow towards the strongest river. Years served has little to do with it."

They glared at each other, but Ellina thought the posture seemed hollow, like a log that has rotted inside, easily crunched with a foot. Here were two stubborn people, each of whom cared deeply, and were determined not to show it.

"I still do not understand," Harmon said. "I thought you were coming to reclaim your men."

"Only because I thought you were dead." The Elder's expression finally unlocked. He looked aged, suddenly, and terribly frail. "After your mother died in battle, I forbid women from fighting our wars. It was too late to save Arana, but I could ensure that other children did not have to grow up motherless. That is the reason I gave, anyway, and it was true, in its way. But my greater motivation was to protect you." He shifted his gaze to the desk, its hard varnish reflecting his remorse. "You were so much like your mother. As a child, you dreamed of knighthood. And oh, you were tenacious. I knew that if you saw other women doing battle, you would be determined to join them. So I changed the rules in the hopes that you would not meet Arana's fate."

"You succeeded," Harmon said, apparently unmoved by her father's speech. "I am no warrior."

"Oh, Harmon." He gave a laugh. "But you are."

"You sound...not angry."

"I am furious," the Elder said, "but it was my mistake for underestimating you. Perhaps I was fighting fate. I will do it no more. You have chosen the path of a military leader, and I can accept that, as long as you do not run away again. I already lost your mother. I cannot lose you, too."

· · ·

Once it was apparent that the Elder had only come for his daughter, Venick, Dourin and Ellina departed to give Harmon and her father a chance to speak alone. Outside, dusk had deepened fully into night, the stars winking from behind high, thin clouds. In the dark were the noises of the city: sheep bells, the crackle of meat over a spit, random laughter.

Ellina found Erol sitting on a stone bench in the center of a plaza. There were six marble statues set along the plaza's perimeter, each depicting a human holding a live torch. Ellina wondered who had seen to those torches, and whether it might have been Erol. She should tell him about the superior flammability of *rezahe* sap. Yet when she came to perch on the seat beside him, they merely sat in silence.

After a time, Erol said, "I'm sorry."

Though he could have been apologizing for any number of things, Ellina knew what he meant. "Farah and I shared no love for each other."

"Still, she was your sister."

Ellina set her forearms on her knees and searched herself for remorse. She found none. "I think," she said, "relationships cannot merely stand on blood ties. They must be fostered. And reciprocated."

The words hung in the air.

Erol said, "I wanted to tell you the truth about your mother and me. I did not know how."

Again, Ellina searched herself. She spoke carefully, trying out the truth of the words as she gave them life. "I think…if you had told me before, I would not have believed you. Though I wish…" Ellina looked at her hands. "I wish I could have known sooner. That it did not always have to be a secret. It explains so much."

Erol mimicked Ellina's posture, leaning forward and twisting his neck to look at her. "You should know that there was another reason Rishiana wanted to push Miria onto the throne. Rishi thought she could wring the humanness out of her. That by making Miria queen, Miria might begin to favor her elven side. But of course, it does not work like that." He looked out between the statues into dark nothingness. "I understand if you would rather not tell the others of our relation. You would not be the first halfling to desire discretion."

This, at least, Ellina could give him. "I am tired of secrets. I want others to know."

Erol nodded. Ellina had not realized, until she saw the tension leave him, that there had been any there at all. He drew his hand up and around the plaza. "Do you recognize these statues?"

Ellina shook her head.

"They are the six founders of Evov, the human conjurors who first created this place. That," he pointed to a slim figure with a neatly trimmed beard, "Was my great ancestor. And yours."

Ellina stood from the bench and went to inspect the statue more closely, reaching to touch the carved folds. Her mother never liked to speak of the past. Most elves did not, actually. History was too much like art. "Will you tell me more? About my ancestors?"

Erol's smile, which always seemed to hover around the edges of his eyes and mouth, split open. "I will tell you everything."

• • •

Over the course of the following days, Evov regained some of its former liveliness. A market emerged, livestock and produce carted in from nearby cities. Refugees mixed with soldiers, elves with humans. Spring was at its height, bringing rain, but the clouds often dissipated by midday, folding away to reveal a bright yellow sun.

Dourin reclaimed Traegar's home. He offered the spare room to Venick and Ellina, though he soon began dropping hints about the queen's palace and its current vacancy. When Ellina refused to acknowledge any of his clues, his probing became more pointed.

"People are starting to wonder who will claim the elven throne," Dourin said one night. He sat before the hearth, Venick in the chair beside him, Ellina on the floor with Bournmay. "They believe it will be you."

Ellina said, "They may believe whatever they like."

"You are the rightful heir."

"And so?"

"Someone must take the crown."

"Maybe not. The mainlands abolished their monarchy. They gave power back to their regions and elected council members to govern their cities."

"Who began warring between themselves," Dourin argued.

"The wars are over now."

"Ellina." He sighed. "The citizens will not wait forever. If you do not return to the palace soon, you will forgo your position."

Sometimes, when Ellina was on the edge of sleep, she envisioned doing as Dourin suggested and accepting the call to queendom. She tried to imagine the way it would be to acknowledge her duty and step into her sister's place, or her mother's. She could do away with old laws and enact new ones. She could keep the world at peace.

But Ellina was awake. She had seen too much death and too much loss to believe duty held a place over her own happiness anymore. She saw it when she looked at Dourin, who lived alone in the home of the elf he had loved, and tried to pretend that was all right, when it was not.

Dourin looked at Venick. "Are you going to say anything?"

"Ellina is free to make her own choices." Venick caught Ellina's eye. "Whatever you decide."

Ellina lay back against Bournmay, propping her head on the bane-hound's belly. "Maybe Venick will become king."

Venick made a spluttering sound. "Maybe I'll *what?*"

"You are a born leader. People are drawn to you. Elves, too. I will happily give you my crown."

"The elflands have never had a king. Also, I'm not an elf."

Ellina was mirthful. "That does not sound like a *no*."

More spluttering.

"It was merely a suggestion." She looked at Dourin. "Well? Would you take Venick as your king?"

Dourin rolled his eyes.

• • •

Three days later, Ellina made her way to a field south of Evov to hunt for milkweed, which Erol required for one of his brews. When the sun hit its highest point, she found a tree with broad, rubbery leaves and came to lay under its shade. She was just thinking she might doze off when a head blocked her vision. "I was told I'd find you here."

Ellina sat up. Grass clung to her braid. She did not bother brushing it away.

Harmon said, "I came to apologize."

The woman sank down beside Ellina, her skirts bunching around her knees. She was quiet for a moment, and Ellina was quiet, giving Harmon time.

"I guess," Harmon said, "I don't really know how to apologize for everything. It seems like, though we had the same goal, my way of reaching that goal often involved hurting you. I don't know you well, and you don't really know me, so I can't just ask for forgiveness and skate by on your good faith." She shot a glance up. "Sorry. Those were my father's words."

"You two seem to be reconciling."

"Yes." Harmon shifted to lean back against the tree. "This war has put much into perspective. It's shown us what's important. But we're getting off topic. My apology—"

"You have my good faith," Ellina said.

Harmon frowned. "But I haven't even tried to apologize yet."

"It's okay."

"I had a whole speech planned."

"Save it," Ellina said, pushing to her feet, "and come help me find some milkweed instead."

• • •

Harmon hosted a dinner. This was supposedly only for the core members of their group, yet when Ellina and Venick entered Evov's open-air courtyard where the dinner would be held, the space was crowded with people.

Ellina tensed. She remembered the stateroom where her mother was murdered, the unexpected press of extra bodies. She remembered a mob beside a river and a band of southerners in a field. Except, then the courtyard gatherers spotted the pair, and everyone broke into applause.

"It seems," Venick said into Ellina's ear, "that Harmon has tricked us again."

Ellina could have been irritated—she did not want a surprise party hosted in their honor—but when Harmon appeared, looking happier than Ellina had ever seen her, Ellina could not find it within herself to be angry. She allowed the woman to sweep in and kiss her cheeks. "I have something for you," Harmon said.

It was Ellina's belongings, the things she had left in Igor before her dash into the Taro: her dagger, her bow and arrows. Clothes, which were mostly human-made. At the bottom of the bag, there was a small glass vial.

Ellina was startled to hold these items again. It felt as if they belonged to someone else.

"It's my fault that you left them behind," Harmon said. "It seemed only right that I should recover them for you."

Ellina thanked the woman, and meant it.

"It is curious," Lin Lill said once they were all seated for dinner, cutting into her potato in straight, deft swipes, "that Evov has reappeared not just for elves, but for humans, too. The city used to be hidden from mankind."

"Erol once told me something about this city," Venick replied. He had a mug of ale in one hand, his ankle tossed over his knee, hair loose. Around them, the dinner party was in its throes, the chatter merry. "He said Evov wasn't always meant to be hidden. The conjurors who built this place didn't intend for it to serve that purpose. Instead, it was supposed to be a haven for those who were lost."

"Are we lost?" Lin Lill asked.

"Yes," Venick answered at the same time Dourin said, "Of course not."

Dourin made a face. "*I* was never lost. I have known where I was the entire time."

Harmon and Ellina laughed.

"This reminds me of the time I got lost in the whitelands," Lin Lill said. "Actually, it is a funny story. That is how I got—"

"Your scar," the others said, almost in unison.

Lin Lill looked around. "Have I become predictable?"

"I always wondered," Ellina said, "how *did* you get that scar?"

"I was just about to tell you—"

"How did you really get it, though?"

Lin Lill touched the mark on her cheek with light fingers. She had told a hundred different stories about her scar, each more fanciful than the next: bear fights, arrowheads, a fall into a well. "It happened while I was playing in the woods with my older cousins," she explained. "No one can say exactly how. I was too young to remember. Actually, when I was a fledgling, I did not even realize the scar was a scar; I thought this was how I always looked."

Venick caught Ellina's gaze. She could tell by the slight tilt to his head, and the way his eyes grew serious while the rest of him remained determinedly nonchalant, that he was seeking her thoughts, which were this: even though Lin Lill's story was not as adventurous as the others, Ellina liked it best, because it was the truth.

• • •

The following morning, Venick found Ellina in Evov's market. "There's been an incident," he said. "With Raffan."

Ellina set down the green glass knife she had been considering. "What incident?"

"Apparently, something was said—by a guard or Raffan, it's not clear—but it turned into a fistfight. Raffan was subdued, and the guards have been reprimanded, but…"

"Raffan's presence is causing trouble," Ellina finished.

Venick sighed. "We can't just leave him in Kenath's prison forever. A decision must be made."

"You wish me to order his death?"

"If you think that's right." When Ellina hesitated, Venick added, "There's always the whitelands. He could be sent into exile."

But Ellina thought that exile was like sweeping a problem under a rug, and that did not seem right, either.

"I think," she said, "he should be given the chance to make a redemption sacrifice."

Venick's startlement was obvious. Redemption sacrifices were an old human custom, one which Venick himself had undergone to earn his place back among his people. "I am not sure an elf has ever performed a redemption sacrifice."

Ellina returned her attention to the knife and gave a slight smile. "So let him be the first."

• • •

That night, Dourin pulled Ellina into his study and explained in soft tones that she and Venick could have Traegar's home for as long as they liked, because Dourin was leaving. To go west beyond the sea, he said. There were other continents out there, entire worlds uncharted, and while he might have stayed for Ellina's sake, it was clear she would be just fine.

"Are you sure this is what you want?" Ellina asked. Her eyes swam.

"Oh, come now. None of that. I will send you gifts. You will not believe the things I find. You'll be so buried in presents, you will forget I was ever gone."

"I will miss you."

"Liar."

"It is the truth."

"Shall I make you say it in elvish?"

"You can try."

"Ah, Ellina." His smile was touched with melancholy. "It is not forever. You know I will be back."

"When?"

Yet they both knew the answer. *When it does not hurt so much anymore.*

Dourin had not had a chance to mourn Traegar properly. "Everything reminds me of him."

Ellina took Dourin's hands. She remembered doing this with Miria, sending her away to never see her again. Ellina felt a stirring of fear, quickly banished. She had let Miria go because it was what her sister needed. If this was what Dourin needed, she would let him go, too.

Ellina spoke the same words Miria had spoken to her. "Be happy."

"And you," Dourin said. "Can you be happy?"

Ellina thought of how Lin Lill did not remember what her face had looked like before the scar. Maybe one day Ellina would forget her old self, too. Maybe, when she looked in the mirror, she would see only the parts she meant to keep.

Ellina pulled her friend into her arms. She told him she loved him, because she did. She warned that she would hold him to his promise to bury her in gifts, and would send Bournmay after him if he failed to see his promise through. She told him they would meet again soon, and hoped it was true.

THIRTY-SIX

Shortly after Dourin departed, Venick and Ellina set off on a trip of their own.

They rode south. The world was new, overflowing. The first night, they did not bother with a tent, but tamped down the earth and spread their bedrolls in the grass. Bournmay disappeared to chase mice through the brush, then returned, panting and bright-eyed. Overhead, the stars seemed endless.

Ellina murmured into the night. "I never answered your question."

Venick turned to squint at her through the dark. "What question?"

"You asked what it would mean if you called me *bournmay*."

"Ellina." Venick chuckled. "That was ages ago."

"Still. If a lover calls a lover *bournmay*, it is more than just an endearment. It is a promise."

"A promise for what?"

"Forever."

Venick shifted to lean on one elbow. "You've had that promise from me all along."

She mirrored his position, propping herself up on one elbow. "And you have it from me."

Venick's tone turned mischievous. "So is that what you're calling us now? Lovers?"

"Come here," she said, "and I'll show you."

• • •

The following morning, sun soaked the meadow. They'd both woken at dawn but were slow to rise. The day was blue, breezy. Ellina lay on her back with her hands behind her head. She hummed a few notes, then allowed her voice to move higher, giving the song belly.

Venick rolled over. He tapped her nose with a blade of grass. "Beautiful."

She shrugged. The music did not come as easily as it once had. There was an underlying huskiness, and a quiver she could not quite steady. "I know it is not what it used to be."

"Ellina, no. Your voice is perfect."

Ellina smiled and decided that yes, it was.

• • •

The next time they stopped to make camp, Ellina pulled the glass vial from her belongings. She walked to the campfire's edge. When Venick saw what she held, his eyebrows went up. "Is that—?"

"The minceflesh, yes."

"You kept it?"

Ellina had, because the world was full of monsters, and she had wanted the poison to make her safe. Now the war was over, but the world still had its monsters. Yet she would not be one of them.

We have no use for a weapon like that.

And they didn't.

She unstoppered the vial, and poured the minceflesh into the fire.

• • •

They continued south. It was strange to travel this way, their pace meandering and easy, with no conflicts looming. They stopped here and there, bathing in bright streams, hunting for berries and fish, lounging with Eywen and even Bournmay, when the hound allowed it.

Still, as they neared their destination, Ellina noticed a quietness steal over Venick. His attention turned inward. When she smiled at him, he struggled to smile back. At last, she could ignore it no longer. "What is it?"

Venick ran a finger along the inside of his shirt collar, pulling. "What if the city isn't there? It might have been abandoned by now. The way we left it—"

"It will be there."

"Even if it is, I told myself that I was never coming back here."

"We all say things we do not mean."

"Yes, but I promised myself."

"Did you promise yourself in elvish?"

"Well…no."

Ellina shrugged lightly. "Then it is not a promise you are bound to keep."

When Venick's home-city Irek finally came into view, Venick let out a long breath. The town was still standing, just like Ellina said it would be, and though it looked smaller than it once had, and war-ravaged, the city was clearly alive; there was a newly built watchtower at the entrance, chickens roaming the streets, citizens out and about. All good signs.

Venick and Ellina rode down the main thoroughfare. People noticed them at once, though Ellina could not be sure if they recognized Venick, or if they were merely noticing Bournmay, who had grown to the size of a miniature horse. In the end, it did not matter. The citizens were curious, but they kept a polite distance. No one attempted to stop them.

When it became clear that Venick was free to roam the city as he pleased, his shoulders fell away from his ears. His movements became eager. He caught Ellina's gaze and smiled.

Venick first took Ellina to the place where his childhood home had once stood, then to the cemetery. Ellina stood a little ways back as Venick set a hand to his mother's grave and then—after only a short hesitation—to his father's. He spoke under his breath, prayers to his gods that Ellina could not quite hear. When he stood, there was an expression on his face she did not recognize.

After, they walked the beach. Overhead, small seabirds painted quick, intricate patterns in the sky. The ocean slowly pulled down the sun.

When Ellina suggested that it was time to return to their horses, Venick shook his head. "There is one more place I want to see."

They followed an overgrown trail down the beach and away from the city. When they reached the cove, Ellina could only stare. It was just as Venick had described from his boyhood, lush with spring, hidden and therefore untouched. The water was clear, the bottom a deep sea green. Colorful fish darted beneath its surface alongside a dazzling array of invertebrates: starfish, urchins, sponges.

"Is it like you remembered?" Ellina whispered.

"You don't have to whisper," Venick whispered back.

"But it's just so..."

"Perfect?"

"Don't you think?"

"It is," he said, "now that you're here."

They climbed from a small overlook to a higher one, shuffling their toes towards the rocky ledge to peer down. The jump had not seemed all that far from below, but now that they had arrived, the water appeared a long way away.

"This was where I learned to swim," Venick said. "Where we all did, when we were boys."

She caught his gaze. "It is quite a ways down."

"That's the fun of it."

"I wonder about your definition of fun."

"Are you afraid?"

"No."

He grinned mischievously. "You first."

She laughed. "*You* first."

"Ellina." He hesitated. "I...have imagined bringing you here. It's something I've wanted for a long time."

His words quieted her, filled her with a feeling that was bright and gentle and new. The sun was in his face. It illuminated his expression, the same one from earlier that she had not been able to name.

She could name it now. That was the look of a man who had only ever known a world at war, who had been born to fight, but managed, against all the odds, to find peace instead. The expression on Venick's face—the one Ellina had not recognized, because it was so unfamiliar—was happiness.

His happiness filled her to the brim. She was bursting with it. She never wanted to look away. "Together, then?"

He smiled, and took her hand.

Acknowledgements

It took four years and so much heart, but my debut trilogy is finally complete.

Every release, it seems as if I have more and more people to thank. Writing has always felt like a solo endeavor, but I'm starting to see that it doesn't have to be. It's good to lean on others, and I'm lucky to have some really great people to lean on.

To my beta readers. You guys are always there for me, even with over a year between books. I'm so thankful.

To my critique partners Catherine, Lya and James, for jumping in mid-series without batting an eye, and offering just as much praise as criticism. I usually do a lot of fretting over my drafts, but I found myself doing less of that this time. I have you three to thank.

To Damon and the team, as usual, for making my cover art dreams come true.

To Jennifer for your proofreading work.

To Nathaniel and Catie for your stellar line editing. (I ctrl+f'ed all the soliders this time. There were six).

To all my readers, and especially to those who've stuck with the series from the first. You're the reason I get to keep doing this.

And finally, to my husband. I struggled a lot this past year, living in one of the dreariest cities in the world during a pandemic with a seemingly insurmountable manuscript deadline. You were the only one who saw me up close through all of it, and helped me through. When I admitted that I was worried you'd get tired of all my antics, you scoffed and said, "We're the same person." It's one of the most poetic things you've ever said to me. I thought, I should put it in a book. And now I guess I have.

Stay Up to Date

For more information on upcoming books releases, visit my website sgprince.com or follow me on Instagram @s.g.prince or Twitter @SarahGPrince.

Printed in Poland
by Amazon Fulfillment
Poland Sp. z o.o., Wrocław

24462173R00217